COWERING IN FEAR

The gunman crouched fearfully, immobile, as Morgan came toward him, whip in hand. The man made a slight move with his hand toward his holster, and Lee Morgan grinned. "I wouldn't try that again if I were you, mister."

CATHOUSE CHAOS!

In the parlor the whores were screaming, running for the stairs, calling for Mrs. Kessler. Morgan jumped over the counter and saw Nelly running down the hall. He grabbed her by the hand and pulled her after him. A gun fired behind them and a bullet ripped into the front door and he turned and saw Mrs. Kessler steadying a double-barreled derringer for a better shot....

Other Buckskin Double Editions:

RIFLE RIVER/GUNSTOCK
HANGFIRE HILL/CROSSFIRE COUNTRY
BOLT ACTION/TRIGGER GUARD

BUCKSKIN DOUBLE:

GUNPOINT

LEVER ACTION

KIT DALTON

LEISURE BOOKS NEW YORK CITY

A LEISURE BOOK®

January 2007

Published by

Dorchester Publishing Co., Inc.
200 Madison Avenue
New York, NY 10016

ISBN 0-8439-2980-4

Visit us on the web at www.dorchesterpub.com.

GUNPOINT

Chapter 1

Inside the Grover land office, Jed Thompson, behind his desk, squinted at the man who came through the front door. The visitor looked familiar, but Jed was not quite able to place the face. The man was tall, lean-faced, and with light-brown eyes, almost amber. He wore a neat suit, expensive silk shirt, and string tie. His boots appeared hand crafted. Jed could also see the buckboard in the street beyond the land office, where a petite young woman sat stiffly and quietly on the seat. On the rear platform were two trunks that obviously carried the belongings of the couple. And the horse, a young, prancing black gelding, also looked expensive.

Thompson waited until the man reached the counter. Then he leaned over and grinned. "Yes? Can I help you?"

"Is the Grover Hotel still here? And can they stable my horse?"

Thompson nodded.

"I'm interested in a spread north of here," the visitor said, "the Spade Bit Ranch; used to belong to Frank Leslie and Catherine Dowd. Does Willie McCormick still own it?"

Jed Thompson looked curiously at the questioner. "You want to buy that old place? It ain't worth the trouble. Sure, McCormick is still there, but he ain't raised any stock in a long time." Then the land office clerk suddenly gaped. "My God, you're Lee Morgan!"

"That's right," Morgan nodded.

"You want to go back into horse ranching up there?" Before Lee could answer, Thompson shook his hand. "I wouldn't waste my time; it ain't worth it. A lot of the grazing land is gone, and so are many of the ranches themselves. Sodbusters have pretty much taken over, and they're still comin' into the Gunsight Gap country in droves. You'd do much better if you kept goin' north to Montana."

Morgan ignored the advice. "Do you think McCormick will sell?"

"He's just an old drunk; letting the place run down. But he's a stubborn man. I ain't so sure he'll sell. Anyway, like I said, the place is in bad shape. You'd need to put a lot of money and work into it to make it decent again. Really, Mr. Morgan, you ought to try somewhere else." He leaned forward and grinned. "I know you probably feel sentimental about the old place, but it just ain't worth it."

"You answered my question," Morgan said. "I thank you for the information."

The land office clerk watched Lee Morgan walk out of the place. The man had surely filled out big and strong since he last saw him here in Grover; and apparently Morgan had also come into some money, judging by the clothes, horse and buckboard.

8

Thompson stroked his chin as he saw Morgan climb atop the seat of the buckboard, tap the horse lightly with the reins, and then move off. Jed Thompson shook his head. Jesse Callaway wouldn't like this; wouldn't like this at all. Callaway had coerced a lot of local ranchers, but Thompson was not sure that the banker would be able to force Lee Morgan into doing anything that Morgan didn't want to do.

Thompson looked at the wall clock: 8:30. Callaway would be at the bank in a half hour. He'd need to get right over there and tell him about the visit from Morgan and Morgan's intention to repurchase the Spade Bit Ranch.

Outside, Lee's buckboard moved slowly up the street, the glossy black gelding in a mild trot. The girl sat silently, looking straight ahead, but Morgan shifted his eyes to right and left, looking at both sides of Grover's main street. Crowds were already thick on the boardwalks that ran in front of the businesses on this main thoroughfare, and horses and wagons were already jamming the streets as farmers and ranchers came in and out of town to purchase supplies. Businessmen were waiting on customers, loading wagons, or simply standing in front of their stores and watching the crowds, occasionally greeting someone they knew or a potential customer.

Soon, Lee Morgan saw the big sign over the main saloon in town—Black Ace. He remembered vividly the first time he had been there with the hands of the Spade Bit Ranch. He had been a raw kid then, who knew very little except how to handle a gun. He had been almost terrified when he'd gone up to that small cubicle with Mary Spots who had given him a sexual experience he had never even imagined. He could joke about it now because he had experienced

9

the same thing and more in dozens of places from all kinds of women. Morgan wondered if Mary Spots was still whoring at the Black Ace.

Morgan had been awed by Mary Spots, but he had been angered and upset by what followed—the challenge by irascible George Peach whom Lee had killed with a flashing draw and shot into the man's chest before Peach could even raise his own gun; and then wounding Deputy John Chook, who'd called him a son of a bitch and had threatened to arrest him after Lee had shot Peach in a fair fight. Morgan wondered if Chook was still in Grover, still a deputy, still picking on those he thought he could take. . .

Morgan ceased his meditations when he reached the Grover Hotel where he pulled his rig next to the curb, dismounted, and tied the reins of his horse around the hitching post. For the first time, he looked at the girl.

"Wait here, Sarah."

The girl nodded.

Inside the hotel, the clerk behind the desk eyed Lee Morgan curiously and then grinned. The man before him looked like someone of means. The clerk seldom saw such men in this town some fifty miles north of the railhead at Boise. "Can I help you, sir?" he asked.

"I need a room for me and my wife," Lee said. "A nice room. We've been on the trail since yesterday and we could use a soft bed, a bath, and a good meal."

"We can give you all of that," the clerk said. "I got a nice room with a good view on the second floor; only two doors from the bath, but it does cost two dollars a night."

Lee Morgan did not answer, merely pulled a wad

of bills from his pocket and peeled off a ten which he handed to the clerk. "This ought to take care of us for a few days."

The clerk stared in awe at the thick roll, but said nothing. He snapped his fingers and a young man came to the desk. "Take this gentleman and his wife to room 21." He looked at Morgan. "Do you have baggage?"

"Two trunks. Then there's a buckboard and a horse. Can you care for them?"

"No problem." The clerk took his register and turned it to face Morgan. "Would you sign in, sir?"

When the visitor had signed the register, the clerk's eyes widened: Lee Morgan! He did not know the man personally, but he had certainly heard of him: of the shoot-outs at the Black Ace, the problems at Spade Bit, and the rumors that this man had run with the notorious Kid Curry and his gang. But wherever Morgan had been for the past few years, he had apparently come back with money in his pocket. The clerk turned back to the bellhop. "After you take Mr. and Mrs. Morgan's trunks to room 21, get the buckboard and horse and bring them around to the stable."

"Yes, sir," the youth said.

Lee Morgan walked outside and helped Sarah down from the buckboard, then watched as the youth took the trunks and put them on a hand truck before going back into the hotel. They followed him through the lobby and up the staircase, the youth taking one step at a time with his burden before he wheeled the trunks down the second floor hallway and stopped at room 21. He unlocked the door, went inside and unloaded the trunks, then handed Lee Morgan the key. Lee gave the youth a fifty-cent piece and the youngster's eyes widened. He had

11

never received so big a tip.

"We don't want to be disturbed. Is that understood?" Lee told him.

"Yes, sir!" the youth answered. "I'll bring your horse and shay around back and brush down your animal."

"Fine." Lee Morgan nodded.

When the youth had gone, Lee shut the door and bolted it. Then he gazed at Sarah, his 20-year-old bride. He had married her in the Klondike two months before returning to Idaho. Sarah had been a whore at the North Star Saloon in Fairbanks, a shapely, smooth-skinned woman who had satisfied him in bed more than any woman he had ever known. Since she married him, she had been docile and obedient, and had devoted herself to pleasing him in every way.

At this moment, Lee certainly felt a rising passion for her. He had not made love to her since they were in their stateroom aboard the *Alaskan Queen,* which had docked at Seattle. He had not been able to touch her all during the train ride from the West Coast to Boise, where he had purchased new clothes for her and for himself, and had bought the gelding and the buckboard for the trip to Grover. But now, at last, they were alone.

Sarah looked at Lee, her blue eyes intense. Desire beamed from them, reflecting the same passion for her husband as he felt for her. She said nothing as Lee walked to the window and pulled down the shade, leaving the room in semi-darkness. Then he came back to the girl, took her in his arms, and kissed her on the lips. She responded fervently, throwing her arms around him and pressing her body close to his. Lee stroked her strawberry blond hair, then ran his fingers down her neck and under her blouse to rub her back. Sarah's right hand slipped into Lee's pants, rubbing his lower abdomen and then his pubic hair. Lee's fever heightened. Dizzied by growing lust, he once more kissed Sarah fervently on the lips, shuttering in ecstasy as she stroked his genitals.

"I want you so bad, Lee," she whispered.

Lee did not answer, moving his right hand around under her blouse until he held her left breast and squeezed hard, almost hurting her. But Sarah did not care. She wanted him too badly. She began to take off his suit coat while he unbuttoned her blouse in a frenzy of desire. Sarah still said nothing but her eyes pleaded, Take me! Please take me!

Lee took off his coat, then his tie and shirt. Next, he unfastened his trousers and let them drop to the floor. Eagerly he helped Sarah, first taking off her blouse, then her skirt, and the petticoat underneath. At last she stood, naked and proud, before her husband, then pressed ardently against him.

Wrapped in each other's arms, they moved as one to the bed and Sarah leaned back, falling on the soft bedspread and pulling Lee after her. They lay there entwined, Lee fondling her breasts while Sarah caressed Lee's swollen cock.

"I love you, Lee," the girl whispered.

Lee did not answer, only kissed her again, drawing her to him more closely until they were submerged in mutual bliss, lost to everything except the satisfaction of their desire.

Afterward, the girl looked intently into Lee's amber eyes as she stroked his chest and he ran his fingers through her long, disheveled hair.

"Lee, what are we going to do?" she said at last.

"Like I said, I'm going to buy back Spade Bit and raise horses again."

"I've never lived on a ranch," Sarah said.

"You'll like it. Plenty of fresh air, open spaces where nobody can bother you; doing what you want. You'll like it."

Sarah settled into a reverie, trying to picture Spade Bit. Lee had spoken of it many times with nostalgia and love. She wondered if life on a horse ranch could really be as wonderful as her husband claimed. But then, nothing could be worse than the life Sarah had led before she'd married Lee. She had known only heartaches since childhood—a father who was often drunk, who often beat her, and had tried once to molest her sexually; a mother who had all but ignored her while she scratched to put a morsel of food on the table. By the age of twelve, Sarah was on her own, working long, hard hours at menial jobs, victimized by a rough, conscienceless employer who hired her, and treated her as a chattel whom men only used to satisfy their lust. She had finally sunk to being one of the whores at the North Star Saloon.

True, the money was good, but she had put up with the worst kind of men: some beat her; others came to her bed smelling like bears, with dirt caked on their clothes and bodies; rough, coarse frontiersmen who often demanded more than she could give. She would always be grateful to Lee Morgan for taking her away from that.

Life on a horse ranch? It would be paradise compared to the life she had left in the Klondike. She had found Lee Morgan so different from the other men she had known—considerate, sympathetic, clean, and willing to spend money on her. Yes, she was lucky indeed.

Sarah awoke from her musings and looked again

into the eyes of her husband. Then she leaned closer and kissed him. "Lee, I love you," she said again.

"I love you, too," Morgan said and kissed her gently on the cheek. Then he rolled over and hoisted himself to a sitting position on the edge of the bed. "I'm going to take a bath now. When I'm finished, you can take one."

The girl nodded. She watched Lee slip on his trousers and walk to the washstand. He took a towel and a cake of soap, then unlocked the door. "Lock it after me when I leave. Don't let anybody in until I get back," he ordered.

"You're the only one I want in here." Sarah smiled.

After Lee had left, she sighed and rose from the bed. She walked over to the washstand and stared into the mirror, then frowned. She was sure that wrinkles had already begun to line her pretty face, the result of her hard life in the Klondike. She tried to smooth them but then pursed her lips. Maybe when she was settled with Lee at Spade Bit, she'd be pretty again. Maybe the fresh air and rural life would rejuvenate her.

Poor Sarah! She could not guess that she might walk into a situation that would be far worse than she had ever experienced before.

Jed Thompson had waited anxiously for the minutes to tick away on the clock in the land office. Finally, the hands reached 8:30. He waited another two minutes, surveying his empty office, before he came around the counter. He slipped on his jacket, reversed the sign on the door from *open* to *closed*, and then left, carefully locking the door after him. He hurried up the crowded boardwalk, weaving around pedestrians. To greetings from some of the local shopkeepers, Thompson only nodded, never stopping. Finally, he crossed the street, avoiding the wagons and horses, and stepped onto the opposite curb. People were already going into the Grover Merchants Bank and Thompson followed. Once inside, he walked straight to the railing that fronted the desk where Jesse Callaway sat shuffling through some papers and glancing at the morning mail.

Thompson felt nervous. Callaway was a busy man, a rich man, and a powerful man. He did not appreciate anyone interrupting him without good reason. Now the land office clerk was not so sure that the reappearance in Grover of Lee Morgan was something that Callaway would want to know. Thompson sighed heavily and leaned on the railing, studying Jesse Callaway's obese frame, his round face, his thinning hair. Thompson had rarely seen the man smile, but then, Callaway had no sense of humor, only a desire to make money, regardless of who got hurt or how close he came to breaking the law.

"Jesse?" Thompson finally spoke.

The banker looked up and frowned. "Jed? What are you doing here?"

"A man came into my office today and I think I ought to tell you about him."

"Well?"

Jed Thompson turned and studied the dozen or more people at the tellers' windows and the busy employees behind them. "You really ought to hear this in private. It ain't something everybody should know."

Callaway shrugged. "All right, come on inside." He gestured towards the door to a private office.

Once within the empty room, Callaway sat at a chair behind a desk and motioned to Thompson to sit in the chair in front of the desk. Callaway leaned forward.

"You know, I don't bring everybody in here; just people who have something special on their minds."

"This is special, all right."

"Well?" Callaway barked.

"Only a little over a half hour ago, this man came into the land office—well dressed, looked like he had money. He had a girl outside in a buckboard that looked new. Nice piece of horseflesh, too."

"I don't care about that!" Callaway frowned irritably. "What do you want to tell me about this man?"

Thompson said, "I thought I recognized him but I wasn't sure, not until he said his name was Lee Morgan. You remember—the son of old Buckskin Frank Leslie? He's come back to Grover to buy back the Spade Bit ranch from old man McCormick."

Callaway's dark eyes widened and he puckered his lips. "Son of a bitch! I figured the law must have caught up with him by now and hanged him. From what I hear, the bastard's been in more trouble than any man I know, running from the law most of the time and traveling all over hell."

"There ain't no 'wanted' poster on him," Thompson told him.

Callaway nodded. "I guess he was too smart." Then he leaned forward and said to the land office clerk, "He may not want that place anyway, once he sees how McCormick let it run down."

"I ain't so sure." Thompson shook his head. "Like you said, he's been all over hell and he probably wants to settle down now. He may not care what the place looks like. He'll be ready to work hard and make a go of it again. I can tell you, he's sure filled out since the last time I saw him. He's a man grown, and I'd guess he's a lot smarter now, with plenty of gumption and experience. He had this pretty young woman with him, like I said, and I'd guess she'll help him."

Callaway shook his head. "We can't let Morgan get the deed to the place. We've hurt McCormick pretty bad and he can't hold out much longer. Others around here surely won't buck us, so it wouldn't be too long before we had that place . . ." He looked at Thompson. "You think Morgan will go out and see McCormick?"

"I reckon so. Maybe even this afternoon. He went to the hotel, I'm sure, because he asked me about the place. He and the girl will probably rest up there this morning, get cleaned up, get themselves a good meal, and then I bet they drive out to Spade Bit." Thompson shook his head. "I still remember what old Man McCormick said when he bought that place from Lee Morgan—'If you ever get homesick, you come back and I'll sell you Spade Bit.' That's what I remember McCormick saying. Maybe one reason the old man wouldn't sell to us was because he still had this idea that Morgan would come back. And now the man *is* back."

"Then we'll have to take care of Lee Morgan before he gets a chance to talk to the old man." Thompson nodded, and Callaway rose from his chair. "Don't say a word about this to anybody else. Just go back to your office. I'll take care of it. And thank you for coming in."

"Sure, Jesse. Any time."

Callaway watched the land office clerk leave, then turned and stared out the office window. He could see clapboard shacks in the distance where

18

immigrant farmers had settled while they tried to get themselves a piece of land. The sodbusters had been coming into Shoshone County for the past two years, looking for acres they could farm or even raise sheep. Callaway had taken charge here, encouraging horse and cattle ranchers to sell out, often quite cheap, in the face of the sodbuster incursions. There was plenty of good ranch land in Montana and in Wyoming, so why waste time fighting and dealing with the sodbusters that took over much of the free range lands? Callaway had done the buying and then got twice or three times the money for the land from eager settlers who wanted to take up farming in this fertile country.

Callaway's business dealings had been excellent and in the past year alone he had made several thousand dollars profit. He had made even more by lending money to these same sodbusters at exorbitant interest rates for the mortgages. Callaway had nothing to lose; if they did not repay the loans, he had only to repossess the land and resell it.

The banker now thought of Lee Morgan again. Yes, the man could bring him a pile of trouble. Who knew where he had been these past years and how much he knew? If indeed Morgan bought back Spade Bit, Callaway would lose the opportunity to make a highly profitable deal. The ranch was on the flats at the foot of the Salmon Hills and abutting the Big Joe River. Callaway could break up the 1200 acres into a lot of small farms, and the restless farmers in the clapboard shacks would vie furiously to buy them for whatever price.

No, Jesse Callaway could not allow Lee Morgan to reoccupy Spade Bit. He would need to stop him, and quickly. He remembered what Thompson had told

19

him—a well-dressed man, a pretty woman, a new buckboard and a good-looking horse. No one could miss this pair on the road that ran from Grover northward past the Spade Bit Ranch. And they would need to thread through Rock Slide Pass, where boulders on both sides of the road could easily hide an army of men lying in wait for unsuspecting travelers.

Callaway would have to move fast; he'd need to station a bushwhacker or two at the pass to take care of Morgan. He hurried out of the office and motioned to a pair of men loitering near the entrance to the bank. Both wore chino pants, dark shirts and vests, Stetsons, and high boots, and gunbelts whose holsters lay low on the thighs, tied tightly. As soon as the two saw the signal from Callaway, they followed the banker back into the private office.

"I've got a job for you and it has to be done today," Callaway said.

The men did not answer, and the banker continued, "I want you to ride out to Rock Slide Pass right away. Be sure you take your Winchesters with you because they're much more accurate from a distance. You're to hide behind the boulders and wait. Some time late this morning or early this afternoon, you'll probably see a buckboard coming north over the St. Marie's Road. A man and a woman will be on it. You shouldn't be able to mistake it."

"What do you want us to do?" one man asked.

"Take care of them," Callaway said grimly. "They'll be on the way to see old man McCormick at the Spade Bit Ranch, and if they get there and make a deal with him, we could be in a lot of trouble. The man is Lee Morgan. Kill him."

"What about the girl?" the other man asked.

"Kill her, too," Callaway said. "No sense in leaving any witnesses around." Then he pointed to the door. "Get going!"

The two men nodded and left the office. Jesse Callaway turned and stared out of the window once more. He squinted, looking at the clapboard shacks some distance away. There was too much money to be made from the fools in those hovels, and Callaway was not about to allow Lee Morgan nor anyone else to deprive him of such profit.

Chapter 2

By noon that day, Lee and Sarah Morgan felt totally refreshed. They had rested and made love for most of the morning, then had bathed, unpacked their trunks, and changed into fresh clothing. Now they walked into the Grover Hotel dining room, where an accommodating waiter served them the special of the day—baked ham, potatoes, fresh peas, coffee, and hot apple pie. They both ate ravenously for they had eaten very little since leaving Boise the day before. When they had finished, Lee tipped the waiter and they left.

Outside, the youth had already brought around the gelding and buckboard. He had obviously brushed down the animal, for the horse's coat shone like satin. As the boy helped Sarah onto the buckboard, he looked curiously at Morgan.

"I'm sorry if I seem nosy, but I notice you have a mighty fine whip hidden behind the seat. Why would you want that?"

"To kill snakes on the trail," Morgan told him.

"It's better than shooting them—more accurate."

The boy was skeptical. He doubted that this tall, strong man would use the whip for such a purpose. But he said nothing, just stood as Lee Morgan tapped the gelding lightly with the reins and the buckboard began to move up Main Street.

Soon they were well out of town and moving leisurely northward over the St. Marie's Road. Both Lee and Sarah felt invigorated. The sun on this late spring day was bright and warm in sharp contrast to the bitter wind and cold they had recently experienced in the Klondike.

As Lee studied the familiar countryside about him, he was glad to be home. He had been a lot of places in recent years—Mexico, Texas, San Francisco, South America, and some places he did not even remember. He recalled his sojourn in Argentina where his old friend Juan McGee had lost his ranch, his daughter, and his life in bitter conflict with the Benudo Indians. Their chief, Cuchillo, had wreaked havoc on the Argentinian ranchers.

In retrospect, Lee Morgan guessed that the horror in Argentina had prompted him to get as far away as possible, all the way to Alaska at the other end of the Western Hemisphere. He had gone from the hot, humid jungles of South America to the windswept tundras of the far north. If the Yukon weather had been harsh, the greedy men who preyed on hopeful prospectors had been much worse. They had gouged these itinerants with their high prices, robbed them without mercy, and often killed them to gain the gold nuggets which the prospectors had worked so hard to get.

Morgan knew that only his experience, strength, and fast gun had saved him from that fate. He had been one of the lucky ones, amassing thousands of dollars worth of gold during his prospecting months, spending only a small fraction of it, and luckily escaping the Klondike with both his life and wealth.

And in the process, he had found Sarah. He had known from the first time he had bought her sexual favors that she was more than just a prostitute; that she was really a lost little girl who had stooped to this trade simply to exist. He had seen her as someone who could be much more than a bedmate; someone who respected and loved him, who would do his bidding, who would make him happy at last.

When it was time to leave the Klondike, he had asked Sarah to marry him. He was sated with travel, women, and adventure and he was now ready to settle down. She had been amazed to learn that Lee wanted her for his wife, but she had never hesitated. Sarah knew at once that Lee Morgan was the only man she would ever love.

As the gelding continued its easy lope up the St. Marie's Road, Lee Morgan took in the surrounding terrain. The view brought back memories. He could see the bare box alders intermixed with the pines of the Salmon Hills reaching back into the high peaks of the Rockies, where snow still lay. The thick green had not arrived yet, and the snow had all but disappeared except for patches that clung tenaciously in some of the shadowed gullies or forest floors. The hardwood trees still were bare, but small, roaring torrents now snaked through some of the ravines of the draws where melting snow had added to the streams.

The road itself was only slightly muddy for the sun had begun to dry out the thawed earth. A slight breeze gently blew the tall brown reeds of the grasslands on either side of the road, but they would be green in another month or two, as would the trees on the slopes.

However, as Lee continued up, he noticed something different, something he had not remembered. He saw endless acres of furrowed earth where there had once been dry gulches, range grass, or wild scrub brush. The land had been plowed. And he could see the log houses of the sodbusters, with stacks of wood in front of them, farm implements leaning against the walls, storage barns and wire fences that ran for miles around the land. He realized that the land office clerk had been right—sodbusters had moved into an area that had once been reserved for horse and cattle ranchers.

Lee turned when Sarah suddenly spoke. "It is pretty out here, Lee. I ain't never seen anything like it—flat plains, and farms, and trees, and mountains, and creeks all in the same place. In Alaska, it was only the tundra and high bare mountains, the same thing all the time, and most of the year just covered with snow, so that a person never did know what was underneath." She squinted up at the sun. "And it ain't nearly as cold here. I can actually feel some warmth from that sun."

"The terrain changes a little up ahead," Lee said. "Rocks and boulders that almost come down to the road. We'll be going through Rock Slide Pass pretty soon, where you won't find one blade of grass or even a scrub brush."

The gelding continued on, loping comfortably, not panting and not tiring. Morgan had chosen well when he bought this animal. But, if he knew anything, he surely knew horses and he was not about to make a mistake.

Soon, small boulders along the side of the road loomed into view, and further up, bigger rocks and rock slopes rose on both sides of the highway. When the road began to turn sharply, Morgan looked at the girl.

"We'll be going through Rock Slide Pass now. Then it'll only be two or three miles before we reach Spade Bit."

The girl nodded.

However, as Lee Morgan approached the pass looking at the high boulders on the hills bordering the road, something grasped his attention. He had seen a flash, like a small explosion with no sound and Lee at once guessed its source—sun glinting on the barrel of a rifle held by someone behind the rocks. A moment later, he saw the flash again. Lee reined the horse to a stop.

"What's the matter, Lee?" the girl asked.

"There's somebody behind those rocks, somebody with a rifle."

"Maybe somebody hunting cats or something," Sarah offered.

"No, not this close to the road," Lee said. "That somebody is waiting for another somebody to come through the pass and maybe ambush him."

"But who'd want to do that? And why?"

"That's what I'm going to find out." He pulled the rig off the road and tethered the gelding to a tree.

He reached into the carrier slot behind the seat and pulled out an empty box and a jug, also empty. Then he took out a blanket and his whip. "Sarah, we're going to have a picnic."

"A *picnic?*"

"Just do as I say. Whoever is in those hills, behind those rocks, won't know what we're really up to. I'm going to leave you in this brake, well hidden, while I go up there to investigate."

The girl nodded as Lee walked around the buck-board and helped her down. They each carried some-thing and, arm in arm, they ducked into the brake towards a clump of pine trees whose thick branches would obscure them from any viewers behind the rocks ahead. Lee spread out the blanket and told Sarah to sit down.

"You just wait here until I get back."

The girl gripped his wrist. "Lee, be careful."

Lee only nodded and patted her hand. Sarah felt a sudden rush of fear as Morgan left her. Lee moved cautiously and quietly through the brake, the whip in his hand. Soon he reached a jumble of rocks, climbed carefully to the top and peered across the road. He saw a man behind one of the boulders, holding a Winchester with the barrel rested on the top of the boulder. The man was obviously waiting to ambush someone coming up the road. But was he waiting for Morgan? Lee had been away a long time; he had practically been forgotten in Shoshone County, so he doubted the hidden gunman could be waiting for him.

He continued a little further north until he came some distance beyond the rocks opposite the road. He then crossed the road and began moving stealthily among the rocks until he came into a position where he could clearly see the man's back, while the man's attention was focused on the road. Lee looked about him, but saw no one else, so he assumed the bushwhacker was alone. Morgan crouched and moved silently closer to the man, finally coming within several yards of the crouching would-be predator. He had long ago learned how to approach a man with stealth and the ambusher had no idea that Lee had come up behind him.

Morgan uncoiled his whip and ran a finger over

the tip. Then he held the whip, ready to snap it as fast and accurately as a rattler. Standing upright, he shouted. "Hey, you!" As the man turned, Lee snapped the whip. The lash moved faster than the eye. The tip of the whip caught the barrel of the Winchester perfectly and jerked the weapon from the ambusher's hand. The ambusher reached for his gun, but once more the whip lashed out with lightning speed, catching the man on the knuckles and drawing blood. The man grabbed his hand and winced; the .45 remained in the holster.

The gunman crouched fearfully, immobile as Morgan came toward him, whip in hand. As the man made a slight move with his hand toward his holster, Lee grinned. "I wouldn't try that again if I were you, Mister."

The man looked at the whip and then moved his hand quickly away from the holstered handgun. Now he stood stiffly, fear in his eyes as Lee Morgan came towards him. Lee reached down and picked up the Winchester, studied it, and then looked at the man.

"You're mighty stupid, Mister. You're lying in wait here to hit somebody and you got a shiny barrel that can reflect sunlight like a mirror with the slightest movement. Hasn't anybody ever taught you about blackening the barrel with graphite so it won't reflect the sun?"

The gunman did not answer.

Morgan held the Winchester in his right hand, after he had transferred the whip to his left. "All right, Mister, what's this all about? Who sent you out here and who were you waiting to bushwhack?"

Still the man said nothing.

Lee Morgan came closer and pressed the barrel of the Winchester against the man's forehead. "I don't have much patience. All I know is that I was the only one coming up that road. If you don't want to talk, then I can only assume that I was the one you intended to shoot, although I can't think of a single reason why you'd want to do that. Now, Mister, under those circumstances, I see no reason why I shouldn't kill you."

Still the man did not answer. He rolled his tongue around his lips. Then his eyes moved, staring up and to the left. A slight glint of relief shone in those eyes. But Lee had caught and interpreted the glance accurately. Someone was behind him, and he whirled and raised the Winchester just as a voice cried out, "All right, Mister, drop it!" However, before the newcomer could make a move, Morgan fired the Winchester, blowing the second man's rifle out of his hand and sending the weapon flying. The astonished cowboy did not wait to do anything else. He vanished quickly behind an outcropping of rocks and in a moment, Lee heard the sound of a horse galloping away.

Lee turned once more to his cowed prisoner. "Your partner ran away and left you to fend for yourself. Now, what kind of friend is that?"

The man ran his tongue around his lips again and his Adam's apple raced up and down his throat. He knew that he was up against an expert. All he had heard about Lee Morgan's prowess with a gun was obviously true, for he had easily disposed of a man who had the drop on him. But worse, Morgan was equally adept with a whip. The ambusher guessed that Morgan would not hesitate to kill him if he did not answer some questions.

"Are you going to start talking?" Morgan glowered at him.

"Honest, Mister," the man threw up his hands,

"we weren't after you. My God, I don't even *know* you. Why would we want to shoot you?"

"Your friend was ready to kill me."

"Only becuase you had me," the man said. "Please, I got no quarrel with you, whoever you are," the ambusher lied, for he knew full well who Morgan was.

"Then who were you after?"

"Somebody we knew; a card shark that cheated us," the man lied again. "A man who robbed us in a poker game at the Black Ace."

"What man?"

"A gambler by the name of Paul something," the man continued to lie. "We were told that he'd be riding out this way from Grover on his way to the minin' town o' Eddiville up north. We didn't even intend to kill him," he gabbled. "We just meant to get our money back 'cause he didn't win it fair and square in that game."

Lee Morgan heaved a deep sigh. The man was cowering, obviously petrified. Perhaps he was telling the truth. Morgan could think of no reason why anyone would want to harm him, so perhaps there was some truth to the bushwhacker's claim. Since he could not prove that this man and his partner were after him, Lee could not in good conscience hurt him.

"All right." Lee nodded. "Maybe you are telling the truth. Where's your horse?"

"Just up there behind them rocks," the man said.

"I'm going to let you go, but without your guns. Since you've got your rifle here with you, I'd guess you don't have any guns with your mount. I'm going to keep your rifle and your sixgun. If you want them back, why, you come to the Grover House where I'm staying and ask to see Lee

31

Morgan."

The man's eyes widened. "Lee Morgan? I've heard of you, and I'm pleased to meet you personally," he said, feigning ignorance. "Believe me, Mr. Morgan, from what I've heard about you, I'd never try to bushwhack you. I want to thank you for lettin' me go."

Morgan cocked his head. "Get out of here."

Lee watched the man scramble away and disappear among the rocks. Then he slipped the .45 into his belt, hooked the Winchester under his left arm, and carried the whip in his right as he descended from the rocks to the roadway. He walked swiftly down the road until he reached his tethered horse. He took one more look at Rock Slide Pass before he walked into the brake. When Sarah saw him, she bounded to her feet and ran toward him with a mixture of relief and apprehension.

"What was it, Lee?"

"A couple of cowhands." Morgan shrugged. "They were waiting to catch up with some gambler who was supposed to be on his way north to Eddiville. He cheated them in a poker game."

"Did they hurt you? I heard a shot!"

"No, I just put a scare into them and they rode off."

Sarah did not say anything. She picked up the blanket, folded it and then accompanied Lee back to the buckboard. Morgan replaced the tool box and jug, put away his whip, and dropped the two weapons inside the storage slot behind the seat. Then he untethered his horse, helped Sarah on the wagon, and boarded it himself.

They said little to each other as they continued the ride north, but now Sarah looked intently at the rocks on both sides of Rock Slide Pass. She felt a sense of relief when they came out of the narrow passage and found themselves again on a straight stretch of road, with flatlands on both sides. But once more Lee saw a sight that had bothered him earlier—the wide stretches of plowed land where there had once been ranches; and log huts where there had once been ranch houses. The scene offered confirmation to what the land office clerk had said—"Much of the ranches and grazing lands are gone; sodbusters have pretty much taken over, and it looked like they're still coming into Gunsight Gap in droves." If McCormick had allowed Spade Bit to deteriorate, why hadn't the old man sold out and moved on? Lee wondered.

Soon he noted the return of grasslands and pastures, and then he saw the rambling ranchhouse of Spade Bit. From a distance, the house did not look bad, although he noted weeds in the front yard, and the rotting posts in many areas of the long fence that abutted the road. When he reached the ranch gate, he found it hanging open on one hinge, obviously in need of repair. Lee could see smoke coming from the chimney and a horse tied to the tether post beyond the front porch, indications that Willie McCormick was at home.

Lee drove the rig into the yard and up to the front porch, then got down and tied the gelding's reins to the post. He helped Sarah off the buckboard, and they both walked onto the porch and knocked on the door. Soon they heard plodding footsteps. The door opened and old Willie McCormick was standing there, squinting at the couple, not certain who these visitors might be. He looked especially hard at Lee, for he thought he had seen this man somewhere before.

"Mr. McCormick," Lee grinned, "don't you recognize me? Lee Morgan."

The old man gasped. His dark eyes widened and he extended his frail hand. "Goddamn, Lee Morgan! So you finally come back, did you?"

"I've had my fill of the vagabond life and I'm ready to settle down. This is my wife, Sarah." He gestured toward the girl. "We came out here to talk to you; see if you still mean what you said about selling me back this spread if I ever wanted to return."

Willie McCormick grinned. "Come in, come in." He ushered the visitors into the parlor and offered them a seat on a shabby divan. Lee Morgan studied the place—the fireplace, the pineboard walls, the oak floors, and woodwork. Everything appeared in need of paint and polish. The furniture was sagging and torn, heavily soiled, and frayed. The old dining table was still in the adjacent room, Lee saw, cluttered with an array of newspapers, magazines, tin cans, scattered tools, wire bales, and other odds and ends. The windows were covered with a haze of grime—Lee could barely see outside.

"The place don't look like much right now," McCormick conceded. "I ain't had but a few horses for some time now, but I'm jus' gettin' too old to keep up. The pastures have been neglected, I admit, and I've been meanin' to do somethin' about that, but it seems I jus' don't seem to find the time. But I can tell you this," he gestured emphatically, "I've been takin' care of your father's grave regular and also the grave of Mrs. Dowd. Yes, sir; I keep the weeds off'n 'em and I put flowers on 'em ever' spring."

"I'm grateful for that," Lee said quietly.

"Now the house here: I know it could use a little

work, but nothin' much. And the barn is still good. I did have the roofs o' the house and barn repaired a couple years ago, so the buildings are dry enough when it rains. But I jus' can't take care o' the place anymore, and things have gotten even worse with all the sodbusters a'comin'."

"Then why didn't you sell out?" Lee asked.

"I give that some thought, too. In fact, Jesse Callaway was out here a couple o' times and offered to buy from me at a fairly decent price."

"Jesse Callaway? Who's he?"

"He took over the Merchants Bank in Grover two, three years ago, and he's been buyin' up a lot o' ranches hereabouts and dividin' them into farms and then sellin' them to them sodbusters. I guess he wants to do the same thing with Spade Bit."

"Why didn't you sell?" Lee repeated.

Willie McCormick shrugged. "Don't know really. It was probably the right thing to do; I'd have a little money and no more responsibility. What few years I had left I could enjoy."

"Well, Mr. McCormick, I came out here because I was hoping I could buy this place back. I'm willing to pay what you paid when you bought it from me. That would seem to be fair."

"You'd be gettin' robbed if you did that," McCormick grinned. "It ain't worth it. It ain't in the kind o' condition that it was when I bought it from you. And I got to be truthful. I lied to you before. I don't have no horses at all, nor any other kind of livestock 'cept for that nag out front."

"Well, if this banker Callaway wanted to buy the place, I'm willing to pay whatever he offered you and maybe even a little more," said Lee. "The truth is, I've been out and around for a long time, going from one place to the next and I was lucky enough to

35

come home with quite a sum and with this wonderful girl here." Lee gestured towards Sarah. "She's more than willing to go into horse ranching with me, and now that I'm older and a lot more experienced, I know that's what I want."

"I'd like to see you do well on this place again," the old man said, "but I'd feel right bad if'n I didn't tell you the whole truth. The sodbusters are all around now and they're hungry for land, especially the flats of Spade Bit. You might have trouble with them. And this Callaway seems to have a passion to get hold o' this place. You could have trouble with him, too; and he's got lots o' friends and influence in the county."

"I've had trouble in a lot of places, but I always managed to handle it," Lee told him. "If I'm on this land legally, nobody is going to run me off. Would you like some time to think about reselling this place to me?"

Willie McCormick stroked his chin. "I don't know if'n I really need any time. I always hoped that maybe you'd come back some day and make this spread into the place it used to be. Maybe that's why I didn't sell out to Callaway." He shuttled his glance between Lee and Sarah and then grinned. "Yes sir, you two are young and strong. You can work hard and that's all this place needs—just some hard work to make it a fine ranch again. If I sell to you, Lee, at least I'll know that Spade Bit will be in good hands. I just wanted to warn you about the trouble you might have; it was only fair."

"I understand," Lee said, "and I'm grateful. How much do you want?"

"I'll take the same as I paid for it," McCormick said. "I got the deed and there's a copy in the county clerk's office in Boise. Once I sell to you, the

36

place is yours, all legal, and you can move right in."

Sarah had been staring about the house with eager anticipation in her blue eyes. She then looked at her husband. "I'd like to move in right now. I can do so much with this place, and I'd sure like to get started!"

"You're mighty anxious, ma'am," McCormick said before looking at Lee again. "Suppose I get the deed and meet you tomorrow morning about nine in the Grover land office. We'll go right up to Jed Thompson and draw up the papers. Then we can go over to the bank and take care o' the cash part o' this with Jesse Callaway."

"That's good," Lee said. "I want to open an account at the bank anyway. I have quite a sum and I don't want to carry it around with me."

"Can we move in right away, Mr. McCormick?" Sarah asked.

"I do have one o' the bedrooms fixed up pretty good."

"Lee?" the girl pleaded.

"We'll see," Morgan answered, smiling.

Willie McCormick rose from his chair. "You two sit right there and let me make us some coffee. For a celebration, like. Guess you're glad to be home, ain't ya?"

Lee Morgan just nodded.

Chapter 3

At nine o'clock the next morning, Jed Thompson was surprised to see Lee Morgan walk into the Grover Land Office. Yesterday, the man had come in only to ask about the Spade Bit Ranch and whether or not the hotel was still in business. Thompson, of course, did not know that Callaway had sent two henchmen out to kill Morgan, and was thus unaware that Lee had foiled the banker's plans. Thompson eyed Morgan curiously and then leaned forward and spoke.

"Mr. Morgan, what can I do for you this morning?"

"There's going to be a land sale. I'm waiting for Willie McCormick. He said he'd meet me here at nine o'clock, so he should be here any minute."

"A land sale, Mr. Morgan?"

"I spoke to McCormick yesterday afternoon and he's agreed to sell me back the Spade Bit Ranch. It's a little run down, I know, but my wife and I will put it back in shape. Do you have a record of the deed

39

here? Willie told me he'd bring in his deed and that a copy of it was at the county seat."

"Y-yes, Mr. Morgan, I—I'm sure it's recorded here somewhere." Thompson was obviously shaken. Callaway had failed to persuade McCormick to sell, but Morgan had a deal in record time. What would Thompson tell the banker when this transaction was over? While the land clerk considered these things, a wagon pulled up in front of the office. An old man got out, tethered his horse, and walked inside. Thompson was sure the man was Willie McCormick. The newcomer smiled when he saw Morgan.

"You're right on time, Lee," McCormick grinned.

"Did you bring the deed with you?" Lee asked, grinning back.

"Right here," the man said, extracting a folded document from his pocket.

"Will we need a notary to transfer this deed?" Lee asked Thompson.

"I'm a notary, and I can do it."

For the next half hour, Jed Thompson went about conducting a business that upset him quite badly. He made up a new deed, writing in a full description of the property and the measurements and location of the spread. Both Morgan and McCormick watched carefully, making sure the land clerk made an accurate copy of the old deed. When Thompson was finished, he handed a copy of the document to the two men and watched them sign it. Then Thompson notarized it.

"You're all set, Mr. Morgan," the clerk said with a forced smile.

But Lee Morgan did not return the smile. "This business isn't finished yet. What about the other copy of the new deed? The one that has to be

40

recorded at the county seat? And I didn't see you record this sale in your own record book."

"Oh, I was going to take care of that," Thompson mumbled. "Later, after you left. Didn't want to waste your time."

Lee Morgan frowned. It almost seemed that this land clerk was trying to put something over on him, that he was not doing all he must do to legally transfer Spade Bit from McCormick to Morgan. He leaned over and looked hard at the clerk. "I don't want to seem too troublesome, but you get that other goddamn copy of this new deed out right now; me and Willie have to sign it, and you have to notarize it. Then I intend to stand right here until you record the transaction and date in your own book."

Jed Thompson felt beads of perspiration dampen his forehead and he could feel his nerves tingle with a hint of fear. It was obvious that Morgan had grown suspicious and Thompson had no desire to have a man like Morgan angry with him. "I-I was just trying to save you some time, Mr. Morgan," he stammered.

"I've got all day and so has Willie McCormick," Morgan barked. "Now you do this goddamn job right or somebody will hear about it and you won't have this job much longer. Understand?"

"I-I'm sorry, Mr. Morgan. I didn't mean to be inefficient."

"Inefficient?" Morgan echoed. "How the hell could you send another copy of this deed to Boise without my signature and Willie's?"

"Yes, yes, of course," Thompson gabbled. He then made a second copy of the deed, his hand shaking as he wrote it out. When he finished, he handed this second document to Lee, who read it over carefully, signed it, and then gave it to Willie McCormick, who also signed it. Then Lee gave it back to the clerk who nervously signed it as well. Morgan didn't budge until Thompson took out a large ledger, opened a page and recorded the sale of Spade Bit and the date in the book. He then looked up at Morgan with a weak smile.

"Everything's been taken care of, Mr. Morgan. I'll see that this duplicate copy of the deed gets to the County Clerk's office in Boise."

But Lee snatched the document. "I'll see that it gets to Boise myself." He then turned to McCormick. "Let's go, Willie; over to the bank."

"Sure," the old man said.

Outside, as they walked up the street, McCormick stroked his chin and then spoke. "I don't understand, Lee. What was that clerk tryin' to do? He knows he has to make two copies of a land sale, one for the buyer and the other to record with the county clerk. Why would he do like he did?"

"There's something wrong, Willie," Morgan said. "It almost seemed like he didn't want to have a record of this sale in Boise, and that he had no intention of recording it in his ledger. Willie," he frowned at the old man, "do you know any reason why somebody would want to prevent me from repurchasing Spade Bit?"

McCormick shrugged. "The place ain't worth a damn right now; that's why I wasn't so keen on sellin' it to you. Like I told you, the only other person interested in the place was Jesse Callaway who runs the bank. But I don't think it'll matter too much to him if he doesn't get it."

"Well, we'll find out when we get there," Morgan said.

Inside the bank, people were already lined up in front of the teller's windows where employees were conducting business. Behind the railing to the right, Jesse Callaway was looking through some papers on his desk and scanning the morning's mail. He wore the same sober look that was perpetually on his face and ignored all the activity beyond the cage. However, as the two men came to the railing, Callaway looked up. His dark eyes widened when he saw Willie McCormick standing there. Then he looked keenly at the young, muscular man with him.

Callaway felt a slight tremor in his obese frame. What was McCormick doing here and who was the man with him? A sense of panic gripped the banker. My God! Had McCormick sold Spade Bit? This man with him couldn't be Lee Morgan? Morgan was supposed to be dead! Soon enough, Callaway would learn the truth, and much to his dismay.

"Hello, Mr. Callaway," McCormick said. "This here is Lee Morgan," he gestured towards his companion. "We just made a deal; Lee's bought back Spade Bit, We just took care o' the deed transfer over at the land office, and now we'll need to take care o' the cash part. Figured you'd help us with that."

Jesse Callaway felt his heart contract. His worst fears had been realized. The banker had not heard from his two gunmen—they had failed to get Morgan and were too fearful and embarrassed to face Callaway. And so Morgan had wasted no time in completing the deal with McCormick. The banker knew that if Morgan was so intent on buying back Spade Bit, he certainly would not sell to Callaway or anyone else.

The banker managed to smile, although a bitter rage boiled inside him. "I'm surprised, Mr.

43

McCormick. When *I* tried to buy that place, you were quite disinclined to sell, but when Mr. Morgan came to you, he got the place in a hurry."

"There was some sentimental reasons," McCormick said. "Somewhere in the back of my mind was the hope that Lee would someday take over Spade Bit again and make a go of it once more. So when he showed up and offered to pay me what I paid for the place, I was willing to sell."

Callaway nodded and looked at Lee. "Mr. Morgan, I must warn you that you might be making a mistake to buy that place. We've had homesteaders coming into the Gunsight Gap country for some time and they're all eager to buy land and take up farming. The've been plowing up much of the free range land, and to be frank, the Gap country is no longer a good place for horse and cattle ranches."

"I can raise plenty of grass for my purposes, maybe twenty or thirty head of good horses," Morgan said. "I won't bother the sodbusters so long as they don't bother me. I'm sure we'll get along."

"Well, they can get pretty testy if a horse or a steer tromps on their planted land," Callaway told him.

"Twelve hundred acres is more than enough for me," Morgan shrugged. "I'll see to it that the animals I raise don't trespass on other people's land."

"Well, Mr. Callaway," McCormick spoke again, "will you take care o' the financial part o' this thing?"

"Certainly," Callaway said. "Come in and sit down."

A moment later, the banker was reading over the new deed, concealing his fury that Morgan now owned the property. He only half studied the document and then looked at the two men. Twenty-six hundred dollars, is that right?"

"Yes," Morgan said. He took the bag he had been carrying and placed it on the banker's desk. He opened it and pulled out wads of bills, much to Callaway's surprise. The banker watched in amazement as Lee peeled off twenty-six hundred-dollar bills and handed them to Callaway. "Count it, give it to Willie, and then make out a receipt for me and a copy for Willie," he commanded.

"Yes, of course," the banker said. He quickly counted the money, nodded, and handed the bills to McCormick. Then he made out a receipt with a carbon that said Willie McCormick had received $2,600 from Lee Morgan for the transfer of a piece of property known as Spade Bit Ranch. He then looked at Willie. "What are you going to do with all that money?"

"Well, I figured I'd keep a little in my pocket and then bank the rest. How do I open an account here, Mr. Callaway?"

"We'd be more than pleased to hold your money," Callaway said, "and we pay 2 percent interest, so your money will be making more money while it's in this bank. You'll get a bank book and anytime you want to withdraw funds, why all you have to do is present your bank book to one of the tellers." He pointed to the old man. "I can assure you, the money will be a lot safer here than on your person."

Willie looked doubtfully at Morgan. "Lee, is that a good idea?"

"Yes, it is," Lee answered. He then emptied the rest of the bag. More bills tumbled atop Callaway's desk, along with a couple of dozen gold nuggets. He smiled at the banker. "I intend to bank my own money here."

Callaway stared at the heap of bills and gold and then at Morgan. "I haven't counted this, Mr. Morgan, but it sure looks like a lot of money."

"I had some luck up in the Klondike," Morgan said. "I've been traveling about for the past few years and then I found a wonderful girl up in Fairbanks. So I figured it was a good time to get married, come home, and settle down. I don't know what could please me more than to raise horses again on Spade Bit. As you see, I've got plenty of money here and I can turn Spade Bit into one of the finest horse ranches in the west, the way it was before."

As Morgan spoke, a new pang of rage stabbed Callaway's insides. Morgan had made his own plans, and it was obvious that he would not sell the property under any circumstances, no matter what the price. The stack of bills and gold on the desk made Morgan a wealthy man who would have no reason at all to sell Spade Bit.

"Would you like to count this, Mr. Callaway?" Morgan asked.

"Yes, I'll do that, but as for the gold, I'll have to weigh and assay it to determine its worth."

"Sure," Lee said.

Morgan watched as Jesse Callaway counted the

bills he had dumped on the table. The banker counted for nearly two minutes and then looked up. "You've got $10,150 here, Mr. Morgan."

"Can your bank take that much?"

"Sure, sure. We have assets of nearly a half million. A lot of it is invested in mortgages and loans, of course, but we have good collateral so your money is safe." He gestured to a man behind one of the teller windows. When the clerk arrived, he handed him the pile of gold nuggets saying, "Weigh these and assay them and then bring them back."

"Yes, sir." The clerk, impressed, hurried off.

"While we're waiting," Callaway said, "we'll make out your deposit applications and a bank book. As I just told Mr. MrCormick," he looked at Morgan, "you'll get a pass book and you can come in anytime to withdraw funds. We'll just check your signature with the one on the application."

"Fair enough," Morgan said.

"I assume the deed transfer has all been taken care of," the banker said.

Morgan leaned over the desk. "It has, no thanks to the land office clerk," he said. "I don't think he's very competent. He gave me the new deed, signed and notarized, but then didn't give us the duplicate copy to sign, the copy that goes to the county clerk. And the man wasn't making any effort to record the sale in his ledger. Do you know anything about that man, Mr. Callaway?"

The banker tightened his jaw. He knew that Jed Thompson had tried to make the best out of a bad situation. Without a copy of the duplicate deed at Boise, and without record of the sale in his ledger,

Morgan would have been left with only his own copy of the deed to prove his claim on Spade Bit. Callaway would have only needed to steal this single copy to erase Morgan's proof of ownership. But again he smiled at Morgan, even as his insides boiled with frustration.

"Jed Thompson doesn't always think straight. I suppose he was just trying to save you time. But you did have the second copy of the deed made, signed, and notarized, didn't you? And Thompson will get it to Boise."

"I have the second copy all right," Morgan said, "but I'm not trusting that fool to get it to Boise. I'm going to take it to the county court myself. I have it right here."

This Lee Morgan was a lot smarter than the banker thought. No doubt he had learned plenty during his years as drifter, and he was not making any mistakes. Callaway could do nothing at the moment but patronize his two new customers, and he soon completed the deposit applications and had Morgan and McCormick sign them. By now, the teller had returned with the gold nuggets.

"These are top grade, Mr. Callaway. After weighing them and assessing them, I'd say they're worth in the neighborhood of $10,000."

"Thank you," Callaway said. He then took a small bag out of the desk drawer and put the nuggets inside. "I can't give a bank book for these nuggets, Mr. Morgan, but I'll give you a receipt on their weight and quality number, with an approximate worth based on today's gold prices. We'll keep the nuggets in our safe. You can take out as many as

48

you like," the banker said, "and we'll merely deduct the weight."

"That'll suit me fine, Mr. Callaway," Morgan said.

Callaway had just handed the passbooks to Morgan and McCormick when a young woman walked up to the railing.

"Are you busy, Jesse?" she asked.

Lee Morgan turned and stared. She was a beauty —sleek, dark hair, clean and shiny; full lips, a smooth, oval face, and most of all the sparkling blue eyes that shone with an energetic vibrancy, a lust for life. She was quite shapely and her attire accented her figure: neat brown boots enhanced her slim legs, a tan riding skirt that flared from slim hips, and a white blouse that emphasized her full breasts.

"I'll be with you in a minute, Sue," the banker said.

The girl now looked at the old man and the young one sitting across the desk from Callaway. She could see that Morgan had been scanning her and she responded with a scrutiny of her own. She liked the light brown eyes, the lean face, and his thick blond hair.

"These two just came in on some bank business," Callaway said. "This is William McCormick and this is Lee Morgan, who just bought the Spade Bit Ranch from Mr. McCormick. Mr. Morgan intends to raise horses again on that spread."

The girl smiled at Lee. "I hope you'll succeed, Mr. Morgan. I know the place used to be one of the most successful horse ranches in the area. My father used

49

to point it out to me whenever we passed the place." Then she frowned. "You wouldn't be the son of Frank Leslie, would you?"

"The same," Morgan nodded. "I gave up the place and sold out to Willie here after the hoof and mouth disease wiped out my herd. Willie kind of took care of the place while I was gone."

"Did you get homesick, Mr. Morgan?" The girl smiled again.

"I guess you could say that," Lee answered.

"Well, this is nice country," the girl said.

"Sue and her father Jim Clemons run the Clemons Trading Agency in town," Callaway said. "As I told you, Mr. Morgan, there have been a lot of changes here in Shoshone County; ranchers moving out and homesteaders moving in to farm and raise sheep. Jim and Sue Clemons have been handling most of the selling and buying, working through our bank."

"We've had our eye on Spade Bit," the girl said, "but if you intend to turn it into a horse ranch again, I guess we can rule it out as a possible parcel."

"I'm afraid that's right, Miss Clemons," Morgan said, rising from the chair as did Willie McCormick to shake Callaway's hand. "Nice doing business with you," Morgan told the banker. After the two men had come around the railing, the girl suddenly touched Lee's arm.

"Mr. Morgan, we deal in all kinds of sales, not only land. If you intend to stock that place, maybe we can get you some good horseflesh to start you off."

Lee Morgan grinned. "I'd like that, Miss Clemons; I'd like that very much."

"If you're short of funds, I'm sure we can prevail on Jesse Callaway to give you a loan," Sue continued.

Morgan only grinned, but Callaway spoke up. "He won't need any loans, Sue. I can't tell you how much he just deposited in this bank, but Mr. Morgan has cash to pay for anything he wants and then some."

"You must have done right well for yourself," Sue Clemons said.

"I was a little lucky, yes," Lee answered.

"You will stop into our office, won't you?" the girl said. "It's right up the street. You can't miss the sign: Clemons Trading Agency."

"You'll see me, Miss Clemons, I promise you."

"Good," said Sue.

The two continued to eye each other as Lee Morgan and Willie McCormick walked out of the bank. A mutual hint of admiration beamed from Lee's brown eyes and Sue's sparkling blue ones. Once outside, Willie McCormick turned to Morgan and grinned. "She sure is a pretty filly, ain't she?"

"I guess," Lee shrugged.

"She had her eye on you, that's for sure," the old man said. "But she ain't no more pretty than your wife, Sarah."

But Lee wasn't listening. His mind was on other things. "Willie, there's something wrong here. First that land clerk tries to botch the paperwork, and I can't believe that with all his experience he would be so neglectful. It almost seemed that he didn't want you to deed over Spade Bit to me. And there was this banker. He should have been overjoyed when we came in to deposit so much money in his bank, but I

51

got the idea that he wasn't too happy about me taking over Spade Bit, either. Then this pretty girl comes in, who runs a real estate office and does business with Callaway. Then there were those bushwhackers on the trail. I'm wondering now if they were really after me. I can't help remembering that the land clerk tried real hard to discourage me from buying Spade Bit when I first spoke to him yesterday."

"I can't go along with your suspicions," Willie said. "You've been to a lot o' places and met some mighty dishonest people, and you just don't trust people any more. Sure, Callaway wanted to buy me out, but that was just routine. It's like he said: Shoshone County is changing. The sodbusters are taking over and the ranchers are moving out. True, he's making some money when these lands change hands, but what banker or real estate people wouldn't? I don't think they care one way or the other if you keep Spade Bit."

"Well, maybe you're right." Morgan nodded, then said, "What are you going to do now, Willie?"

"I don't know." Willie shrugged. "I suppose I'll go back to Spade Bit and pack up my personal belongings and move out of the place. I'll probably take a room at the boardin' house here in town."

"Would you want to work for me?"

"Work for you?" the old man repeated, astonished.

"Sure." Lee grinned. "You know something about horses, and you certainly know everything about Spade Bit. I also need a couple of more hands, some good strong men. Do you think you could find a couple for me?"

Willie McCormick nodded. "I can take care of that, Lee, but I really can't run the place myself."

"You wouldn't have to do much. The other hands could do the bull work. Is the old bunkhouse still there?"

"It wouldn't take much to get it in shape," Willie admitted.

"Then you will work for me?"

McCormick shrugged. "Why not? I'd probably wither away and die if'n I just sat around doin' nothin' besides drinkin' liquor and gamblin'. Before you know it, I'd be sick and broke. I got a little more business in town, but tomorrow I'll find the help you want."

"Find me a couple of men you think would make good hands, who know about horses. I'll pay $30.00 a month and board. I'd also like you to find an all-around housekeeper who'll do the cooking and take care of the ranch house."

"And what'll you be doin'?"

"I've got to go to Boise to record the deed. I'll likely be gone for two or three days."

"What about your wife? You want me to take her out to Spade Bit?"

"If you don't mind."

"It's all right with me," Willie said. "And don't you worry none about hired help; I'll take care of things. I'll meet you at the hotel about noon to pick up your wife. That okay?"

Lee nodded and left the old man. Then he walked

to the Grover House, up the stairs, and to Room 21. Sarah leaped from her chair, happy to see him. She smiled and came towards him. "I missed you, Lee. I'm glad you're back!"

Lee grinned at his pretty wife. While he had admired Sue Clemons at the bank, she couldn't hold a candle to his Sarah. He took her in his arms and kissed her, immediately aroused by her body pressed against his. She led him to the bed, where she sat down and Lee sat beside her.

"Sarah, I have to go to Boise to bring our duplicate deed to Spade Bit to the county clerk's office. I'll be gone for two or three days. Meanwhile, I've asked Willie to stay on and to hire a couple more hands along with a housekeeper."

"We don't need a housekeeper, Lee. I can take care of that," she protested.

"You'll have to do your share," Morgan said, "but there's too much work for you alone. Willie will be here about noon to take you to Spade Bit, and I'll ride out to join you as soon as I get back from Boise."

An ecstatic beam flashed from Sarah's blue eyes. She threw her arms around Lee and squeezed hard. "I can't wait to get to that ranch; I just can't wait!"

Lee reached into his pocket, extracted a wad of bills, and gave his wife twenty dollars. "This ought to get you anything you need until I get back," he said.

The girl took the money, but then looked fervently into her husband's eyes before she kissed him and caressed his chest. She smiled at him. "It's almost like I'm at my old profession, but you know that ain't true."

"No, it isn't," Lee said.

"We're not leavin' for a while," the girl whispered, kissing Lee on the ear and making him tremble. "This here is a nice, soft bed."

Lee Morgan rose from the bed, walked to the window and pulled down the shade. Soon, they were both naked and enjoying mutually passionate bliss on the soft hotel room bed.

Chapter 4

The two men standing before Callaway in his private office were embarrassed and very uneasy. The banker's thick neck was red with anger, irate lines cut through his moon face, and a burning irritation came from his dark eyes. The pair had seen their employer in a rage before, but not as intense as it was now. Callaway first pointed to the shorter of the two men.

"Marnie, I can't believe you let this happen to you; a man sneaking right up behind you and disarming you with a whip."

"He was fast, Mr. Callaway, awfully fast," Marnie whined.

Then the banker glared at the second taller one. "And you, Slim, how the hell could you let Morgan do that to you when you had the drop on him?"

"It's like Marnie says—he was awfully fast. Honest, Mr. Callaway, I never seen a man so fast. He come up with that rifle like lightning and fired before I even seen the Winchester move. He'd have

57

killed me sure if I didn't get out of there."

"He was just as fast with that whip," Marnie added.

"Well, at least you had the good sense to tell him you were waiting for somebody else, and not for him."

"He believed me, he did," Marnie said emphatically. "He didn't have no idea at all that it was him we was after."

"All right, all right." Callaway gestured impatiently, then glared at his two henchmen. "I'm going to give you another chance. Morgan intends to leave town again, going to Boise to personally record his new deed to Spade Bit. I want you on the trail south of here, maybe at Snake Pass, to wait for him. Be thorough this time. Don't ask any questions. Shoot first, and when you get him, make sure you get that deed off of him."

"We won't let him fool us this time," Marnie promised.

"Then move out now. I suspect he might head for Boise soon and figure to stay on the trail tonight so he can get to Boise early in the morning and then come back here. He's anxious to get working on that spread."

"Do you have any idea when he'll be leaving Grover, Mr. Callaway?"

The banker glared at Marnie. "I don't give a damn when he's leaving. You two get your asses out to Snake Pass and you wait for him, if you have to sit there for a week. And make damn sure you get that deed!"

"We'll get it," Slim promised.

Lee Morgan spent the bulk of the morning in bed

with Sarah. Then both he and his young wife bathed and dressed in clean traveling attire and went to the hotel dining room for a meal before Lee had the bellhop bring their bags downstairs. Lee carried a small bedroll that had a change of clothes.

The hotel boy brought Morgan's rig and gelding to the front of Grover House and held the reins until Morgan and Sarah came out of the hotel. Lee gave the boy a quarter tip, and the youth smiled, thanked Lee, and left. Lee swung his bedroll behind the seat, then put his rifle and whip there. Only a moment later Willie arrived with his small wagon. Lee helped Sarah aboard, threw her bags in the back, and kissed his wife, then stood and watched the wagon move off.

He was about to get into the buckboard when a woman called out to him, "Hello, Mr. Morgan, going somewhere?"

Lee turned to see Sue Clemons standing on the boardwalk. She looked even more attractive than he remembered her in the bank. She had also changed her clothing and was now clad in a traveling skirt and close-fitting jacket. A black Stetson completed her attire.

"You look like you're off somewhere yourself," Morgan said.

"I will be if you agree," the girl said.

"Me?" Lee asked, surprised.

"Who was that pretty woman I saw going off in that wagon?" Sue asked.

"My wife," Lee said. "She and Willie are going out to Spade Bit. I'll join them when I get back from Boise."

"Boise?" Sue Clemons cried. "I may be heading there myself. After you spoke to me in the bank, about the horses I mean, we sent a wire to a breeder

59

we know just north of Boise. He's got excellent animals. I asked if he had good stock to start a horse ranch. He wired us right back; said he had some good studs and mares, any breed you want. I can tell you, Mr. Morgan, this man has real fine stock; the best. But it does cost money. You'd probably have to pay about $1,000 for five animals, but you won't be sorry. I came looking for you because I was told you were staying at the Grover House. If you were agreeable to my suggestion, I intended to take the afternoon stage and go right down there to make the deal for you."

"I'm inclined to trust your judgment, Miss Clemons. All right, I'll go along with what you said." He leaned forward and looked at the girl with an amused twinkle in his amber eyes. "You don't have to take the stage. You could ride along with me. But I'll be staying on the trail tonight, and maybe you wouldn't be willing to do that—to be out on the trail alone with me all night, I mean."

The girl smiled and leaned closer to Morgan. "I'm not afraid if you aren't—but what about that pretty wife of yours? Would she mind?"

Lee grinned at the girl again. "She can trust me as I trust her. If you're all packed, we'll just get our things and then leave. But you'd better bring a blanket."

"My bag is right up the street at our agency office. I've also got a bedroll in the place; it's just up the street, right on the road out of town."

Within the next half hour, the buckboard carrying Lee and Sue had pulled out of Grover. Soon they were moving leisurely southward, the gelding trotting at a comfortable pace.

The terrain south of Grover pretty much

paralleled the landscape to the north—a mixture of flatlands, mountains in the distance, creeks, tall grass, and long stretches of forest. But even to the south, Lee Morgan had seen the same transformation in the terrain, more and more log or clapboard houses, the domiciles of sodbusters, and more and more plowed lands. Lee did, however, spot a few cattle ranches here and there, mostly small places, and he did see a couple of horse ranches. Apparently, some men were still clinging tenaciously to their old ways.

Lee Morgan could not help feeling a tingle inside him with the ravishing Sue Clemons next to him. When she smiled, he felt his nerves grow taut, and when she looked at him, her dazzling blue eyes almost mesmerized him. He could not help but notice her long, slender legs and the firm breasts that strained against her jacket. Still, he made no overtures to her, even though she had shown a keen interest in him. He was happily married to a girl who satisfied him in every way, he reminded himself sternly.

Lee remembered the many women he had met and made love to during his travels. Some had satisfied him completely, while others had engaged him in a mere biological exercise. He tried to keep his mind on Sarah, who was now his only love.

Lee and Sue Clemons talked of many things as they rode, getting acquainted and discussing their backgrounds. Sue said that she liked the trading business, an enterprise that gave her a chance to leave two parties satisfied, a buyer and a seller, and one that gave her a chance to help people, especially strangers who came to the area needing something. She had met an array of different folks and had found most of them to be essentially honest and easy to deal with. No, she had no steady beau, and she did not frequent saloons, gaming tables, or places of ill repute. She tended to her business and she found that most fulfilling. She generally spent her evenings at home with her father, playing the piano, or listening to the phonograph. When Lee bluntly asked her if she had ever had a lover, she only smiled impishly.

And what of Lee Morgan? Sue Clemons had heard of him, his fast gun, his wandering life, and rumors of trouble with the law and the companionship of outlaws. And she had also heard that he had left saddened women in dozens of places, and that he had killed countless men, and fought a hundred fights. Were these rumors all true?

Exaggerations, Lee assured her. Yes, he had traveled to many places; to Texas and San Francisco, and Mexico, and Argentina, and most recently to Alaska where he had luckily made a gold strike to return home with a handsome bundle of money. He had met Sarah there, and she had prompted him to reevaluate his life.

And what did Lee plan now? Would he stay in Grover permanently? Raise horses at Spade Bit for the rest of his life? Maybe also raise a family?

"That's my intent," he told the girl. "I've kept on Willie McCormick and he's going to hire some hands while I'm away at Boise."

"I've never been very far from Grover," the girl said. "Oh, I go to Boise quite often, but beyond that I've only been to Denver a few times and once to Kansas City. But I've never been to the big, sprawling cities like San Francisco, or Chicago, or New York. I guess I'm just a country girl at heart. I'm content to spend the rest of my life in Grover."

"A very pretty country girl," Lee Morgan said.

The girl leaned over and rubbed her shoulder against Lee. The touch sent a thrill through him and he realized that this pretty companion had aroused in him an excitement he had often experienced before. But when she ran her soft, warm fingers down his arm, he recoiled slightly. The girl took the hint and moved away from him.

As the buckboard approached Snake Pass, Marnie and Slim again waited behind some boulders. This time they had taken Lee's advice to graphite the barrels of their Winchesters so that they could emit no tell-tale glints to warn anyone approaching the pass. Marnie stiffened when he saw the buckboard coming towards the pass.

"There he is, and he's got a woman with him," he hissed to Slim.

"Must be the same girl who was with him last time," Slim said. "Well, we got our orders. They both get it 'cause we don't want no witnesses."

The two men crouched behind the rock with their rifles aimed ánd waited for the buckboard to come within range so they could shoot with a maximum expectation of accuracy. But then, Slim's eyes widened and slapped Marnie on the shoulder so hard that his companion winced from the blow.

"Jesus Christ, Marnie, Jesus Christ!" Slim hissed.

"What the hell's the matter with you, Slim? You gone loco?"

"Don't you see who's on that buckboard with Morgan? Can't you see? That ain't the girl who was with him yesterday. That's the Clemons girl, the woman who works with Jesse Callaway."

Now Marnie also squinted hard at the approaching buckboard and his eyes also widened.

"I'll be a son of a bitch! It *is* the Clemons girl." He turned and looked anxiously at his companion. "What are we gonna do, Slim? How the hell can we kill that girl? Christ, she not only works with Callaway, but he's got a thing for her. He'll hang us by our balls if we shoot that girl!"

"Let me think, let me think," Slim said quickly. He looked again at the buckboard that was now coming into good, close range, and then he heaved a deep sigh. "Marnie, how the hell are we supposed to know who the girl is on that buckboard from this distance? It won't be our fault if we mistook her for the other one. We'll just have to kill her, too."

"I don't know, Slim, I don't know." Marnie shook his head.

"Marnie, if we don't do the job this time, you know damn well what Callaway will do to us. And I must tell you, I like this job and the good pay. We hardly do any work at all and we get plenty o' money. No, I say we kill both o' them."

"Yeah, you're right, Slim." Marnie crouched deeper and pushed the barrel of his Winchester further over the rock. Then he took a steady aim, getting Lee Mogan into his sights. Meanwhile he spoke to Slim. "You get the girl. I'll take Morgan."

"*Me?*" Slim gasped.

"We'll have to shoot together," Marnie said.

Slim shuddered. He did not like this idea at all, killing a girl who worked for Callaway, shooting somebody that Callaway wanted. He licked his lips nervously, but knelt beside Marnie and aimed his own rifle, sighting in on Sue Clemons next to Lee Morgan. Without warning, Slim fired, but his nervousness had thrown off his aim and the shot missed, popping out a chunk of dirt in front of the gelding.

On the road below, Lee Morgan acted instinctively. Before Marnie could take his own shot, Lee veered the frightened horse quickly to the right and off the shoulder of the road as the second shot also chopped out a chunk of earth. Morgan whipped the gelding hard and drove the buckboard over a rough square of grassland and into a brake, the wagon bouncing over the rough terrain. When he pulled the horse to a stop, they were quite well hidden from the road.

Lee quickly got Sue off the wagon and dragged her into a clump of scrub pine. The girl was terrified and shaking as Lee dropped her to a sitting position on the damp ground.

"Why were they shooting at us? Why?" she gasped.

Lee patted the girl's hand. "I don't know, but I'm sure as hell going to find out! That's the second time in two days I've run into bushwhackers."

"Y-you mean somebody's trying to kill you?" the girl's eyes widened.

"I didn't think so yesterday, but I think so now." He reached into his holster and pulled out his forty-five. "Here, take this. If you hear anything, don't hesitate to shoot. I'm going up there to see who those ambushers are."

"P-Please," Sue Clemons gripped her companion's arm, "don't go! They might still be waiting for you—for us."

"Don't worry," Lee said. He took his whip and rifle from the buckboard, swished the lash to make sure it was pliant, then cocked the Winchester. "You wait right here for me; I'll be back." The girl licked her dry lips but said nothing. She stiffened fearfully as Lee disappeared into the woods. Then she scanned the area about her for possible

65

attackers.

Lee Morgan had run into ambushers many times before and he had long ago learned to deal with them. He moved cautiously through the trees, silently, stealthily, until he had come some distance south from the spot where the shots had come from. Now he squinted from behind the trees, trying to get a clue to the whereabouts of the ambushers. He saw nothing, but he guessed that they were somewhere behind the rocks on the other side of the road. He dashed across the highway, dropped again, then squinted upwards, but still saw nothing.

Now Lee began a slow, quiet climb towards the rocks, his rifle and whip ready. He stopped suddenly when he heard stones cascading from the rock area some two hundred yards to his left. They were in there, all right, and he would get them.

Above him, behind the rocks, Marnie and Slim sat on the ground in utter dismay. They had failed again. Marnie accused his companion of firing too soon and too impetuously. The shot had alerted Morgan and the wily man had quickly veered away to avoid Marnie's bullet. Now he was hidden in the woods somewhere, perhaps searching for them. They dared not remount and go onto the open road. They were too familiar with Morgan's ability with a gun after receiving a personal demonstration yesterday.

"Goddamn it, Slim," Marnie cursed, "now we're in real trouble! Callaway will have our hides for sure, and we dasn't even leave here until dark. If Morgan spots us, he'll pick us off, even from a couple hundred yards."

Slim did not answer.

Lee had heard Marnie's lament and he was stunned. Callaway? The banker? He had ordered

Lee's assassination? Good God! Why! What had Lee ever done to this banker? Lee simply could not understand, but at least he was now aware of an implacable enemy. Another thought struck him. Clemons Realty had worked with Callaway and his bank. Would Callaway be so callous as to kill Sue Clemons just to get him? He would only find answers when he captured these two ambushers. He waited, hoping to hear one of the bushwhackers speak again so he could better pinpoint their location. The man Marnie soon accommodated him.

"Why the hell did you shoot so soon? If you'd waited until they got a little closer we'd have got them for sure."

Slim did not answer. He was too rattled and upset.

Neither man knew that the person they dreaded was now within a short distance of them as Lee Morgan continued his stealthy advance. Suddenly, Lee rose full length, peering over a rock at the two men huddled behind another boulder. "Drop those rifles and drop them quick!" he ordered.

Slim reacted instinctively and raised his Winchester. But he had not even got it halfway up when a rifle shot struck him squarely in the chest. A surprised look was pasted on his face as Slim tumbled over and fell dead, stretched out on his back amid the stones and pebbles. Marnie gaped at his companion and then stared in horror at Lee Morgan.

"P-please, please! D-don't kill me," Marnie said as he tossed his rifle aside, raised his arms and pressed his back against the boulder. He sat immobile as Lee Morgan came forward.

Lee threw his own rifle down and then tossed his whip from his left hand to his right. Next, he ran the fingers to his left hand over the lash before he reared back and snapped the whip. The tip struck Marnie's hand like a rattler's fangs and cut a gash across the palm. Before the man was even aware of the sting, the lash came out again, ripping open Marnie's shirt and leaving a gash just above his ribs. The man had barely reacted to this second cut when still again the lash came, this time slashing his right ear, causing blood to roll down his neck. Marnie was terrified as Lee came closer.

"Now you listen, you bastard," Lee growled. "You better give me some answers or the next time I use this whip, I'll be taking out your eyes. I heard you mention Callaway. Why does he want to kill me?"

Marnie could not answer from sheer terror.

"Are you going to start talking, or will I use this again?"

"P-please, p-lease," Marnie pleaded again. "I'll talk! It was Callaway. He hired us to kill you. He wants the Spade Bit. He figures he can get a good profit from sodbusters if he has that land. Yes, I'll admit it now; we was supposed to get you yesterday, too. He told us to try again now; kill you and get the copy of that deed you're carrying."

"That son of a bitch," Lee cursed. "And he'd even kill Sue Clemons, somebody who was helping him make money in the sale and purchase of land?"

Marnie nodded. "What are you gonna do to me?" he asked anxiously.

Lee Morgan pursed his lips. "I ain't got no choice." He picked up the man's own Winchester and aimed it at Marnie.

Marnie threw up his hands. "My God! You wouldn't just kill me like that, in cold blood!"

Lee only shrugged. Then he fired. The shot blew

68

open Marnie's face and blood spewed like a suddenly broken water pipe that shot out a thick red liquid. The man keeled over and lay in the pool of his own blood. Lee raised the rifle again, and rolled both men on their backs with his boot. He then fired two shots, about two seconds apart, into the chests of the two dead men. It would not look good if somebody found them shot in the back.

Morgan left them there among the rocks, and scrambled down to the road. He walked quickly to the brake where he had left Sue Clemons, then stopped abruptly and cried, "Miss Clemons, don't shoot! It's me, Morgan!"

"Come on in."

The girl waited until Lee had come into the small clearing, then lowered the .45 and hurried up to him, throwing her arms around him. "Thank God you're all right! You're all right!"

Lee Morgan grinned. "Were you worried?"

The girl's face hardened and she glared at Lee. "Yes, I was worried. I was fearful for you and for myself. Who knows what those men up there might have done if they got you?" Then she frowned. "I heard several shots."

"I had to kill them. When I reached them, they tried to shoot me and I had no choice."

The girl nodded. Then her pretty face sobered. "You saved my life."

"Mine too," Lee answered.

She stroked the fringes of his buckskin jacket. "You're a brave man, Mr. Morgan, going up there and risking getting your head blown off. Who'd want to kill you—or me? Who?"

"I don't really know. As I said, I had to kill these men before I could learn anything from them," Lee Morgan lied. "But I think we're out of danger now.

69

We'll ride on until dark and then camp for the night."

"I have to admire you, Mr. Morgan."

"Lee; just call me Lee," Morgan grinned.

A few moments later they were again aboard the buckboard and once more moving south towards Boise. They did not say much to each other, for the recent trauma had still left Sue Clemons shaken. But the girl occasionally glanced over at Lee, a growing admiration beaming from her bright blue eyes. Soon she moved closer to him, resting against his side. She rode that way for some time, then looked up at her companion.

"Lee," she half whispered, "I think I like you."

"I couldn't be more pleased," Lee grinned, "but we'd both best remember that I got a real loyal wife waiting for me back at Spade Bit."

The girl sighed, then squinted up at the growing dusk. The sun was gone now. "Will we be stopping for the night soon?" she asked.

"Pretty soon," Lee answered.

Finally, when darkness had totally enveloped the landscape, Lee pulled off the road and onto a rutted path where fishermen often drove their wagons or horses to fish for bass on the Payette River. He found a good clearing, dry and soft, and unhitched the horse and tethered the animal to a tree. Then he gathered firewood and started a fire. He took out a pan, some cups, metal plates, forks, biscuits, a pot, and coffee. The girl watched as he mixed the coffee into the pot with water and placed the pot over the fire, then drop slabs of jerky into a pan and place this over the fire as well. Soon they were eating biscuits, hot jerky, and drinking coffee. Sue ate slowly, looking at Lee's lean face, sporadically dark or bright from the firelight. Then she smiled. "You can do a great deal more than simply deal with ambushers, can't you?''

"I do what I have to," Morgan said.

Later, after they had eaten and Sue had washed the utensils, and as the fire diminished to dying embers, Lee crawled into his bedroll and Sue slid into her own. However, neither of them immediately fell asleep. Lee stared at the embers but even in the darkness, he sensed that the girl's eyes were riveted on him. He finally looked back at her but only grinned, making no move to come near her.

Sue Clemons heaved a sigh. "Good night," she said before she rolled over and pulled the blankets closer around her body.

Lee Morgan scowled. For the first time, he was almost sorry he was married . . . .

Chapter 5

Dawn had broken with clear blue skies in the wilds between Grover and Boise, with an array of birds chirping in the trees. Lee Morgan opened his eyes and saw the still slumbering Sue Clemons across from him, beyond the ashes that had been last night's campfire. For a moment he was not sure where he was, but he then remembered that he was on his way to Boise and that he had taken the girl with him. Lee shivered slightly for there was a chill in the air at this early morning hour. When he looked at the girl again, he remembered his wife and wondered how she had fared at the Spade Bit on her first night there. He wished Sarah were with him instead of Sue Clemons.

As Lee slid out quietly from under his blanket, the morning cold stabbed him. He walked over to the girl and pulled her blanket closer around her. She stirred slightly, but she did not awake. Morgan stood erect, trying to smooth his trousers and buckskin shirt that had become crumpled from sleeping in them all night. After he had slipped on his boots, he gathered some kindling and wood and soon had a fire going. Then he took the coffee pot and walked the few dozen yards to the river where he filled it with clear water.

The girl was still sleeping soundly when Lee returned to the campsite. He put some coffee into the pot and hung it on an improvised support, then placed the frying pan over the flames and laid several strips of bacon in the pan. Soon, the aroma of sizzling meat mixed with the smell of burning wood radiated through the forest.

"Mm, that sure smells good."

Lee turned, to see the girl wide awake now and peeking from under her blanket. She had a friendly smile on her face and an admiring gleam in her eyes. Lee returned the smile, then said, "I didn't mean to wake you up just yet."

"I simply can't get over your many talents," Sue Clemons said.

"I'm going down to the river bank to wash up," Lee said. "I won't be long." The girl nodded and watched him move off. He had left the campfire deliberately for he wanted to give the girl a chance to dress in privacy. He washed his hands and his face, and had brought his straight razor with him to give himself an improvised shave—no suds and no mirror. But Lee had learned to shave without such needs. By the time he came back to the campfire, the girl was fully dressed.

"Will we have breakfast soon?" she asked.

"Five or ten minutes," Lee said.

"Good," Sue answered. "That'll give me time to wash up a little, too." While she was gone, he stirred the coffee, getting a good mixture as the water boiled, and turned over the bacon strips so they'd be done on both sides. The girl meanwhile had washed up at the river bank and then combed her hair as best she could. When she stood up, she tried to smooth out some of the wrinkles in her skirt and blouse. Finally, she came back to the campfire and smiled at Lee Morgan.

He handed her a tin plate with bacon and a biscuit, then gave her a cup of hot coffee. "This isn't much, but it'll hold us until we reach Boise. Then we can get ourselves a good restaurant meal," he told her.

"Like I said, Lee, you're a man of many talents."

"After a while you learn to have to be able to do a lot of things for yourself if there's nobody else to do them," he said, staring at the girl. Yes, she was pretty, even with her somewhat rumpled clothing, hastily washed face, and hurriedly combed hair. Sue Clemons noted the stare and smiled at him again.

After breakfast, she gripped Lee's hand as he started to clean up. "You get the horse and buckboard ready and I'll take care of this," she suggested.

"Are you sure?"

"I'm not exactly a cripple," the girl said. "I feel I should do something, after you did all the cooking last night and again this morning."

Lee Morgan nodded and rehitched the gelding to the wagon, after feeding the animal some oats he had brought with him. Occasionally, he watched the girl who moved briskly and efficiently as she gathered up the cups, plates, pot, pans, and eating utensils before walking off to the river bank to wash them. Lee had finished his own chores before the girl got back and doused the fire with water from the coffee pot.

Soon, they had packed the buckboard, clambered on the front seat, and left the campsite. Again Lee drove leisurely south along the St. Marie Road. They talked as they continued south, the girl questioning Lee on his many adventures. When she asked what had been his worst experience, he needed to stop and think, but then decided the jaunt to Argentina was probably his most agonizing disappointment. He had gone into partnership with a rancher, Juan McGee, whom he had befriended, intending to help him deal with hostile Benudo Indians under the vicious chief named Cuchillo.

"You can't believe how fierce the Benudos are," Lee said. "They have no respect whatever for human life and they relish torture."

They had caused wholesale destruction and death at the McGee ranch, raping, pillaging, and burning, then killing anything that moved. Lee had been out looking for them at the time the band had caused this havoc, and he finally caught up to them, but only after they had ravaged and murdered McGee's pretty daughter, Sarita. Morgan had killed some of the Indians, but he realized that his efforts had been a total failure.

"The Indians in our own west are not as savage as the Benudos," Lee said. "And of course, our Indian problem is over now, but it's still going strong in South America."

"Will you ever go back there, Lee?" the girl asked.

"I doubt it," Morgan answered. "I've seen enough poverty, inhumanity, and greed to last me a lifetime. I think I'm making the right decision in coming back here to settle on Spade Bit."

"I'm glad," the girl said, leaning back and staring up at the sky.

They continued for most of the morning and when the sun was getting high in the sky, radiating a pleasant warmth, the girl turned to Lee. "The breeding farm is only one or two miles away. We should be there before noon."

"I'm looking forward to it."

The ride continued for about another half hour before Lee Morgan saw the sprawling spread with many corrals that held horses. In the fields beyond, more horses could be seen. He could surely get the stock he needed from this ranch, Lee decided.

When Lee reached the entrance to the spread, he saw a big sign overhead: Chapman's Horse Ranch. He urged the gelding forward into the place, past several corrals and up to the front of the long, low-slung ranch house. He dismounted from the buckboard, tied the horse, then helped the girl down. A burly man came out the front door and onto the porch. When he saw Sue Clemons, he grinned, came down the steps, and pumped her hand in a warm greeting.

"My God, Suzanne, you sure got here in a hurry!"

The girl cocked her head towards her companion. "This is Lee Morgan. He's the customer I told you about in my wire."

"Glad to meet you, Mr. Morgan," the burly man said, shaking Lee's hand as well. "I'm Joe Chapman, and as you can see I raise all kinds of horses for sale."

"I can see that you have quite a selection."

"Are you going to start from scratch?" Chapman asked.

"Yes," Morgan answered.

"Well, I can tell you that we've found certain breeds very popular now," the rancher said. "A lot of people like Morgans for saddle horses because they're strong and they can go long distances without tiring. But for the past couple of years or more, there's been a big demand for work horses, like Percherons and Clydesdales. The homesteaders who've been coming into Shoshone County are always looking for them."

Lee Morgan listened and nodded.

"Now," Chapman gestured, "it depends on *why* you want to raise horses. If you want to make a good profit on it, I'd suggest you start with work horses because there's a big demand for them right now, and the demand will get bigger as more homesteaders come into Idaho."

"To tell you the truth, Mr. Chapman, I'm more interested in raising horses for pleasure than making a profit," Lee said, "so right now I'm not particularly interested in work horses."

"Then I suppose you'd want saddle horses," Chapman said.

Lee nodded.

"Of course," the burly man gestured, "there's also a market for saddle horses, like I said, so you could still make a profit with them. The Morgans are real easy to break. And the name ought to suit you real well," Chapman added with a grin.

"I'll need four mares and a stallion," Lee told him.

"Come on out back to my Morgan corral," Chapman gestured, "and you can take a look at what I've got. The mares are one and two years old, so they should foal for a good many years. I got a real good stallion that will breed those mares like rabbits." He grinned.

Lee Morgan returned the grin.

As they walked behind the long ranch house, Sue Clemons held Lee's arm. "Chapman is the best, Lee.

No low stock. All his animals are clean, healthy, and strong. If he gets any bad ones, he won't keep them around. He'll sell them off to skinners who pass them off for a cheap price on the unsuspecting."

Morgan did not say anything, but when he reached the corral, he had only to take one glance to know that the animals were of high quality. His eyes focused on a big roan stallion. The animal's legs looked exceptionally strong, his back was broad and full, and his head was held high, almost haughtily. Without a doubt, this was the best of the stallions in the corral. Joe Chapman could not help noticing the stare, and he nodded at Morgan.

"That's the best, the one you have your eye on; Upway Don, we call him, because he's the king in there. He's two years old and he'll have a long, productive life if you take care of him. But I have to tell you," Chapman added soberly, "I can't let that animal go for under $400."

"That's fair enough," Lee said, after a moment's hesitation.

"All right," the man said. "Then I'm willing to give you any of the mares you pick out for $200.00 each."

"Joe," the girl said, "I told Mr. Morgan that he could probably get all the stock he wanted for about $1,000."

"That's true, and I could have given him five horses for that price, but not the Don; not *that* animal."

"It's all right, Mr. Chapman," Lee Morgan said. "I don't mind paying extra for a superior animal."

Chapman grinned. "I can tell that you know quality when you see it."

"In fact, I'll need a couple more horses, for my

79

hands to work around the ranch, and a work horse to pull a wagon."

Joe Chapman pursed his lips pensively for a moment, then pointed at Lee. "Tell you what I'll do. If we close the deal for $1,500, I'll throw in a couple of mustangs and a real strong Percheron that can pull three tons."

"We have a deal," Lee grinned, gripping Chapman's hand in a firm handshake.

"Joe," the girl spoke again, "Mr. Morgan here has considerable funds in the Grover Merchants Bank. Suppose he has Jesse Callaway transfer $1500 from his account to your own account at the Boise County Bank?"

"That would be fine, just fine," Chapman said. Then he turned to Morgan. "I can have these animals delivered to you by the end of the week."

"No." Lee shook his head. "It might be a while before I have my barns and corrals ready to house them. I'll wire you as to when I want delivery."

"All right," Chapman nodded. "As soon as I get your telegram, I'll have the animals sent up to you. Where do you want them delivered?"

"To the Spade Bit Ranch on the St. Marie's Road, about ten miles north of Grover."

Chapman frowned. "As I recall, we used to sell stock to somebody up there at one time; Frank Leslie, I think his name was."

"That was my father. I've been away for quite a while, but I intend to make a go of the place again," Lee told him.

"Well, I wish you a lot of luck."

After closing the deal, Lee and Sue went into the ranch house with Joe Chapman. He seated them in chairs before a big oak desk, then drew up the papers: a bill of sale for each animal and other information needed to cement the pact. When Chapman had finished, he and Lee both signed, with Sue as a witness. He then rose from his chair behind the desk, again shook Lee's hand, and expressed his pleasure at doing business with him. He hoped he could accommodate Morgan again some time, and told Lee that if he had any trouble with any of the animals, if they were not all Chapman said they were, he'd make good on anything he sold.

After Lee and Sue left the horse ranch, they continued on into Boise, a bustling cow town, where people jammed the streets. Corrals were filled with cattle, and some with horses. The railroad ran through the city so almost all the ranchers in Idaho now brought their stock here for shipment. Lee noted that huge warehouses had also sprung up to hold corn, wheat, and rye that farmers were now producing for shipment to the cities of the east and west coast. The town had really mushroomed during the years that Lee Morgan had been away.

His first stop was the county courthouse, where he duly recorded and left the deed copy to prove that he was again the owner of the Spade Bit Ranch. Then Lee took the girl to one of the better restaurants in town where they ate a tasty meal of ham, potatoes, vegetables, coffee, and pie. By early afternoon, Lee had completed his business in Boise and they started back northward to Grover. Sue had enjoyed these hours with Lee. Besides, she had done well with this customer. On a $1,500 sale, the Clemons Trading Agency would get a commission of $75.00.

Lee and Sue stayed on the trail until nightfall, and once again bedded down by the embers of their campfire. But Lee made no overtures to the girl, who was torn between attempting to seduce him, and remembering that he was a married man who seemed actually to care for his wife.

Late in the morning of the day following Morgan's visit to the horse ranch and to Boise, Jesse Callaway stood on the boardwalk in front of his bank. The sun was again beaming down from a clear sky, radiating an unusually pleasant warmth for this time of year, so the obese man had taken a break to enjoy the fine morning before turning to his routine.

Callaway was about to go back inside when he saw a rider coming up the street, leading two horses that carried bodies draped over the saddles. He squinted carefully and then his eyes widened. He recognized the two dead men. The bodies were those of his henchmen, Slim and Marnie. He blinked, unable to believe his eyes. It should have been Lee Morgan's body draped over a horse, but instead his two employees had been killed.

Callaway jostled through the crowd of pedestrians on the boardwalk towards the deputy sheriff's office, where the rider was leading his caravan of two dead men. The banker saw the horseman pull up to the small jail and tether the three horses, while Deputy John Chook, who had long ago recovered

82

from the bullet he had taken from Lee Morgan, stared at the man and then at the bodies. Jesse Callaway came within ten or fifteen feet of the jailhouse and stood there listening.

"What's this all about?" Chook asked.

"My name is Carlisle, Henry Carlisle. I work on one of the ranches down near Snake Pass, north o' Boise. A couple of hunters found these two men about dawn this morning." Carlisle cocked his head at the bodies. "They were both killed at pretty close range, lying in a jumble of rocks off the road. My boss asked me to bring 'em into Grover and tell you what happened out there."

"Do you have any idea who killed them?" the deputy asked.

The man shook his head. "Nope. But from what the hunters told us, I got an idea these two dead men were apparently hiding behind some rocks to take a shot at somebody coming up the road. I'd guess they missed their quarry, and then somebody found them and killed them."

"Goddamn!" Chook hissed, astonished.

Now Jesse Callaway came up to the deputy. He looked at the rider, then at the bodies, and then at Chook. "Those two men worked for me, John," he said.

"For you?" the deputy frowned. "What the hell were they doing out there in them rocks, maybe waiting to bushwhack somebody, as this man says?"

"I have no idea," Callaway lied smoothly.

"Well, we'll have to look into this," Chook blustered. He turned to Carlisle. "Better take the bodies over to the mortician. He's right on the next

83

street, on the corner; you can't miss him: DuBois Mortuary."

The man nodded, untethered the horses, climbed on his mount, and then moved slowly away. When he was gone, Deputy Chook scowled at Callaway. "Are you sure you have no idea what those two men were doing at Snake Pass?"

"As I said, they work for me, but not twenty-four hours a day," the banker said. "I can't account for every minute of their time."

"The rider who brought them in thought they might have been lying in wait to hit somebody comin' up the road. Why would they do that?"

"How do I know?" the banker shrugged. "Maybe they didn't think I paid them enough and they wanted to make some extra money on the side." Maybe they weren't waiting to ambush anybody; maybe they just were riding up there and got bushwhacked themselves."

"Well, I'll look into it," Chook said. "I'd appreciate it, Mr. Callaway, if you'd come into my office when you get a chance and tell me all you can about those two men. It might help me in my investigation."

"Sure, John," Callaway said. "I'll come in this afternoon."

Jesse Callaway walked away from the jail, but he could feel himself shaking. He had known of Lee Morgan's prowess but he could not believe that the man could be that good, to avoid an ambush twice. He was certain that Morgan had killed Marnie and Slim. But how? And of course, if he had avoided this second trap, he had no doubt

84

reached Boise to record his deed. If indeed Morgan refurbished Spade Bit and made a success of the place again, other ranchers would be encouraged to stay on and the business of buying and selling land for a good profit would come to an end.

Callaway had reached the Black Ace. He nonchalantly peered inside and saw a man sitting alone at a table, drinking whiskey from a bottle. The banker ducked inside and walked up to him. "Brady, would you mind coming to my private office? I have a job for you."

The man shrugged, took another swig of whiskey, then rose from the table. Within ten minutes he was standing in Callaway's private office while the banker sat behind his desk. The man waited before Callaway gestured and then spoke. "Brady, I need a gunman, a good one. Somebody who won't make a mistake."

"There are lots o' gunmen around, Mr. Callaway. You don't need me to find you one," said Brady.

"None of those I know are good enough. I need one who is sure to do what he has to—and maybe is a leader as well, who can rile up enough people to cause a lot of trouble for someone. I need somebody who can draw faster than the eye can see, with a spiel better than Daniel Webster, and with the leadership qualities of a Calhoun."

"You sure want a lot, Mr. Callaway," the man grinned. "Well, I can tell you, there's only one man I know who fills those qualifications—Billy Paxton. Last I heard, he was in Wyoming chasing off a bunch of sodbusters for the Cattlemen's Association. Those that Paxton and his boys didn't drive off, he killed. I ain't never heard of Paxon failing in a job."

"Then that's the man I want," Callaway stated.

"Do you know his price?" Brady laughed. "Why, he'd wipe you right out with his fees! He has four steady boys that work with him, and they ain't but an eyelash slower than he is with a gun."

"I don't care what it costs," Callaway said. "If you can get him up here to do a job for me, I'll give you a hundred dollars—fifty now and the rest when this Paxton and his boys get here. In fact, if you can get him here within a week I'll give you a $25.00 bonus."

"But what am I going to tell him, if I find him?"

Jesse Callaway reached into a drawer and pulled out a checkbook. He wrote quickly on one of the checks; date; name: Billy Paxton; amount of $500.00 and his signature, drawn on Callaway's own Grover Merchant's Bank. "You just give him this check and tell him there'll be a lot more for him and his men if he can do the job I need to have done." Brady whistled when the banker handed him the check. Then he counted the five ten dollar bills that Callaway gave him. "How soon can you leave?" Callaway asked.

"I'll take the early stage to Boise, and the first train tomorrow to Cheyenne. That's where Paxton must be now."

"You aren't to say a word about this, do you understand?"

"Whatever you want done, is none o' my business. Nobody will know why I'm goin' to Cheyenne."

Callaway watched Brady leave his office, then stood up and looked out the window at the array of clapboard shacks in the distance. There was too much money to be made from those anxious sodbusters inside those hovels. Even if he had to pay this Billy Paxton a couple of thousand dollars to get rid of Lee Morgan, it would be worth it.

Chapter 6

Lee Morgan arrived back at Grover about mid-afternoon, and none too soon, because dense clouds had accumulated overhead, hanging low with the threat of rain. When Lee reached the Clemons Trading Agency office, he helped Sue down from the buckboard and untied her bag and blanket from the rack. He offered to carry the gear inside, but she waved him off with a smile.

"It's all right, Lee. I can handle it. What are you going to do now?" she asked.

"Ride out to Spade Bit. My wife is already there and Willie McCormick probably has things going strong by now. I really should be helping out."

"You will stay in touch, won't you?"

Lee Morgan pursed his lips. He and Sarah would be busy at Spade Bit, where they'd be working hard. "I'm sure we'll meet again, although I'll be mighty tied up on the ranch for some time," he said.

"I understand," the girl said. "Well, when you're straightened out, you come back and see us, won't you? Maybe we can help you buy some other things you might need.''

Lee Morgan nodded and watched Sue walk into the agency office. He stood immobile for a moment, a frown on his lean face. Damn it! He was sorry he had met this pretty girl. He had come back to Grover with Sarah to settle down, to forget about other women as he tried to forget about his previous adventures over the past years. But he could not deny the desire he felt for Sue Clemons.

Lee sighed and began to clamber onto the seat of his buckboard, when someone tapped him on the shoulder. Lee turned to face Deputy John Chook who was looking sharply at him.

''Don't I know you?'' the deputy asked. ''You sure look familiar and I rarely forget a face.''

Lee Morgan studied the man and then nodded. ''Yes, but it was a long time ago, and it was something I'd just as soon forget.'' Then he grinned. ''It was in the Black Ace Saloon, when I was a lot younger. Morgan's my name; Lee Morgan.''

''I'll be goddamned!'' Chook gasped. ''What the hell are you doing back here in Grover?''

''I bought back Spade Bit from old Willie McCormick and I intend to start raising horses again. I just came back from Boise to record my deed for the place, and I stopped off to buy some new stock.''

''Yeah, I remember now.'' Chook scowled. ''You still go around bothering other people's women and playing loose with a fast gun? A lot of people around here still haven't forgotten what you did to Peach and how you shot me. You were a pretty wild kid.''

Lee Morgan studied the man. He recalled how irate Chook had been in the saloon that night, but in retrospect, Lee felt no guilt. He had not started any fights—he had just defended himself. He had no reason to make excuses for his actions.

"Look, Deputy," Lee said, "what took place in the past is over and done. It's forgotten as far as I'm concerned. I've been doing a lot of traveling for some time and now I just want to go back to my old homestead and settle down. Is there anything wrong with that?"

"No, I can't say there is; and I hope that's *all* you want to do." Chook stroked his chin, for another thought had struck him. He knew that Jesse Callaway had wanted Spade Bit badly. Callaway must have been furious when old man McCormick had sold the place to Morgan instead. Those two dead men he had seen today had worked for Callaway. Their bodies were found among the rocks at Snake Pass, and Morgan no doubt had gone through Snake Pass on his way to Boise. Had Morgan done those two in when they tried to bushwhack him? Chook had no proof of this, nor was he inclined to bring up the subject, at least not at the moment.

Still, Deputy John Chook felt fearful. Lee Morgan was obviously strong and determined, no doubt hardened from years of traveling and also probably an even better shot than he had been in the Black Ace on that day so long ago. Chook also knew that Callaway was a determined man, too, and the banker had the money to hire anybody he wanted to help Callaway to get what he wanted. Was there going to be trouble between Callaway and Morgan? Would hired guns be coming into Grover to dispute the ownership of Spade Bit? It could mean range war, with a lot of people hurt, and Chook didn't look forward to that. Grover and the Gunsight Gap country had been quite peaceful in recent years and the deputy liked it that way. It made his job much easier.

Chook stared hard at Morgan. "There isn't going to be any trouble now you're back, is there? I mean, there are a lot of homesteaders around here now and they won't put up with stock from local ranchers stomping all over their plowed fields. The day of the free range is over."

"Listen, Chook," Morgan said. "If there's going to be any trouble, I'm not the one who'll start it. I've got 1,200 acres out there, more than enough for my purposes, and there won't be any need for my stock to roam. Most of the land is well fenced and I intend to make repairs where necessary. If the sodbusters leave me alone, I'll leave them alone."

"Fair enough," Chook said.

"Now if you'll excuse me, I have to get out to my ranch. I'm anxious to see my wife and to start working on the place."

"Fine, Mr. Morgan," the deputy said. "I wish you and your wife a lot of luck." But there was little sincerity in the tone of his voice.

By three o'clock, Lee Morgan was well on his way to Spade Bit. He looked about warily as he approached Rock Slide Pass, for he remembered only too well how the two cowpokes had tried to ambush him here. However, he saw nothing suspicious, so he rode through in relative confidence. He drove leisurely for another hour and soon reached Spade Bit. Someone was raking the yard in front of the ranch house, while someone else appeared busy in the barn. He also spotted Willie McCormick on the front porch, replacing some rotted floor planks.

McCormick looked up and grinned as Morgan came into the yard. He hurried down the porch steps to meet his new employer, took the reins of the gelding and tethered the horse to a post. As Lee climbed off the buckboard McCormick offered him a handshake.

"It's about time you got back! We've been working around this place like jackasses, all of us, including your pretty wife. How did you make out in Boise? Did you get any horses?"

"Yes, I got some fine animals and they'll be shipped up here soon." He scanned the area and then grinned. "You're coming along nicely."

"Oh, we got a lot of chores finished," McCormick said. "The barn is pretty well set, and the housekeeper I hired and your wife have done quite well inside the house. Of course, there's still a lot more work to be done. We'll likely need some new tools to move along faster." He added, "We can even give you supper. Matilda—that's the housekeeper—will be doing the cooking." He gestured at the man working in the yard. "That's Clem Corcoran—used to work for a rancher up north near the Colorado Mission country. The other man I hired is Hank Goyette; used to work as a wrangler on the Land Brand Ranch. Matilda Maynard also worked at the Land Brand as a housekeeper. So, as you can see, Lee, I hired experienced people, and they're all three good workers."

"How did you manage to find them so quick?" Lee grinned.

"No trouble," Willie said. "There's a lot o' folks out o' work in the Gunsight Gap country, what with so many ranchers selling out. And them home-steaders sure as hell have no need to hire 'em. They couldn't afford to hire anybody, even if'n they wanted to."

"Well, let's get my stuff inside," Lee said, "then

you can stall the gelding and the buckboard." He looked up at the gray clouds. "The rain has held off so far, but I think we're still going to get a storm."

McCormick helped Lee to unload his belongings from the wagon and to carry them inside. Matilda met Lee and Willie and she curtsied with a smile. "I'm sure glad to meet you, sir," she said to Lee. "Your wife is sure a hard worker! Mrs. Morgan has got the main bedroom all cleaned up spic and span, with clean sheets and blankets on the bed. You can put your clothes inside the dresser drawers, because they've all been cleaned out, too. I've been working on the rest o' the house; got the kitchen taken care of, one of the other bedrooms, and the dining room cleaned up. I ain't got to this parlor nor the other rooms yet, but I promise I'll have them spruced in another day or two."

"I'm sure you've been doing a fine job," Lee said.

"I didn't expect you 'til tomorrow," Matilda said, "so I wasn't plannin' much for supper, jes' some rabbit stew, if you don't mind that."

"That'll be fine, Matilda," Lee said.

The women curtsied again. "And I want to tell you, Mr. Morgan, I'm sure grateful for this job. I didn't know what I was gonna do after the Land Brand went bust. I've been doin' the best I could since last summer, and it sure is a pleasure to have a steady job once more. I can tell you, I'm a good cook and a good cleaner. You won't have no trouble with me at all. Whatever you want, all you have to do is ask."

Lee Morgan studied the housekeeper: middle-aged, a little obese, with her dark hair now graying. Wrinkles crisscrossed her almost circular face, the result of advancing age and a hard life. However, her dark eyes were bright and lively. She wore a

94

simple print dress and an apron, with old sandals on her feet. Lee liked her.

Then Sarah came into the parlor, wearing an old cotton dress she had found somewhere. Perhaps it had belonged to Catherine Dowd. Sarah also wore a bandana around her head. She ran up and kissed Lee, overjoyed to have him home, happy she was involved in his new life.

"You look busy enough, Sarah," Lee said.

"I intend to pull my weight," the girl said proudly. Indeed, Sarah had worked hard all her life. Now she was eager to be an ideal wife to Lee Morgan, not only to satisfy his biological needs, but to cook for him, keep house, and offer him all the other comforts he deserved. Still, she felt a little threatened. Matilda could probably tend house and cook better than she could. But Sarah had made up her mind to show Lee that he had not made a mistake in marrying her.

"I'm glad to see you pitched right in," Morgan said.

"I'm truly enjoying myself!" The girl smiled again.

Willie McCormick gestured to Lee. "Let's go outside and look around. I'd like you to see what we've done so far and what else we have to do."

"That's a good idea," Lee said.

"Lee, do you want me to go with you?" Sarah asked.

"You seem to have enough work to do right here," Lee said. "Maybe you can help Matilda with supper."

After a tour of the ranch, he was more than satisfied. Willie and the two hired hands had done a good job thus far. They had cleaned the barn, the bunk house, the shed, and the tool house and had disposed of tons of accumulated junk.

Clem had already begun to repair some of the fences, and Hank, who had been working on the front yard, had swept and prepared a dozen stalls in the barn.

At supper in the big kitchen, Lee found the rabbit stew tasty. He grinned at his wife when Matilda told him that Sarah had helped her to prepare the meal. "You were real lucky to find a girl like her, Mr. Morgan," she told him.

When Lee reached across the table and touched Sarah's hand in appreciation, the girl lowered her eyes modestly, but with a warm feeling inside.

At the dinner table, Willie formally introduced the new hands to Morgan. Both Clem Corcoran and Hank Goyette expressed pleasure in finding steady work again and both promised to work hard and do whatever Lee Morgan asked of them. They boasted of their long experience of working on ranches, and hinted that they were pretty good with guns if they needed to use them.

After the meal, Lee took Willie aside. "You did a damn good job of hiring. I like all three of them. They'll be a real help in restoring this ranch."

"Glad to hear you say that, Lee," the old man said.

Alone, in the near darkness of the bedroom this first night in their new home, Sarah wasted no time in cuddling close to her husband, rubbing his chest, and reaching over to kiss him. Perhaps he had felt lust for Suzanne Clemons, but Sarah was here now, a willing wife. No need for a guilty conscience. He shuddered and felt desire grow inside of him when she reached down and ran her fingers through his pubic hair.

Lee needed no further encouragement for he was now fully aroused. He pulled Sarah close and kissed her passionately on the lips. The girl responded as passionately, straining her body against his, kissing him again. Then she took Lee's hand, slipped it inside her nightgown and placed the palm on her breast.

"Stroke me, Lee," she whispered.

Lee gently caressed first one breast and then the other, prompting her to moan ecstatically and push herself even closer to him. Then Lee moved his hand down and slipped it under her nightgown, pulling the garment over her head and flinging it on the floor.

Both could feel their hearts beating frantically. Their nerves tingled, and passion burned fiercely within them. Fervent anticipation made Lee dizzy. Sarah kissed her husband deeply again, then swung one of her soft, shapely legs over him. Lee ran a hand up and down the leg, then moved on top of Sarah, spreading her legs as he massaged one of her breasts again.

"Take me, Lee, take me!" she whispered eagerly.

Lee Morgan kissed her again as he entered her, breathing heavily. Sarah moaned in ecstacy.

When they had finished, Lee Morgan rolled over on his back, his arm under his wife's head, while she ran a finger about in small circles on his bare chest. They had been quiet for a long time, when Sarah spoke very softly.

"Lee, are you sorry you married me?"

Lee Morgan looked at her, amazed. "It was wonderful, getting Spade Bit back, but to have you in the bargain—I can't believe that kind of good fortune!"

The girl smiled, content, and reached over to kiss

him again.

Lee had meant what he said. They made love again with the same ardor for half the night before they finally fell asleep.

In the morning, Lee Morgan drove into Grover right after breakfast, to the telegraph office. With conditions at the ranch much better than he had anticipated, he intended to send a telegram to Joe Chapman and ask him to deliver his stock at once, for he was ready for them. When he completed this chore, he walked across the street to the grange store and ordered feed, to be delivered to Spade Bit as soon as possible. He would have the horses here within the next two or three days and needed to be certain he would be prepared.

When he finished his business, he debated whether or not to visit Sue at her office. However, as he walked towards the place, he hesitated. No, he had too much to do and he should not involve himself with her right now. As he walked back to his horse, he met Jesse Callaway standing in front of his bank.

"Hello, Mr. Morgan," the banker said with a forced smile. "Things going all right for you?"

"Just fine, Mr. Callaway," Lee answered. "Spade Bit's getting back in shape and I'll have several horses coming up from the Chapman Horse Ranch in two or three days."

"What kind of animals?"

"Saddle horses. Got myself some real good Morgans."

"Glad to hear it," said Callaway sourly.

Lee tipped his hat to the banker and then mounted his horse.

Callaway watched Morgan ride off and frustration

98

erupted him again. The man had wasted no time, and he seemed quite pleased with his progress so far. Each passing day would make things worse for the banker. He only hoped that Brady would succeed in hiring Bill Paxton.

By late morning, Lee Morgan had completed his business in Grover and returned to Spade Bit, where he found his four employees already hard at work. When Lee came into the parlor, he saw his wife working along with the housekeeper, dusting and sweeping, moving furniture and cleaning windows. Lee grinned.

"My God, Sarah, you're keeping yourself real busy."

"You got a real hard working wife, Mr. Morgan," Matilda said.

"I expected you back about this time," Sarah told Lee. "I've made some soup for the noonday meal."

Lee Morgan grinned and kissed her gently on the cheek. "You're a wonder, Sarah," he said. The girl smiled, warmth radiating through her. He appreciated her and that's all she wanted.

For the next few days, Lee, Sarah, and the others worked constantly about the ranch. The horses Lee had bought arrived on schedule and were settled into the barn. Then he and his wranglers went about breaking the horses. Clem and Hank did a quick and capable job of taming the mares. Lee himself decided to break the Morgan stallion.

An instant respect sprang up between Lee and Upway Don. The animal stared intently at this tall, muscular man, and Morgan returned the stare as fiercely. Still, the horse would give no quarter when Lee mounted him. Sarah and the ranch hands stood behind the corral fence, watching the harsh contest between the strong-willed, obstinate, powerful stallion and the equally stubborn and determined man. Upway Don bucked and stomped, reared and twisted, snorted and jerked, obsessed with throwing this tenacious rider from his back. But Morgan accepted the challenge, riding out the stallion's rage. The battle between animal and man continued for nearly an hour, neither willing to give an inch. The spectators watched in awe, although Sarah feared that the horse would throw her husband and perhaps trample him to death.

But finally, the horse gave up the battle. Too spent to fight anymore, he trotted slowly around the corral with his last ounce of strength. Lee, exhausted too, finally dismounted and stroked the horse's sweat-drenched neck. Upway Don lowered his noble head and pawed the ground with one hoof in a last gesture of defiance, then stood quietly. The stallion had accepted Morgan as his master.

Lee gave the gentlest of the mares to Sarah, and Clem began giving her riding lessons. By the end of the first week at Spade Bit, Lee Morgan could not have felt more satisfied. He had four loyal, hard-working employees, a loving wife who would do anything for him, some fine horses, and the physical condition of the ranch was improving with each passing day. He told himself that he had made a wise decision in giving up the life of a drifter and settling down on his old homestead.

But storm clouds were gathering, and the tempest would not be generated by Mother Nature, but by greedy men.

On the eighth day, while Lee Morgan began another busy morning at Spade Bit, a visitor walked into the Grover Merchants Bank and then into Jesse

Callaway's private office. The banker stared at the man with a mixture of curiosity and satisfaction. The newcomer wore an immaculately tailored suit, a fine Stetson, silk shirt, and string tie. He reminded Callaway of a wealthy businessman or a successful lawyer, except for the gunbelt he wore slung low on his hips, the holster tied firmly about his thigh. This slim man, perhaps in his early thirties, had a narrow face with deep, penetrating gray eyes and exuded an aura of confidence.

"I sure appreciate your coming here, Mr. Paxton," the banker said.

Paxton grinned. "If anybody's rich enough to give me $500.00 sight unseen, I'd be a damn fool not to make a special trip."

"If you can do this job for me," Callaway said, "there's another $1,500.00 for you—maybe even a bonus."

"I'm listening," Paxton said.

After he had offered the man a seat, Callaway told his story and what he wanted Paxton to do. Callaway admitted that he had been turning a fair profit in buying out ranches and reselling to homesteaders. Those sodbusters who lacked cash could get loans from his bank at exorbitant interest rates. A most choice place was Spade Bit, 1,200 acres, but Lee Morgan had returned to reclaim his old homestead. Morgan had money and would never sell.

Callaway needed this piece of land and he needed Morgan out of the way—killed if necessary. The banker had already tried to finish him off twice, but Morgan had foiled him on both occasions. Thus, only the best, a professional like Paxton, could do away with the man. Would Paxton do it?

The visitor leaned over the desk and grinned. "I'm

surprised at you, Mr. Callaway, using hacks to do this kind of job. I can tell you right off that the best way to do this is to rile up the sodbusters around this Spade Bit Ranch. Make them believe that Morgan will have his horses running wild over their growing crops and ruining any potential harvest. It works either way," he continued. "If it's ranchers who want to rid themselves of sodbusters, we use the opposite approach—tell them the farmers will steal their cattle and ruin their grazing lands. People are mostly like the range grasses, Mr. Callaway; they bend whichever way you make the wind blow. In this case, the wind will blow towards this Morgan —he's a threat to the farmers and will bring about their destruction if they don't do something about it. When we get finished, those sodbusters will descend on that place like a wild mob. They'll burn and destroy and kill. This Morgan—does he have any famiiy?"

"I don't know," Callaway said.

"Well, we'll find out." Paxton shrugged. "If he's got a wife and young ones, they'll have to be killed too. You don't want any heirs left around. Then you can just buy the ranch from the county, and I'm sure you have enough influence hereabouts to get it for a good price."

"You mean there has to be more than Morgan that's killed?" Callaway asked, frowning.

"That's how it'll have to be," Paxton said calmly. "But it won't be any of your worry. Me and my boys will take care of everything. However, I must tell you that the full price is $3,000. You gave me $500. I want another $500 now and the balance when the job is done."

The banker licked his lips nervously and did not answer.

102

"Now Mr. Callaway," Paxton grinned, "you didn't make me come all the way from Cheyenne for nothing, did you—me and my boys? They're apt to get mighty riled."

"No, no, of course not," Callaway said quickly. "All right, $3,000." Then he took out his check book, but Paxton gripped his arm. "I want the next $500 in cash, if you don't mind."

Callaway nodded, but he felt perspiration dampen his face. Suddenly he felt panic. What had he done? Was gaining Spade Bit really worth a range war with widespread destruction and killing? Paxton had mentioned such things as casually as if he was discussing the weather. But Callaway knew he could not back out now. He only hoped he could learn to live with the tempest he had paid to unleash on the Gunsight Gap country.

When the banker looked up again, he saw Billy Paxton leaning over the desk, a grin still on his face. "The cash, Mr. Callaway."

The banker nodded and reached into a drawer of the desk from which he pulled out a wad of bills. Sweat covered his hands as he peeled off ten fifty-dollar notes and handed them to the slim man before him. Paxton shook his head after he had counted the bills.

"You shouldn't look so worried. You don't have to do a thing; just sit back and let me and my boys take care of everything. No one is ever going to know that you're the one who hired me."

Jesse Callaway did not answer.

"Nice doing business with you," Paxton said, tipping his hat. Then he left the private office. Callaway never stirred from his chair. He felt the perspiration pouring down his face and wiped his forehead with the back of a trembling hand.

Chapter 7

Billy Paxton had gained notoriety as a regulator. He had four men in his employ, all of them top gun-hands, willing to do anything for the right price, and quite fearless. Besides Paxton's gang, several other so-called regulator teams operated in the west, profiting by the conflicts that arose among horse and cattle ranchers, sheepherders, and farmers, all of whom were vying for control of the open range.

Paxton's reputation was well known and he would hire out himself and his team to the highest bidder. He had worked for cattlemen's associations to rid an area of encroaching sodbusters or sheepherders. He would hire out on another occasion to grange farmer organizations to chase ranchers off the land; on one occasion he had even worked for sheepherders. Paxton's mode of operation was quite standard. He and his men were good orators who could convince naive farmers or ranchers that they faced a perilous threat and must act to protect their own interests. Then he and one of his men would organize and lead vigilante groups made up of those whom they had incited, bringing on a confrontation that was designed to chase off the alleged offenders.

Since regulators were usually excellent gunmen, most farmers and ranchers were easily awed and subsequently cowed. Rarely did Paxton's adversaries prevail, so he satisfied those who hired him and enhanced his reputation. Paxton had never heard of Lee Morgan, but even if he had, he would have been unconcerned. He had been too successful in his career to lack confidence, no matter who his opponent might be. Paxton saw the problem of Lee Morgan as merely an annoyance that must be overcome. He had nothing personal against the man, but would simply be doing a job for which he would be well paid.

After his discussion with Jesse Callaway and with another $500 in cash in his pocket, he met with his four employees, all top guns: Percy Logan, Kid Proctor, Ben Parker, and Buck Lewis. The four men had worked for Paxton for over two years and were considered top-quality regulators. They would be paid well for this job, which Paxton believed they could complete within two weeks.

Now they sat around a table in the special suite of the Grover House (only the best for Paxton) drinking from two bottles of good whiskey, while Paxton spoke. "This job won't be much different than any other—maybe easier because we only have to deal with one man and a single ranch instead of a bunch of them. From what I've learned so far, sodbusters have been pouring into this area, driving out most of the ranchers. They want this land and they want it bad. All they have to hear is that a horse rancher will let his animals run wild over their farms and they'll be up in arms. They've got to be convinced that this Lee Morgan is out to ruin them because he thinks the sodbusters have no right to free range land."

Paxton took a swig of liquor and then continued, "I want all four of you out tonight, up north near the Spade Bit ranch, and I want you to ride all over the farmland up there. By tomorrow, those sodbusters will be wild; they'll come into town and start complaining. Then we'll convince them that Morgan's horses were responsible, and that this was just the beginning. As usual, we'll offer to help them, and when they agree, we'll organize them and go out to Spade Bit. Maybe we can scare Morgan off, but if not, why we'll just keep the pressure on. We'll go all the way, if necessary—kill the man, any family he has, hands we can't drive off, and then burn his property."

"Do you have the set-up, Billy?" Kid Proctor asked.

"Yes," Paxton answered. "I got a map that shows the farms around Spade Bit. The man in the land office was very accommodating—he pretty much does what our employer wants. Now," Paxton gestured and looked at the four men around the table, "any questions?"

"No, I guess not," Percy Logan said.

"Then let's get this job done tonight. We'll meet back here tomorrow morning. I suspect that by noon there'll be a lot of angry farmers in town."

The four gunmen left Grover well after dusk, carrying rocks in their saddle bags for added weight and their horses wearing deep cleat shoes, the type generally used to scale very harsh or steep terrain where a mount needed to get a firm foothold. The cleats would tear up sod quite well. They moved at a leisurely pace, not only to keep their horses fresh but to arrive at their destination no earlier than midnight, when the sodbusters and their families would be sure to be asleep after a hard day's work. The farmers had already plowed their acres preparatory to planting. They had worked long and hard and would be infuriated to discover their plots trampled by the hoofs of galloping horses.

As expected, Paxton's men found the farm houses totally dark and quiet. They singled out the four farms that lay on the south perimeter of the Spade Bit Ranch and approached the newly plowed land quietly and stealthily. Then, on signal from Percy Logan, they whipped their horses and galloped across the fields of the first farm, churning up the earth. The noise finally awoke the farmer and his family but before he could come out of his house to see what had happened, the intruders had ridden away into the night.

Paxton's men carried out the same operation on the next farm, and then the third and fourth. The owner of the last farm, Michael Campion, turned angrily to his wife.

"Godamn it, it's happened; just what I was afraid of! I knew we'd have trouble when that new owner brought those horses in here. He's lettin' 'em run wild!"

"What are you going to do?" asked his wife.

"I'll wait 'til mornin' to see how much damage they did. Then I'll go into town and get the law to do something about this."

So Billy Paxton had already successfully begun his job. By dawn, all four farmers surveyed their acres and cursed vehemently. They would need to do their plowing all over again. When they investigated further, they found gaps in the fence that separated their properties from Spade Bit land, along with easily noticable hoofprints. The evidence pointed directly at Lee Morgan, just as Paxton had intended.

By midmorning, Michael Campion and his three neighbors rattled into Grover aboard Campion's heavy wagon. They went immediately to Deputy John Chook to voice their complaints. That man who had taken over Spade Bit was allowing his horses to run wild over their property and Chook had to do something about it. Chook was surprised. Morgan had assured him that none of his horses would be allowed to infringe on the surrounding farms. So Chook did what almost everyone else did in the town—he consulted with Jesse Callaway.

After Michael Campion and the others had left, Chook hurried to the bank, found Callaway, and explained that some farmers had complained that Morgan's horses had trampled their fields.

"Come into my private office," Callaway said.

Inside the next room, Callaway told Chook to sit down. "John, you're to do nothing about this; *nothing at all.*"

The deputy frowned. "Nothing? I don't understand . . ."

"You don't have to understand. I'm just telling you not to do anything about this. Don't go out to those farms, don't go and see Lee Morgan, don't check with your sheriff in Boise, don't take any action at all."

"But, Jesse, if I don't, this could lead to range war," said Chook, perplexed.

"It's a problem between Morgan and the farmers. They can work it out for themselves or fight it out for themselves."

"But I'm a lawman,' Chook protested. "I can't allow trouble to start if I can prevent it."

Callaway's thick neck reddened. "I'm telling you again, just stay out of it! Do you understand? Don't do a thing." He leaned forward. "I've been taking good care of you, haven't I?"

Chook sighed. "All right, Jesse," he said reluctantly. "I won't do anything. If those farmers come back, I'll tell them I'm looking into it."

"Fine." Callaway nodded. "That's exactly what I want you to say."

Billy Paxton was more than satisfied by the initial efforts of his men. He planned to send them out again that night to trample the two farms that abutted the west boundary of Spade Bit. "Do the same thing there—and for good measure, go back over the farms you hit last night. And make sure you take care of the fence and leave a trail of hoofprints."

"Don't worry, Billy," Ben Parker said, "we know what to do."

"Billy," Buck Lewis now spoke, "I think some farmers came into town this morning to complain to the deputy. Do you think that lawman will listen to them and do something about it?"

Billy Paxton grinned. "He won't do a thing. Our employer will see to that."

"This man who hired you must have considerable influence," Lewis said.

"If he didn't," Paxton replied, "we'd be pretty

foolish to work for him. After you do your job tonight and these farmers get even more riled up, they'll come running to the deputy again, but they won't get any satisfaction. Then they'll no doubt hold some kind of meeting. I'll make sure I find out where that takes place and we'll take the next step. We'll join them, tell them we're buyers who are looking to buy wholesale crops this fall at a good price, but that maybe this isn't the right place if they're going to have trouble with ranchers who might ruin their harvests."

"That one always seems to work," Kid Proctor said.

"When they're hot enough, we'll offer to help them confront this man Morgan who's been giving them so much trouble." He shuttled his glance between Percy Logan and Kid Proctor. "You two will go with those sodbusters to Spade Bit. All right with you?"

Logan shrugged. "Won't bother me none."

"Then you boys better get ready for your work tonight."

Percy Logan and the other three set out once more after dusk to ride northward. Again they weighted down their mounts and again used cleat shoes on the animals. They began at about midnight, riding over two more farms, galloping over the other four again, and cutting the fence in several places along the western lateral of the Spade Bit ranch.

The next morning, more angry farmers came into Grover to demand from Deputy John Chook that he do something about the horses stampeding over their lands. When Chook merely told them that he would look into it, the farmers became more incensed, and decided to take the law into their own hands.

Paxton had been completely accurate in anticpating the reaction of the farmers, for that very evening some two dozen of them met at the grange hall in Grover. Michael Campion seemed to be the leader and he bellowed angrily and loudly that something must be done about the Spade Bit. Only after Paxton and his henchmen arrived, now dressed in neat business suits, did the grumbling stop while the sodbusters looked curiously at the visitors.

"I hope we ain't interrupting," Paxton said to Campion. "My name is Howard Pacquette and these gentlemen are my business associates. We represent the Wholesale Produce Corporation out of Kansas City. We've come here because we're looking for a good source of fresh produce. We heard that Shoshone County was an excellent place because the rich land here would grow excellent crops. We are told that your grange association would be meeting here tonight, so we're taking the opportunity to talk with you. We're willing to pay as high as a dollar a bushel for beans and fifty cents a bushel for wheat, if your harvest is as good as we were told."

The sodbusters gasped. The price was generous indeed.

"You've only got to get your crops to the railroad at Boise," Paxton continued. "Our corporation has its own freight cars to haul produce east to Kansas City. Are any of you fellows interested?"

The question was the cue for Ben Parker to speak. "Howard, you might just ask them about the rumor we heard in town—that they're having trouble with ranchers. You know we can't deal here if we can't be sure a harvest will come on time and in good condition."

Paxton nodded and looked at Campion. "Well, sir, do you have any such trouble?"

"A little," Campion admitted, "but we aim to squash it before it gets out of hand. That's why we're meeting tonight—to decide what to do about this here horse rancher."

"Horse rancher!" Parker feigned a gasp. "They're the worst. They got no consideration at all. You can't make them keep their animals penned. The only way to deal with somebody like that is to drive him out yourselves. We know—we've had this experience before—in Wyoming, Kansas, and a lot of other places. And usually the local law doesn't do anything about it."

"Then we'll drive him out!" Campion cried.

"Now, if you fellows think you'd like to deal with our corporation, why we'll help you," Paxton said. "My two associates here," he pointed to Logan and Percy, "know how to deal with people who don't control their herds. They've had plenty of experience. They'd be glad to join you in dealing with this horse rancher who's giving you trouble."

"You'd do that?" Campion stared at Logan.

"Sure," Logan grinned. "After all, we're just as interested in a good harvest here as you are. We can both make considerable money if you can deliver us a good crop."

The others in the room nodded, spoke to one another, and apparently liked this idea. One of them looked at Campion. "That's a mighty good offer, Mike. Maybe we should go out to that place tomorrow—all of us." He looked at Paxton. "Would your people be willing to go with us?''

"Absolutely," Billy Paxton said, smiling broadly.

The next morning, Lee Morgan arose early. After he washed and dressed, he ate a hearty breakfast with Sarah and two of his hands. However, he noted that Willie McCormick was not there.

"He got out real early, Mr. Morgan," Clem Corcoran said. "He wants to check the fences again to see if any of them need any more repair."

Morgan grinned. "Old Willie is even more conscientious than I am."

"Are we going to work on the barn again today?" Hank Goyette asked.

"There's still a few rotten boards that need to be replaced," Lee said.

"Do you want me to help, Lee?" Sarah asked.

Morgan grinned and leaned over to pat his wife's cheek. "I want you to practice riding your mare this morning. You're doing right well, but I want you to be as good as possible so we can take long rides together."

Sarah nodded, smiling.

As Lee and his two hands left the house and started walking towards the barn, they saw Will McCormick galloping furiously towards them. Morgan frowned. Why was the old man lathering his horse like that? He, Clem, and Hank waited until McCormick reached them and reined his horse to a stop.

"Lee, I think we've got some real trouble," he said, a worried expression on his weathered face.

"Trouble?"

McCormick nodded. "The fence has been cut in

114

four or five places on both the south and west quarters. There's lots of prints and the plowed fields beyond our place have been trampled something terrible."

"My God," Lee hissed. "Did our horses get loose to do that damage?"

"Wasn't Spade Bit horses." Willie shook his head. "Them animals were wearing cleat shoes, the wrong kind in open country like this, the kind that can do a lot o' damage to newly plowed land."

"Son of a bitch!" Lee cursed. It was apparent that somebody was out to get him by riling up the farmers, hoping to drive Lee out. And who else could it be but Jesse Callaway? Lee guessed that angry farmers would soon be confronting him, for if what Willie said was true, the sodbusters would naturally conclude that Lee's horses had caused the damage. He turned to Goyette.

"Hank, saddle the stallion for me. I'm going to ride with Will to take a look at that fence."

"Yes sir, Mr. Morgan," the ranch hand answered.

Five minutes later, Lee mounted his horse and loped over the open fields with Willie McCormick. Ten minutes later, McCormick was showing him the fences. Morgan also looked at the plowed fields beyond. They looked as though a herd of buffalo had stampeded over them. Then he studied the hoof prints that led from the fields to his own property and out again.

When Lee had finished his inspection, he turned to McCormick. "Willie, we're going to have visitors—maybe this morning. We're going back to the house to arm ourselves and wait."

"The sodbusters?" McCormick asked.

Morgan nodded. "They're going to blame us for

this, but we both know that none of our horses were involved. But somebody wants to put the blame on Spade Bit."

"Who?"

"That's what I intend to find out," said Lee, "But I have a pretty good idea. Come on, let's go back. I want to make sure that Sarah is safely out of the way if there's going to be trouble."

A few hours later, Lee first heard and then saw a parade of wagons coming up the road—three of them, with half a dozen men in each wagon. There were also four riders on horseback. Clem, Willie and Hank checked their rifles, while Lee fingered the whip he held in his right hand. The four men stood firm, watching the riders and wagons pull up in front of the house. The men in the wagons carried an array of weapons: shotguns, old rifles, blunderbusses, and small .22s.

When the visitors came within twenty or thirty yards of the house, three of the riders loped slowly forward. In the lead was Michael Campion and almost abreast of him were Percy Logan and Kid Proctor, now dressed in trousers, shirt, kerchief and ten gallon hats. Both men wore side arms that hung low on their thighs.

"Are you Lee Morgan?" Campion glared at Morgan.

"What if I am?" Lee answered.

"We got a complaint," Campion said. "For the past two nights your horses have been runnin' wild over our farms. We worked hard on these lands to raise crops on these acres and we paid damn good money for 'em. We ain't gonna tolerate no horse rancher lettin' his animals run loose all over the country."

"My horses don't run anywhere except on Spade Bit land," Lee said quietly.

"That ain't what we heard," Campion said. "We're told that horse ranchers are the worst kind o' neighbors. They ain't got no consideration at all for farmers who work hard to feed their families. We didn't just come here to warn you, Morgan. We came here to tell you to get out of here. There ain't no more room for ranchers. This is all farm country now, and we aim to keep it that way."

"Who the hell are you?" Lee asked.

"Mike Campion, that's who. I own the farm to the south o' here." He looked down at Willie. "Willie McCormick knows me; we been neighbors for the past couple o' years or so. Willie, we got on well. Why did you want to sell this place? Morgan's gonna bring us nothin' but trouble. You should o' sold out to Callaway like ever'body else."

Willie McCormick looked hard at Lee Morgan as a suspicion formed in his mind. So that was it! Jesse Callaway was behind this in an attempt to drive Lee out, since he had tried unsuccessfully to buy the place from Willie himself. But would the banker go to so much trouble just for the sake of one piece of land?

Lee Morgan looked at Campion. "You're crazy. My horses were never on your land. Cleated horses trampled your farms, not my animals. My horses don't have cleated shoes. Somebody's trying to make trouble between us."

Campion turned and looked at Percy Logan. "You were right, Mr. Logan; this man with his trespassin' horses said just what you thought he'd say. I must

117

admit, you know these kind o' people real well."

Lee Morgan looked at Logan. "Who the hell are *you?*"

Percy Logan loped forward, with Kid Proctor at his side. "My name is Percy Logan and I'm associated with the Wholesale Produce Corporation out of Kansas City. We're up here looking into the possibility of buying the harvests from these farmers." He gestured towards the men on the wagons. "We know about horse ranchers like you who have no regard for the rights of the farmers, so we've advised them to convince you to give up this ranch. Surely, Mr. Morgan, you can see for yourself that this is farmland now; the ranching business is finished.

Morgan looked at the low-slung holsters on Logan and Proctor and scowled. "Why, you sons of bitches," he growled, "you look like nothing more than a couple of hired guns. Who's the bastard who's paying you to work up these sodbusters?"

"I resent that, Mr. Morgan," Logan protested. "We're honest businessmen."

"Sure you are," Lee jeered. He looked at Campion. "Can't you see that you're being set up to start a range war? Somebody's paid these two cutthroats to get me off this land!"

The slighest hint of doubt crossed Campion's face and he licked his lips. Meanwhile, Clem Corcoran edged slowly forward, staring intently at Percy Logan and Kid Proctor. Logan saw the hesitation in Campion's eye and he quickly spoke again.

"You're the one using a ruse, telling lies to fool these poor men," he blustered at Lee.

"Maybe they're stupid enough to believe you, but not me," Lee said.

Suddenly both Logan and Proctor whipped out their six-shooters, fast and straight. The farmers on the wagons stared in awe at the quick draws, while Morgan's three hired men moved back a step or two. However, Lee stood firm and never flinched. He only grinned at the two men while he fingered the handle of his whip.

"Now, Mister," Logan threatened, "you take back what you said or we might have to do something about it."

Lee looked at Michael Campion and the suddenly silent men on the wagons. Logan had called out this horse rancher who had supposedly allowed his horses to trample their fields. They waited eagerly for Morgan's reaction. Would he back off?

Then, with even more speed than the two gunmen had drawn their six-shooters, Lee lashed out with his whip. Two quick strokes and within a second, before anybody knew what happened, the tip of the whip struck with abrupt, uncanny accuracy, snapping both guns out of the astonished gunslingers' hands, leaving sudden welts on the fingers of both Logan and Proctor. The two men stared as though some invisible, supernatural force had suddenly disarmed them. The farmers gasped with equal awe.

Total silence reigned in the space before the Spade Bit ranchhouse. Then Lee took a few steps forward, but the riders and the farmers in the wagon made no move at all. Finally, Morgan spoke to Campion, "I'm telling you straight, my horses didn't do that damage and somebody's trying to involve us in a range war. Now I'd advise you and your friends to get off my property." He looked at Logan and Proctor. "The same goes for you two."

119

Kid Proctor licked his lips, rubbed his bleeding knuckles, and at last found the courage to speak. "Do you mind if we get our weapons?"

Lee grinned and flicked his whip again. "If you think you're man enough to retrieve them, go ahead and try."

Proctor pursed his lips, then cocked his head at Percy Logan. Without a word, the two men whirled their horses and galloped off. When Lee turned to Campion, he too whirled his horse and trotted away without a word. The other farmers turned their wagons and clattered off behind him. A moment later the parade was out of sight.

Clem Corcoran came forward. "Mr. Morgan, I got to tell you something. I recognized those two gunmen, the one called Percy Logan and the other one. The second man is Kid Proctor. They both work for Billy Paxton."

"Billy Paxton?" Lee questioned. "Who is he?"

"He's the worst, Mr. Morgan, the worst. He has an outfit that calls themselves regulators. They hire out to cattlemen groups tryin' to get rid o' sodbusters or grange associations tryin' to drive off ranchers. Somebody must want to drive you out bad to bring Billy Paxton here. His price comes real high and he won't stop at nothin' to get a job done. Paxton don't care what he does. I was with a ranch in the Colorado Mission country where some ranchers hired him to drive some sodbusters from their farms. He did a real good job. There ain't one farm left around there."

"That bastard must be pretty desperate," Lee said grimly.

"Who?" Hank asked.

"Jesse Callaway," Morgan answered. "From

what Campion said, he's been buying up all the land around here—all but Spade Bit. Guess I'd better have a little talk with him."

Chapter 8

Lee worked steadily during the rest of the day, saying little to his wife and even less to his hands. He had been gripped with a growing anger as the day wore on, smarting from this apparent attempt by Jesse Callaway to do him in. He had been even more irritated by Billy Paxton's two gunslingers. By evening he had decided to confront not only the banker, but Paxton as well. He was silent at the dinner table and after dinner, said nothing to anyone but retired from the dining room and went into the parlor.

After she had helped Matilda clear away the dishes, Sarah also came into the parlor, sat in a chair, and began to sew. She occasionally glanced at her husband, who ignored her for the most part. Though Lee had made her stay in the house that morning, she had learned about the confrontation from Willie McCormick. He had told her of the two men who had accompanied the farmers and who were in the employ of a notorious regulator, and

123

what the business of a regulator was.

Sarah had only sewed one seam on a shirt when she finally spoke. "Lee, are you going into town tomorrow?"

Lee Morgan looked up. "Yes, I have to."

"You won't get into trouble, will you?" she asked anxiously.

"I'm not the one looking for trouble," Morgan said, "but I've got to square this thing. I've got to deal with the men who are responsible for this, make them understand they can't scare me, nor force me off this ranch."

"Maybe you should go to the law," Sarah said. "There must be a lawman in Grover."

"Sure—John Chook," Lee said contemptuously. "He's probably in the pay of the man responsible for what happened this morning, just like everybody else in Grover."

"Lee, I don't want anything to happen to you," Sarah said. "I can't remember when I've been so happy as now, on this ranch, and seein' how happy you are; seeing what nice people we have working for us. I'd hate to see anything happen to this wonderful life we're staring together."

"That's why I've got to go into Grover," Lee said grimly.

Sarah only nodded. Yes, she understood that he would have to confront his enemies, make them see that he would not be frightened or cowed. Sarah knew from experience that those who did not stand their ground were beaten at the start. McCormick, the other hands, and Matilda were loyal to her husband, but she was not sure they would stick by Lee if things really got bad.

The next morning, Lee buckled on his gunbelt.

124

Clem Corcoran saddled Upway Don and brought the stallion from the barn. The horse stood quietly as Lee mounted.

He looked down at Sarah and at Clem Corcoran. "I may not be back tonight; depends on how much business I have to do in town. I have to see a few people, order some things for the ranch. However, I'll definitely be back sometime tomorrow."

Sarah reached up and gripped her husband's wrist. "You will take care of yourself, won't you, Lee? You won't get into trouble?"

"I'm not looking for trouble," Lee said quietly. "But if it comes looking for me, I won't run away."

The two stood and watched as Lee whirled Upway Don about and cantered off. They remained there, looking after him, as Lee reached the road and then put the horse into a hard gallop as he headed south towards Grover—and Jesse Callaway.

Lee reached the town a little after mid-morning. Main Street was quite busy. Farmers on horseback and in wagons had come to buy supplies; men on horseback cantered through the street; merchants were busy with customers. Pedestrians ambled along the boardwalk on both sides of the main thoroughfare. The two cafes in town appeared busy, and Lee could hear the clang of metal on metal from the blacksmith shop.

He stopped first at the small jail, walked inside, and found Deputy John Chook sitting behind his desk looking through some papers. The lawman looked up when the visitor entered the room, and his eyes widened. He had not expected Morgan here this morning, nor did he like the low slung gunbelt the man wore.

"Morgan. What can I do for you?" he asked.

Lee leaned over the desk and peered hard at the

deputy. "Chook, do you happen to know about the little trouble I had yesterday? Some angry farmers came onto my property and accused me of letting my horses run roughshod across their lands. They brought a couple of gunmen with them."

Chook licked his lips. "I—I didn't know about that."

"Like hell you didn't!" Morgan said. "I suspect they'd come in here to see you but you didn't do a damn thing about it. Did Callaway tell you to stay out of it?"

"Callaway?" Chook barked. "He's got nothing to do with me!"

"He tells you what to do, I suspect, just like he tells a lot of other people in this town what to do."

"That ain't true! Nobody tells me what to do except the sheriff in Boise," Chook protested.

"You've had this job a long time, Chook, and I guess you like it. Now, from what I understand, Callaway hasn't been here but a few years. If you don't tend to your business, I could see the sheriff in Boise and give him an idea of what's going on—you doing what Callaway wants, ready to let a range war start because he says so; you sitting back and closing your eyes to trouble that's brewing." Lee pointed emphatically. "You may as well know something, Chook. Nobody's going to chase me off Spade Bit, short of killing me. And I guarantee that you'll have a lot of other dead men on your hands before you bring in my corpse. Do you understand?"

Chook squirmed nervously. "What—what do you want me to do?"

"I told you a couple of gunmen came out to my place with those farmers yesterday, and I understand they work for a man called Billy Paxton, a so-

126

called regulator, who uses his own gun and the guns of his henchmen to drive honest men off their lands. Somebody hired this man to drive me off Spade Bit, and I'm pretty sure it was Jesse Callaway."

"H-how can y-you say that?" Chook stuttered.

"Real easy," Lee said. "Now you'll have to make up your mind. Are you going to play Callaway's game, or are you going to do your job?" He paused. "I suspect that Mike Campion came to you as soon as he found his land trampled, isn't that right?"

"Yes," Chook admitted, "and I told him I'd look into it, and that's just what I intend to do."

"You're a goddamn liar!" Morgan snapped. "You don't like me, and if Campion complained to you about my horses stampeding over his lands, why, you'd have been right out to my place to look into it and hope that Campion was right, so you could come down on me. There's only one reason you *didn't* do that, Chook—Callaway told you to stay out of it. He wants me dead and he doesn't care how many of those sodbusters die with me, just so long as he gets his hands on Spade Bit."

"I don't want no range war, Mr. Morgan, honest I don't," whined Chook.

"Then you better make up your mind which side you're on—law and order, or Jesse Callaway. I have business in town today and among other things, I intend to see Callaway and have it out with him."

"W-why don't you let me t-take care of it?" Chook offered nervously.

"*After* I talk to him," Lee said.

The deputy did not move as he watched Lee Morgan leave the jail. Morgan would make more trouble than he could ever handle, and if a range war erupted, Chook would have to answer to the sheriff and perhaps lose his job. He lowered his head and rubbed his forehead, agonizing over this dilemma.

Lee Morgan took Upway Don to a livery stable. He had only gone a half block up the street when a woman standing in front of the Black Ace called to him. "Hey, Mister, are you Lee Morgan?"

Lee turned and saw the prostitute called Mary Spots. The tall woman was a little more hefty now, and her narrow face had lost much of its youthful smoothness. Wrinkles had begun to etch her forehead and neck, and cheeks, not very well hidden by a heavy coating of rice powder.

"I'll be damned! Mary Spots!" Morgan grinned.

The woman studied him. He had matured into a tall, strong, handsome man, with a vibrant gleam in his eyes and a confident appearance. "I 'spect you don't have to pay for whores anymore, do you?" she grinned. "I'd bet you can get all the women you want to do whatever you want. But tell me, do you still like the French kind?"

Lee Morgan only grinned.

"No, I doubt that you've had any need to take up with pigs or whores." Then she took his arm. "Come on inside—my treat. I'll buy you a drink."

Morgan eyed the woman with a hint of amusement. "The last time I had anything to do with you, one man got killed, another almost got killed, and I just about ended up a wanted man."

"That was a long time ago," Mary Spots said. "Nothin' like that will happen now. We'll just have us a nice little talk."

Lee shrugged and walked into the Black Ace with Mary, who sat herself at one of the many empty tables. She gestured to the bartender, who brought over a bottle of whiskey, two glasses, and a syphon of soda water. Mary Spots never took her liquor straight. The bartender eyed Morgan curiously, but said nothing. He didn't look like one of Mary's usual customers.

For nearly an hour, Lee Morgan and Mary Spots sat talking and sipping their drinks, catching up on old times. Lee spoke of all the traveling he'd done after he had left Spade Bit, and of his satisfaction in coming home, rebuilding his ranch, and hoping to settle down in peace at last.

And what of Mary Spots? Things were still the same with her. She was at the same old business, still taking lustful men upstairs, and always regretting that she had not found something more. She told Lee that she hoped to quit the business soon. She had saved some money over the years, and besides, even the crudest of men now preferred younger women.

"It was real nice to see you again, Lee Morgan." Mary Spots smiled. "I hope you and your young filly have a happy life out there on Spade Bit." Then she touched his arm and frowned. "But, Lee, won't you have trouble with the sodbusters? They won't like a horse ranch in their midst."

"I hope to settle that," Lee said.

"I'd hate to see you have trouble."

Lee did not answer. Instead, he looked up and stared hard as he saw five men come into the Black Ace and go over to one of the tables. They were dressed like cowboys, and all of them wore low-slung holsters. One of them, the slim man with the narrow face, told the bartender to bring glasses and two bottles of his best whiskey. Lee immediately recognized two of the men as Logan and Proctor, and he guessed that the man who had ordered the drinks was Billy Paxton. After studying the five men for a moment, he turned to Mary Spots.

"I think trouble just came," Lee said, cocking his head toward the men.

Mary glanced over and her eyes widened. She guessed that they were professional gunmen. Mary Spots felt a hint of panic. Could Lee Morgan handle these hardcases? She did not know what kind of experience Lee had developed since he had come into the Black Ace that evening so many years ago as a raw kid, but no man could be foolish enough to take on the five men at that table. She gripped Morgan's wrist.

"Lee, I don't know if you've got a case against those fellows, but only a total fool would face down five men like that!"

"I don't intend to start any trouble," Lee said. "I just want to talk to them."

The woman released his wrist and he rose from the chair and ambled over to the table, standing there silently. Billy Paxton and the others glanced at him, Logan and Proctor actually glaring. Lee looked at their holsters and said, "I see you found yourselves some new Colts."

"What do you want, Mister?" Billy Paxton asked.

"You mean to say your two boys here didn't tell you about me? Tell you what happened out at my ranch yesterday?"

Now Paxton smiled, but coldly. "So you're Lee Morgan. Yes, they told me about you. I can only say you're making a big mistake trying to hold onto that place. We didn't rile up those farmers, although I did allow two of my men to go with them to try to talk sense into you. We're strangers here, but we can sure tell that this area has changed from ranch country to farm country. I never yet saw a place

130

where farmers and ranchers could live peaceable side by side, and I suspect you're alone against a mob of farmers. There's plenty of ranch country up Montana way or down in Wyoming. You'd be very wise, Mr. Morgan, if you sold out that place and took your horses somewhere else."

"Jesse Callaway would like that, wouldn't he? And you'd like it too, because then you'd get paid off," Lee said.

"I don't know what you're talking about,' Paxton said.

"Like hell you don't," Lee growled. "Callaway would do anything to get Spade Bit. The two hoodlums he hired to finish me off are dead now, so he went all out and pulled in you and your gang. And I bet your expert services don't come cheap."

"I have to tell you, Mr. Morgan, I don't like that kind of talk."

"The truth always hurts, doesn't it, Mr. Paxton?" Lee scanned the others about the table, and then looked again at Paxton. "You're all no good sons of bitches, who ought to be hanged by your balls."

"Who the hell do you think you are, talking like that to us?" Buck Lewis suddenly rose from his chair and went for his gun. However, Lee lashed out with his arm, striking the man's wrist viciously, and Lewis drew away, wincing from the pain. He quickly recovered however, and cocked his arm to throw a punch. But Morgan struck first, a hard punch to the stomach that doubled over the regulator. Then Lee lashed out again with a left that struck Lewis squarely on the jaw, sent him reeling backwards against the bar, and then sliding to the floor on his rump. He was all but unconscious, blood streaming down his face.

"That wasn't smart, Mr. Morgan," Paxton said,

very quietly.

Lee leaned over the table and glowered at the regulator. "It wasn't smart to rile up those sodbusters either; nor to send out two of your hoods to intimidate me. I don't know how much Callaway is paying you, Paxton, but if you persist in making trouble for me, you'll go back where you came from draped over your saddles."

"Is that a threat, Mr. Morgan?" Paxton said. When Lee did not answer, Paxton shrugged. "Threats don't bother me, nor my men. You'd be wise to give in, and save a lot of trouble for everybody."

"I'm leaving you with this one warning," Lee told him. "If you send your men to my place again, they'll come back in pine boxes."

"I believe you, Mr. Morgan," Paxton said. "Except that you may not be alive to see it. I know what I'm talking about. The smartest thing you could do would be to sell out Spade Bit and move elsewhere. I'd guess you'd get a real good price for it."

This time, Morgan did not answer. He simply scanned the five men at the table once more and then walked off, sitting down across from Mary Spots. She looked at him with a sense of awe and then spoke in a half whisper. "My God, Lee Morgan, I don't believe this! What you said to them and what you did to one of them—you should be dead on the floor by now!" She gripped his hand tightly. "Please don't look for more trouble. I'm speakin' to you as a friend now, not somebody lookin' for a customer. You can believe how pleased I am to see you, and how happy I'd be to see you settle down. But there's a thousand places as good as Spade Bit —no one place is worth getting killed for."

"Nice talking to you, Mary," Lee said, rising from his chair, "and thanks for the advice. But I have to do what I have to do. If I'm lucky, everything will work out."

Lee left the woman sitting alone at the table. Billy Paxton and his men sat silently and watched him leave the saloon. Then Paxton turned to Percy Logan. "Now I believe what you said about how fast he is. Still, there's a goddamn rich payday at the end of this job, and no bastard like Morgan is going to do me out of that money. We're going to talk to those sodbusters again, and this time we'll really work them up. Then, when you go back to Morgan's ranch, you attack—no more talk. I want to see dead everything that moves on that place."

"Morgan's got a wife, maybe even kids," Logan put in.

"I said *anything that moves*," Paxton repeated emphatically.

"It's your show, Billy." Percy Logan nodded.

Jesse Callaway was less than happy when Lee Morgan walked into his bank, strode over to the railing, leaned down and glared at the banker. Callaway could see that the man was angry. Still he forced a weak smile. "Mr. Morgan. What can I do for you?"

"In your private office." Morgan cocked his head towards the door.

Callaway was about to suggest that they could talk out here, but the fire blazing in Morgan's amber eyes made him think better of it. He rose from his chair. "If that's what you want." He led Morgan through the door, offered him a chair in front of the desk, and then went around and sat behind it. "You look quite upset. Is there some way I can help you?"

133

Callaway said.

Morgan leaned towards the banker. "Listen close, Callaway, because I'm not going to repeat it again. I'm the one who killed your bushwhackers at Snake Pass, but before I did, I overheard them say that you hired them to do the job. I can also guess that you hired Billy Paxton and his killers. Don't play games and try to deny anything. You must want Spade Bit awfully bad to go to all this trouble and expense, get two men killed and maybe bring on a lot more bloodshed. I can tell you right out, not you nor anybody else is going to get me off Spade Bit, not for any kind of money, or with any kind of threats. The only way I'll leave that ranch is in a box —but you'll need a hell of a lot more boxes to carry the men I kill before they get me."

"Now please, Mr. Morgan, you're making some wild . . ."

"Shut up!" Morgan interrupted brusquely. "I told you not to play games with me. I'm telling you to call off your dogs and to forget Spade Bit, because if you persist in trying to take it away from me, a lot of people are going to get killed. You'll not only have the sheriff of Shoshone County in here asking questions, but federal marshals, too."

"That would be the last thing I'd want—killing and destruction. I live here, I have a good business that gets better every day. Why would I want the kind of trouble you're talking about?" Callaway asked innocently.

"Because you've got an obsession with Spade Bit. The best thing you can do, Callaway, is to make sure that Paxton and his men don't come near my property again. That's the only way there'll be peace." Lee rose from his chair. "I've said what I came to say. Now it's up to you, but I can promise you, if trouble comes, Banker Jesse Callaway might also end up in a pine box.''

Callaway did not answer. He licked his lips nervously as Lee walked out of his office. Striding through the bank, Lee almost bumped into Sue Clemons, who had just completed some business at one of the teller windows. She looked at him soberly, touching his arm.

"Lee, can I talk to you? Outside?" she asked. Once outside the bank, she tucked her arm through his and hurried away with him. When she reached an area with no crowds, she stopped and turned to him. "Is it true? You were confronted with some angry farmers at your place yesterday?"

"They claimed my horses stampeded over their plowed land," Lee told her.

"I'm so sorry," the girl said.

"My animals didn't do it. I was set up because an influential man in this town wants Spade Bit, and he'll do anything to get it," Lee said.

The girl frowned. "You mean like hiring those two ambushers on the way to Boise?"

Lee nodded. "That was just the beginning. He's hired some hardcases to get me now. But I just had a talk with the man who wants my place. Maybe I convinced him to call this whole thing off and forget Spade Bit."

"Who, Lee? Who in this town would want to do this to you?"

"I'd rather not say," Morgan answered. "I'm hoping it will blow over before there's real trouble. I'll have to talk to these farmers myself, show them how I've been repairing my fences to keep my horses off their property." He smiled. "I appreciate your concern, but don't worry about it. I think everything will turn out all right."

Now the girl smiled too. "Our house is just up the street. It's about noon time. Would you let me give you some lunch?"

Lee Morgan grinned. "Sounds good to me."

The Clemons home was quite neat, large, and clean. Sue Clemons showed Lee through the house, ending with the living room where there was a piano that Sue played for her own amusement, two big bookcases loaded with volumes, for she and her father read extensively, and a phonograph and records. On the fireplace mantle was a framed photograph of a good looking woman—Sue's mother, who had died some years ago.

After the tour of the house, the girl led Lee to the kitchen, where she prepared lunch, some ham sandwiches, coffee, and apple pie. As she worked, Lee spoke.

"I ought to get some things like that for my ranch —a phonograph and a piano, I mean. They'd be a good diversion for Sarah and me on long winter nights. I suppose you could get such things for me, too, couldn't you?"

"Yes, anything," the girl answered. "And there are a couple of piano teachers in town who could teach Sarah to play, if she doesn't know how, and an instrument shop that can order phonograph records."

"I'll have to give that some thought," said Lee.

After lunch, Lee accompanied Sue back to the Clemons Trading Agency office. She invited Lee to visit her again, when her father was home, and to bring his wife with him. They could have a pleasant evening. They stopped in front of the office, and Sue planted a quick kiss on his cheek, smiled, and then disappeared inside. Lee moved on, intent on finishing his business in town before the day was over.

Chapter 9

Billy Paxton had remained calm during his confrontation with Lee Morgan, and while he had tolerated the embarrassment to one of his men, Paxton was really enraged over the incident. He now felt a personal anger against Morgan and would stop at nothing to destroy the man and Spade Bit along with him.

As Lee had hoped, his talk with Jesse Callaway had influenced the banker. Callaway now had second thoughts about killing Morgan and trying to get Spade Bit. He wasted no time in meeting with Billy Paxton to call the entire thing off. The price in human lives might be high, the banker told Paxton, and Callaway did not want serious trouble in the Gunsight Gap country. However, Paxton would have none of it.

"A deal's a deal," he told Callaway. "When I start a job, I don't quit until the job's finished."

"I'll pay you the $3,000," Callaway said. "I just want to call this off."

"It's too late, Mr. Callaway," Paxton answered. "Morgan has made a fool out of a couple of my men and he's going to pay for it. If you insist on calling it off, I'll have to expose you, let everyone know that you're the one who called me in on this."

Jesse Callaway was trapped. He now feared Billy Paxton more than he did Lee Morgan.

Paxton ordered his men to make still another visit to the farms surrounding Spade Bit. By morning the sodbusters would be ready to shoot first and ask questions later. Then Paxton and his men would lead them to Spade Bit.

Meanwhile, after his pleasant visit with Sue Clemons, Lee went about town to conduct his other business. He purchased a freight wagon that the seller promised to have delivered to Spade Bit within two days, and also new tools he would need on the ranch and special equipment for his horses. He finished these chores by midafternoon and returned to the livery stable to get Upway Don.

Lee reached Spade Bit about dusk, much to Sarah's delight, and just in time for a good supper of roast chicken, potatoes, peas, and hot apple pie. He and Sarah spent a quiet evening, then retired early and made passionate love. Lee was tired and in a deep sleep when the midnight riders again galloped over the fields of the surrounding farms.

At midmorning the next day, Willie McCormick came up to Lee, a sober look on his face. "They were out again last night, Lee. I found more cut fence and busted posts. The farms off our west and south quarters were trampled again."

"Son of a bitch!" Lee cursed.

"Do you think Campion and the others will come back here?" Willie asked.

Lee Morgan squinted towards the road, then studied the surrounding landscape. "There's nobody in sight now, but they probably will show up. However, I had a talk with Callaway yesterday and maybe I convinced him to call off his dogs. If he does, we won't see those so-called regulators back here with the farmers, and maybe we can talk some sense into Campion and the others."

Willie McCormick nodded, but he didn't have much hope.

However, bad trouble was brewing. By sun-up on this bright day, Billy Paxton had set his next plan in motion. He had sent out Percy Logan and Kid Proctor to call on Michael Campion and some of the other farmers again. When Logan reached the Campion farm at about eight o'clock, he saw just the sight he had expected. Michael Campion and two neighbors were walking slowly over his trampled fields. The farmers looked up when the regulator trotted into the yard before the low clapboard farmhouse.

Percy Logan dismounted, tethered his horse, and ambled towards the field where the three farmers stood. He studied the churned-up earth, then spoke to Campion. "How long are you going to stand for this?"

The sodbuster said, "That Morgan claims his horses didn't do it."

Logan laughed. "Now come on, Mr. Campion, who the hell else could it be? Do you know of any wild horses in this county that would stampede over your land? Do you think night riders are rampaging over your farm? It's got to be those horses from Morgan's ranch. And remember, if we can't be sure you'll have a good crop on time this fall, the Wholesale Produce Corporation will have to look

141

elsewhere. Too bad." He shook his head sadly, then reached down and fingered some dirt. "This is such good soil; it'll grow damn good stuff and we'd be willing to pay well for it."

Campion and his two neighbors looked at each other; then Campion turned to Logan. "What do you expect us to do? Morgan drove us off the other day."

"He may be good with that whip," Logan said, "but that's all. You've got to think of yourselves and your families. Are you willing to stand by and see your crops ruined because a horse rancher can't control his animals? Are you willing to go bust, when you got a chance to make some real money this fall?"

Campion again looked at his companions. "We can't let this happen. What do you want to do?"

"Well," Logan said, "my associates are talking to some of the other farmers in the area. I think we ought to go back to the ranch again, but this time we won't do any talking. We'll just go in there and take care of the place and anybody who gets into our way. We'll drive off those horses, even kill them if necessary."

"My God!" Campion gasped. "You want to start a range war?"

"Morgan already started it," Logan pointed out. "You got no choice. It's either him or you. You'll only be defending your property, which you surely have a right to do. You heard the man the other day. He was unwilling even to talk to you, and he threatened you if you didn't get off his land."

"I don't know . . ." Campion hesitated, shaking his head.

Now Logan shrugged casually. "It really don't matter to the Wholesale Produce Corporation. We can go somewhere else. There's plenty of farmers who'll jump at our offer. If you're content to see your land ruined, no crop this fall, and no money, why, that's your decision." Logan started to amble away. "I'll just tell Mr. Paquette and the others that we'd best get out of Grover and look elsewhere."

"Wait!" Campion cried sharply. Logan stopped and waited for the farmers to catch up with him. "All right, we'll do what you say. But we can't speak for the others."

"I'm sure they'll also see the truth of the matter. Now get your weapons and a wagon, and we'll all meet at Rock Slide Pass—say, in about two hours. All right?"

"We'll be there," Campion promised.

Meanwhile, Kid Proctor and Billy Paxton himself had been talking to other owners of homesteads in close proximity to Spade Bit. Paxton and his fellow regulators enjoyed the same success as Logan had, with Michael Campion. After all, money was of first importance to everyone, and especially to farmers who were struggling to eke out a successul living on the land. The image of good hard cash for their fall crops from a big produce distributor was a dream come true for these men and they were easily convinced that Morgan was a threat to their livelihood which needed to be removed.

By noon, farmers in wagons were coming onto the open flats near Rock Slide Pass. They carried their usual array of weapons: rifles, shotguns, old blunderbusses, whatever they had handy. Billy Paxton had also talked some of them into bringing oil-soaked torches that they would use to set fire to the buildings of Spade Bit. Three wagonsful of men had assembled, about twenty farmers. On horseback were Billy Paxton, Percy Logan, Kid Proctor, and Ben Parker, all wearing side arms and carrying rifles in scabbards on their saddles. Also on horseback were Michael Campion and two other farmers. Buck Lewis had not shown, since he was still nursing a broken jaw, the result of his encounter yesterday with Lee Morgan.

Before the motley army of sodbusters started out, Billy Paxton addressed them. "I know that what we suggest you do is not easy. Nobody likes violence nor destruction. We know that nobody likes to hurt a neighbor. But," he gestured emphatically, "Lee Morgan is not just a neighbor; he's a tresspasser who has no regard for your rights. If you attack him and destroy his ranch, you'll only be acting in self-defense. You have rights and nobody has a license to deprive you of these rights. Nobody can fault you if you take steps to protect yourselves and the future of your families. Since the law won't help you, you must take the law into your own hands."

Many of the farmers still felt uneasy. They were not men of violence. Still, Paxton and his men convinced them that an attack on Spade Bit, the destruction of this ranch and its horses, was the only way to make certain that they could grow their crops and raise their families in peace.

Shortly after noon, the parade of horses and wagons started north on the St. Marie Road. Paxton had given them clear instructions. They were not to hesitate, not to waste time talking to Morgan. They must act quickly and give no quarter. They must burn the buildings, drive the horses out of the barn and kill them, and shoot anybody who tried to stop them. This was the only language that men like Lee Morgan understood. And if they had to kill

Morgan or any of his hands, then so be it.

But Billy Paxton had already promised himself that he would personally take care of Lee Morgan. He was still smarting from what had happened at the Black Ace yesterday. If word ever got out that Paxton had been cowed by one man, and while Paxton had four men with him, such gossip would ruin his reputation and he could not allow this to happen. On this one point he was adamant: no matter what else happened today, Lee Morgan must die, slain by Billy Paxton himself.

Ten miles up the road, on Spade Bit, Lee was relaxing since the morning had passed uneventfully. He had eaten his noon meal, and at about one o'clock had gone into the horse barn to help Willie McCormick replace some rotted timber. Clem Corcoran and Hank Goyette, meanwhile, were repairing the tool shed in preparation for the arrival of more equipment from Grover. For the time being, Morgan ignored the problem of the broken fences, promising himself to take care of that later.

Matilda and Sarah Morgan were inside the ranchhouse. They had washed the dishes and cleaned up the kitchen and were now engaged in other household chores.

None of the people on the ranch were aware of the grim procession coming up the road. Billy Paxton led the parade cautiously, moving at a relatively slow pace to keep horses and wagons as quiet as possible. Kid Proctor rode ahead as scout, and the man soon came back to Paxton with an elated grin on his face.

"Goddamn, Billy, there's nobody around at all! They must all be indoors in the house or the barn. We can hit them before they even know we're there."

"Good," Paxton said. "You lead that first wagon to the barn and I'll take the second wagon to the house." He looked at his two other cohorts. "Percy, you come with me and, Ben, you go with Proctor. I want those torches lit as soon as we come into the yard and I want the barn and house set afire right away. When the horses come out of that barn, you get those sodbusters started killing them off. When Morgan and his hands try to interfere, we'll just shoot them down."

The other regulators nodded.

Soon they reached Spade Bit. Paxton held them up while he peered around. No one was in sight. He motioned to Proctor. "All right—you know what to do. And you too." He looked at Logan. The two men nodded, trotted back to the wagons and told the farmers to light their torches. When all was ready, Paxton cried, "Let's go, let's go! Remember, no quarter!"

Only then did the heavy rumble of wagons and galloping hoofs of horses draw the attention of those on the ranch. Lee Morgan and Willie McCormick dashed out of the barn, just in time to see the group of men storming into the yard with their torches. Hank Goyette and Clem Corcoran ran from the tool shed to investigate the racket, while Sarah and Matilda came out of the house and stood in astonishment on the porch, staring in terror at the invaders.

"Take cover, take cover!" Lee Morgan shouted to Sarah. Before he could speak again, Billy Paxton and Percy Logan opened fire with their six-shooters, but missed, although they had struck the planks on the front porch, prompting Matilda and Sarah to drop to the floor. McCormick ducked behind the open door of the barn, while Corcoran and Goyette squatted behind a wood pile at the side of the house. Lee himself zig-zagged to the side door, avoiding the flying lead. Once inside, he grabbed his rifle, already loaded, and burst out the side door again to drop next to the wood pile.

Now the regulators, the farmers and the Spade Bit hands began an exchange of fire, but Paxton and the others failed to hit the three hands who were sheltering themselves, while the hands themselves, hardly gunmen, did not hit any of their attackers. During the furious exchange, Paxton ordered the farmers to dismount from the wagons to set the buildings afire with their torches. The farmers hesitated, but Billy Paxton glared at them.

"You sons o' bitches, do you expect us to do all your work for you? We're holding off these trespassers, so you men get your asses out of those wagons and do what you're supposed to do!" He then aimed his own guns towards the wagons, filling the sodbusters with fear. The farmers quickly decided that they'd be safer from the erratic shooting from the Spade Bit hands than they would be from Billy Paxton.

The farmers got out of the wagons, scurrying forward, crouching, and trying to reach both the barn and the house with their torches. Four of them were heading for the barn and six towards the ranch house. Lee Morgan had reloaded his Winchester repeater and he stood upright, brazenly exposing himself to the regulator's gunfire. He raised his rifle, aimed and shot with lightning speed and knocked the sixgun out of the hand of Percy Logan, who first gaped at the flesh wound, then blinked at Lee Morgan. The farmers with their torches were stunned by the uncanny accuracy and stopped dead in their tracks, holding their torches aloft.

"You bastards better get out of here or you'll all be dead," Lee shouted.

But Billy Paxton now fired quickly at Morgan, skimming the bullet off Lee's shoulder, drawing blood and forcing Lee to drop to the ground. The regulator leader screamed at the farmers. "You cowardly sons o' bitches, *get moving!* Burn that goddamn barn and that house!"

Ben Parker and Kid Proctor continued to fire heavily and recklessly, keeping the ranch hands and Lee Morgan pinned behind the wood pile. Proctor had even forced some of the farmers to unleash volleys of fire, however inaccurate. Despite the withering barrage, however, Lee Morgan again stood up, this time crouching warily. He turned to McCormick, who was behind the open barn door.

"Willie, get inside and turn those horses loose! If those bastards set the barn afire we could lose all of them."

"Sure, Lee," the old man answered, and ran into the barn.

Lee squinted at the uneasy farmers who were still advancing with their torches. He aimed his rifle and let loose at the nearest sodbuster, hitting him squarely in the chest. The man fell backward and landed flat on his back, abruptly dead. The next torchbearer gasped in horror, but then he too caught a slug from Lee's Winchester. The shot struck him on the temple and spun him around. He staggered like a drunk while blood poured down his neck, his arm mechanically waving the torch. Then the torch fell and the farmer collapsed to the ground, also dead.

Lee now turned his attention to the sodbusters heading for the house. He aimed for the man in the lead and with one shot caught the would-be arsonist

148

in the neck, almost tearing out his Adam's apple. The man gasped, his eyes widened, and he dropped the torch to grab his wound, then buckled to the ground, squirming in the dirt like a wounded cougar before he lay still in death. The other farmers heading towards the house with their torches suddenly about-faced and hurried back to their wagons, ignoring the shouted curses of Billy Paxton.

The regulators now shot wildly at Lee, who zigzagged deftly. The horses suddenly emerged from the barn at a gallop, clouds of raising dust, as Willie McCormick drove them into the open land behind the house. The diversion enabled Lee Morgan to scramble to the side of the house, scale the wall and get onto the roof, where he slid behind the west slope. He now had an overall view of what was going on.

Lee stared in horror as Sarah ran down off the porch to attend to the dead farmer in the yard. She had barely stepped into the yard, when she caught two slugs from the blistering gunfire. One bullet struck her in the chest. The second bullet hit her in the forehead and her face was suddenly covered with blood. She gasped once, staggered a few feet, then collapsed to the ground. There was no doubt that she was dead.

Overcome by rage and grief, he fired like a madman, wounding two more farmers. His next shot struck Ben Parker square in the chest, opening a chasm that poured out streams of blood. The regulator fell to the ground.

Now Billy Paxton followed Clem Corcoran who was frantically seeking cover. Paxton caught Corcoran with two quick shots to the head and the ranch hand spun twice and then fell over. His body jerked twice, his legs flew upwards, then he lay stiffly prone.

Hank Goyette stared at the bloody corpse and panicked. He would have darted away, but he dared not leave his cover behind the woodpile. However, Lee had gained the upper hand atop the roof and now let loose with six more quick shots, striking the wagons and sending splinters of wood flying through the air. The accuracy of his aim told the farmers that only death would await them if they remained any longer. The teamsters whirled about and clattered the wagons quickly out of the yard, tossing away their torches. An angry Billy Paxton shouted after them, but they ignored him. Paxton could not stop Campion from leaving, either. He too had had enough.

Paxton still hoped to finish off Morgan, but one of his men was dead and Morgan had also downed four of the farmers. The next shot from Lee's Winchester caught Percy Logan in the arm, numbing the limb as the man dropped his weapon. He winced in pain and turned to Paxton.

"B-Billy," he panted, "w-we got to get outa here!"

"I want to get that son of a bitch!" Paxton growled.

"He'll kill us all, Billy," Logan insisted. "Let's go!"

When a shot from the roof whizzed by Billy Paxton's ear, he no longer hesitated. "All right, let's get out of here!" Neither of his two surviving henchmen balked. They and Paxton turned their mounts and galloped south along the St. Marie Road.

In the sudden quiet, Lee Morgan climbed numbly off the roof. His horses were safe in the pastures; his buildings were still intact, but one of his men was

dead. And Sarah—Sarah! A sobbing Matilda
Maynard was now bending over the body of Lee's
young wife. He stood erect, staring down at her.
Then slowly he knelt and reached out to touch her
hair. Hank Goyette and Willie McCormick came
over to him, but said nothing.

Finally Lee stood up and walked away, stooping
when he had moved about ten yards. He was blinded
by tears. Willie McCormick came up to him.

"I don't know what to tell you, Lee," the old man
said in a croak. Lee nodded, and McCormick patted
him awkwardly on the shoulder. "We'll take care of
her. We'll see that she's given a decent burial next
to your father and Miz Dowd."

"I'd appreciate that," Lee answered gruffly.

At dusk, the two remaining hands and Matilda
Maynard had dug graves for Sarah and Corcoran.
They had previously loaded the dead farmers and
the slain Ben Parker on the buckboard and covered
them with blankets. They would take the bodies into
Grover in the morning.

Lee Morgan read from the Bible as he buried his
wife and Corcoran in the small plot where his father
and Catherine Dowd lay. Then he and the others
walked slowly back to the empty house.

Chapter 10

News of the Spade Bit shoot-out did not reach Grover immediately. The stunned farmers, who had seen three of their neighbors killed and many more wounded, said little as they rode from the horse ranch in horror. Most of them now regretted their rash act, not because they felt any empathy for Lee Morgan, but because they had seen the futility of such actions. They would return to their clapboard and log farmhouses, realizing they had made a terrible mistake by listening to Billy Paxton and his men.

Michael Campion would have the most agonizing chore. Since he had been the one who had encouraged his fellow farmers to attack Spade Bit, he would be the one to notify the families of the dead men that they had lost their breadwinners. All of the farmers would spend a tormenting night and perhaps still be too shaken in the morning to work their lands. Most of them gave in to the sobering thought that nothing could be worse than this needless waste of human lives. If they had learned anything, it was to leave Lee Morgan alone and try to live peacefully once again.

Billy Paxton had suffered a blow. One of his men had been killed, another injured, and he had been forced to retreat from Spade Bit, despite his overwhelming number of men. Who in Shoshone County would ever listen to him again? And worse, Paxton realized that when the shock of the Spade Bit bloodshed forced authorities to take action, the farmers would quickly blame the regulator and his men. Paxton had also received a sober lesson: Lee Morgan and his guns were not something to take lightly.

The regulator had already received a thousand dollars from Jesse Callaway, not all he wanted, but a healthy amount considering he had failed in his mission. He knew Callaway was unlikely to ask for its return. Paxton believed his best course now was to make himself scarce. As soon as he returned to Grover House he packed his things for a quick departure with his three surviving cohorts.

"Where'll we go, Billy?" Kid Proctor asked.

"Not far," Paxton answered. "Down to Boise. We still have business with that Lee Morgan."

"Billy," Percy Logan spoke soberly, "maybe it'd be best to leave this thing alone. Ben's dead, and there ain't no use of any more of us getting killed or hurt."

Paxton's eyes flamed. "No son of a bitch is going to do this to me. He's made fools of us and he's going to pay. I'm not going to rest until I see that man dead. If the rest of you don't want to join me in this, then I'll do it alone."

The regulator leader's three companions now felt a tinge of agony. They wanted to forget Morgan,

Gunsight Gap country, and Idaho itself. But Paxton was the one that good payers hired, not them. Paxton could command the high prices that allowed them to live in comfort. If they deserted him now, they would be losing a good thing. Thus, while they might try to dissuade their leader from doing anything more in Shoshone County, they would have to follow him in this obsession, no matter how senseless.

Still, they would try to change their leader's mind. "Billy," Kid Proctor said, "when word of this thing gets out, lawmen will cover on Grover like locusts and those scared sodbusters will blame us. Is it worth trouble with the law just for one man?"

"Proctor is talking sense, Billy," Buck Lewis said. "I wasn't there today, true, but the killing at that place will make an awful lot of people unhappy. The law don't like to have angry people on their backs. They'll demand some kind of action."

"I don't think these sodbusters have the guts or the influence that those cattlemen in Wyoming have," Logan said. "They wouldn't support us, and they'd leave us to take all the guilt."

Proctor had continued packing his bag while he listened to the pleas of his men. Now he looked up from his saddlebag with eyes like steel. "You boys may think you're talking sense, but if Lee Morgan gets away with this, we may all be out of a job. You, Percy," he pointed at Logan. "You wouldn't be able to have the prettiest whores in Cheyenne anytime you wanted one. And you, Kid, how would you pay for the fine liquor you're so fond of. And Buck, how can you support your gambling habits without money?"

No one answered.

"Who'd hire us if they found out that one man and

a couple of ranch hands took us on and whipped us?'' Paxton continued. He then shuttled his glance between Logan and Proctor. "Morgan disarmed you two with a mere whip after you had the draw on him. Don't you think those sodbusters will spread word of that? And you, Buck, you were gonna take on Morgan and then he flattened you. Don't you think those people in the saloon will be talking about it? If I don't get Morgan, nobody's likely to hire me again, at least not for the price I've been getting up to now. And you boys will be out of work. Is that what you want?''

Paxton's men remained silent.

"No," Paxton said, "the only way to stay in business with good pay is to kill Lee Morgan. If Morgan is dead and they know we got him, everything else will be forgotten. I say we go to Boise and take rooms there," Paxton said. "There may be a lot of lawmen crawling all over Grover and Gunsight Gap, but within a few weeks, a month at the most, things will have cooled down. That fight today at Spade Bit will be history. People will forget it. Then, we'll come back, bide our time, and kill Morgan, even if we have to bushwhack him.''

Finally, Percy Logan sighed. "Whatever you say, Billy.''

"Good," Paxton said. "Then we'll pull right out."

"You mean now?" Kid Proctor asked. "Right this minute? I'm starved. I'd like to get something to eat.''

"The sooner we're gone, the better," Paxton said. "We'll stay on the trail tonight, but we'll stop and have a hot meal on the way out of town.''

The three cohorts agreed. They packed their horses, checked out of Grover House, and stopped at the Grover Cafe for a meal. Then, as darkness descended, the four men quietly left town and disappeared to the south.

The first real news of the shoot-out in Grover came the following morning. At Spade Bit, Lee Morgan and his surviving hands awoke early. Willie McCormick got the buckboard and Appaloosa ready to carry the dead men in to the mortician. Lee Morgan felt sick, still agonizing over the loss of his wife. He did not speak to Matilda as she served breakfast, and she said nothing to him. When he finished his meal, Lee walked outside where Willie was preparing for the ride into town. Only then did Morgan speak.

"Willie, take Hank with you. Stop at the jailhouse and tell Deputy Chook what happened. He's more likely to believe two men than one."

McCormick nodded and signaled for Hank Goyette to climb on the buckboard. Lee Morgan stood motionless in the yard, saying nothing, watching the riders and their morbid burden leave what was left of Spade Bit. Lee stared until the buckboard was out of sight. Somehow he had lost some of his fervor for this place. The trauma of the day before had left a disheartening feeling inside him.

Lee Morgan made no move to do anything. He returned to the house and slumped in a parlor chair. Matilda came into the parlor, but he neither moved nor acknowledged her presence. She left again but returned a few minutes later and placed a steaming cup of coffee on the stand next to Lee's chair. Lee ignored the offering and rose from the chair.

"Mr. Morgan?" Matilda looked questioningly at his blank face.

"I'm going out, Matilda," Lee finally said.

"Going out? Where?"

"To visit my wife's grave."

The housekeeper threw her hands to her mouth to muffle her sudden gasp. It was too soon after the burial to be visiting the grave. As Lee left the house, she worried that his grief over the tragic death would cause him to ignore Spade Bit and forget about his work. She was suddenly fearful that she might once again be looking for employment.

Willie McCormick and Hank Goyette rode slowly down St. Marie Road and arrived in Grover nearly two hours later. By now, the town was alive with morning bustle: people crowded on the sidewalks, businessmen toiled in their shops, and horses and wagons raised dust on the street. People had no notion of what the buckboard carried, since a large tarp hid the four bodies neatly laid out on the rear platform. McCormick weaved through the crowded street and then pulled up in front of a well-kept building with a sign slowly rocking in the breeze above the porch: DuBois Morticians.

Hank Goyette found DuBois inside the place, working on a body with his assistant. "Will you come outside? We got some customers for you."

"Customers?" DuBois huffed angrily. "We don't refer to the dead as customers." He cocked his head to his assistant who followed him outside and to the back of the buckboard. Willie McCormick pulled back the tarp to reveal the four bodies. DuBois gasped. He recognized one of the men.

"My God, that's Clem Harrington! I buried his mother only a couple of months ago." He stared hard at McCormick. "What happened here?"

"I think you better get Deputy Chook, Mr. DuBois," Willie said.

The mortician nodded and then gestured to his aide. "Run over to the jailhouse and get Chook." As

158

the youth ran off, the man said to McCormick and Goyette, "Help me get these men inside."

Fifteen minutes later, Hank Goyette and Willie McCormick were sitting in Chook's office, relating the events of the shoot-out at Spade Bit. The deputy listened in dread as the Spade Bit ranch hands described the event.

"That don't say much for you, Deputy," McCormick said. "Didn't the farmers come to you first? That's what I'd have expected."

Chook nodded. "I told them I'd look into it."

"I guess you didn't look into it fast enough," McCormick said. "Now you got a real problem on your hands. How are you goin' to explain what happened up here to the sheriff in Boise? How are you goin' to explain your delay in takin' some kind of action?"

"I was busy," Chook lied. "I had to take care of some other things."

McCormick leaned over the desk. "Deputy, nothin' you had to do coulda been more important than stoppin' a bunch o' sodbusters from takin' the law into their own hands, led by a bunch o' professional gunmen. I don't envy you, Chook."

The deputy rolled his tongue around his lips to mitigate some of his nervousness. Finally he found enough courage to speak. "I want to thank you for comin' in and tellin' me what happened. I'll go over to DuBois and take a look at those bodies. Then I'll start an investigation."

"Sure, *now* you'll start an investigation," McCormick scoffed before he rose from his chair and turned to Goyette. "Let's get outa here!"

The bodies had not been in DuBois' funeral parlor long before word of their presence spread through Grover. The young aide who worked for DuBois had

159

not only heard fragments of the story from the men who brought in the corpses, but had heard more details as Chook and DuBois talked when the deputy had come to view the bodies. Chook had barely left with DuBois to walk to the jail to make a report when the youth darted out of the funeral parlor to spread the story all over town. The listeners in turn spread the story to others, embellishing the report.

Within an hour, everyone in Grover knew that a range war had started to the north of Rock Slide Pass, with dozens of men killed and many buildings burned to the ground. Residents stormed the jailhouse for more information, but the harrassed deputy would only say that there had been some trouble at the Spade Bit Ranch, adding that the reports of death and destruction were greatly exaggerated. He promised that he was looking into the incident and would spread the word when he found out the real truth of what had happened. Chook was finally being forced to lock his office door to get away from the curious.

The news of the Spade Bit shoot-out inevitably reached the ears of Jesse Callaway, and he reeled in apprehension. Guilt swelled inside him, for he knew that he had initiated this event. But even worse, he realized that Lee Morgan knew it, and wondered if Morgan would come looking for him, seeking revenge after the death of his wife. Callaway made certain that he had a loaded revolver in his desk drawer and he began wearing a gunbelt whenever he went outside. He would no longer move about unarmed.

Callaway left the bank and hurried over to Grover House to find "Mr. Paquette," the alias Billy Paxton had used. He walked nervously into the hotel and up to the desk clerk. "Pardon me, is Mr. Paquette in? It's important that I see him."

"I'm sorry, Mr. Callaway, Mr. Paquette checked out last night."

"Last night?"

"I thought it was kind of strange, leaving so late," the desk clerk said, "but who are we to tell guests what to do? He and three of his associates left, but I didn't see the other one. However, Mr. Paquette paid Mr. Parker's bills, too, so I assume he went with the others."

Of course the desk clerk wouldn't see Ben Parker, Callaway thought. He must have been killed in the shoot-out. "Do you know where Mr. Paquette was going?"

"No, he didn't say."

Jesse Callaway thanked the clerk and then left Grover House. When he got into the street, he peered about warily, expecting Lee Morgan to suddenly emerge and attack him. Then he scowled. Billy Paxton had failed and had just run off, taking $1,000 of unearned money with him. If trouble started with Lee Morgan, Callaway would have to find some way to deal with it alone. He walked back to his bank, trying to make himself inconspicuous. Once inside, he told one of the tellers that he would be conducting all business in his private office from now on instead of at the desk behind the railing. If Morgan came storming into the bank, Callaway would have a better chance to defend himself inside the private room instead of out in the open.

News of the shoot-out had also reached the Black Ace Saloon. The men drinking and gambling chattered like squirrels about the event, mixing fact and fancy as they talked. Mary Spots could not help overhearing the news and she gasped in disbelief. Lee

Morgan had taken on several hired guns and a band of farmers, and had come out on top. However, Mary was sad to learn that Lee's wife had been killed during the skirmish. She remembered how he had expressed pleasure in getting back Spade Bit and being able to share it with his pretty young wife, whom he adored.

Mary Spots went over to one of the men at the bar. "Are you sure about that? Are you sure that's what happened?" she asked.

"It's the truth, sure enough," the man answered. "They say Morgan was so fast and accurate, he woulda picked off every last man who came onto his place if they didn't get out of there pronto."

"But his wife was killed?" Mary asked.

The man nodded gravely. "That's what we've been told."

"But Morgan killed one of the gunmen who went out there with the sodbusters and wounded a couple more," another man at the table said.

Mary Spots asked no more questions, mulling over what she had heard. So Lee had not been able to avoid the trouble he had hoped to escape. Mary sat alone at a table, drinking more than she should have, and cutting down on the amount of soda water she usually mixed with her whiskey.

She was tempted to ride out to Spade Bit to try to console Lee. She knew how bad he must be feeling. Yes, she should go out there to see him. Mary Spots poured herself another stiff drink.

The news also reached the office of the Clemons Trading Agency. Both Mr. Clemons and Sue listened in disbelief as the postal carrier delivering the morning mail spoke of the massacre at Spade Bit. The carrier was one of the few people in town

162

who had a quite accurate account of what happened. He knew that five men had died—a gunman, three farmers, and one of the Spade Bit ranch hands. He also knew that Lee Morgan's young wife had been shot and killed. He also knew that Morgan himself had not been hurt, nor any of his property destroyed, and that Morgan had not been driven from his ranch.

When the postal carrier finished his story, Sue Clemons looked at him incredulously. "Mr. Morgan's wife was killed?" she whispered.

"Yes, Miss Clemons. I was told he's already buried her."

"Oh my God, my God!" Sue gasped.

"That Morgan must be some kind o' man," the carrier said, shaking his head. "I don't see how anybody could take on a mob like that and come out a winner. Those gunmen skipped out o' town last night, I hear."

"Yes, he's quite a man," Sue answered, her blue eyes now reflecting a faraway look.

"Well," the carrier shrugged, "I still have other mail to deliver."

After the man left, Sue turned to her father. "Dad, do you mind if I take the afternoon off? I'd like to ride out to the ranch and see Lee. He could use some sympathy right now."

"Do you have a feelin' for that man, Sue?" her father asked shrewdly.

"I—I'm not sure," Sue confessed. "I just feel that I ought to go and see him."

"All right, girl," her father nodded. "But I have to tell you, don't get too involved with Mr. Morgan. I'd hate to see you get hurt."

"I can take care of myself," Sue assured her father.

The Clemons's closed their office at noon and retired to their home at the end of the street to have lunch. When they had finished, Clemons said he would return to the office to take care of business. He repeated his warning as he left: Don't get hurt.

After she had washed the lunch dishes, Sue changed into riding clothes—a leather skirt, blouse, and leather vest. She also donned her riding boots, and a wide-brimmed hat. She walked to the stable to have the groom saddle her favorite mare. "This animal is good and rested," the man said, "but don't run her too hard."

"I won't," Sue promised.

By one o'clock, Sue Clemons trotted out of town. Soon she was cantering up the St. Marie Road. She was anxious to see Lee Morgan, and for more reasons than simply expressing sympathy. Still, she restrained the urge to move at too fast a pace that might tire her horse. At about mid-afternoon, Spade Bit came into view. As she veered into the yard, the place looked deserted and she panicked. Had everybody left? She trotted up to the house, dismounted, and tethered the mare to a post. Then she came up the steps, onto the front porch, and knocked at the door. She heard shuffling feet inside.

A moment later, Matilda Maynard opened the door.

"Hello," the girl said. "Can I see Mr. Morgan?"

The housekeeper studied the visitor's riding attire, her shapely figure, and her pretty face. "I don't think he'd be in the mood to see anybody right now. We had some bad trouble yesterday and his wife was killed. He's real depressed."

"Please, ma'am, I came all the way out from Grover. Just tell him it's Sue Clemons. I'm the one

164

who helped him buy his horses. I'd really like to see him."

Matilda studied the girl again. "Well, he ain't in the house, anyway."

Sue Clemons frowned. "Where is he?"

"He's out back," the woman cocked her head. "The small cemetery plot at the north end o' the pasture." She threw an almost pleading look at the girl. "He's bad, Miss. He was out there at his wife's grave this morning, and now he's out there again this afternoon. He wouldn't eat a thing all day. He didn't do nothing except mope, and ride out to the cemetery. Willie and Hank tried to talk to him after they got back from Grover, but he wouldn't listen to them. Maybe you should ride out there and see him. Just take the path behind the house and follow it to the end. You'll run right into the cemetery."

"I'm obliged to you, ma'am," Sue said. She left the porch, untethered the horse and mounted again. She then trotted around the house to the rear, and soon found the path. While she rode, Sue studied the vast expanse of range land, squinting until she saw the west boundary far in the distance. Yes, Lee Morgan certainly had plenty of room to exercise and graze his horses. He would have no need to let them roam over the surrounding farms.

The girl rode on for nearly ten minutes before she saw the big roan stallion, Upway Don, his reins tied to a tree. Then she saw two white markers jutting out from the ground. And finally she could see Lee Morgan himself, kneeling in front of a freshly turned grave. The girl dismounted and led her horse to another tree where she tethered the mare. She walked quietly into the small cemetery. It was surrounded by a white fence that was somewhat in disrepair. There was a second recently covered grave, no doubt the burial site of the ranch hand who had died.

If Lee heard her coming, he didn't acknowledge it. He continued staring down at the mound of earth. She knelt beside him, but he still did not look at or speak to her, though he must have been aware of her presence.

He did not react, even when she put a soft hand on his shoulder. Then she finally spoke. "Lee, I'm so awfully sorry; I just had to come and tell you that."

Still, Lee did not respond.

The girl ran her fingers down his right arm. "Please, Lee, won't you talk to me?"

Finally, Morgan turned and looked squarely at her. "It wasn't right, Sue—it wasn't right! Sarah never hurt anybody, never. But they killed her. Do you know she ran right out in the yard, in the open, to help one of those sodbusters who was shot? She just wanted to help the man, and they shot her dead!"

"I know how hard this is on you, Lee, and you have every right to feel bitter. But what's done is done and you've got to get on with your life. You've made a good start here. Don't throw it away. I'm sure your wife wouldn't want that."

"It doesn't make any difference anymore what she wants. I don't intend to rest until I get revenge on those gunmen."

"They've left town, from what I heard in Grover, and nobody knows where they went," Sue said. "There's been enough bloodshed, Lee. I know how you feel and I can't blame you, but if you harbor a grudge for the rest of your life, *you'll* be the one who gets hurt most." She looked down at the grave. "I don't think Sarah would want that either."

Lee Morgan rose to his feet now, and looked down

at Sue Clemons. "I know you're talking sense, but I'm just too hurt to listen to you."

The girl too rose and gripped Lee Morgan's hand. "I only want to help, Lee, believe me. I don't want anything else. I'll admit I've had a—feeling for you, but the last thing in the world I'd want was to have anything happen to your wife. But you'll have to accept it. All you can do is remember Sarah—remember the happy times you shared.

"I'm going to order the best headstone I can find," Lee said gruffly.

Despite the somber occasion, Sue smiled. "The Clemons Trading Agency can help you with that, too."

A faint grin suddenly crossed Lee's melancholy face. "I believe the good Lord sent you out here. You must be tired and hungry. Let's ride back to the house and I'll have Matilda fix us something."

"I'd like that," the girl said.

Fifteen minutes later, they pulled in front of the ranch house. Hank Goyette was surprised to see them come in together. He was even more surprised when Lee asked him to take Upway Don and Sue's mare into the barn and brush them down while Lee took the visitor inside for some refreshments.

"Yes sir, Mr. Morgan," Goyette grinned. He was glad to see his boss come out of his shell and guessed that the girl had helped him in this.

Inside the house, Matilda was equally surprised when Lee asked her to make some coffee and bring some rolls. She was pleased when Lee invited Sue to stay for supper and Sue accepted.

As they ate their evening meal, Lee began issuing instructions for chores tomorrow: finish painting the shed, sharpen the rest of the tools, store supplies, and do a host of other things. McCormick and Goyette were elated because Lee had come back to reality. Matilda too was happy at the change in him.

For nearly a month Lee worked harder than ever, frequently taking time to visit Sarah's grave. Sue Clemons had become a frequent visitor to the ranch, ostensibly to report her efforts in buying items that Lee needed on the ranch. She relished these visits, for they gave her the chance to see and talk to him. The girl felt fervent admiration for Lee Morgan—perhaps she was even falling in love with him. She could make him laugh and make him feel at ease, and thus enabled Lee to cope with his grief and anger.

Meanwhile, the Shoshone County sheriff and two federal marshals had launched an investigation into the shoot-out at Spade Bit. Lee, though he blamed the farmers, conceded that they had probably been incited to make their incursions by the gunmen led by Billy Paxton. Michael Campion and the other farmers insisted that they would have never indulged in this reckless act if Paxton had not talked them into it. The farmers promised to do whatever possible to make amends to Lee Morgan, while Lee himself was content to drop all charges against the sodbusters.

The Shoshone County sheriff ruled that the true culprits were the missing gunmen, who would be prosecuted—if they could be found. The lawmen had taken the easy way out: blame Paxton and his men and close the case. The sheriff reprimanded Deputy John Chook, ordering him to take swift action in the future to avoid any potential trouble. Chook was relieved. He had gotten away with a mere slap on the wrist. He informed Jesse Callaway that he would no longer do his bidding and endanger his job. Callaway hardly complained, for he himself was grateful that he had not been involved in the investigations which might have sullied his business reputation and perhaps even resulted in his arrest. He hoped he would never lay eyes on Billy Paxton again. However, he still went in fear of Lee Morgan, despite reports that Morgan was now settled into a quiet, reserved life.

By early June the massacre at Spade Bit had been all but forgotten around Grover. The farmers were busily tending to their new crops and Lee Morgan continued to work on Spade Bit. There had been no further trouble between them and the sodbusters were happy to leave Lee Morgan alone.

But the peaceful atmosphere that prevailed in northern Shoshone County proved to be only the calm before a new storm.

Chapter 11

Without a doubt Sue Clemon's support and sympathy had much to do with calming Lee down and enabling him to resume a normal life. They had seen each other frequently during the past several weeks since the shoot-out and, despite his grief at the loss of his wife, Lee had become quite close to the girl. Sue herself had already developed a deep infatuation for Lee, so it was inevitable that their relationship would intensify.

On a pleasant evening in June, Lee Morgan rode into town to accept an invitation to Sue's home for dinner. He told Matilda, "I don't know how long I'll be gone, but don't worry if I'm not back tonight. I might stay over at Grover House and ride home in the morning."

"You just enjoy yourself, Mr. Morgan," Matilda answered, smiling.

Morgan left Spade Bit in the late afternoon, but he did not arrive in town until well after dark. The main street of Grover was crowded with men who had worked hard all day and had come into town for a little diversion. A din of noisy crowds and the tinkle of piano notes drifted from the saloons, including the Black Ace. As Morgan loped past the place, Mary Spots was standing outside, leaning against the railing. She cried out, "Lee! Lee Morgan! You sure look grand tonight."

Lee reined his horse and looked down at the woman. "You must be putting in a long day," he said, grinning.

"You sure look fine," Mary said. "I want to tell you, I'm so sorry about what happened out at your ranch. I intended to come out there and try to help you out, but I just didn't have the gumption to do it."

"That's all right, Mary."

"Why don't you come inside? I'll buy you a drink," she offered.

"I'd like to," Lee said, "but I've got to meet somebody."

Mary Spots studied the man's neat attire and grinned. "Must be a woman," she said. "Well, that's good. I know it's hard to forget bad things, but you can't stop livin.'" She rested a hand on Lee's. "You take care yourself, hear? And if you need anything, you'll always know where to find me."

"I appreciate that, Mary Spots."

Lee tipped his hat, turned his horse and continued to the street. He soon reached Sue's address—167 Main Street. The two gas lamps on either side of the front door were lit, a signal that the occupant was expecting company. A glow of light radiated from the windows of the front parlor. Morgan had barely dismounted when Sue Clemons came out of the door and onto the porch.

172

"Lee, you're right on time and you sure look handsome."

"And you're pretty as a picture," Morgan answered as he studied the girl. She was wearing a blue cotton dress with a tight bodice and a deep V neck edged with lace. The dress fit her snugly and accented her voluptuous figure.

"Just take your horse around to the stable and Ben will take care of it," Sue told him.

Morgan nodded and rode around the house to the stable, where a groom came up to him. "Do you want to leave that animal here overnight?" the man asked.

"I doubt it," Lee said. "I'm visiting the Clemons. Miss Clemons told me to bring my horse here."

"Oh, fine," the man said. "I'll take care of him and you can pick him up any time."

Lee walked back to the Clemons house, where Sue was sitting on the porch railing, waiting for him to return. When she saw him she stood up. "Come on inside. Lee." Once inside the parlor, she offered him a chair and Lee sat down. "I'll have dinner ready soon and I promise you the two of us will have a good meal."

"The two of us? What about your father?" Lee asked.

"He had to go to Boise. He won't be back for a couple of days."

She disappeared into the kitchen, and Lee sat alone for perhaps ten minutes, when Sue finally returned. "Everything's all ready, Lee," she said. "Come into the dining room."

It was an excellent meal—roast beef, boiled potatoes, some fresh peas, cherry pie, and coffee. After the repast, Lee retired again to the parlor while Sue cleaned up the kitchen. When she joined

173

her guest about a half hour later, she played some songs for Lee on the piano, then played some records on the phonograph. As they sat together and listened to the music, Sue cautiously moved closer to Lee on the sofa. He did not move away.

"This sure is a nice home, Sue, and that phonograph music is very pleasant, as was the meal. You once told me that I was a man of many talents, and you have many talents, too. And you're pretty, also."

The girl's face sobered and she looked intently at Morgan. "Lee, do you like me?"

"Indeed, I do," he answered.

"I'm glad," the girl said. She reached out and touched his hand, and Lee felt a sensual thrill. When he looked at her and saw the intense yearning in her wide blue eyes, he leaned over and kissed her on the lips. She threw her arm around him and pressed herself closer to him.

"I don't want you to forget about Sarah, Lee," she whispered, "but I care so much for you. I just can't help it."

"I care for you, too, Sue," he said.

"Will you come with me, Lee?" she asked. When Morgan hesitated, Sue rose from the sofa, took his hand, and urged him to his feet. Then she put her arm around him and led him to a good-sized bedroom on the first floor. The room was almost dark save for the dim light of one oil lamp on the bureau.

"The bed's nice and soft, Lee," she whispered.

Despite his love for his wife, more than a month had passed since Sarah's death, and he was still a man with needs and desires. He had been attracted to Sue from the first time he had seen her, but he had always kept his distance. There was no more need to do that. He was a widower and lonely, very lonely. As for the girl, she saw no reason to conceal her desire for him.

"Sit down with me, Lee," the girl whispered again. She led him to the bed and he sat down next to her. She nestled close to Lee and put her arms around his neck before kissing him.

"You sure have a way of arousing a man," Lee Morgan said. He gently moved the girl away from him and then took off his jacket and string tie. He had left his gunbelt in the parlor. Lee pulled her close to him. "I want you, Sue."

"I'm glad," she said. She slipped her arm from behind his neck and ran her fingers over his chest, then downward until her warm hand rested on his throbbing erection. Lee shuddered at the sudden thrill of her touch.

With one hand he unbuckled his belt, while Sue slipped her hand inside his shirt and caressed his bare chest. Lee slid his own hand inside the neck of her dress and touched one breast, squeezing the nipple. The girl quivered in response and pressed her lips closer to his, pushing her slim body against him as she unbuttoned her dress and allowed Lee to slip it off her shoulders and down to her waist.

Lee was breathing hard, and so was Sue. Lee quickly undressed and Sue removed her dress and undergarments. Naked, they fell back on the bed, caressing and fondling each other, kissing with a fervent passion. Lee pressed himself against her warm, soft body and she threw one of her slender legs over his own.

"I want you so bad," the girl whimpered. "I need you so much!"

Lee Morgan pressed the girl gently on her back,

and then kissed her hard on the lips. She responded by reaching down and seizing his swollen cock. His mouth moved down, to suck first one breast, then the other.

"Oh, Lee, please!" She panted. "Now!"

Lee entered her then, sending them both into dizzy, ecstatic bliss.

They spent the night in Sue's soft bed, making love again and again. Not until well after midnight did they fall asleep, embracing each other.

Lee awoke in a stream of sunlight coming through the bedroom window in the early morning. Sue was still sleeping soundly, one arm around him, and he gently removed it, then turned and squinted at the clock on the bureau. Seven o'clock. He had certainly slept long beyond his usual tme.

Lee was about to get up when Sue suddenly reached over, grabbed his neck and pulled him close to her. She smiled and kissed him. "Good morning, Lee."

So they did not get out of bed just yet. Instead they made love again. When they were satisfied, Lee watched while Sue arose and put on a robe.

"I'll get you some breakfast, Lee, while you wash up and dress. There's soap and water on the washstand there," Sue said.

Lee did as she suggested, then went into the kitchen where Sue was frying eggs, and bacon and boiling coffee. She smiled when she saw him.

"Breakfast will be ready soon."

"You're really something, Sue," Lee said. "You're the best thing that could have happened to me after the trouble I had. I don't know how I'm ever going to repay you."

"You already have," she replied with a warm smile.

He kissed her gently on the cheek. "I'd like to stay here all day, but I have to get back to the ranch. There's still a lot to do out there."

"When will I see you again?" Sue asked.

"You know you're welcome to visit Spade Bit anytime. And I'd like to call on you from time to time, if you don't mind."

"Sounds good to me. Now sit down and have your breakfast," the girl said.

After Lee had finished his meal, he went into the parlor, took his gunbelt and buckled it on. Sue, still in her robe, walked right to the front door. "I'll be out to see you as soon as I can," she promised.

"And I'll be in town to see you at the next opportunity," Lee said. "Maybe we'll have some more business down Boise way and we can travel together again."

"I'd like that," the girl answered. "In fact, I'm going to work on it; there's always a lot going on in Boise!"

Lee Morgan grinned and left the house. When he reached the stable, the groom looked at him curiously. Lee had left the animal there all night, and he suspected that Morgan had done more than visit with Sue Clemons. But he said nothing; it wasn't any of his business.

"I brushed your horse down and fed him," he told Lee.

"I appreciate that," Lee said, handing the man a dollar bill. "This ought to cover everything."

The groom grinned, delighted, then he watched Morgan mount the stallion and trot out of the stable. Lee Morgan rode leisurely back to Spade Bit. He felt grateful to Sue Clemons. She had proved to him that life did, indeed, go on.

Two days later, on a quiet early summer afternoon, Michael Campion rode into the yard of Spade Bit, where Lee Morgan was planting some hedges. Lee looked up, surprised by the visit, while Willie McCormick came out of the barn, equally curious.

"Mr. Morgan," the sodbuster said, "I learned something today that I think you should know. Billy Paxton is back in town with his three gunmen. They're stayin' at the Grover House. I came here to tell you that me and the other farmers hereabouts didn't ask them to come here, and we have no intention whatever of havin' anything to do with 'em again. If they try to talk to us, we won't listen to a word. We all appreciate the peace that has come here now, and we're satisfied that you're keepin' your horses on your own land. We wanted you to understand that."

Lee Morgan nodded, but uncontrolled rage suddenly disforted his lean features. "I appreciate what you said, Mr. Campion." Then he turned to McCormick.

"Willie, saddle Upway Don for me."

"Don't do it, Lee; don't go into Grover," Willie pleaded. "They'll be waitin' for you."

"Willie is makin' sense," Campion said. "If Paxton and his boys intend to start any more trouble here, we'd best let Deputy Chook take care of it. He's learned his lesson, and he won't sit back and do nothin' this time."

"I appreciate your concern, Mr. Campion, but I have to take care of this." Lee again turned to the old man. "I want my horse saddled. Now you do it while I go into the house and change."

Willie McCormick knew there was no sense arguing with Lee. Campion also knew that further discussion would be futile. Both men watched Morgan go into the house. Then McCormick went to the barn, while Campion turned his horse and clattered out of the yard.

Lee changed his clothes and buckled on his gunbelt.

When Lee came out of the house, Matilda looked at him with a mixture of awe and fear. She knew well enough what he intended to do, for Willie had told her. While she had confidence in her employer's ability, she was not sure he could win out this time against several gunmen. And of course, if he got killed, she would be out of a job again.

Matilda followed Lee out to the front porch. She saw Willie McCormick holding the reins of Upway Don. The animal pranced restlessly, tossing its head and pawing the ground. But the horse stood motionless as Lee mounted and looked down at Willie.

"Don't worry. I guarantee that nothing is going to happen to me."

Willie did not answer, but handed Morgan the whip the old man had also brought out of the barn. Lee coiled it and slipped it over the pommel of his saddle. Then he checked his Winchester before slipping the weapon back into its scabbard.

"Be careful, Lee," Willie said softly. He stepped back and watched Morgan whirl the horse and gallop out of the yard. Matilda too watched with an uneasy look on her face, and Hank Goyette had come out of the barn. They stood silently and motionless until horse and rider were out of sight. No one said anything, simply shuffled off to resume their chores. Yet each in his own fashion prayed that Lee Morgan would return safe and sound.

Lee Morgan arrived in Grover at about four o'clock. The street and boardwalks were relatively empty now, for the bulk of the day's business had been completed and the evening rowdiness had not yet begun. The sun was still high in the sky. He walked his horse slowly up the street, the hoofbeats reverberating since he was all but alone on the thoroughfare.

The few pedestrians about eyed Lee curiously, for everyone knew of his reputation and of how he had put the attackers of Spade Bit to flight. He had come halfway up the street, in front of the Black Ace, where Mary Spots was again outside the saloon, leaning against the hitching rail in front. Mary knew that Billy Paxton and his boys had returned to Grover—in fact, one of them was inside the Black Ace drinking.

As Morgan passed the saloon, he saw the woman and the apprehensive look on her face. He guessed that she knew why he had come to town, and Lee also surmised that she knew the whereabouts of Paxton and his men. Morgan veered his horse to the rail, dismounted, and tied his horse. Then he glared at Mary Spots.

"All right, where are they?"

"I don't know what you're talking about!" But Mary's anxiety was clearly etched on her face. When Lee glanced at the swinging doors of the saloon, she stiffened.

"Are all four of them inside?"

Mary Spots gripped Lee's arm. "Don't go in there, please don't!"

"Let me go, Mary."

"Please don't go in there. There's only one of them there—that Buck Lewis that you hit that day. I have no idea where the others are."

180

Lee Morgan did not answer. He stood in the street in front of the swinging doors, and called out, "Buck Lewis! I know you're in there and I'm calling you out. If you're not a coward, come on out here and make sure you're wearing a gun. You hear me? You're a no good, sneaky son of a bitch, and if you've got the gumption to say I'm wrong, then come out here."

Inside the saloon, all eyes focused on Buck Lewis. The gunman's Adam's apple slid up and down his neck like a yo-yo, and he quickly downed another shot of whiskey. He felt more sweat on his face when he head Lee shouting again. "Are you coming out here or do I come in to get you?" Lewis's lips suddenly felt chapped and he rubbed them nervously. The men in the saloon were staring expectantly at him.

"Somebody's called you out, Mister," one of them said soberly.

Buck Lewis took a deep, rasping breath, downed another shot, then rose from his chair. After straightening his gunbelt, he walked slowly out of the saloon.

Meanwhile, Mary Spots darted up the street and into the jailhouse to warn Deputy Chook of the gunfight. Chook said he would get right on it, but when Mary left, he returned to his desk. He would not go outside until the fight was over. He knew if he interfered he would surely get himself killed. He drew a bottle hidden inside the desk and took a long draw on it. Then he rose from the desk, took a rifle from the rack, and walked outside. Standing on the boardwalk, he stared intently at Morgan in the street and then watched as Buck Lewis emerged from the saloon.

Mary Spots had continued running up the street

181

and ducked into the Clemons Trading Agency office, where she ran to the desk and grasped Sue Clemons's arm. "He'll get himself killed, Miss Clemons." The whore was well informed of just about everything that went on in Gunfight Gap territory, and she knew of the close relationship that had developed between Lee Morgan and Sue Clemons since the death of Sarah Morgan.

"What are you talking about?" Sue asked.

"Lee Morgan," Mary Spots said. "He's called out one of Paxton's men, and if somebody don't do somethin', Morgan will get himself killed for sure. He might take the one he's called out, but the others will get him."

Sue Clemons dashed out of the office and squinted to see Morgan and Lewis confronting each other. Both men stepped backward until they were about twenty yards apart. Others now lined the board-walks, for Morgan's shouts had drawn the curiosity of businessmen and their patrons. They ogled the two men with their low-slung holsters and their fingers that danced as if playing notes on an invisible piano.

Jesse Callaway had come out of his bank and he stared intently at the two men preparing for battle. Sweat broke out on his round face, but there was still hope. Perhaps Paxton's man would take out Lee Morgan and his worries would be over for-ever.

Only two men now stood in the dusty street. Their shadows lengthened by the waning afternoon. Both men now stood rigid, alert, waiting. Finally, Morgan spoke.

"Anytime you're ready, coward."

"You did the calling, Mister," Buck Lewis answered.

"You did the murdering," Morgan snapped back.

The exchange of shouts echoed through the street. The spectators stood fascinated, for they knew that within the next few seconds one of these men would be dead.

Buck Lewis felt his nervousness swell, for Morgan's eyes were too calm, too alert. Everything he had heard about this man served only to increase his anxiety. He glanced at the awed onlookers and knew he could not back down. If he allowed Morgan to draw first, he would have no chance at all. With his left hand he wiped the beads of sweat forming on his forehead.

"I'm waiting, killer," Morgan cried.

Buck Lewis suddenly went for his gun. He had barely pulled it from the holster when Morgan got off two quick shots that struck his opponent in the chest. The shots resounded in the otherwise quiet street. Lewis flew backward with two quick steps, spun around, and fell lifeless.

Morgan stared at the shape sprawled on the ground. He quickly replaced his gun in its holster and ambled slowly back to the boardwalk in front of the saloon. Those inside who had been peering over the swinging doors retreated intinctively although Morgan did not enter the Black Ace.

Jesse Callaway fell a pang of distress and returned to pace the floors inside his bank. Sue Clemons and Mary Spots ran swiftly up the boardwalk and stopped in front of the saloon where they stared at Morgan, who was now next to his horse. None of them said anything. Deputy John Chook hurried up the boardwalk from his jailhouse, filled with relief that the gunfight was finally over. He had surely played it safe.

Chapter 12

A few people ambled into the street to stare at the dead man, including Deputy John Chook, who turned the body over with his foot. He then saw the heavy blotches of blood staining the man's shirt and the gun still clutched tightly in his fist. He glanced at Morgan who was now near his horse, then turned to the group of spectators. "Will a couple of you boys carry this man over to DuBois's place?"

Three men immediately complied, hoisting the body to their shoulders, and shuffling away with the burden. Chook then walked slowly toward the Black Ace until he was beside Lee. "Morgan, that was a foolish thing to do."

"It was a fair fight," Morgan answered. "He didn't have to come out."

"I'm not questioning that," the deputy said, "but it don't look good having gunfights in the middle of Grover's main street."

Mary Spots glared at the lawman. "I told you about this, Deputy. Why didn't you get over here and stop it?"

But John Chook did not answer her, for he knew that the call girl suspected the truth: he had been too squeamish to get involved, and he had conveniently waited until the gunfight was over. Chook turned again to Morgan. "You know that the man you killed was linked up with Billy Paxton. When Paxton hears about it—why he's likely to come after you himself. You might have made a mistake taking that man out."

Morgan grinned at Chook. "Then why don't you look up this Paxton and tell him to get out of town so there won't be more trouble. Anyway, if you find him, aren't you supposed to arrest him and his boys? Didn't your sheriff say that Paxton and his followers were the ones responsible for that shoot-out at my ranch?"

John Chook did not answer at once. He felt his nerves tighten. The last thing the deputy would try to do was make an attempt to arrest gunfighters like Paxton and his men. He straightened with an air of bravado. "Well, I can see that you didn't do anything illegal, so I'm not going to hold you. As for Billy Paxton, I'll take him in if I find him." He then doffed his hat to Sue Clemons and Mary Spots and walked back to his jailhouse.

Sue Clemons stepped up next to Morgan and gripped his arm. "I'm sorry this happened, Lee. I thought you'd let bygones be bygones and just get on with taking care of your ranch."

"No matter what, Sue," Morgan answered, "they killed my wife and I just can't let them get away with it."

"But that's the law's job," Sue said. "Those men are wanted and when the law catches up to them, they'll surely be arrested and prosecuted."

186

Morgan huffed. "The way the law around here works, they'll never see a day in jail."

"Lee Morgan," Mary Spots said, stepping toward him, "I'm not sayin' you can't take care of yourself, but there's still three more of those men around Grover. When they find out you killed one of theirs they ain't gonna give you the chance to call them out; they'll know better. They'll bushwhack you! Don't go out lookin' for them. Let the law take care of them."

"She's talking sense, Lee," Sue Clemons said.

Morgan shuttled his glance between the two women before he spoke. "I appreciate the concern of both of you, but I'm going to handle this my way. I have to find the rest of those men and settle this thing once and for all." He now looked hard at Mary Spots. "Where are they, Mary?"

The prostitute hesitated but then answered. "I—I don't know."

"Mary Spots, you do know," Morgan said. "You knew about Buck Lewis in the saloon. He was sitting there drinking, and I suspect you approached him to drum up some business. I'd even guess he told you something about the others, and how they were going to get me. Isn't that so, Mary Spots?"

The woman did not answer.

"The Grover House?" Lee asked. "Is that where the rest of them are?"

"I swear, Lee Morgan," the call girl said, "the man never told me where the rest of them were."

Morgan studied the woman's face and saw she was sincere. He then nodded. "All right, I believe you."

"Lee," Sue Clemons said, "will you come with me to the cafe and have some coffee and a roll with me? Would you do that, please?" The girl's motive was obvious. In the quiet of the cafe she might calm him down and maybe even dissuade him from going after Paxton and the others.

Lee Morgan looked at the girl and saw the distress and fear in her eyes. Yes, he owed her that much. "I need a good stiff drink," he said, "but I'll settle for the coffee."

"That's a good idea, a fine idea," Mary Spots said. "You go along with Miss Clemons. She'd be a lot better company than me and that rotgut they sell inside." She nodded toward the entrance of Black Ace. She felt relief when Lee Morgan and Sue Clemons moved off, walking arm and arm up the boardwalk. She let out a sigh and went inside.

There had been someone else watching the duet walk toward the cafe. The man called Brady, the man who had first brought Billy Paxton to Jesse Callaway, had been standing just inside the swinging doors of Black Ace. After the two had disappeared from view, he came out of the saloon, glancing at Mary Spots with a pensive look in his eyes. He did not speak to her, but as soon as she went inside the saloon, he hurried up the boardwalk, almost in a run.

Brady darted inside Grover House and hurried up the stairs to Room 24 where he rapped on the door. When no one answered, he knocked again and then cried in a loud whisper, "It's me, Brady. Let me in, Paxton."

A moment later, Percy Logan unlatched the door and ushered Brady inside. Billy Paxton and Kid Proctor were sitting at a table, with shot glasses and cards scattered over the surface. Paxton looked up at the interrupting visitor and almost scowled.

"Brady, what do you want?"

"I got to tell you what happened, Mr. Paxton," Brady said. He looked at the other two men before staring at Paxton again. "Lee Morgan came into town this afternoon, lookin' for blood. He must 'a found out you were back. He stopped at the Black Ace and called out Buck Lewis. Morgan killed him in a gunfight."

"Killed Lewis!" Kid Proctor hissed.

Brady nodded vigorously. "Now he's after the rest a' you. He blames you for the death of his wife and that trouble at his ranch, and he's out for revenge. He won't stop 'til he gets all of you."

"The bastard!" Billy Paxton scowled. "Lewis was sure dumb to tangle with that man alone. But it doesn't matter. I want Morgan as much as he wants us. That's why we came back to Grover. Where's the son of a bitch now?"

"Well, that girl, Sue Clemons, who runs the trading mart with her father, took him over to the cafe for some coffee. Morgan is likely to be there for a while because I think the girl is going to try hard to talk him into forgettin' the rest of you."

"The cafe," Paxton mused, stroking his chin. "It wouldn't be good to go in there and start shootin'. A lot of others might get hurt and then we'd really be in trouble. We could wait 'til he comes out of there and bushwhack him, but we might hit the girl, and that wouldn't set good with the law, either." Then he grinned and shook his head. "And it *sure* as hell wouldn't be a good idea for one of us to call him out. If he's fast enough to get the draw on Buck, then we'd likely end up at the mortician's, too."

"All three of you could go," Brady pointed out. "He couldn't get three of you."

"No, that's a bad idea, too." Paxton shook his head. "We'd look real bad, three of us taking on one

189

man. People would say it took three of us to get him, and our reputations would suffer for sure. Besides, Morgan would probably get one of us, maybe two before we got him.'

"What'll we do, Billy?" Kid Proctor asked.

"I'm trying to think," Paxton said.

Percy Logan said soberly, "I still say we ought to give it up. Forget about Lee Morgan and pull out. It just ain't worth it."

But Paxton's face hardened and he scowled at Logan. "No, goddamn it! I came here to get the son of a bitch, and I'm not leaving Grover until he's dead. It's got to be that way, Percy."

The three regulators mulled over the situation, trying to come up with an idea that would work. Brady had also been thinking. He leaned over the table toward Paxton. "I got an idea for you if you want to do it."

"I'm listening," Paxton said.

"A hostage," Brady said.

"A hostage?" Proctor huffed. "That'd be the worst thing we could do."

"Not the one I'm thinkin' about," Brady said. "Mary Spots. She ain't nothin' but a whore and everybody in town knows it. Most folks, especially the so-called good folks in Grover, ain't got no use for her or her kind. They wouldn't care if somebody kidnapped her, or even killed her. One of you could drag her into the street, call out Morgan from the cafe and you'd have a shield."

Paxton shook his head in disgust. "Brady, you must be crazy. Morgan won't give a damn what we do to that over-the-hill whore."

Now Brady grinned. "You're wrong, Mr. Paxton. Mary Spots showed Morgan some mighty good times in bed. He'll remember that. When Morgan came back to Grover he got real friendly with her; not to buy her services, but somethin' more than that. They acted like they liked each other real well, like old friends. Morgan sure ain't got no lust for Mary Spots like he's got for the Clemons girl, but he admires her and thinks a lot of her. You take her hostage and I guarantee he'll come runnin' to help her, especially if he knows it's one of you who's got her."

Billy Paxton stroked his chin again. Then he looked at his two companions. "What do you boys think?"

"Could be," Kid Proctor agreed. "I remember that mornin' in the Black Ace. They was sittin' together and they sure had an admiration for each other that had nothin' to do with goin' to bed."

"Yes." Paxton nodded. He looked at Brady. "All right, we'll give your idea a try. You think Morgan will be in the cafe for quite a while?"

"I'm sure he will," Brady said.

The regulator nodded again. "One of us will go to the Black Ace, rile up the storm with Miss Spots, maybe claim she cheated him, then drag her up to the front of the cafe. And you, Brady, run in to the cafe and find Morgan. Tell him that one of us is in the street beating up this whore and threatening to kill her. He'll surely come out, and if what you say is true, he won't draw with the whore in his line of fire. While he's standing there wondering what to do, why we'll push the woman away and kill Morgan

191

before he knows what's happening."

"It just might work," Percy Logan said. "That oughta do real well."

"I'll go get the whore," Percy Logan said. "He made me look like a fool and I'd like to be the one to finish off that bastard."

"Well, I'd have liked to do it myself," Paxton said, "but it might be better if one of you did it, instead of your boss."

Percy Logan checked his six-shooter, put it back in his holster, and adjusted the belt. As he and Brady started out of the hotel room, Paxton rose from his chair. "Me and Proctor are coming out too. We'll stay hidden, but we'll back you up in case you need us."

Logan and Brady left the hotel and hurried to the Black Ace Saloon. Mary Spots was there, leaning against one of the gaming tables while she filed her fingernails. Logan motioned for Brady to leave before approaching Mary.

Logan suddenly took her by the shoulders and shook the astonished woman violently. She gaped in shock as he then unleashed a loud tirade. "You dirty whore, robbin' me like that! I paid you but you stole the money out a' my pants up in that room. You ain't gonna get away with this, you no good bitch."

Mary Spots blinked in amazed horror. Others in the saloon merely looked at the two near the gaming table but said nothing and made no move to intervene. They watched, amused, as Logan grabbed Mary roughly by the arm and dragged her out of the saloon, still screaming angrily. "No

192

goddamn two-bit whore is going to rob me and get away with it."

As soon as Logan and the woman were outside, Brady left from the saloon. He watched Logan haul Mary Spots into the street, shaking her and hitting her in the face, until she started to bleed. That was Brady's cue. He hurried up the boardwalk and into the cafe where Morgan sat quietly at a table with Sue Clemons. The man rushed up to the Spade Bit owner.

"Are you a friend of Mary Spots?" he asked.

"What if I am," Morgan said.

"Well, some cowpoke just dragged her out of the Black Ace, and he's beatin' the hell out of her in the street."

Then Morgan heard the maldictions shouted from the street. "You no good whore!" the voice yelled. "Take that, you bitch!" Then a scream from Mary Spots. "And this too, you filthy slut!" There was another slap and another scream. Morgan rose from his chair. Sue Clemons tried to grab his wrist to restrain him, but he broke free and hurried into the street. As planned Logan now had Mary directly in front of the cafe. Morgan could see blood on the woman's face, and he could see Logan shaking her furiously while he threatened her. Logan had ripped away part of her dress, exposing one of her breasts. He was also brandishing his six shooter, aiming the barrel toward Mary Spot's head.

"Hey, what are you doing there?" Morgan cried.

"You stay out of this," Logan shouted. "This bitch did me wrong and she ain't gonna get away with it."

"You're crazy, mister," Morgan said. "Whatever else she is, she's honest."

"Like hell," Percy Logan retorted. "She took advantage of me and robbed me, and now she's gonna pay for it."

"Let her go," Morgan cried.

Logan grinned smugly at Morgan. "You come any closer and she'll be dead." He pressed his six-shooter barrel against Mary Spot's head. "Now back off and stay out of this." He baited Morgan. "This thing ain't nothin' but an old whore. She ain't worth a dime anyway. Look at her! She's just a washed-up bitch. I did her a favor drawin' blood. It does a better job 'a coverin' up her pruned, ugly skin than that cheap mascara she's wearin'. Ain't that right, mister?" Logan grinned again.

"I said let her go," Lee said.

"And who the hell are you in that get-up?" Logan continued to bait Lee. "You some greenhorn dude tryin' to look like Billy the Kid? Watch yourself or some drunk will call you out and leave you for dead."

As Lee took another step closer, Logan pressed the barrel even harder against the prostitute's head. Morgan stopped abruptly, but then a sudden realization struck him. The man holding Mary Spots was Percy Logan, one of those who had started the trouble at his Spade Bit. Fire suddenly came into Lee's eyes and rage swelled inside him. He now saw this man as the one who had actually shot and killed his wife.

However, Lee Morgan was calm enough to know

that boiling anger never helped in a life-and-death confrontation. He took a deep breath to steady himself. He would have to wait for the right moment. He would need patience. He had to mark time until Logan took the gun away from Mary Spot's head. Lee knew the man had some kind of plan. Logan would wait for an excuse to shoot Morgan at the first opportunity. Who among the spectators now crowding the boardwalks could really say that Lee had not gone for his gun?

"Well, you dude bastard, do you want to make somethin' out 'a this?"

But Lee did not respond. He had only to say one disparaging word and the man would shoot. No, he must bide his time. He simply stood immobile and quiet, and Logan was noticeably irked. "Has the cat got your tongue, Mister? Are you too scared to speak up? You afraid to rescue this whore bitch?" He then slammed the tip of his gun into Mary Spot's check, drawing more blood. "There now, don't that cover up her wrinkles better than mascara?"

But still Lee Morgan did not reply. He simply remained stiffly erect, and Logan's irritation increased. The regulator finally spoke again, almost unconsciously drawing the gun away from Mary Spot's head and holding the weapon in front of him. He had made the fatal mistake Lee was waiting for.

Before the ogling onlookers knew what happened, Lee Morgan drew his gun and fired two shots. The first slug stung the weapon out of Percy Logan's hand. The second shot caught the regulator squarely in the chest, blowing away tatters of blood-soaked shirt. Logan reeled backward and fell flat on his back, spread eagle.

The grateful Mary Spots, now free, cowered and started to run. But then, she saw a rifle barrel peeking out from behind a wall and she cried out quickly, "Lee, look out! Look out!" Morgan dropped flat on his belly, as did Mary Spots. Two shots rang out, both of which whizzed across the street and lodged in the tether post in front of the cafe. Instinctively, Lee Morgan rolled over twice, just before two more shots came from a rooftop and hit the dirt where Lee had just been.

Lee Morgan squinted and saw the man on the roof. He raised his gun and squeezed off a shot just as the man moved away. Still, the shot had grazed the shoulder of Kid Proctor, who scrambled swiftly away. Billy Paxton, who had been behind the wall, also retreated and disappeared through the alleyway.

With the shooting over, Lee Morgan hurried over to Mary Spots, with Sue Clemons right on his heels. The girl helped Morgan lift Mary Spots to her feet. Sue took out a handkerchief from her dress pocket and wiped away some of the blood from Mary's face, trying to soothe her with comforting words.

"You saved my life, Mary," Morgan said to the prostitute.

"You were worth it, Lee," the woman answered with a grin, despite her bloodied face.

"Lee, let's get her to the doctor," Sue Clemons said.

They had just started to leave when Deputy

Chook arrived, looking from the beaten Mary Spots to the body of Percy Logan. As usual, the lawman had managed to arrive when the shooting was over. "What happened here?"

Ironically, Brady stepped forward. "I seen the whole thing, Deputy; seen it all. That man," he said, pointing to the dead man, "just come in the Black Ace and, for no reason, began shoutin' at Mary. He dragged her outside, and beat her up. Mary didn't do nothin'. Then, Mr. Morgan here came out 'a the cafe and told this gunman to turn Mary Spots loose. But the man only called them names and brandished his gun. Looked like he was aiming to kill both Mary and Mr. Morgan." He gestured toward Lee. "Morgan had no choice. He shot this fellow to save Mary Spots—maybe himself, too."

"Well," Chook said, "if that's the way it was, then Mr. Morgan did only what he had to do; did the only decent thing." The deputy again found himself asking spectators to take a body to the mortician. Four men quickly picked up the slain man and carried the body off.

One of the spectators now looked at Chook. "That wasn't all of it, Deputy. After this thing in the street, a couple 'a bushwhackers tried to kill Mr. Morgan. They run off when Mr. Morgan shot back."

"I'll have to look into that," John Chook said.

"Sure, Deputy, you look into it," Morgan said in disgust. Then he and Sue Clemons took Mary Spots to the doctor's office. Chook and Brady, along with the others, watched the three depart.

The uproar on Grover's main street during the

waning June afternoon created a stir for some days to follow. Grover's citizens were surprised at Lee Morgan's ability with a gun, and they even admired him for saving Mary Spots. Brady had been wrong to think that no one cared for the prostitute. In a sense she and others like her offered an important service that deterred many rough, crass men from molesting the "good" girls in town. Yet, many of the same citizens who showed an admiration for Lee Morgan's efforts, also developed a sense of uncertainty. Was it wise to have a man like Morgan in their midst? A man who's reputation might draw hordes of real gunfighters to Grover to call him out and disturb the serenity of Grover?

Deputy John Chook did not try to catch up to the bushwhackers who had shot at Morgan on Main Street. Chook must have suspected that the ambushers were Billy Paxton and Kid Proctor, the only survivors of the five regulators who had come into Grover to get Morgan.

The incidents on that June afternoon had given Billy Paxton second thoughts about his obsession with killing Lee Morgan. He had lost three men and had even failed to get him in an ambush. As before Billy Paxton decided to leave Grover in a hurry.

"It ain't no use, Billy," Kid Proctor told his leader. "That Morgan has a charmed life. I'm sayin' again what I always believed: we'd best leave this thing alone and ride as far away from here as we can."

Paxton conceded. "You're right. We failed here and we're likely to get ourselves killed if we keep trying to get Morgan. We'll just have to mark this caper up as one that didn't work out."

"You're talkin' sense, Billy," Kid Proctor said. "I say we get right out 'a Idaho, go back to Wyoming, or even Oklahoma or Texas to sell our services. Somewhere where we ain't likely to find anybody like Lee Morgan."

The two left in the night, stopping only to camp and disappearing somewhere inside the vast expanse of the west. They were not particularly worried about Lee Morgan coming after them, although that was a possibility. They were inclined to believe that Morgan, with his problem in Shoshone County over, would simply settle down on his ranch.

As for Lee Morgan himself, he had now found in Mary Spots a loyal friend, someone who would do anything for him. With the crisis over, she hoped Lee would remain at Spade Bit for good.

"I know what a hurt that was, losing your wife and then needing to deal with those killers," Mary told Lee, "but it's all behind you now. Sue Clemons is a fine girl and I think she loves you, and I believe you care for her."

"Yes, I do have a deep feeling for Sue," Morgan conceded.

"Then, give some thought to remarrying," Mary Spots said. "You're not likely to have any more trouble and you can concentrate on livin' a long and happy life. I happen to know that you've got three fine and loyal people workin' for you out there, and I can tell you, you'll always have a good friend in me.

If you ever need anything, I'll sure as hell be there."

"I'll give some thought to what you said, Mary Spots."

Jesse Callaway continued to fear Lee Morgan. He was mildly surprised when Morgan came to see him with a somewhat friendly look on his face. Callaway ushered Lee into his private office and listened. "Mr. Callaway, I knew from the start that you were behind all the trouble I had. I lost my wife because of you. But, some people have convinced me that I can't hold a grudge for the rest of my life. I just came to tell you that I'm willin' to let things go now, although I doubt that I can ever forget what you tried to do."

"I swear, Mr. Morgan," Callaway raised his hand, "I've learned my lesson. I was a fool, the worst fool who ever lived. I got too damn greedy and now I realize what greed can do. But I also swear, after I called in this Billy Paxton, I wanted to call the whole thing off, but he wouldn't listen; he insisted I go through with it. I'd take an oath on a stack of Bibles that that's the truth. I was afraid of guns, Mr. Morgan. And I can tell you, I'm willin' to do anything to make up for what I did."

"I know I shouldn't, Mr. Callaway, but somehow I believe you. But I promise you," Morgan said emphatically, "if you ever try to hurt people again, you won't even live to regret it. And if I ever hear of you trying to cheat anybody, you'll have to answer to me."

"Like I said, Mr. Morgan, I learned my lesson."

Morgan nodded and left the banker's office. Jesse Callaway felt a deep relief, as though every illness a man could have had suddenly swept out of his body.

There still was Sue Clemons. Morgan now felt a deep affection for her. He knew she felt the same fondness for him. If he asked her to marry him, he knew she would quickly consent. However, Lee Morgan was not sure he felt the same love for her he had felt with Sarah, so he warily avoided the subject of marriage, even though she willingly accommodated him in body and soul. After a night of sexual bliss with the girl, and as he prepared to ride out to his ranch again, Sue Clemons gripped his wrist. "Lee, what's going to happen now? Between you and me, I mean?"

"I don't know, Sue," Lee Morgan said.

"You must know how much I care for you. It's been two months since your wife died. Don't you think you should consider a new life?"

"Sue, I'll never forget how much you did for me during my grief and anger," Lee Morgan said. "No man could have expected anything more. There isn't any way I could ever repay you."

"There is, you know," the girl said, holding the collar of his shirt.

"I got to think a little more, Sue," Lee answered. "Please give me a little more time. I know it isn't fair to ask you that, but I need more time."

"Sure," Sue Clemons answered with a forced smile.

"If you feel that my hesitation isn't right, and you don't want to see me anymore, I'll surely understand."

"No, Lee," the girl said, "I'll always want to see you as long as you still want to see me."

Lee Morgan nodded, kissed the girl gently, then mounted Upway Don. Sue Clemons stood in front of her house and watched Morgan ride off. She remained still until he was out of sight. Once on the open road and heading back to Spade Bit, Lee squinted up at the clouds and then some birds that were frolicking without inhibitions in the sky. He wondered.

LEVER ACTION

ONE

Coming over the top of the pass, heading for home, Lee Morgan looked for the chimney smoke of Spade Bit in the distance. They had been away for a week, buying horses. There were heavily-timbered ridges between the pass and the ranch, but the sky was blue and cloudless and he should have been able to see smoke drifting up from the cookhouse and the main house. There was no smoke.

"What's up?" Sid Sefton asked, riding up to where Lee had reined in his horse. Bud Bent, Charlie Potts, and Wesley Ford were moving the newly bought horses down from the pass.

Lee pulled his hat brim low to shade his eyes. "I don't know," he said. "You see any chimney smoke down at the ranch? There should be some smoke."

Sefton squinted against the sun. "Ought to be. But it's a right windy day."

"Up here it's windy," Lee said. "Should be still

7

enough down below. I'm going on ahead. Hold the horses a mile out. I'll lose off three spaced shots if it's safe to drive them in.''

Sefton was Morgan's top hand. He nodded and Lee toe-touched his stallion's flanks and came down from the pass at a fast clip, dodging rocks, and when the trail was clear he urged the animal to a gallop. The ranch was three miles distant and the stallion covered the ground in minutes.

Lee reined in when he was still five hundred yards out. It would take something heavy, a Sharps Big Fifty or a Remington Rolling Block, to bring him down at five hundred yards, and at that range a shooter would have to be better than good.

There was no wind, no sound except for a red squirrel twittering at the base of a mountain ash; that close to a working ranch there should have been sounds: the cook chopping stove wood or rattling pots, one man calling to another, a door banging open or shut. There should have been something, but there was nothing.

He took the stallion off the trail and walked it out far and wide, circling the ranch buildings. Now and then he stopped and listened. Then he came in from the far side where the pines grew in close and cover was good. He felt a sudden chill when he heard the squawk of buzzards over carrion. He slid the Winchester out of the boot, then getting clear of the pines, he saw what was left of Spade Bit: the main house a burned-out ruin with only the stone chimney still standing. His eyes jumped to the bunkhouse, the cookshack, now piles of blackened rubble. Closer in he saw the dead men, his men sprawled where they had been shot.

McCorkle, the old Scotch cook, lay all twisted up, as if he had died in agony. Old Mac's face was more skull than face, and the buzzards had been at the body. The face and neck and hands had been eaten away, and there were tears in the cook's shirt where the buzzards had gone after the meat of his chest.

Standing still, stunned into immobility for an instant, he watched the buzzards come flapping back again. He raised the Winchester, then let down the hammer: too soon to signal the others to come in. He slapped his hat against his thigh and the buzzards lumbered into awkward flight; gorged with human meat, they didn't go far. They watched him with fierce red eyes as he came forward to check the bodies of the three men he had left to guard the home herd. There was nothing to check: they were nothing but bloated, half-eaten corpses. Next, not wanting to do it, he started to look for the body of his new woman, Maggie. He didn't find it, not in the ruins of the main house, not in the pines where she might have been dragged and outraged.

It was a cool day in the high country, but the stink of rotting bodies was terrible. Guns and gunbelts had been stripped from the bodies of the three men, and even their boots were missing.

The corral was about a hundred yards from the bunkhouse. Past there lay a long stretch of mountain meadow that went over the top of a low ridge and down the other side, good grazing for his horse herd. Sure thing, he thought, except there's no herd left. The corral gate was closed and inside dead horses were everywhere. Here the stink was enough

9

to knock a man down.

Drained of feeling, he went inside and a quick look told him that not all the herd had been destroyed. He made a quick count and stood there trying to make sense of what had happened. They had taken twenty horses, the best of the herd, and slaughtered the rest. Why had they done it like this? It made no sense. Indian trouble was long over in Idaho, but even if the raiders had been Indians, they would have run off every animal on the place. Same for white horse thieves: good horses were big money and this herd had been top quality horseflesh. Not a horse he owned wouldn't have fetched a good price.

He raised the Winchester and squeezed off three spaced shots. There were no ambushers here, no one to be wary of. They were long gone, their bloody work far behind them by now. Not Indians and not horse thieves, he thought, and not some bitter enemy from the past. God knows he had plenty of enemies, yet he didn't think this was the work of somebody that hated him. Somebody that bitter would steal the whole herd or kill the whole herd. It would be one or the other.

The hell with the herd! Where was Maggie? He hadn't wanted to think about her but now he did. Truth was that himself and Maggie didn't get along all that well, but that had nothing to do with the here and now. He didn't love her the way he'd loved his dead wife Sarah, and he knew she didn't love him. What happened was he needed a woman and Maggie wanted to cut loose from the waitressing job in Boise and at the time, two months before, it was a fair enough deal for both of them. In bed she was all

10

a man could ask for, and then some; trouble was they couldn't stay in bed twenty-four hours a day, and when Maggie got up and got dressed she turned into another woman. A fussy, house-proud woman with too many ideas about how the ranch and their lives should be run. But tired of her or not, he would go and search for her. It was something he decided without thinking.

He was walking back to poke through the ruins a second time when he spotted the sheet of paper nailed to a tree. He tore it loose and read what was lettered on it in pencil:

LET ALL TRAITOROUS MORMONS AND GENTILES BEWARE. DEATH AND DESTRUCTION TO ALL WHO OPPOSE THE TRUE MORMON CHURCH ETERNAL DAMNATION TO ALL OUR ENEMIES. IF YOU ARE NOT WITH US YOU ARE AGAINST US. GOD IS ON OUR SIDE AND WILL BRING US VICTORY. THIS IS THE LAND OUR FATHERS FOUGHT AND DIED FOR AND WE COMMAND YOU TO LEAVE IT. REMAIN HERE AND YOU WILL DIE BY THE BULLET OR THE ROPE.

Lee folded the paper and put it in his pocket. The first shock had worn off and now the blood pounded through his body in a killing rage. The Jack Mormons had paid him a visit, renegade Mormons, killer Mormons expelled from the church because they refused to obey the new anti-polygamy laws that

11

made it a crime to have more than one wife. This was Idaho not Utah, and Spade Bit was seventy miles north of the Idaho-Utah border, but he knew about the bloody-handed Jacks. Everybody along the borderline lived in fear of the Jacks and their woman-stealing raids. They needed young "wives" and so they came down from their strongholds in the snow-capped, fog-shrouded mountains and took them, some hardly more than children. Driven by a fierce hatred of Mormons and Gentiles alike, they killed and burned and robbed, and only the young women were spared, to be roped and dragged into the half-explored mountains to the southeast.

That's where Maggie is, he thought, far back in the mountains or on her way there. Now that she was in danger, he was able to think of her with more affection. She had some New England book learning, not as much as she liked to pretend, just enough to make her put on airs, and though he didn't object to the feminine touches she added to the house, there were times when her airs and graces plain got on his nerves. Life on Spade Bit was not to her liking, but she didn't come out and say so. Maggie was too smart for that, knowing full well that if Lee hadn't taken her home with him, ten to one she'd still be waiting tables in that Boise hotel.

Lee heard the new horses coming in from the trail. Sid Sefton rode in first, slid down, looked around with no expression on his face. It took a lot to shake this hard man, but suddenly his face seemed to crumble and he said in a whisper: "Sweet Jesus Christ!" Saying nothing else, he walked over to Lee. His sun-browned face was an ashy color and one

12

eyelid twitched. Lee handed him the sheet of paper without a word. Sefton read it and handed it back.

Lee said quietly, "They killed the boys and took Maggie. They took twenty horses and slaughtered the rest. Guess they couldn't handle more than twenty on the mountain trails."

"Yes," Sefton said. "They hide deep in the mountains."

Bent, Potts and Ford drove in the new stock. Like Sefton, they had been with Lee in the old days. They had stayed on with the new owner, McCormick, when a hoof-and-mouth epidemic killed off the herd and Lee was forced to sell out. They were still there when Lee came back, a long time later, with enough money to buy back Spade Bit, the only place he really wanted to be. He had come back to *this!*

"Jack Mormons did this," Lee said roughly. The three hands were too shocked to say anything. "Quit your gawking and get the new stock up to the meadow. Rope corral will hold them till we clear out the dead animals. Go on now before the stink spooks the animals."

Sefton stayed with Lee. "Never knew the Jacks to raid this far north," he said.

"Must have wore out the border country," Lee said. "It figures they would. Now they're coming north. Greener pastures up this way."

Sefton took a sack of Bull and papers from his vest pocket and rolled a smoke with one hand. The loose-packed cigarette burned fast as he sucked in the acrid smoke. Tobacco smoke helped to kill the stink, but not by much. Sounds of horses and men drifted down from the upper meadow. The sun was

13

warm and Spade Bit had the peace of death.

"What do we do?" Sefton asked. "We start right off maybe we can catch up, rig an ambush."

"No chance of that. They have too much of a head start. Look how far gone the bodies are. Mac and the boys got killed maybe five days ago."

Sefton ground the cigarette stub into the dirt. "Got to do somethin', Lee."

"I'll do something. Just have to figure out what it is. I mean to go it alone, Sid. I don't see there's any other way. Word is there's no way to take the Jack settlement by direct attack. Nobody even knows for sure where it is. I hear tell they're holed up so tight they can't be got at. Guess the army would move on them if there was any chance of winning. You know what happened to that bunch of ranchers and farmers went into the southeast mountains. Was no more than a month after the raiding started."

Sefton nodded. "Read about it in the Boise paper. They got massacred. Fifty went in, two came out."

"That's what I'm saying," Lee said. "Entire party ended up in a box canyon, Jack scouts watching them all the time, didn't have a chance. Two men that escaped were watching their back trail."

Sefton said, "Could be they got massacred 'cause they didn't know what they were doing. Men forget how to fight or maybe they never learned. We're different, we been fightin' all our life. Indians, rustlers, a few times the law. We got a few real good men. You and me and the boys. A fightin' force could be built round that."

"It wouldn't work," Lee told him. He wanted to get on with burying the dead. "I'm not sure a

14

hundred fighting men could get the job done. My guess is there are places in there so narrow only one or two riders can get through at a time. Even if we found the right trail, we'd be single-filed to kingdom come. They could snipe at us, bring down rockslides. Bastards could pick us off from high up, then we'd find them gone if we managed to get up there. Their big advantage is they know that wild country and we don't."

Sefton kicked a chunk of charred wood in helpless anger. "It's a hell of a thing."

"Let it go for now," Lee said.

Ford and Bent rode down and sat their horses, waiting for orders.

"Climb down," Lee told them. "We'll get started with the burying. Out where Buckskin Frank and Catherine are buried. Old Mac and the others were Spade Bit people."

Buckskin Frank Leslie and Catherine Dowd were buried in a grassy clearing back in the pines. Buckskin Frank had gone there first, dying of his wounds after he killed Kid Curry, worst of the Wild Bunch. Catherine Dowd, who loved Frank Leslie all her life, shot a fine horse called Dandy and had the animal buried at the foot of Frank's grave.

"That's some kind of Injun business," one of the older hands said at the time. "Guess she means old Frank to have a good horse in the hereafter."

But he said it in a whisper because no one ever questioned what Catherine Dowd did. Then, some years later, she died too and was buried beside the man she loved.

Ford found a shovel with a fire-blackened blade

15

and they packed the bodies out to the burying ground and took turns digging the graves. Lee dug Old Mac's grave by himself. McCorkle had been a good old boy as well as a good cook. Old and irritable, racked with arthritis, he worked hard and never complained about anything important. He had been a loyal friend.

"So long, Cookie," Lee said and began to fill in the hole. They got all the graves filled in and stood there in silence. They hadn't wrapped the bodies in blankets because saddle blankets were all they had and they were going to need them. It was as quiet as only a graveyard can be. The wind blew up a bit and rustled the branches of the trees.

"Ain't you goin' to say a few words?" Wesley Ford asked Lee in a plaintive voice.

"No prayers," Lee answered. "You want to pray over them, stay here and do it. Just don't take too long. We got to clear the corral, burn the dead animals."

"Wes," he said to Ford. "Get on down to Zimmerman's Crossing and buy up all the coal oil they got." Zimmerman, a German, kept a general store on the Bridger River about ten miles to the south. He also operated a ferry so he got the travelers coming and going.

Lee gave Ford two fifty dollar gold pieces. "Zimmerman will lend you a wagon on my say-so. Get a water barrel, house building tools, crosscuts, axes, hatchets, plenty of grub. Figure out what we need."

Ford looked puzzled. "What's the barrel for? We got a fine deep well."

Lee turned some of his anger on good-natured

Ford. "Don't talk like a God damned fool. Sons of bitches've probably poisoned it. It'll have to be looked at. You want to drink some, see if it's safe?"

"Not me, boss." Ford ran to his horse and vaulted into the saddle. Nobody smiled because nothing was funny that day.

Thirty-six dead horses had to be burned. Good horses as good as any in the state. A lot of money was tied up in the bloated, stinking carcasses, but Lee wasn't thinking of money. To him the small horse herd had represented a new start in life. Since he was forced to sell out he had battered around North and South America, even the Klondike; and in all that time in Washington State, Mexico, the wild cow country of northern Argentina, there had been only one purpose: to get enough money to start over. Finally the Klondike had brought him luck and he came back full of good feelings and a hunger to make a go of it this time. And now . . .

"Let's get to it," he told the hands. "We'll burn them in six piles. Soon as they're piled we'll cover them with all the brush and deadwood we can find."

He turned to Bud Bent. "Use your machete till Wes gets back with the axes. Fires will have to burn long and hot."

Bent, who had spent time in Mexico, carried a heavy-backed machete in a scabbard behind his saddle-gun. The thick blade was long and sharp without being razor-edged. A razor-edge would dull or gap if you used it for cutting wood. It was different when you swung it at a man's neck.

Lee said, "We'll take the corral apart and stack the posts and rails away from the fire. After that

17

comes the hard part of it."

Sefton spat. Bent and Potts shrugged or grunted. Nobody there was looking forward to roping and dragging dead horses. The dead horses were crawling with maggots and ants; there was the dull buzz of blueflies. But worst of all was the smell.

Stripped to the waist, they worked the rails clear of the posts, then stacked them at a safe distance. Rooting up the posts took longer because they were buried deep. They worked steadily until the entire corral had been taken down and moved away.

Lee told Potts to make a fire and cook a pot of coffee. No one felt much like eating though they had grub—beans, bacon, flour—left over from the horse buying trip. While they drank bitter black coffee, the buzzards, never far away, flapped down for another banquet. Suddenly, Bud Bent, an even-tempered man by nature, jumped to his feet yelling obscenities and started blasting with his six-shot Remington revolver. The hammer clicked three times on empty before he started to reload. He hadn't hit anything.

"Quit it," Lee ordered without getting up. "You're wasting ammunition and making noise. Drink your coffee and never mind the fucking birds. Time to saddle up and get to work."

They worked in pairs: Sefton with Potts, Lee with Bent. Lee pointed to the places where he wanted the carcasses piled. There was no need to tell the men to cinch up tight; they had already done that. It was dirty work but simple enough. The hind legs of the dead animals were roped together before they

18

mounted up and wound the long end of their ropes around steel saddle horns.

The ropes twanged tight and the first carcasses came sliding across the hard-packed dirt. When one was in place, they went back to get another. It put a terrible strain on saddle horns and ropes, but they held, at least for the time being. They had to hold, Lee thought. We have to get this rotten business over with before I can even start thinking about the Jacks and how to rescue Maggie.

He thought about her as he worked. It had always been in the back of her pretty red head that, given time, she could get him to marry her, sell the ranch and then they could move away to another ranch close to some big town. And she would say: "With your energy and experience you'd be an important man in no time. Of course I'm not thinking of myself, not that I wouldn't enjoy being able to entertain nice, respectable ladies and being invited in turn to their homes . . ."

Hours dragged past like a dog with a broken back, and the first three piles were already in place when he called a halt. "Got to water the rest of the horses," he said. "They'll be no good if we don't."

They rode up over the meadow ridge and down to the clear, cold stream that came from the mountain. It was good to wash the sweat off and to drink the sweet water. Then they went back to the job they hated.

Sometime later Lee looked at his old silver-backed stem-winder, his dead father's watch. Wes Ford should be getting back soon if the Jacks hadn't hit

Zimmerman's place. The Jacks could have followed the river north from east Utah knowing beforehand that Zimmerman sold guns. If so, he could kiss the coal oil and other stuff goodbye. But what the hell, even that wouldn't be the end of the world. He would make do; he had done it before. Good water was just over the ridge and there was enough grub and coffee to last a day or two. Brush and deadwood would burn the horses if they fetched enough of it. Doing it that way would take a lot longer, but it could be done.

The sun was on a westward slide and they were still dragging wood to burn the horses. Bud Bent, who had the only cutting blade, stopped the downward swing of his machete. "Wagon coming," he said.

Lee had already heard the rattle of the wagon on the rutted trail. Sure enough it was Wes Ford and they crowded around when he drove in, water sloshing from the poorly fitted barrel-lid. Cans of coal oil were lined up in three rows.

"Got everything you told me to get," Ford told Lee, proud of himself. "Zimmerman was like to piss his pants when I told about the raid. Says he wants the mules and wagon back tomorrow. Could be he's fixin' to pull out."

Lee didn't like Zimmerman, didn't give a damn what he did. For now they had everything they needed and tomorrow the men could throw up a cabin and start clearing the ruins. He wouldn't be there to oversee the work, but Sid Sefton would make sure it was done right. He would ride out at first light, and so far that was the best plan he had in mind. He would head south and see what happened.

The sinking sun threw a red glow over everything and the wind blew hard as it often did at that time of day. "We'll start the burning," Lee told Sefton. "May have to fetch more wood, but now we got the axes to cut it."

There were twenty cans of coal oil, more than enough to get it done. The men waited in silence, knowing that this could be the end of Spade Bit. Lee was a good boss and paid good wages, but there was no guarantee that he could fight his way back from this disaster. They knew—because he made no secret of it—that a good part of the Klondike money had gone into buying back the ranch and the purchase of the first small herd.

"One can to a pile," Lee ordered. "When the fires burn down a bit, soak them again."

Ford came down from the meadow after hobbling and tethering Zimmerman's mules. Lee asked him if he wanted to burn horses or to cook. Ford was a pretty fair cook when he put his head to it, and there had been times when he'd pitched in when old McCorkle was flat on his back with what he called the rheumatics.

He said he'd rather cook and Lee warned him to do it a long way from the horse burning. "If you don't, everything will taste of coal oil."

Sefton was standing by when Lee turned to him. "Everything's wetted down," the tophand said. "No call for you to take part in it. They were your horses."

The night was thick with the smell of coal oil.

"No," Lee said. "I want to light the first match, so I can keep the picture in my head. It'll be a help in the hard times to come. If ever a Jack asks me for mercy I want to remember the men they murdered here, the animals they slaughtered. And then I'll know what to do."

They walked to the corral where Bent and Potts were waiting, their boots wet with coal oil. "Dry them off, for Christ's sake!" Lee said angrily. "Then stay the hell out of the way."

The first wood match flared and he tossed it into the heaped-up brush. Flame boomed up and engulfed everything and the heat was fierce. Lee touched off the next fire and the next and the next. No one said anything because there was absolutely nothing to say.

Far back from the fire, on the other side of the main house, Wes Ford was yelling at them to come and git it.

TWO

Lee was awake long before sunup.

Greasy smoke still curled up from the mounds of burned horses, and it looked like no more burning had to be done. Now it was just a matter of letting the fires burn out and cool before the bones were buried. All signs of the fire would be obliterated by scraping the hard topsoil clean and spreading fresh dirt. The corral would be put back the way it was, then it was best to wait a few days, get rid of the stink, before the new-bought horses were driven down from the meadow.

Pale light glimmered in the east as he walked up to the meadow to look at the fresh stock. Least he had something left. Sefton, who had taken the last watch, could see him well enough, and there was no challenge. Sefton had just come back from checking the herd and now stood by the rope corral, a blanket draped over his shoulder, a .44 caliber Winchester in his hand.

The grass was wet and patches of fog hung in places. It was cold.

"How goes it?" Lee asked, thinking he ought to be on his way but wanting to let the men sleep a little longer. They were bone-tired, had earned their rest. But there were things to be said before he rode out.

"New stock's been restless," Sefton told him. "Quieter now than before. You get much sleep?"

"Enough."

"Me too. You figure out yet what you're going to do?"

"Kind of," Lee said. "If that doesn't work, I'll try something else."

Sefton pulled the blanket tighter around his shoulders. It was as wet as the grass. "Like what?"

They began to walk around the rope corral. Lee said, "There's been talk the Jacks will take in anybody that agrees to convert to their kind of Mormon. Like as not, a few more diehards will join them, misfits or religious fanatics. Probably what they're really looking for are hard cases with gun experience: outlaws, killers, army deserters, the general run of wanted men. You can see how some of them would be tempted to join the heavenly band. A safe place the law can't get at must look sweet. Question is, is it true?"

"It's true."

Lee was surprised. "How the hell do you know?"

Sefton said, "There was an article about it in the Boise paper." Years back some schoolteacher Sefton romanced had taught him to read. Since then he'd been reading everything he got his hands on, especially newspapers.

"Don't believe everything you read in the Boise *Sentinel.*" But Lee hoped Sid and the *Sentinel* had it right.

"Story rang true, the way they wrote it. Man that wrote it, Edgar Upton, stays close to the truth, the way I heard it. Got a reputation to protect and so forth. You fixin' to pass yourself off as a bandit?"

Lee took a cigar from his shirt pocket and put a woodie to it. Darkness was fighting off another day. In the corral the horses were settling down at last, worn out by jittery nerves.

"I might do that," Lee said, savoring the first smoke of the day. "A few years back I used to know a hold-up man and rustler looked something like me. Name of Ben Trask. Same age, give or take a year. Ben was one of Don Luis d'Espana's *pistoleros* same time as me. Drank a lot, talked a lot in the *cantinas.* After Don Luis booted him out for being drunk too often, he tried to get back in the bandit business. *Rurales* caught him half-dead in the desert, hung him from a barrel-organ cactus."

Sefton was testing the top rope of the corral. "Taking his name could get you killed quicker than anything."

"Not too likely. Ben was just a ham and beaner, never an important member of the outlaw fraternity. They'd hardly know him this far north."

"You don't know that for sure." Sefton sounded angry. "How do you know he isn't in the Jack army by this time?"

Lee said, "I know I have to get in there. Anyway, didn't I just tell you he was hung by the mounted police? You're thinking maybe I should just make

25

up a name and a story to go with it. Ben Trask suits me better. I recall how he sounded, how he acted, his little peculiarities. Knowing a man's history makes it easier to take his name, become the man himself."

"Could be," Sefton said reluctantly. "Only thing wrong with it though, which is you can't just ride into the mountains with a sign on your chest saying Howdy folks, I'm Ben Trask, the border bandit, and I'd like to enlist in your devil's brigade. Even if you had some way of identifying yourself, such as false army discharge papers, the Jacks wouldn't buy a pig in a poke. You wouldn't have anybody to vouch for you. You could be anybody, a U.S. marshal, a Pinkerton, an army spy. My friend, the Jacks would kill you out of hand. I was in their shoes, that's what I'd do."

Lee smiled in spite of himself. "Just the same, there has to be some kind of clearinghouse for these law-dodgers, a place where somebody looks them over, takes their measure and sends them ahead or maybe does away with them."

"Does away with them, I'd say. But all right, you get to the Jack fortress or whatever you want to call it. Then what?"

"I don't know, Sid. Getting there comes first."

"This so-called go-between, if there is one, how do you mean to smoke him out?"

"If he's there I'll find him," Lee answered.

Sefton wasn't good at hiding his feelings, which was why he was a poor poker player. Lee knew he was peeved at being left out of this. Now Sefton asked, "You're dead set against my idea for recruiting a war party of men done wrong by the Jacks?"

Lee waved his cigar stub and it glowed red in the gray morning light. "That's right, old friend. Come on, Sid, we got ranch business to discuss."

Sefton wasn't to be put off so easily. "We'll discuss it directly. One last question and I'll button up. Question is, you want me to come with you? No farmer war party, just two so-called law-dodgers 'stead of one. You'd have somebody to watch your back. It would give you an edge you don't have now."

Down below men were rolling out of their blankets. The sound of their voices carried on the still morning air. Time to get going, Lee thought. He liked Sid Sefton but this conversation was going nowhere. He had to set him straight or go on wasting time.

"Look Sid, I need you here. So you're not going unless you want to go by yourself. And that's the end of it. Bud, Charlie and Wes are good men, but they'll work better with you giving the orders. I'm depending on you to look after Spade Bit while I'm gone. There's nobody else. Not too much money left, but I'll give you the best part of it to get the ranch in some kind of shape. Stay on guard. Zimmerman will spread word of the raid, and with me gone it's possible greedy men will believe me dead and the ranch waiting to be grabbed off by anybody tough enough to hang onto it."

Sefton stuck out his jaw, something he did without thinking when he was ready to fight or thinking about it. Lee trusted him as much as any man in the world. "They'd better not try it," Sefton said.

"Watch yourself all the same. Leaving out Old Mac, we're short three men and there's not the wherewithal to replace them. Boise Northwest National has five hundred and sixty dollars on deposit, and that's the end of the money. I'll give you a letter to the manager, but don't go yourself if you run short. Send Wes instead. Conaway, the manager, knows him."

Sefton stared at the horses in the corral. "You sound like you're drawin' up your will?"

"I did that last night by the fire. Just in case, you understand. You never know how things turn out."

Sefton didn't like to hear that. "Tear it up, Lee. Wills bring bad luck."

"Horseshit! If I get killed you and the boys get the ranch. But you'd be in a bad fix without a legal paper to back it up. Come on, leave the horses alone, they're settled enough. I want the men to hear the rest of it. Besides I want my God damned breakfast."

The fires were dying in the smoke-blackened corral, and it still smelled bad, but nothing like the day before. Rain and sun and hard work would return it to normal. Wes Ford was dishing up bacon and biscuits when they got down to the fire. An iron coffee pot bubbled in a bed of coals. Lee and Sefton filled their battered train cups with coffee and they all hunkered down to eat.

"Boys," Lee started off. "I mean to go south and do something about what happened here. Don't talk, just listen. Sid is to be full boss while I'm gone. What he says goes. In spades. If I don't get back in three months, then you'll know I'm dead. That in mind, I made a will last night leaving you all equal shares, but Sid remains boss. That's written in the will. You can sell your share and pull out, but not inside of a year, and you can't sell your share to outsiders. Have to keep it in the family. Naturally you can pull out anytime you like, but if you do it inside of a year, your share stays behind and you get nothing but final wages. That plain enough for you?"

Charlie Potts was offended. "God blast it, Lee, we all been working together for years. Nobody's goin' to make trouble, with you gone." Ford and Bent nodded their agreement. "We'll have the place all fixed up when you get back," Potts finished.

"I'm counting on it," Lee said. "Now finish your breakfast and get to work."

He wasn't sure where he was going and wasn't sure there wouldn't be trouble no matter what Charlie Potts said. Except for their saddles and guns and a few personal possessions, none of the men had owned a thing in their lives. He knew he could count on Sid; the others—well, they were human after all and the thought of becoming property owners might bring a change. Shit! What was he going on about? Bickering, a few fistfights among the men were the least of his problems. Landgrabbers or a return visit from the Jacks—there was real trouble.

Taking a pack animal would make life less of a hardship on the trail, but it didn't fit into the picture of the desperate law-dodger traveling fast and light. He packed a coffee pot and small skillet, coffee, bacon, jerked beef, canned beans. He rolled his blanket and ground sheet in a rubber slicker; the rain could be hard and cold in the mountains. His weapons were a .44 caliber Winchester, one of the new-fangled lever action five-shot Winchester shotguns, a single-action Colt .45.

The lever action shotgun was an interesting weapon that had been introduced by Winchester Arms the year before. He liked weapons and he liked this new shotgun. Winchester sold it mainly to sheriffs and police departments and called it the "alley cleaner." It had been used effectively in prison riots when a lot of fast, heavy lead was called for. Some men said it had some tendency to jam, but it hadn't jammed on him, and he had put it through some hard testing. It worked fine if you bought the best ammunition, and he did.

The men were scraping their plates when he mounted up. They waved, he waved back, and then he was gone. No man would have been able to get him to admit the excitement, but it was there all right, and maybe the quiet, hardworking life didn't suit him as much as he thought. Buckskin Frank, his father, had been like that, always saying he wanted to retire and put the hell-raising and gun-fighting behind him and spend the rest of his life raising horses. Except that wasn't easy for a man of his restless nature; if violence and danger didn't catch up fast enough, he went out to meet it. Then came the time, as it did to all gunfighters who can't or won't call it quits, when he met it once too often. Maybe this is my turn, Lee thought calmly, and put it out of his mind.

Pocatello, forty miles distant, was the only town

of any size on the way south, a wild railroad and ore processing center on the Portneuf River near its junction with the Snake. Nowhere as truly wild as the old Kansas cowtowns, it was surely wide-open enough to have a cathouse frequented by local badmen and law-dodgers wanted in some other part of the country, but not in Idaho.

He left the trail before he got to Zimmerman's Crossing—the German would want to gab about the raid—and picked up the river a few miles south. On its way to join the Snake, the river wound through hills thick with larch and pine, and the trail followed its course.

For the first five miles he saw no one; getting closer he passed farm wagons, a few lone riders, a party of Basque shepherds without sheep on their way to town. Lee was in the horse business, so he had nothing against sheepmen. The Basques were a fact of life in Idaho, and all but the meanest, sheep-hating cattlemen had learned to let these dangerous herders alone.

After another hour's ride he could see the smoke of Pocatello far off, then the river made a wide eastern sweep, while the trail branched off and went straight down to the new trestle bridge that ran into Main Street on the other side.

It was about two o'clock when he crossed the bridge; the river below a dirty yellow from the muck the ore plant dumped into it. Smoke from locomotives, their bells clanging, hung over the long, wide expanse of railroad yards east of town. Pocatello was a town of go-getters and civic boosters and there was a new red-brick town hall;

31

there was even a theater.

A man fitting a new pane to a broken store window told him where he could find a livery stable. "A right turn the next corner, two blocks down from there to Fremont Street, and you'll find a whole slew of 'em. Catling's the best of the lot. Real up to date. Got lockers for you valuables. Padlocks costs you a dollar. You get fifty cents refund when you come back."

He put away his horse and other belongings and went back to Main Street to get a mug of beer and something to eat. The five-stool restaurant provided pork chops, apple sauce, mash and gravy, and when he got through, passing up what was sure to be bad coffee, he went next door to a beat-up saloon with the usual long bar on one side, tables and chairs on the other. Only one man occupied a table, a half-drunk cowhand with a bottle and glass in front of him, his boots testing on a saddle as worn-out as he was.

At that time of day the saloon was quiet except for a handful of men in bib-overalls or canvas work suits. They were talking at the bar or feeding nickels into gaming machines set against the end wall. The three-fruit machines whirred and clanked without paying out any jackpots. A dusty, battered player piano had an out of order sign daubed in black paint. Below the sign some wag had added in pencil: SO IS MY WIFE. Behind the bar a portly bartender walked the duck-boards, collecting empty glasses and beer mugs and dumping them in a zinc trough. Gaboons were placed along the footrail, but most of the spit was on the sawdusted floor. A saloon with no upstairs and no women, it looked like the kind of place it was.

Halfway through the second beer, Lee crooked a finger at the bartender. Change still lay on the bar and Lee pushed a fifty cent piece toward the bartender. "Where they keep the women in this town?" he asked.

"Depends on how much you can spend, mister." The bartender glanced at Lee's soiled wool shirt, thorn scarred leather vest, sweat-stained Stetson. "No offense intended, but you don't look too flush unless you're one of them essentric millionaires you read about in the *Police Gazette.*" The bartender chuckled at his own stale wit. "Mister, I'd say Mrs. Kessler's down by the river'd be about right for you. Kinda rough—got a great big Irish clodhopper for a bouncer—but I would have to say Mrs. Kessler's."

"Mrs. Kessler's down by the river?"

"Just south of the bridge, down a flight of steps and there she is, right where the paddlesteamers tie up. A big old yellow frame house the color of dog vomit, set back from the landing. Tell 'em Eben Claypool sent you. Only don't come back here cryin' if somethin' happens to you. I ain't got no shares in the place."

Looking at the whorehouse from the bottom of the dock steps, Lee gave the bartender full credit for describing it accurately. It was the color of dog puke and probably hadn't been painted since the town was founded. The house was three storeys high, no bullet holes scarred the windows, and that was all that could be said for it. A huge, plug-ugly, check-suited Irishman, who looked like an ape with clothes

33

on, unbolted the door when Lee knocked. Set on the back of his bullet head was a derby a size too small for him. The suit and the derby were yellow, like the house. He looked like an ex-trooper or a railroader turned whore bully. His little pig eyes, rimmed red like a boozer's eyes, regarded Lee with mindless hostility, and given the chance, this roughneck would rather fight than fuck.

"What did ye want?" he growled in a city-Irish brogue. His breath smelled like a week-long poker game.

"A poke," Lee said.

"Oh ye did, did ye? Well let me tell ye somethin', boyo. They'll be none a that durty talk round here. Conduct yerself like a gintleman or take yerself off, do ye get me meanin'? An' ye'll have to check the pistol before goin' upstairs. First rule of the house. Last but not least, no rough stuff or ye'll have me to deal with."

Lee didn't want to give up the Colt but he said all right.

"Ye bet yer balls it's all right," the hooligan said, still wanting to fight. "Payment in advance, no exceptions. What's that ye say? Are the girls clean here? Damn right they's clean. Doc looks 'em over once a month. Never ye mind the girls. Are ye clean yerself? Well for yer own information and eddyfica-tion, ye'll be gettin' a short arm inspection when ye get upstairs. Charges are two dollars for ten minutes and so on. Stay as long as ye like pervided ye behave yerself."

Lee gave the thick mick the Colt and saw it shoved into a pigeon hole behind a wooden counter.

A few other guns were there before his. Then he was ushered into a hot, stuffy parlor with faded flocked wallpaper, a threadbare Turkey carpet, brass-bottomed oil lamps with flowered chimneys, and six whores sitting on two long red sofas. A small, thin woman with a pinched face and a green velvet dress came out of a door marked office and caught a blond, young whore trying to hide a garish dime novel under a cushion. The whore, almost white-blond, got red in the face when the madam glared at her.

"Welcome sir," the madam said to Lee, doing her best to smile. "I am Mrs. Lorena Kessler. I take it Roger has explained the house rules?"

Lee decided Roger didn't look like a Roger and Lorena didn't look like a Lorena. Spike and Lizzie would be more like it. Lee nodded and Mrs. Kessler showed him into her office. He guessed it wouldn't be ladylike to accept poke money in front of the girls.

"Make yourself at home, sir," Mrs. Kessler said. "You'll be with us for how long?"

Lee put a five dollar bill on the desk; already on it were an imitation marble clock, a cashbox, a framed and tinted photograph of a fat man with a handlebar mustache. The fat man was probably the late Mr. Kessler.

"I'll take five dollars worth," Lee said.

"Make it six," Mrs. Kessler said. "For six you get thirty minutes of pleasure. Drinks are available by the bottle or glass. Those six lovely ladies out there are available. Choose the one you like, Mr. . . . ?"

"Ben Trask," Lee said.

"Pleased to meet you, Mr. Trask," the madam

said. "Haven't seen you before, have I?"

Lee knew this old bitch had a mind like a bank examiner: stiff and cold and full of facts. More to the point, he knew some madams curried favor with the local law by turning in wanted men, especially important law-dodgers with a big price on their heads.

"Just passing through," he told her.

He had already chosen the whore he wanted, the full-bodied towhead with a liking for dime novels. Not more than nineteen or twenty, she still had some spirit left. Time would wear her down, but so far she hadn't sunk to the liquor or morphine that kept so many whores going from day to day. He smiled at her and she smiled back, standing up to do her duty by Mrs. Kessler. She had the whitest-blond hair he had ever seen.

"Watch my book, will you?" she said to the whore sitting next to her. "Don't let old Lorena take it."

The other whore yawned behind her hand. "Watch it yourself, darlin'."

Lee's whore took the tattered book with her when they went up to the second floor to a small, narrow room with nothing in it but a double brass bed, a table, chair, wash stand with china jug and basin, a cheap pine wardrobe. An oiled paper shade covered the window and the little room smelled of sweat, lilac water, and sex. On a shelf set high on the wall were a few bottles of scent and face powder.

The whore kicked off her shoes, undid her back buttons with practiced ease, and slipped off her blue silk dress. She hung everything on the back of the chair, then climbed on the bed, opened her legs wide, bounced her backside a few times, and was ready to go to work.

"Come and get it, big boy," she said. "Any way you want it is all right with me. Back or front, makes no difference. You want to suck my thing, there it is waiting for you." Lee was taking off his clothes. "You want me to suck you, just say the word. You've had suck jobs naturally, but tell me this, you ever had a brandy and cream suck?"

"Sounds nourishing," Lee said, his cock standing up straight when he took off his trousers and underpants.

"I find it so," she said. "If you want that you'll notice I don't spit out after you come. Here's how it's done: I take a swig of brandy, a swig of cream but don't swallow before I take you in my mouth. Brandy by itself would be too raw on your member, only the cream cuts it, see. Of course you have to pay a lot extra for a brandy and cream suck. Has to be ordered from downstairs. If that don't tickle your fancy, hows about my special hum suck?"

"How's that?"

"I hum while I'm sucking you and the vibration . . ."

"I take my pleasure the old-fashioned way, me on top of you. After that, we'll see."

"Yep sure fine," the whore said. "The customer is always right 'ceptin when he tries to take his pleasure with a leather belt. Had a kinda old fella try that a few weeks ago. Had to holler for Roger and have his bare ass whupped right out onto the docks. Roger tossed his clothes after him."

"Talkative, ain't you," Lee said with a grin.

37

A return smile from the whore. "My way of puttin' fellas at their ease. Makes them feel at home, it not bein' so cut and dry. You can call me Towhead if you like. That's what everybody calls me, count of my hair. I'm friendly and you should be glad I'm available. Come on over now. I got to skin you back, make sure you don't give me a dose. Roger calls it a short arm inspection. Army talk, I guess."

She skinned him back and clucked her tongue approvingly. "Clean as a whistle, mister. It'll be a pleasure to do you."

"Call me Ben," Lee told her, positioning himself between her muscular thighs. She had a shaved muff and her love lips glistened with vaseline. He steadied himself with one hand and pushed in right to the hilt. Her muscles tightened and relaxed, while her legs closed around the small of his back. Her hands roamed all over him, stroking his hair, his backside, his tightened-up balls. She bucked her ass and her entire body quivered as he drove in and out of her like a piston rod and soon they were dripping with sweat, soaking the sheets.

Lee didn't realize how wound-up he was until he began to fuck her. This was his first paid-for poke since Maggie came to live at Spade Bit, not that he felt any need to be faithful, and it wasn't because Maggie didn't love him, and even if she had that wouldn't have stopped him if he was away from home and wanted a woman and the need wouldn't wait. It had been none of that. After Sarah was murdered by farmers egged on by the landgrabbing banker Callaway, who swore Spade Bit horses were going to trample their crops, he had buried himself

38

in work, the only way to dull his grief. After Maggie came he had gone on working like a madman, but fucking Maggie as if he'd never get another fuck in his life . . .

"Oh Jesus, you're like a stallion," Towhead whispered in his ear. "It's like you're halfway up my body. That big dingus of yours feels like it can't get enough of me. Christ! I think it's coming out my mouth. That's it, that's it! Bring it right out to the tip, then shove it in—*hard*—all the way."

In and out, in and out, his stroke quickened and he larruped it into her until the brass bed creaked and shook and her fingers dug into his backside and her head rolled from side to side. Her eyes were closed and clean pink tongue stuck out between her teeth. Now her ass bucked so hard that he had to pin her arms to the bed to steady her for his relentless thrust. "Come with me, Ben," she gasped. "Please come with me. Oh my God, I'm coing to come. Come now, Ben. I want to feel your hot come shooting into me."

Her body convulsed and so did his, and he kept on thrusting until he was drained and his cock began to soften, but he didn't pull out, and in a while it grew stif again and they did it again. "You're runnin' up quite a bill," she whispered. "You sure you can pay it?"

"Sure can," Lee said, "and it's worth every penny."

For a whore, Towhead was a great actress, at least in bed, and that was where it counted. Later, after they did it for the third time and he couldn't do it anymore, they lay side by side and talked.

She was an Oregon apple picker's daughter, she said, which might or might not have been true. It was Lee's experience that every whore had a yarn. She was of Swedish descent, she said, which was probably true. Her father and brothers had tried to rape her, had raped her, in fact, so she decided she might as well get paid for getting poked. Her dream was to save enough poke money to open a dressmaking shop in Eugene, Oregon. Men friends, nice customers like Ben, often gave her a little extra to help her on her way.

"I'll be glad to help you," Lee told her.

"How much, Ben? Course you can give me as much or as little as you like. Real nice men have given me as much as fifty dollars."

Lee knew he was taking a chance by asking her if she knew about the law-dodgers that went into the northeast Utah mountains to join the renegade Mormons. But when he asked her, she showed more interest than surprise.

"You mean you're an outlaw, Ben?" she said, sitting up in the sagging bed. "A bandit or a train robber, a real desperado?"

She had her story and he had his. He told her he was from Colorado, had shot a drunken bully in self-defense, but this man had powerful friends and they were out to hang him or jail him for life.

"They'll get me sure if I don't find a place to hide for a while. Man in my home state told me about these outlaws going to Utah to join the Jack Mormons. He was wanted too, for cattle rustling, and he asked me if I knew where these Mormons had their hideout and how to get there. Course I didn't know any more than he did, but it gave me ideas. One last thing this man said was there was some agent or go-between could arrange for a man to join. You ever heard of such a man?"

Now her look was guarded, but she said, "I don't know myself. There might be somebody that does."

"Somebody around here?"

"Maybe right in this house. But listen, I don't want to get mixed up in anything that could get me in trouble. So I can't promise anything, see? I wouldn't mind if you gave me the fifty dollars before I said anything more. Give me the fifty and we could talk more like real friends."

Lee reached over, took fifty dollars from his pants and gave it to her. A little threat was needed, so he made it. "Towhead, darlin', I wouldn't like it if you were telling me tall tales."

That frightened her a little. "Oh no, Ben, I wouldn't do such a thing. We're friends, ain't we. No, this person, this girl I'm talkin' about, is one of the house girls here. She calls herself Nelly Apple-yard, so I guess she is. Tell you the truth, she doesn't belong here at all. Her man friend sold her to Mrs. Kessler, and now she just mopes and cries all the time instead of makin' the best of it. That Clem Haney was worse than an outlaw."

"He *sold* her?"

"Sure he sold her. It's done all the time in this business. But like I said, she can't get used to it. She cries all the time even when Roger doesn't beat her. Oh he doesn't beat her so marks or bruises will show. He used a rubber hot water bottle filled with sand, hits her on top of the head till she goes

41

unconscious. Mrs. Kessler hates her because the regulars shy away from her. No life, no spirit. I guess she even cries when some man tries to poke her. Men have demanded their money back. That doesn't set well with the old bitch downstairs.''

"Why don't they just let her go?"

"They got two hundred invested in her."

"But if she's not earning money?"

"They'll kill her anyway, Roger will, some night when he's murderin' drunk. He wants to do it and it'll be an example for the rest of us ladies. Not long ago, one late night, he took her out and held her out over the river at the end of his arms. She came in all white and shaking and threw up on the carpet. You can imagine how Mrs. Kessler took that. I tried talking to her on our day off, told her that brute paddy is going to kill you, you don't get out of the doldrums. I wasn't just talking, Ben. She'll disappear some night and later they'll find her in the river and decide it was suicide, if there's even that much interest. Nobody will give a damn. Women in the Life kill themselves every day. But us ladies here will know that Roger killed her and we'll behave. You're damn right we will. Nobody can do anything about it, not even me, and I like the poor soul.''

Lee started to get dressed, but Towhead pulled him back into bed. "Maybe I can help her," Lee said. "I want to talk to her."

Towhead's smile was tired, a little bitter. "You just want information, Ben, or am I wrong. Can you help the poor kid, or is that just talk? Don't get mad. We all got to look after ourselves."

"I want to talk to her. Could be she's got nothing to tell, but I'll help her if I can. Men beating up on women rubs me raw. None of my business, you think. I could make it my business."

On the other side of the wall bedsprings squeaked and there were footsteps in the corridor. Business was picking up as the day wore on toward nightfall.

Towhead raised up in bed and looked at him. "You can't talk to her in my room. Wouldn't be possible anyhow. You start trouble and Mrs. Kessler will tie it to me. I won't let you bring her to my room even if you tell Mrs. Kessler you want her for a three-way. The old bitch will catch on when she thinks about it. She's mean but she's smart. Sorry Ben, I don't want to end up in the dirty river."

This time Lee got out of bed and stayed out. "All right, after I leave you I'll go downstairs and say I want another girl. I'll look the girls over and chose her if she's available. That way there's nothing to connect you."

Towhead got dressed as fast as only a whore can undress. "She'll be available, you bet. Always available is her main problem. You can't miss her: kind of small, pale, with weepy blue eyes. If she isn't available it's because some bastard wants to abuse her. Mrs. Kessler doesn't mind that. But if she isn't there, have a drink and wait. The men that choose her don't keep her long."

Lee pulled on his boots. "Thanks, I'll do what you say. Be seeing you sometime."

"Not likely," Towhead said, "and not here."

THREE

Lee went downstairs and the girl described by Tow-head still sat forlornly at the end of the couch. Some of the whores he'd seen earlier were upstairs with customers. He glanced at all the whores left in the parlor, and some smiled, some yawned, and then he settled his bill with Mrs. Kessler. The madam put the money in the cashbox and said, "Thank you, sir, and please call again."

"I'd like another girl," Lee said.

"Oh." Mrs. Kessler raised her eyebrows. "Didn't you like the young lady you had?"

Lee winked. "Liked her fine. But now I'd like to try something else. Lately I been in places they got few women of any kind and would like to make up for lost time."

Mrs. Kessler was pleased to find such a pleasant, prompt-paying customer. "Well why not? You're a healthy young man. I can see that. They're out there waiting for you. This time there's no need to pay in advance. Pay when you're ready to leave."

The whores whispered and giggled when they realized he was going to pick a new poke. Nelly Appleyard looked up at him, then back at the floor. Her face was pale and drawn and there were dark smudges under her eyes. One of the whores burst out laughing when he stopped in front of the Appleyard girl and said, "Let's get acquainted, missy."

There was more laughing and Mrs. Kessler came out of the office looking mean. "What's the laughing about?" she demanded to know.

Frightened, the laughing whore said, "This gentleman just picked Nelly. Oughtn't of laughed, I guess."

"But you found it funny?"

The whore squirmed under Mrs. Kessler's dark, mean eye. "Guess I'm feeling silly today."

"I'll talk to you later, Angelica," the madam threatened, turning to Lee. "You may find this young lady a little shy."

Lee went into his country shitkicker act. "I like all kinda ladies, God bless 'em."

Towhead came downstairs and took her place on the sofa, and for all the notice she took of Lee, she might never have seen him before.

"Go along now, Nelly," the madam said. Nelly Appleyard went with Lee, and some of the whores giggled in spite of themselves. Mrs. Kessler told them to be quiet or they'd know the reason why.

Going upstairs the girl stumbled and Lee kept her from falling. She mumbled her thanks and he told her to think nothing of it. Her room was on the third floor.

"No call to be scared of me," Lee said, opening the door she pointed to. "Nobody's going to hurt you."

Once inside, not looking at him, she began to fumble with her buttons. Lee said, "You don't have to do that." He kept his voice low. "All I want is to talk to you."

He sat her down on the chair and he took the bed, facing her. It could all be a waste of time. The thug who deserted her, actually sold her into whoredom, could have told her anything or nothing.

"What do you want, mister?" Her thin voice was made thinner by despair.

Nothing was to be gained by dragging it out. "I want to know where Clem Haney went after he left here?" But you never knew about women: she still might have a soft spot for the son of a bitch. "I'm no kind of law, no kind of hired killer gunning for your man. Where did he go?"

"He's not my man, not anymore." Her voice was so faint that he could barely hear it. "I don't what you want, mister. What's he got to do with you?"

Lee told her he was a wanted man trying to hook up with the Jack Mormons only he hadn't been able to do it. Big money could be made if he joined the Jacks. Better than that, he'd be safe from the law, which would stop looking for him if he stayed out of sight for a year or two. The look on her face told him no further explanation was needed.

Not being beaten or threatened gave her a little courage. "How'd you hear about Clem?"

"Clem told a fella that told me. Us law-dodgers gossip like old women, like for instance such and such a fellow robbed a train with three other fellas.

Such and such a fella got hung, got shot. Or the talk could be about a fat bank waiting to be robbed. Or what big rancher is hiring on gunslingers. Business talk, you could say. Where did he go? I can help you, make it worth your while."

Nelly Appleyard reached over to take a towel from the washstand, dipped in the water jug and pressed it against her forehead.

Though she was young, about twenty-four, her face was haggard, as if she had given up hope. Not much given to pity, Lee pitied this forlorn woman.

But he had to push her because she was so scared of everything. "I *can* help you, Nelly, if you tell me where Clem Haney's gone to. I know he's gone to be vetted by the Jack Mormon agent. Clem liked to talk, is my information. He must have told you where this agent is located. Tell me and I'll take you out of here, stake you to a train ticket and enough money to keep you going till you get a job—whatever."

She looked at him with teary eyes. "Clem said nothing, he just left. Look mister, whoever you are, can't you see I can't help you? I don't want to get in worse trouble then I'm in. I'm nothing but a greasy whore in a whorehouse. If you want a poke or a suck, there's the bed."

Lee still hoped to break her down, no matter how hopeless and bitter she was. For an instant there had been a faint look of hope in her eyes, and then it was gone, driven out by fear and mistrust. She wanted to believe him, but her misery got in the way.

Kindness hadn't worked, so he decided to be

brutal. "All right, girlie, you don't trust me because you don't trust me because you don't know me. How about the Irishman and the old hag downstairs? You ought to know them well enough by now. You know that vicious bastard will kill you sooner or later. Get on his bad side once too often and he'll murder you. He broke you in, am I right? The whore bully always breaks the new girls in no matter how many men they've been with. His way of putting his stamp on them. But that's nothing compared to what he'll do when the killing mood is on him. He'll throw you in the river when he's tired kicking and beating. If he hasn't beaten you senseless, you'll be glad to drown. You want to take some time to think it over?"

She nodded, he said nothing.

It was getting dark and Lee stood up to light the handing lamp. He trimmed the wick and put the chimney back in place. A paddleboat hooted on the river. Nelly Appleyard had her eyes closed, her hands clenched tight in her lap. Finally she spoke.

"How can you get me past Roger? You don't even have a gun."

"Never mind the gun. I'll get it back. What kind of gun does Roger carry?"

"A big, heavy gun with a short barrel. Sometimes I see him with his coat off. The gun is in a holster under his arm."

Could be a Colt .45 with a cut-down barrel, Lee thought. Or a breaktop five-shot .455 British Webley, a stubby gun with a hell of a wallop. Could even be a Colt Lightning double-action .38 To a woman a double-action .38 might look bigger than it was.

"What if there's nothing to tell?"

Lee was getting sick of her. "You got plenty to tell. Make up your mind. You're scared Roger will come after us, after you after I get you out. Not a chance. I'll cripple the son of a bitch so bad he won't be able to walk to the shithouse. I'll put him on crutches for the rest of his life. One more time: where did Haney go?"

"Eutaw Springs. He went to Eutaw Springs to meet a man named John Spargo who runs a trading post." The words came out in a rush, as if she couldn't say them fast enough. "That's the truth, I swear it. Clem said this man Spargo was the one who decided who joines the Mormons, who doesn't. Clem bragged about how they'd be happy to take on a big man like him."

Lee thought: And if they aren't glad, if Spargo isn't pleased with what he sees, all Clem will get is a bullet in the head and a deep grave. Because that was certain to be the way they handled it, so there would be nobody around to talk about it. Recruits were sent on ahead or they disappeared. No loose ends. It made good sense from where the Jacks stood.

Talking seemed to calm her a little, though she continued to dart nervous glances at the door, afraid the Irishman would come crashing through at any moment. She stopped talking and he waited.

She said, "I'm just telling you what Clem told me. You can't blame me if he told me a lie."

"I'll chance it."

"Clem says it's not even a town. He said Spargo's saloon and trading post is all there is. You ever heard of the place?"

Lee knew she was talking to cover her fear, to put off having to go downstairs to face the whore bully's gun and maybe die in front of it. Panic would take hold of her again if they didn't go soon.

"It's time to leave," he told her. "I'll go down first, you'll be right behind me. I'll settle up with Mrs. Kessler and start to leave. Take your place on the sofa and don't move till I yell come ahead. Don't get scared if there's a lot of noise out where Roger sits. Get out fast no matter what I'm doing. Get out and wait close-by. I'll be right behind you, that's a promise. If not, get to the train station as fast as you can."

He handed her fifty dollars, enough to take her far from Pocatello. "Just don't panic," he said.

The office door was open and Mrs. Kessler was talking to a runty man who was twisting a silk hat in his hands. Lee said he was leaving and wanted to settle up. The runty man went out ahead of Lee. Mrs. Kessler closed the door.

Lee went out through the archway that led to the front door where the Irishman sat on a stool by a peephole. The Irishman took a swig from a flat pint bottle before he eased his wide backside off the stool. He didn't like Lee and maybe he hated the whole world because he was nothing but a drunken whore bully and knew it and didn't like it. Now he was slightly drunk.

"You was upstairs a long time, wasn't you? Had

50

trouble gettin' it up, haw? Ye can tell ol' Roger. Might be able to give ye the benefit of me wide experience with women."

Lee knew he had taken on a load of whiskey, but he talked without slurring and his movements were steady. Booze wouldn't slow him down all that much.

"Some other time," Lee said calmly. "I'll take my gun."

"Certainly sor, Yes indeedy sor." He guffawed. "Take care ye don't shoot yerself in the foot, sor. T'would break me heart, ye did yerself an injury."

Laughing to himself he went behind the counter where the checked guns were kept in wooden pigeon-holes. He put Lee's Colt on the counter and folded his arms. More than ever he looked like an ape with clothes on.

Lee picked up the Colt and said, "You made a mistake, mister. This isn't my gun. My gun is a brand-new Remington .44. Take another look and you'll find it. Or you want me to call Mrs. Kessler and have this straightened out?"

A darker shade of red colored the Irishman's booze-mottled face. He roared like an injuried bull. "What the hell are ye tryin' to pull. Ye gave in an old Bisley Colt, ye got back an old Bisley Colt." He unfounded his arms and leaned forward, hands flat on the counter. "Now get the hell out of here before I get cross."

Lee swung the heavy pistol and smashed the Irishman on the head just above the forehead. He swung up and down and hit the Irishman in the same place. A short, savage chop broke the Irishman's nose and blood spatterred like rain. Another man would have dropped like a stone, but the Irishman stayed on his feet, fumbling for his shoulder holster. His Webley .455 was coming out cocked when Lee brought the Colt down like a club and broke the Irishman's wrist. The cocked double-action clattered to the floor and fired as the hammer came down and the Irishman scrambled to grab it up with his good hand. Lee hit him twice on the back of the neck and his face hit the floor and he lay still.

"Come ahead, Nelly!" Lee yelled. "Nelly, come ahead!" In the parlor the whores were screaming, running for the stairs, calling for Mrs. Kessler. Lee shouted again, then vaulted over the counter and kicked the Irishman in the side of the head. There was nothing personal in the way he shattered the Irishman's leg bones by stomping on them until he felt them grinding under his boots. For good measure, he kicked the Irishman's kneecaps loose. He jumped over the counter and saw Nelly running down the hall. He grabbed her by the hand and pulled her after him. A gun fired behind them and a bullet ripped into the front door and he turned and saw Mrs. Kessler steadying a double-barreled derringer for a better shot. He put a bullet close to her head and she ducked out of sight.

A paddlesteamer with only one light showing was moored at the landing; it was quiet up and down the dark river. If anybody heard the shooting, they hadn't come running to see what it was about. He helped her up the steps to the bridge, where Main Street began and naphtha lights flared white in the darkness. A town with so many saloons was late getting to bed and there was considerable traffic in the street and on the bridge. No city policemen were in sight.

The girl was trembling all over. Lee tightened his grip on her arm and told her to take it easy. "Nobody's coming after us. Take my arm and walk slow like we're out for an evening stroll. It's only ten o'clock. Go slow, I said. Talk, smile, you can manage to do that."

"Yes," she said.

On the next corner a city policeman stood shifting his weight from one foot to the other. Going past they got more and more than the usual bored look policemen give people, and then the bridge and the whorehouse were far behind and the girl stopped shaking and trying to look over her shoulder.

Then her questions came in a string, as if she had been saving them. "What if Mrs. Kessler sets the law on us?" Mrs. Kessler stayed very much on her mind. So did the Irishman. "Is Roger dead? Did you kill him? If he dies will we be sent to prison for a long time? Why should I be sent to prison? He was a very bad man."

Lee said Roger wasn't dead and the law wouldn't be coming after them. "You were sold like a slave and kept as a slave. There's nothing to worry about. Mrs. Kessler won't go near the police. How can she? The police want nothing to do with Mrs. Kessler or her place. Mrs. Kessler will see doctoring Roger as a business expense or else she'll throw him out and get herself another bully. Forget all that. Where do you want to go?"

"I have to think," she said.

All along Main Street the saloons racketed with life musicians, player pianos, mechanical harps. Pocatello was a mixture of the old and the new. Horses were hitched under the new-fangled naptha streetlights, and there were signs advertising painless dentists, Eagle Lock typewriters and horn gramophones. On the second floor, in a commercial block, a chiropractor advertised his services with a pair of giant hands manipulating a gigantic spine. It would take more than a chiropractor to put Roger together again.

"I want to be on the first train out," she decided.

"To where?" Lee asked her. "The ticket agent will want to know that."

"The first train, any train. I wish you were coming with me."

Lee didn't want to get into that. "You'll be all right as soon as you board the train. But he wasn't sure this weak-willed woman would ever be all right. She would take up with some other glib bastard and it would be like that for the rest of her life. In the end, it had nothing to do with him.

He put her on a train for Salt Lake City and went back to get his horse. Time to be gone before Mrs. Kessler rounded up a bunch of thugs and put them on the streets asking questions about a tall man and a pale lady.

Clear of the town, he rode south on the road that crossed the Idaho-Utah line and went straight down to Ogden and then to Salt Lake. Northeast of Ogden were the mountains where the Jacks were holed up, or so it was said. According to Clem Haney, if you could believe anything he said, Eutaw Springs was

54

in the foothills that ran up into the western slope of the Rockies. The Jacks had the Rockies at their backs, no way to get at them there. But he wasn't betting that the Jacks hadn't found and mapped an escape route, even if it meant climbing up into the peaks and down the far side. The original Mormons had been some of the bravest, most daring explorers in the world; this bunch of renegade bastards came from the same venturesome stock.

But for now there was nothing to do but find out if Eutaw Springs existed. It wouldn't be on any maps. He would stay on the road until he was about ten miles north of Logan, then swing east and cut along the south end of Bear Lake, the biggest lake in northeast Utah. Past the lake, he would have to feel his way.

Once he reached the Idaho-Utah line, he would have to watch his step. This was country that had suffered Jack raids and naturally people would be suspicious or everybody and anybody. In normal times, a lone rider wouldn't be seen as any special threat. Nowadays a lone rider could be an advance scout for a Jack raid. Any inquiries he made, at this ranch or that, would have to be made in the full light of day, which was no guarantee that he wouldn't be shot from ambush by a jittery rancher before he got close enough to ask questions.

A good road and a bright moon made travel easy. Close to the Utah desert, it hardly ever rained in southern Idaho. He would be about eighty miles from Spade Bit when he reached the borderline. Long before now the boys would have fixed up the corral and started clearing the ruins. Tomorrow or the next day they get started on the cabin. He hoped to see Spade Bit again.

He stopped to drink water and to splash some in his face. He had gone more than twenty-four hours without sleep. Times past he could have gone longer than that, but helping to drag and burn thirty-six dead horses was back-breaking work, and the few hours restless sleep he got the night before had done nothing to rest him. Sleep, what he got of it, hadn't come easily, and there were nightmares that brought sweat in spite of the cold mountain air. Towhead and the bed-tussle had released most of the tension, and his hot hatred of the Jacks had cooled to the point where he could control it. A man who couldn't control himself was a likely candidate for killing. A man didn't have much of a chance when hate governed his every move. Yet the hate was there, and it would stay with him for the rest of his life. In this, he was very much like his father, who never found it possible to stop hating a man because he was dead. Once, talking of a man he had tracked down and killed, Frank said, "I wish I could restore him to life so I could kill him again."

Tiredness was making him groggy. East from the road he would find a place to unspool his blankets after he watered his horse and put the animal on a long tether so it could graze. He was hungry, but not hungry enough to risk a campfire in this country; morning would be time enough to cook coffee and fry bacon.

On both sides of the line the country looked much the same and it took a look at his watch to let him know he had to be in Utah by now. For all his traveling, he didn't know this part of the country, though it was less than a hundred miles from Spade Bit. He yawned. God damn, it would be good to sleep.

He wondered how Maggie was faring. For somebody with such "respectable" notions, it was a hell of a fix to be in. He yawned a bone-cracking yawn. What the hell did respectability mean? If respectability meant turning into a mealymouth psalm singer and tightwad, then he wanted no part of it, and he sure as hell wasn't about to get married again, least all to Maggie, who could only get worse once the knot was tied. There had been hints, of course, dozens of them, but he had turned a deaf ear when the subject came up. Maybe it was time to stake Maggie to a new start and send her packing. If I get her back, if we live through this, that's what he'd do. He would miss her in bed, but the world was full of women and he would find someone to take her place.

Trying to remember everything he knew about Ben Trask didn't do much to keep him awake. Ben was originally from Colorado and though he claimed to be from Texas he didn't have the slow Texas drawl, which was all to the good because Lee knew he was no kind of playactor. One way or another, it was nothing to fret about. Except for the famous badmen, most small-potato outlaws and gunslingers told so many stories about their past lives that nobody gave a damn.

He came to the trail that went east from the Logan road. It was rutted by wagon wheels and probably went east to the Mormon farms on the flat side of Bear Lake. It should take him to the lake and then he would ride south to get around it.

Here, off the road, there were no farmhouses, no lights far back in the bare brown hills. Moving on, he spotted a stand of scrubby trees with a shallow creek on the far side of it. Past the trees the creek made a bend and lost itself in stunted hills. Under the trees, protected by shade, was enough grass for his horse.

He saw to the animal, unspooled his bedroll and fell into a deep, dreamless sleep, with his hand resting on the lever action shotgun.

FOUR

When he rolled out in the morning, he could see the mountains to the east. Far back were the peaks vaulting into the sky. Set against the cloudless blue sky, the peaks looked jagged and flatsided, like the painted scenery he'd seen in theaters.

He cooked a big breakfast and as he moved on the country began to change; the arid country fell behind. Mountains closed in as he rode, but they were nothing like the mountains on the far side of Bear Lake. These were real mountains, the grand-daddy of all mountains, the Rockies, and the Jacks were in there somewhere, far back and high up, thinking themselves secure from any attack.

By afternoon, he figured he was about halfway to the lake. Bear Lake was a big lake; how big he didn't know; it might take a while to get around it. Not a patient man by nature, he could be patient when he had to. The Jacks wouldn't run away, and neither would Maggie, and whether she liked it or not, she would have to suffer along with the other captive women. She would have been raped many times by now, for the Jacks were a horny bunch, but it wouldn't kill her. It might make her hysterical, as old Mac the cook used to say; poor Maggie, with her airs and graces, should have stayed in Massachusetts.

Lee was watering the stallion from his hat when the three farmers came out of the brush. Big rocks were scattered through the brush, and they had been in there, watching him. He heard them coming before they showed themselves. If they had wanted to kill him from cover, they could have done it long before they started making so much noise.

Most farmers couldn't shoot for beans, but with three men shooting at him from a rest position, at least one bullet would have found its mark.

He turned to face them, careful to keep his hand away from his gun. The two older men were bearded; the young one had a week's black stubble on his face. They looked like farmers, but you never knew; a closer look at their weapons told him they were just farmers. The Jacks had the money to buy better weapons. The older men carried breech-loading, single-shot Army Springfields, worn and battered and probably bought from some traveling gun dealer. The young farmer had a Big Fifty Sharps, the buffalo gun. All wore farmer clothes, black and dusty.

Lee looked at their weapons. "Don't have a lot of money," he said. "Ninety-seven dollars and an old silver watch. Take what you want. It's not worth dying for."

The young farmer, not much more than twenty, took a tighter grip on the Sharps. "What the hell are you talkin' about, mister? You think we're road agents?"

"You mean you're not?"

"He thinks we're road agents," the young farmer said. He had a high voice and his laugh was high-pitched. "Don't that beat all."

"That'll do," one of the bearded men ordered. "Nothing funny about it. What're you doin' here, mister?"

Lee looked at the rocks sticking up out of the brush. They might have left their best shot back there, ready to drop him if he made a wrong move. They might be smart enough to do that.

"Who wants to know?" Lee asked. "Is this a private trail, or what? You got something against strangers?"

"Depends," the bearded man answered. "Depends on what kind of a stranger you might be. You have the look of a gunman to me."

"You said it right, Jacob. He sure looks like a gunman." This was from the third man, who hadn't said anything. "Ask him what his business is. Ask him what he wants."

Lee didn't know why the man couldn't ask his own questions. But he left it to Jacob, who seemed to be leader of this threadbare outfit.

It came out that the others were Paxton and Ike.

"You better speak the truth," Ike warned. Ike was the youngster. Lee knew he was ready to use the Sharps, maybe wanted to use it. Young Ike was a farmer, but he had the makings of a killer; people

61

might be talking about him in a few years. Ike wanted to catch him in a lie, or what he decided was a lie. It would be hell drawing against a cocked Sharps.

Lee told them he was Ben Trask from up in Idaho and was searching for his sister, Isabel. Ike started to say something, but was shushed by Jacob. "Isabel took up with a drifter that figured to marry into her share of the ranch. Wasn't no share, but he didn't know that. If she had a share it would become his property. So he thought. Guess she told him—lied about it—to keep him interested. I ran him off with a shotgun, but he came back by night and took her with him. Iz was always wild, always kicking the traces. They could be married by now, but I mean to take her back a widow. I hope to find her in Lake-town."

Ike gave out with his shrill laugh. "You don't believe in young love, mister?"

Jacob said angrily, "Shut your mouth, let him talk." He spoke like the others except for a slight foreign accent.

"It's all bullshit," Ike jeered. "You got eyes, you can see this fella don't own no ranch. Look how he's got up. Don't even have a clean shirt. He owns a ranch, why don't he have riders to back him?"

Jacob was quiet in contrast to the babbling kid, and he had clear, gray intelligent eyes: a Bible reading German or Scandinavian. Lee knew the solemn farmer would kill him if he thought he had to, or he would try, and if he succeeded he would speak some appropriate verses over the grave.

"Boy has a point," he said. "You got no men siding now."

"My sister is family business. Not right to drag hired hands into a family quarrel. I look after my own in my own way. You look like a man would understand that. What's this about anyway?"

"What it's about is Jack Mormons and you could be a gunman fixin' to join up with them. You don't know the Jacks been raidin' along the border of your state?"

"Sure I know. Bad news travels. It was in the papers. What've Jacks got to do with me? I told you I was looking for my sister."

Ike whinnied. "More likely his runaway wife, his so-called wife. Maybe his runaway grandmaw. He's lying, I tell you. What say we lay a rope acrost his back. That'll get him to talk in a hurry."

Jacob paid him no heed. "You say your sister's in Laketown. Why there? There's nothing there. A one-sided street, is all. How'd you get Laketown in your head?"

Lee said, "My sister mentioned this fella's father had a ranch around there. She was mad at me, said they could go there if I wanted to be mean about the marriage."

Jacob didn't frown, didn't do anything. "That can't be, mister. Ain't no ranches down that way. Some farms. It's farmin' country. Maybe your sister didn't get it right?"

"I don't know," Lee said. "She said a ranch."

"A chicken ranch," Ike sneered. "Five thousand head of Rhode Island Reds. Down there they got to wear snowshoes so's not to be hip-deep in chicken-shit.''

Jacob put an edge in his voice. "Hold your tongue, boy. What's your sister's fella's name?''

"He said he was Andy Jackson Belford. Came by my place with a busted leg. Said a rattler spooked his horse. I let him have a spare bunk with the hands till the leg mended. My sister Isabel fussed over him, swallowed his lying stories, finally decided she wanted to marry him. Not entirely her fault. It can get lonely for a woman up there.''

It could go any way, Lee knew. Finally it would be Jacob who made the decision.

"You tell it straight enough,'' Jacob said deliberately. "Or you could be a champeen liar. I got to think a minute.''

Ike cut in with, "He's lying. Every word he's sayin' is a lie. Look him over good. He's nothin' but a saddlebum gunman lookin' for work. That fine horse don't belong to him. He stole it.''

The stallion was grazing on sun-dried grass about fifty feet away. Lee called the animal and it raised its head and came to him. Lee scratched the animal between the ears and it whinnied, wanting to get back to grazing. A word from Lee sent it away.

"It's your animal sure enough,'' Jacob admitted. "That don't prove your story. You got anything to prove your name? Old bill of sale with your name on it? Tax akcessment? A piece of paper of that nature?''

Lee pretended to get mad, not mad enough to get shot for it, just mad enough to show he had some guts. "You know a law says a man has to prove who

64

he is? Carry documents and papers like they do back in Europe. My grandfather used to say a man had to carry them or get locked up. You sound like maybe you came from over there, mister. I'm surprised you'd want to start that horseshit in a free country."

Jacob squared his shoulders, looked pretty peeved. "I'm as good an American as you. Maybe better."

"Making a point," Lee said. "No offense intended."

Jacob relented. "None taken."

"Then what's the verdict? Listen to me a minute. You better listen, mister. I'm resting my animal, minding my own business, and you people come out of the bushes like bushwhackers and I'm supposed to tell my whole history. What gives you the God damned right?"

Jacob was wavering, wanting better proof that Lee's story was true. Ike wanted to kill him. Not too bright, Paxton just listened to what was being said.

Jacob said in his slow voice, "We got to be extra careful, don't you see? It's been hell and damnation down this way. Was a time a man could ride these roads and not a finger would be raised to him. Now that's all changed, with no man trustin' another without he knows he knows him real well. We got to stop ever'body comes into this country. You sound like a decent white man, only there's a big hole in your story. Which is, how come we didn't see your sister and this man you say she's with?"

Lee shrugged. "Maybe she lied to throw me off. They don't have to be in Laketown."

"You said they was," Ike cut in. "You said that."

Lee shook his head. "I said they could be in Lake-town, close to there. I meant to take a look, ask questions. Then look someplace else if I came up dry."

Ike gave out with his womanish laugh. "You wouldn't come up dry on a chicken ranch. Maybe your brother-in-law's old man raises hogs as well as chickens."

Keeping his temper, which was real enough, Lee spoke to Jacob. "You tell sonny here to watch his mouth or I'll shove that buffalo gun up his shithole. What kind of man are you, letting a man be bad-mouthed with your gun on him?"

Ike took a step forward before Jacob ordered him back with an angry shout. "Stay back, I told you. You want me to send you back to the farm? I'll do it you don't stop jawin' like the fool you are."

Jacob stared at Lee. "I think you better turn about and go back. Your sister, this man, wasn't through here. They'd a-been stopped. This road is watched night and day. I'd a'heard about it one way or another. We can't let you go on. Every gunman throws in with the Jacks is one more miserable thing we got to deal with. That's how it is, the situation bein' what it is. Go back."

Lee's voice was hard and flat. "Nobody turns me around on a public road. You want to kill me, then do it. You want to commit murder, here I stand. Tell you one thing, mister. I get out of this I'll put the law on you, swear out a complaint."

Jacob stood his ground; he was a tough old bird.

"Swear out all the complaints you like, Sheriff knows where to find me. Go on back."

Lee knew the other man was ready to yield. A lifetime of law and order still had its hold on him. "I won't do it," Lee said. "Only way to stop me is to kill me."

Ike said quickly, "Let me kill him. You're so holy-joe, you don't have to do it. I'll even do the buryin', you don't want to dirty your hands."

Jacob swung the old Springfield toward Ike. "You shoot this man I'll shoot you. The both of you get back in the brush. You got wax in your ears, or what?"

Jacob's voice rose to a shout and Ike slouched away, trailed by Paxton.

Jacob turned to Lee. "You still fixin' to set the law on me?" His attempt at a smile was pretty poor. "Don't mind it if you do. It's your right. Wish there was some law around here. Send the sheriff if you like. He'll come. It's safer than takin' on the Jacks."

"Forget the sheriff," Lee said, liking the old farmer. "You been having a bad time of it, I can see that."

Jacob said mournfully, "Not much we can do about it except watch the roads. We turn back some, but that's not to say they don't get past by cuttin' acrost country. Or they come down from north of Bear Lake and get into the mountains from there. Wild country north of the Lake."

Lee whistled for his horse. "I'll be going."

Jacob looked after him.

The sun was gone and the road sloped down and

he saw the scatter of lights that was Garden City, the dull shine of the big lake beyond it. He circled the town, not wanting another set-to with nervous, suspicious locals, and got back on the road a few miles south of it.

High up, the road followed the lake except where a rockface cut down into the water, and in places like that the road climbed higher, but where it was possible, the road stayed with the lake.

After a while the mountains fell back from the lake and there was a long, wide stretch of green country, good farming country, that ran dead ahead until it was lost in darkness. Far back from the road were the lights of a few farmhouses. They might be showing lights, he thought, but there were men with guns waiting in the dark. Men taking the first watch as soon as night closed in.

A dog barked and far away another dog replied. A pale moon drifted behind massed black clouds. No one challenged him and he made good traveling time.

Late that night, even with a clouded moon, there was enough light to see Laketown's one-sided street set high above the lake. The lake was fed by rivers and creeks and melted snow from the mountains, and the town was set high above the shore so spring floods wouldn't wash it away. Only one light showed, and if Laketown had some kind of law, that was probably it. Now came the part he didn't like, asking about John Spargo. There might be nothing to it if Spargo wasn't under suspicion—in this country a man didn't have to do much to be suspected of something—but he had to go down and ask, else he could be wandering for days. If trouble waited down there, he couldn't duck it by just asking where Eutaw Springs was. Clem Haney said there was nothing there but Spargo's trading post and saloon, Spargo himself, and maybe a woman and a hired man.

Smart thing—maybe—would be to go right to the town law, probably a marshal, and ask him; asking a bartender or storekeeper came to the same thing: the marshal would know in minutes and there would be questions as to what this stranger was doing in nervous country that got few strangers.

He decided to stay with the story of the flighty sister, because Jacob might be having second thoughts along about now. There was a chance he might follow along to see how the search was going.

But there was no trouble with the marshal, none at all. Old and stiff at sixty or so, most likely he'd been in the job for twenty-five or thirty years. Settled farming country, where there were no ranches, no sheepherding, seldom new serious trouble and Marshal Purdy Boykin—his name was on a faded sign beside the jail door—must have led a nice full uneventful life before the Jacks came. Trouble was the last thing he wanted with anybody.

Lee slept for four hours and was up early. Still too early to go down into town. From high up, screened by brush, he watched the town and the road coming from the north. Nobody came or went. On the far side of the lake, its flat gray surface reflecting the morning light, were the foothills, the bottom rung of the mountains that rose higher and higher to become fog-shrouded peaks. Now and then he caught a glimpse of the peaks through drifting clouds. It was cold where he was, but it was colder up there, where the snow stayed all year, and it looked like it was raining.

The town began to wake up. Cookstove smoke spiraled up from chimneys' a man came out onto a porch and pitched a basin of slop-water into the street; a blacksmith started pounding iron.

Lee led his horse down through the brush, then mounted up and rode into town. No one was in the street when he got there and knocked on the nail-studded door of the marshal's office. Down the street he heard a window being pushed up. He knocked again and a crabby voice told him to hold his hosses.

A dead-bolt scraped back and the door opened a crack. A lined gray face with gray stubble and wire-rimmed glasses on it looked out at him.

"What? What's it you want?" Marshal Purdy Boykin wanted to know. His voice quavered as if he expected to get a bullet for an answer.

Lee said, "Sorry to bother you so early, sir, but you're the man I got to see. My sister Isabel ran off with a man . . ."

The door opened most of the way and Lee saw an elderly man in a red flannel undershirt blinking at him. The hot smells of coffee and bacon drifted out.

"All right, come in," the marshal said grudgingly. "You say your sister run off with a man. Run off, wasn't abducted. Well now, how does that concern the law, here or anywhere? But take a chair, why don't you, and I'll listen to what you got to say."

The marshall put on a shirt and hat and sat behind

70

a battered oak desk. He buttoned two buttons of the shirt, but didn't tuck it into his pants. His tarnished badge was pinned to the left pocket of the shirt. The pot-bellied stove glowed red and the office was hot and smelly. Close to the stove, on a table with a sheet metal top, stood an old iron coffee pot and an equally old fry pan with bacon and sliced potatoes in it.

"Don't let me keep you from your breakfast," Lee said.

On the wall behind the desk a sheaf of yellowed reward posters hung from a spike. The poster in front had a police—or prison-made photograph—of some oldtimer wanted for stagecoach robbery. Lee couldn't make out the date of the crime, but it couldn't have been recent.

"I will eat, you don't mind," the marshal said. He filled a coffee cup and ate his bacon and fries straight from the pan. He had good manners and didn't talk with his mouth full. When he got through, he said, "You can't be from around there or I'd know you. Same would hold for your sister."

Lee said, "We're from up in Idaho. Man she ran off with is a rascal and I aim to take her back."

The marshal had little interest in flighty sisters, but he felt he had to ask, "What would bring them here? This town is as dead as Kelcy's Nuts. You saw for yourself what it's like. You sure you got the right place?"

Lee said he had the name of the town right. "I didn't expect to find them in town. This rascal that enticed my sister said he was going to talk business with a man named of John Spargo runs a trading post at a place called Eutaw Springs. Ever hear of it or him?"

"I know him," he said laconically. "Not well, just by sight. Though I haven't laid eyes on him in—I don't know—three or four months. Comes to town now and then he needs something he don't stock at the post."

At least he exists, Lee thought. Spargo was a living, breathing human being and not the invention of some law-dodger's whiskeyed imagination.

"Glad I didn't come this far for nothing," Lee said.

"Don't be too glad. Wasn't no report of a strange woman passin' through here with a man or by herself." Then the marshal checked himself, thinking maybe he was getting into something he wanted to stay out of. "Course they could have got to Spargo's place by a different route. Or they could have come through late at night. People do come through at night, not many, a few. I can't see every blessed thing that goes on, can I?"

"A man has to sleep seven or eight out of the twenty-four."

"Right you are, young man. As for getting to the Springs, it's a good piece from here, east of the lake, far back in the foothills. Sounds like a town or settlement, but it ain't. Just Young John Spargo, son of Old John Spargo, and his trading post and saloon. Old John started the business in the late Thirties before the trappers killed off the fur animals. Still some trapping can be done in the mountains—animals are coming back—but you got to work hard to do it. Trapping or no trapping, Young John, as

72

he's called, hangs on there. Must make some money with the post and saloon. Course Old John was pretty well fixed by the time he died."

"You been there?"

"Not in years," the marshal said. "Had to go lookin' for a man that murdered his wife—caught her layin' down for this brother—and took to the mountains. Couldn't find him, it was winter. Come spring we found him froze to death. That was one tough search, I can tell you. Course I was a lot younger. That was thirty years ago and ain't been to the Springs since then. But I ain't finished tellin' you how to get there. County road, a rough trail up the east side of the lake. You'll pass a few farms, then nothin' north of there. Up the middle of the lake it gets to be real bad country not fit for nothin'. Stay on the lake trail till you come to a worse trail goin' east into the hills."

"I'll find it," Lee said.

"You will after I finish tellin' you," the marshal said irritably. "Take that trail—there's about fifteen miles of it—and you'll come to Spargo's place smack-dab against the foot of the mountains. Can't miss it. It'll be lookin' right at you."

Lee thanked the marshal and started to leave. At the door he turned and said, "One last thing, marshal. On the way in here from the Logan road three farmers held rifles on me, wanted to know if I was on my way to join these Jack Mormons I been hearing about. I thought the Jacks were way west, in the mountains north of the Great Salt Lake. You got Jacks around here?"

The marshal drank coffee just to be doing something. "I don't know anything about no Jack Mormons," he said after straring into his cup for a good fifteen seconds. "They may be sheriff's business or territorial business or army business, but they ain't my business. I'm strictly a town marshal. If there are Jacks in these parts, and I'm not saying there are, they don't bother the town and they don't bother me. We like to have it like that."

So that was it. Laketown and the marshal had struck some sort of arrangement with the Jacks. Maybe it hadn't been talked, but a deal had been made. As long as the Jacks didn't burn them out, the townspeople and the marshal saw nothing, heard nothing. That was why the marshal hadn't asked questions, why nobody ran to gawk at him as he rode in.

"Close the door as you go," the marshal said before returning to the rest of the breakfast.

A few people looked at Lee as he mounted up. Nobody said "Mornin'," nobody did anything but look and quickly look away.

He had been saving the stallion for this last stretch of country. Now he urged the big animal to a gallop when he saw the first of the farms the marshal had mentioned. It was well back from the road, with trees planted north of it to break the wind. He guessed most of the farmers in the lake country were Mormons, but a few Gentiles would have moved in to farm since the government forced the Mormon leaders to open the Utah Territory to settlement. But Mormon or Gentile, the farmers along here, like the townspeople, had made some kind of deal with the Jacks, otherwise they would have been burned out. This wasn't so unusual when he thought about it. For one reason or another, badmen of one kind or another, often held back from raiding too close to home.

Two hours later he was clear of farm country. Here the trail got very bad and it had few signs of use. At times there were long stretches of rocky broken country between him and the lake. The trail dipped and climbed, but mostly it climbed, and the hilly country on that side of the lake was covered with sagebrush and greasewood and occasional patches of pinon pine.

The trail grew narrower as he went inland from the lake, and soon he was high up enough to be able to look back at the lake, though he couldn't see the western shore because fog had settled in during the late afternoon. There was fog on the lake and heavier, wetter fog up ahead and it began to rain, and when it showed no sign of letting up, he unrolled the slicker and put it on. The long loose skirts of the slicker kept his saddle and weapons dry. So close to the mountains, the rain was very cold, and it beat down as if it meant to go on forever.

He was hungry and to dull his hunger he smoked a cigar, shielding it against the rain, but it got wet anyway and he threw it away. He had hoped to make Spargo's place by nightfall, but there was no chance of that.

The trail continued to wind up into the hills. Later the rain turned to drizzle and that stopped and everything dripped. He knew he risked getting shot if he ventured into Spargo's place after dark, and it would be dark and late when he got there.

It was close to dark, and raining again, when he came to a fork in the trail with a signpost standing beside it. SPARGO was lettered on the flatboard, and that was all. This was where Spargo land began, or where the original John Spargo decided it began. Back in the Thirties, even before the Mormons came, there would be no one to dispute his claim, and now, more than fifty years later, this country had no more value than it had then. He still had fifteen miles to go, no use even trying to get there before morning, so he used the last of the light finding a place to spend the night: a deep, brushy hollow off the trail, with plenty of leftover rainwater for the stallion to drink and the sparse grass there would have to do.

He draped the rubber ground sheet over a bush and crawled in under it wearing the slicker. Building a fire, even a small one, was dangerous. Under the slicker his clothes were damp. Using the saddle as a pillow, he managed to sleep.

It rained several times, but he stayed dry enough.

FIVE

Next morning, in gray light, he was saddling the
stallion when two men rode by, heading for Spargo's
place or the mountains. They didn't see him because
the light was thick and there was some mist and he
was in good cover. The two riders were up high and
outlined against the eastern light. Not that he got
much of a look. They were riding hard and were gone
in seconds, but he figured he'd know them again.
Sure as hell they weren't farmers or lawmen or they
would have used more caution. They could be Jack
scouts returning from a mission; any renegade
outfit, any fighting outfit, was only as good as the
information it gathered. Yet, from the look of them,
he figured they were law-dodgers hoping to get the
nod from Spargo. Didn't much matter what they
were unless they were chasing him.

He gave them thirty minutes start, let them get
well ahead, before he mounted up and moved on.
Later he topped a ridge and there was a bowl shaped

valley below. He dismounted, climbed up the safe side of a big rock, and used binoculars to look for places where he might be bushwhacked. If they were waiting, he didn't spot them.

He rode with the Winchester in one hand, the reins in the other. The stallion was well trained, but horses were just plain dumb no matter how many tricks they learned, and a sudden burst of gunfire could throw the animal into a blind panic that could kill or cripple both of them.

He eased his way down the slope and started across. Down below floodwater covered the trail and he walked the stallion through it, waiting for rifles to crack. But nothing happened and halfway across the trail came out of the water and it began to climb and there were plenty of places where they could be stretched out with their rifles pointing at him. Still nothing happened.

Out of the little valley, past places where an ambush could hardly fail if they knew their business, he decided they had nothing to do with him. Just the same, experienced ambushers sometimes picked unlikely places, so now and then he reined in and scouted the country ahead before he went on. The sign he picked up from the trail told him they were still traveling fast.

Spargo's place, when he finally saw it, was located at the base of a high, smooth rockface that sloped out at the top to make an overhang that protected it from the wind and weather. The main building looked like three log cabins joined together many years in the past, and it was tarred against damp rot. There were two outbuildings and a big, solid stable, and a crapper stood back in the pines. Pines grew in close except where they had been cleared in front to make a big wagonyard. The spring, circled by willows, was at the base of the cliff. It bubbled up at the bottom of the cliff and the overflow created a small pool that in turn spilled over and was lost in sandy soil. A big weathered sign above the main building stated: JOHN SPARGO & SON/SALOON & TRADING POST/FURS BOUGHT OR TRADED/SUPPLIES SOLD.

Lee didn't spot a lookout, but he knew one was there. One of the outbuildings faced the trail and the man sitting in shadow stood up and gave a shout that brought two men hurrying from the main building. The lookout didn't show himself, stayed where he was. Lee knew he'd be shot out of the saddle if he did anything.

One of the men who faced him was short and barrel-chested and wore a thick untrimmed beard. Lee figured that was Spargo. He was dressed in rusty black, coat and trousers, and he wore a round-crowned, preacherish hat and a dirty white shirt without a collar. He had a heavy pistol in a plain black holster and he had his hand on the butt. The other man, old and stooped and dressed in ragged buckskins, carried an old 15-shot Henry rifle, nicked and scratched by hard use, but otherwise well kept. Like Spargo, he was bearded, but his beard was far from virile and hung down from his emaciated face in dirty, lifeless strands. Lee could hear his mumbling: a loony.

Behind the two men, framed in the doorway, was a young girl with cropped hair, wool shirt and worn

Levis. Lee couldn't get a good look at her. He waited while Spargo looked him over. He took his time, then said, "Who are you, mister, and what brings you here?"

Coming from his beer keg chest his voice sounded as a bear might sound if a bear could talk. The matted black beard grew so high on his face that it looked like he was wearing a mask.

"I'm looking for John Spargo," Lee answered. "I have business with him."

"You're looking at him," Spargo said. "What do you think your business is? Say it short and sweet."

"Word's out you're looking for men. I want to hire out my gun to the Jacks. You said keep it short."

The girl had moved forward in the doorway. She had short brown hair, a heart-shaped face, copper-studded, and she wasn't as young as he'd first thought. The rubber-handled Colt .38, the Officer's Model with the swing-out cylinder, looked too big for her, even when belted high as it was.

"Never heard of them," Spargo growled. His rumbling voice carried without effort.

The old man gave a crazy laugh.

Spargo said, "I run a saloon and trading post and nothing but. Still you're here so come on in so we can talk. Just leave the animal, it'll be looked after."

The girl stepped aside to let them in. She was mad about something or else her face had a naturally sour look. Spargo gestured for Lee to go first and he went into a big, wide, low-ceilinged, smoky room with a rough plank bar—boards laid across very old whiskey barrels—and a scatter of tables and chairs.

The two men Lee had seen on the trail that

morning now sat at a table with bottles and glasses in front of them. They looked at him with no particular interest. Both were in their middle-thirties, wore range clothes, cartridge-studded gun-belts, and looked like the law-dodgers they were. A third man not with the other two stood in the center of the room with his hand on his beltgun. Spargo told him to sit down and he went back to his table and picked up his glass with his left hand, still looking at Lee.

Spargo jerked his thumb toward a table at the end of the bar, set well away from the others. He wasn't friendly or unfriendly; his flat, rumbling voice didn't give anything away, and there was nothing particularly violent about him. But Lee knew that he was about as dangerous as a man can get.

"We'll be more private here," he rumbled.

The old man sat at one of the tables with the brass-framed old rifle across his lap. The girl stood by the door with her hip stuck, her hand resting on the butt of the high-holstered .38. One of the men Lee knew from the trail took out a deck of greasy cards and began to deal to himself. Lee wondered if Clem Haney had been here and where he was now. Only two things were possible: he was buried deep or in the mountains with the Jacks.

Spargo put a bottle and glass on the table and sat down. "How'd you hear about this place?" He watched as Lee poured a trickle of whiskey. He wants to see if I drink too much, Lee decided.

Spargo wore brass shirt studs instead of buttons and he hadn't washed himself or his shirt in a dog's age. "Keep it simple," he advised Lee.

"I'll do that," Lee said.

"Wait." Spargo turned as the card dealer threw the cards down, lurched over to the girl and whispered something. There was a slap and a hard push and the law-dodger's spurs dug into the floor and he crashed down on his back. He was red-faced and cursing and reaching for his gun when the girl's gun came out fast and already cocked.

"Try it," she said.

The old man cackled and Spargo slapped the table with the flat of his hand. "Quit it!" he bellowed. "You there, card shuffler, pick yourself up and go back where you was. Do it now."

The floored badman went back to his table, slopped whiskey into his glass, tossed it off. His partner leaned across the table and tugged at his shirt sleeve.

"You done good, Missy," the old man said to the girl.

It got quiet again and Spargo said to Lee, "You was about to say how you heard of this place. Keep it short now."

Lee said, "An army deserter told me. Happened in a saloon in Leadville, Colorado."

Spargo's face registered nothing. "He just up and told you he was a deserter. You just met the man, so you say, and all the same he told you he was on the run. Why would he do that?"

Lee knew Spargo was just stringing him out. No way any of it could be checked. Spargo watched his face intently, as if he thought he could read the truth there.

"He was footless drunk," Lee went on. "Said he

82

was on the run from Fort Sherman and knew there was a place he could hide and never be found and make money at the same time. Being hunted myself, I asked where this place was. He got crafty and winked and changed the conversation. I figures he was busting to tell me—tell somebody—and when I said it didn't matter a damn he still kept silent, but after more whiskey he got loud and cantankerous. Who the hell was I to doubt his word, and so forth? Then he came right out and said he was going north to join the Jack Mormons.''

Lee couldn't see much of Spargo's dark eyes, but he sensed resentment. ''They don't like to be called that, mister.'' There was a pause. ''That's what I hear. Go on.''

''I told this drunk I never heard of these Mormons —who were they? He told me in dribs and drabs, holding things and then letting them out the drunker he got. A mishmash of a story, but he was so convinced he got me convinced. I asked him how he planned to join these people? If they were raiding and killing and all the rest of it, why would they trust a stranger? A few drinks later he told me about this place.''

Spargo said, ''He mention me by name?''

''No. That he absolutely couldn't tell me. A big secret. You know how drunks are. I figured he didn't know. But he did say there was a Mormon agent in Eutaw Springs, Utah, who passed on everybody that wanted to join up. Guess that would be you, Mr. Spargo.''

''You guess wrong. This deserter, he say how he heard of Eutaw Springs?''

"Not in so many words. I didn't press it too hard or he would've got huffy about it. Mostly he talked like he knew things other people didn't know. Conclusion I came to was he just heard rumors he wanted to believe."

Spargo stared at Lee. "And you come all this way on the word of a loudmouth drunk?"

"I figured there might be some truth to the story. It was worth taking a chance. What did I have to lose? I needed a place where I could lay low for a while."

Still staring, Spargo said. "What you do to make the law so determined?" He scratched this thick of beard every time he asked a question. "Shoot the Governor of Colorado?"

Lee wondered why Spargo was hedging so much. He knew he'd be killed, anyway they'd try, if his story sounded fishy. Maybe Spargo was one of those men who can't say anything straight.

Lee said, "I killed two men while I was stealing horses belonged to the Circle X in West Texas. A big outfit. One of them was the owner's son. Man has political pull so the law's working harder than usual."

Spargo scratched his dirty beard. "You say the law knows you come north?"

"No. I rode clear across Kansas with nobody following along. On the prairie you know if somebody is behind unless they're an Indian tracker. I think I'm in the clear for now."

Spargo growled, "I wouldn't like it if the Texas law, any law, followed you here. You say not, but I don't know that. We'll let that go for now. A word of caution: don't get cocky. Here your guarantees don't mean a thing.''

Spargo scratched his beard. ''You have to kill those two men? Or was you just havin' fun?''

''They came at me from nowhere, in the dark. There was enough light for them to see me. I shot the both of them, then got in close and shot them on the ground.''

''You don't look like a killer. Which don't mean you ain't killed a man or two. There's a difference though.''

''Never claimed to be a killer,'' Lee said. ''They could've killed or wounded me, brought me down, got me hung. What do you think, Mr. Spargo?''

''About you?'' Spargo stroked his beard when he wasn't scratching it. Messing with his beard was what fist-pounding and arm-waving were to preachers and politicians. It kept him busy all the time. ''I don't know what I think about you. Haven't made up my mind.''

Lee knocked over his chair getting up. He threw a silver dollar on the table. ''I'll be on my way. Looks like I came here for nothing.''

Spargo didn't move. ''You ain't going no place, sonny. Sit down and keep your temper.''

Lee remained standing. Here was where he'd find out for sure. ''Who's to stop me?''

''Me, I'll stop you. Me and him—and her.'' He meant the old man and the girl. ''Don't let his age fool you. A word from me and he'll put five bullets in you so fast you won't even know you're dying. Sit down. I'll decide when I'm good and ready.''

Lee sat down. ''How long do I wait?''

"Didn't I just tell you? You wasn't invited here or drug here. You come on your own free will. You're here and here you stay till I decide. Getting me mad won't help your case. Clear?"

"As day," Lee said.

"Good." Spargo stood up. "I like men that see the sense of things when they're explained. Now sir, we got a few rules here has to be followed. No wandering off, might get lost. No mixing in with the other men. Keep your distance. Like for instance you wouldn't want to get friendly with a man turned out to be a wrong 'un. No card playing for fear of fights and gunplay. The man that pulls a gun in here, less he's pushed, will get shot. Had two men had a gun dispute a while back. Now they're not here."

"You'll have no trouble with me, Mr. Spargo."

"I knew you was a right-thinkin' man." Spargo lowered his voice even more. "That man over there that bothered the girl. Now that was a fool thing to do, cause it's obvious she waint no whore. That man for what he done is down in my black book and as for yourself don't think sweet-talkin' will work where grabbin' didn't. Try that and you'll have me after you not to mention the old man. His granddaughter there is the apple of his eye."

Lee glanced at the girl and she glared back at him. "I'm not that dumb. It wouldn't be worth it."

"It would if you got away with it." Spargo never smiled. "You're tired and want to sleep, bunks are in there." He nodded to a door. "Want food, the girl will fix it for you. We got beef and venison and smoked ham. Only I got to tell you everythin' cost

86

more than you'd pay in a reg'lar restaurant."

"You want to see green?" Lee asked. "I got about a hundred dollars."

Spargo glanced at Lee's money. "That should cover it. You didn't have to say how much. I'd a-trusted you for it."

Sure you would, Lee thought. I have a fine stallion and a saddle that cost two hundred dollars.

"Everything here is for sale except the girl," Spargo said. "But should Missy take a fancy to you, well then that's her business. But put it out of your mind, it ain't goin' to happen. If you don't want to bunk in with the other men and listen to them snoring, there's some cubicles with doors so a man can sleep in peace. Good value for the money."

"Suits me," Lee agreed. "Can you have the girl fry me up a steak and cook a pot of coffee. What number cubicle?"

"Only three cubicles, ain't got numbers, take your pick. Grub'll be ready in a minute. You go ahead."

Spargo spoke to the girl called Missy and she went into the lean-to kitchen built into the side of the house. In there she slammed things around. Lee waited while coffee and steak smells came out of the kitchen.

The law-dodger who'd been shamed by the girl was putting away liquor at a good rate. Some of the whiskey slopped on the table, dripped to the floor. The sullen outlaw's partner kept on trying to settle him down, but it didn't do any good because now he wanted to beat up the girl more than he wanted to poke her. He scowled at the old man, then at the kitchen, and kept drinking. Spargo had gone into the other side of the building, probably where the supplies were stored. That law-dodger's going to get himself killed, Lee decided. And his partner, if he butts in, is going to share the same grave.

The girl strode across the room with the food tray. Her face was flushed and sweat beaded her upper lip. It looked like she was hopping mad all the time. She slammed down the coffee pot and steak platter.

"You want sugar for the coffee?" She threw out the question like a challenge.

Lee shook his head. "How much?"

That made her angrier. "You settle with Spargo. I'm not waitress."

Lee took the whiskey and the food into one of the so-called cubicles. A narrow space had been partioned off against the back wall of the bunk room. Two cubicles had rickety doors and the third hidey-hole he looked at wasn't as beat-up as the others. It was about the size of a jail cell in a mean jail. The bunk room smelled bad, the cubicles a little less so. No table, no chair, nothing but a plank bed with a thin mattress and a torn blanket. It would do.

He propped himself against the wall and started on the steak. He was reaching down to take the coffee pot off the floor when there was a knock. He eased his gun in its holster and called out, "Come in."

It was the girl and she held out tin salt and pepper shakers. "You forgot these," she said. "I salted and peppered the meat. Some people like it saltier."

"It's fine as it is." It wasn't all right, it was too God damned salty, but he didn't say that. He noticed the she closed the door when she came in.

She stood there doing nothing. Her face was sun and wind burned and her light eyes were even lighter against the reddish tone of her skin. A small, good-looking woman about thirty, or a few years past it. The rough life had aged and lined her a bit, but she would have been welcome in any man's bed. Her shirt was too big for her, but her breasts filled it out.

She still hadn't said anything.

Lee said, "Maybe I could use more salt and pepper," and felt like a fool after he said it. Soon he'd be saying things such as "Nice weather for this time of year."

She came close enough to hand him the shakers. Their hands touched and she drew back, but didn't leave. She stood with one hip thrust forward, something she did without thinking, and he felt a stirring in his pants. He crossed his legs but she was on to him.

She said, "Spargo says you call yourself Ben Trask."

"It's my true name. What's yours?"

"Missy. Missy Landry. It's French. That's my grandfather out there. His grandfather came from France. You ever been to France."

"Never have. How about you?"

It was the wrong thing to say. She flared up. "You know God damned well I never been to France. Who are you to poke fun at me?"

"Nobody. I wasn't poking fun."

"I been to Salt Lake though. My grandmother was born there and wanted to see it before she died. We spent ten days there and she died there. I came back here and been here ever since. You ever been to

Salt Lake?"

"Never got the chance," Lee said.

"At least that's one place you haven't been," she said.

The steak was terrible with even more salt added to it. "Lots of places I ain't been to."

"My grandmother taught me to never say 'ain't.' It's not good English. My grandmother could read from beginning to end, didn't have to puzzle out the words."

Lee drank some coffee, which wasn't any better than the steak. "What happened to your mother and father? Just asking?"

"You can ask," she said. "They left and never came back. That was when I was eight. Maybe they died or maybe they didn't want me. My grandmother raised me, taught me to read. She's been dead for sixteen years."

"You like it here?"

She didn't like the question and her sudden, fierce look said so. Lee noticed that her hand always came to rest on the butt of her gun when she got mad, he way of telling the world that she wasn't going to take any shit from anybody.

Lee decided the coffee wasn't as bad as the steak. The man who got this girl was going to get a rotten cook. "You don't have to tell me a thing," he said.

She frowned at him. "I've got nothing to hide. I wouldn't mind leaving here. Sparago knows that. Years ago, when I was a kid, he thought we should get married. I said no and he dropped it. Now he's getting old and has settled into his own rut. Same with me. My grandfather can't live forever and when he dies I'll have to leave. It's leave or stay here for the rest of my life. Spargo says he'll leave me his money if I stay."

Lee shrugged. "You'll think of something."

"I'm thinking about Spargo's money," she went on. "Grandfather says he has some put away and I'll have that. How much he won't say. I'd leave now if he'd go with me. Except he won't. Nothing could drag him away from these mountains. He was here before Spargo's father. A long time. Says he's the last of the mountain men. I guess he is. All the others are dead. He knows these mountains up and down, backward and forward."

The old man must be the guide, Lee thought. Spargo sizes up the outlaws and the old man takes them in if they pass the test. How the girl fitted in he had no way of knowing. But it was likely, the old man being so old, that she would go along too.

He wondered if she had ever been with a man. Many men must have tried, but that gun on her hip and the old man always around, she might still be a virgin. Lee didn't know if he'd ever had a rassle with a virgin. They said you could tell, but he wasn't so sure about that.

Looking at her and feeling like it, he was ready to risk a brief ride in the hay. Spargo said what Missy did was her business. He was so matter of fact about it that he probably didn't care. But you never knew. There was the 15-shot Henry to think about. The hell with the old man and his ancient Henry. You took your chances when you wanted something badly enough.

But nothing happened.

"Mr. Trask . . . Ben," she said with some hesitation. "I think you like me because you have a bone in your pants for me. I'm used to rough talk, so don't mind me. You'd like to do it with me and I with you. But not here, not with those men out there. Later, maybe. Would you like to poke me when I'm more prepared for it?"

Did she mean some night on the mountain? It would be better in a bed, but he'd take it any way he could get it.

"I'd like that very much," he said honestly. He didn't ask what she meant by "later." He didn't ask because he knew she was saying things she'd never said to any man. He thought he knew. And of course he could be as wrong about her as the lunatic up in Bridger County who jumped off a bluff was about his homemade wings.

"I'll be going now," she said.

Right after she left he heard somebody guffawing in the saloon. The laughter was loud and forced and ill-natured. The ugly tone was unmistakable even coming as it was from a distance. Then he heard Spargo's rumbling voice and it got quiet. A door slammed.

Lee went out and Spargo and Missy weren't there, then he spotted them through the windows, walking away from the house. They went out of sight. Lee turned to go back to his hidey-hole.

"Jackass braying woke up, did it?" the old man asked in his toothless, crazy voice. His own laugh was more of a wheez. He laughed until tears ran out of his faded blue eyes. "Next time the jackass does that throw him a fork of hay."

Lee ignored him, turned to go. Behind the woman-shamed drunk outlaw said, "The old man's got a real big mouth, but you got nothin' a-tall to say. Now why is that? It ain't sociable that you won't let on how she is. Is she a good poke or just fair to middlin'? Is she loose or is she tight, so on and so forth?"

He sounded very drunk and Lee wanted no truck with him. He half-turned, not enough to get back-shot. He knew the drunk was going to push it no matter what he did or said. The third man, sitting by himself, took his bottle and glass and went into the bunk room. No sign of Spargo or the girl: they are having a long confab.

The first hard push came. "How was she?" the drunk said. "Does she suck cocks? Matter of interest, y'unnerstan'."

"What's that you say?" The 15-shot Henry came up off the table. The old man had been mumbling. Now he was silent. "You talkin' about my grand-daughter, you dumb jackass son of a poxy hoor. I'm goin' to stop your mouth for good."

The drunk was too drunk to be afraid of the rifle. Or else he thought the old man wouldn't shoot without Spargo's say-so. That's what he thought. He said, "You ain't goin' to kill nobody. You ain't goin' to risk your meal ticket killin' without orders."

"I'll be told quick enough. You wait." The old man backed out holding the rifle. "Young John comes back you'll whistle a different tune. Draggin' my little girl's name in the shit bucket."

The door slammed and Lee was left with the two outlaws. Their gun-rigs marked them for gunslingers and he didn't doubt they were fast enough. He knew the drunk would get to it in a minute. No way to head it off, no way to duck it. Spargo, unless he happened to be close-by, wouldn't get there in time to stop it.

The drunk's partner said something, but the drunk stood up anyway and was quick enough for a man with half a bottle in him. "I ask you is the women a good poke. You don't say nothin'. You think you got a crotch claim on the woman. Like hell! You don't look like you could poke your mother!"

Lee just looked at him. The other man got up and moved back from the table. Lee knew he was fixing to knock over the table and use it as a shield if this turned into a gun battle. Saloon fights often did. The drunk grinned when he heard his partner move.

"You can stay out of this," Lee said.

"Got to side my brother," the other man said, sounding tired as if he'd backed his loudmouth brother in too many stupid fights.

Outside there was a yell and the drunk went for his gun. It came out fast with the hammer going back when Lee drew and shot the drunk's brother in the chest. He was sober so he got it first. He took the bullet through the lung and still managed to pull his gun before he staggered and fell forward on his face. His gun fired into the floor. The drunk got off a shot and missed. Lee shot him twice while he was still earing back the hammer for a second shot. He sagged and folded and fell. On the floor his dying brother was still clawing for his gun. Lee took aim and shot both men in the head. Spargo came bulling through the door with his gun in his hand.

Lee stayed where he was. Spargo came across the room with the old man behind him. The girl had her .38 drawn. Spargo said, "Drop it, mister."

Lee held his Colt dangle by his side. "Don't crowd me, Spargo. They asked for it and they got it. That right, Mr. Landry?"

"Mr. Landry!" The old man was startled. "*Mister* Landry! He's tellin' the truth, Young John. They come down hard on this fella, the drunkard did. Forced him to a fight."

Spargo let down the hammer and holstered his gun. So did the girl. The old man stooped over the bodies, stepping in blood. He scuffed his blood-wet boots in the sawdust.

"Couldn't be deader," he announced.

"You and Lem get rid of them," Spargo told the old man. "Trask, you sit down."

Lee sat at Spargo's table by the end of the bar. Spargo got coffee from the kitchen, asked Lee if he wanted whiskey.

"Had enough," Lee said.

"That man you killed had too much. I watched the whole thing through the window. Could have stopped it, but wanted to make sure if you could handle it. I'd already decided to get rid of them, send them back. The quiet one had somethin' to him, but the drunkard—was his brother—would have got him into trouble. Did get him into trouble one last time."

"Then you know I didn't start it?"

"The old man told me. I saw it for myself."

"Does that mean I'm all right with you?"

"I guess so," Spargo said. "But from here on in, when I tell you to do somethin' you do it. I told you to shake the gun and you didn't."

"I thought you were fixing to kill me," Lee said. "I thought I'd kill you while you were killing me."

Spargo waved the matter aside. "Probably I'd have done the same. Forget it. There's more important things to talk about. Missy and the old man will take you in. It's a long, hard journey and some of it is walkin'. Expect some blisters, my friend. A bit late in the season for real heavy snow, but nature don't run like a train schedule. You could get a light fall, you could get ten feet. Don't start bellyaching if there's snow four feet over your head."

"I'll manage," Lee said.

Spargo frowned. "Don't interrupt. And don't downgrade the old man and the girl. They can go places you wouldn't think possible. In the mountains the old man especially is like a goat. Go all day, go all night if he has to. Listen hard to what I'm going to tell you next. Which is you can't join the Jacks and then decide the life doesn't suit you and you want to go home. Can't be done. You know too much by then. No exceptions. Nobody leaves— ever."

"I hear you," Lee said.

"Oh sure. It's easy to say yes," Spargo said. "Easy to say yes here in a room with a good steak under your belt and prob'ly feelin' cocky cause you just dropped two men. I know you're feelin'. Fine with me, how you feel. Here you ride out anytime as long as you pay me for room and board. We shake hands and it's been nice to make you acquaintance.

96

With the Jacks that don't work. Go against orders and it's the end of you. They tell you to kill your brother you've got to do it. They're like an army in there. Only one general, everybody else is soldiers. You got any doubts, now's the time to lay them on the table."

"No doubts," Lee told him. "I'm ready to go any time."

"All right then," Spargo said. "You leave first thing in the morning. You know what I like about you, mister? You don't ask too many questions. Most men in your place would've."

More probing: Spargo never stopped. "Would you have answered them?"

"Hell no, not hard questions. I don't know. Could be you'll like it in there. Good food, good accomodations, no shortage of women. Only don't go jumpin' women you ain't supposed to. They hang you for that."

Under the cliff it got darker faster than out in the open, and the room was full of shadows when Spargo got up to light a brass lamp that stood on a shelf behind the bar. The smell of gunsmoke remained and so did the smell of death.

"Don't be expectin' the old man or the girl," Spargo said. "They got their own cabin. I sleep in there." That was the supply part of the building. "Me and them will be taking turns on the watch during the night. You got enough liquor in there? Be sure now. I wouldn't want you stumblin' about in the dark. Use the chamberpot you get the call of nature. Don't go outside."

"I get your meaning," Lee said.

"Sure you do," Spargo said. "Now I would think this is a good time for you to go to bed."

Spargo followed Lee into the bunk room where the lone man lay snoring. He didn't just blow out the light there, he took it with him.

Lee took off his boots and stretched out on the bed. Except for Spargo's light the house was in darkness.

SIX

They started into the mountains after Missy cooked a big breakfast—hamsteaks, pancakes, biscuits, canned peaches, coffee—that the old man said would have to last all day. Cooking on the trail was for slowpokes; there wasn't time for eating till night came.

The early morning wind whipped against the log buildings. At that gray hour it had a lonesome sound. Lee and the old man were eating when Spargo came in from the last watch. Missy sat down to her own breakfast after giving Spargo his.

"Eat your fill, young fella," the old man advised Lee. "Then put all you can on top of that. Man's got to eat like an animal in the mountains. Pity humans can't store up food like bears. Bears'll eat till they're larded with fat. That'd make life a lot easier in the mountains when the tempertoor gets down there. Only thing wrong with it: a man'd get so fat he couldn't hardly move."

"Eat your breakfast, Grampa," Missy said.

The old man, who hadn't been eating, now shoveled in the greasy food as fast as he could swallow. He had no teeth to chew anything, so he cut everything into small pieces and swallowed without chewing. His faded eyes were bright with the thought of going into the mountains. His thin body quivered with a taut wire.

Spargo stomped his feet on the floor, making the dishes rattle.

"Cold can't be that bad, Young John," the old man said. "What you got to worry about? You'll be dozing by the stove whilst we're out there in the mountains freezin' our hind-ends off."

Spargo forked more ham onto his plate. "You wouldn't stay behind if you could."

The old man didn't like the way the ham was disappearing and he speared three pieces for himself. The platter was just about cleared, but Lee didn't want any more. Missy just picked at her food, something that didn't escape Spargo's attention. But he said nothing.

"You never said a truer word, Young John," the old man said. "Up there in the high country it's like I'm a young man again. There ain't no place like it in the whole God damned world. You can have your feather beds and potbelly stoves and all the rest of it and good luck to you. It's me for the mountains an' the free life."

Spargo grunted.

Lee was sure the old man wouldn't have asked the question if he hadn't been so excited. It came out before he knew it. "That other fella ain't comin' with us?"

Spargo gave the old man a hard stare. "No, he ain't. Changed his mind, is goin' back where he come from."

Lee didn't miss the way Spargo lowered his voice after he glanced at the bunk room door. The man had been snoring in a whiskey sleep when Lee came out to breakfast. So long stranger, he thought. Soon you'll be sleeping sounder that you are now. He guessed Spargo would kill the man in his sleep.

Spargo's cold stare had silenced the old man and killed his appetite. But that didn't last more than a few minutes and he was back to gabbing about the high country while he gummed the last of the biscuits.

"Best you be off," Spargo said abruptly, still staring at the old man. He's wondering how much longer he can trust him, Lee thought. Spargo was a cold-hearted son of a bitch and it would be a pleasure as well as a public service to kill him. That was just a thought. Spargo wasn't important. He was just a go-between, a man who leeched off others and made money doing it, but by himself he was nothing much. If the Jacks were killed or scattered, he would find something else to do. But whatever it was, it was sure to be dirty and cruel.

The last thing he said to Lee was, "Sure you wouldn't rather pay your board bill with that shotgun? I'll give you back your money and a little extra."

"No thanks," Lee said.

Spargo looked at him from behind his tangle of coarse black beard. "Mister, I could take it if I liked. This is my place and you're beholden to me. You don't know how beholden. I could take it any time I took a notion to. What do you think of that?"

The old man and Missy were mounted up. It wasn't light yet and the wind was brutal. The pack mule brayed in complaint, pulling on the lead that Missy held.

"I think you couldn't," Lee said, then wheeled his horse to follow the old man who was starting on his own. Missy and the mule brought up the rear. Spargo shouted something, but it was lost in the wind.

They followed the red-brown cliff for most of a mile and the old man turned in his saddle and pointed to a break in the rock. It didn't look like more than a wide fissure, but when Lee got closer he saw that it went clear through the rock. At first it was near dark in there, but then it began to widen and the light got better and they began to climb. It was a hard climb until they got to the top. They had come up through the inside of the cliff using a sort of natural stairway. Lee had never seen anything like it before. The cliff fell away by stages from the top and instead of going up they went down through scrub oak and blackthorn bush and the trail showed some signs of recent use. My horses have been through here, Lee thought, but it was no wonder they hadn't been able to take the whole herd. It could be done, of course, if they took the time to do it, but these were men always mindful that to be

102

trapped too far from their stronghold was to be destroyed.

Now they were on a long narrow plateau seamed and riven by ravines and gullies. It stretched for miles and far away, past the end of it, the mountains rose up, and past those mountains were higher mountains. They were climbing step by step, though there were long stretches where the trail made a sharp descent. But inevitably it climbed again and kept climbing and after five hours travel the mountains Lee saw from the top of the cliff appeared to be no closer. He knew that was because he had never been here before; nothing up here was familiar; there were no points of reference. On the other hand, the old man—knowing these mountains—could judge distance within a few miles, that is, if he needed to judge it at all.

They rode in silence except for the old man's singing. It looked like he knew only one song and he sang the first two lines over and over: *My father was a grizzly bear/My mother was a beaver*. The first two lines were all he remembered or else he didn't like the rest of the song.

Canada geese flew over, high up, and the old man yelled and waved at them. Then he went back to singing, but now the first two lines were: *My mother was a mourning dove/My father was a gander*. His papery old voice was lost in the vast spaces of mountain and sky.

Lee wondered what part, if any, the old man and Missy had in the killing of the men Spargo rejected for Jack membership. It was hard to think of Missy as a killer, but the old man was half-savage in spite of his dead wife's book-reading, and killing would come easy to him. Whatever it was, they were there when the killings took place, and not much else mattered.

In the late afternoon, when the sky was rolling with dark clouds, Missy's horse stepped in a hole and she lost her hold on the mule. The mule ran kicking and braying through the brush, ripping the pack and scattering supplies and bedding over a wide area. This happened a few miles from the end of the plateau.

"Oh you devil, you God damned wicked devil!" the old man howled. I'm a-goin' to kill you, shoot you, hang you, cut out your black heart and eat it. Of all the miserable, cantankerous, ornery dumbbastard craytures God put on this earth!"

The mule brayed from five hundred yards away, defying the old man, not wanting to be lost or abandoned, but showing his independence.

"Stay back," the old man warned. "I'll go argue with the rotten, evil son of satan. I think this time he's a-goin' to get it. I think at last his hour has come."

They watched from a distance while the old man edged in cautiously to where the mule was kicking up dirt and gravel. This was a scene that had been played many times before, and so the mule bolted and stopped, bolted and stopped, and the old man kept coming, holding the wide loop of the rope down by his side. He hid it from the mule though the mule knew it was there. The mule watched the old man out of the corner of his eye and didn't try for another short run until the rope swung out and dropped around its neck and was jerked tight. Then it ran the length of the rope and stopped.

"Ain't he a beauty though," the old man said when he came back leading the mule. The mule brayed, showing long, yellow teeth. "If there's a more treacherous, unreliable crayture in the Utah Territory I'd like to see it. You know why I'll never see such a beast! 'Cause it don't exist, nor never has." He continued his love song to the mule while Lee and Missy dismounted and started to gather up what they could find of the scattered supplies.

Night was closing in fast. Thunder clouds were rolling down from the north and the old man said they should leave what they couldn't find handily. Now that damage had been inflicted, the mule stood still while the old man roped and balanced the pack. They got going again.

Now Missy rode beside Lee, something she hadn't done earlier, with the villainous mule training behind. Missy had got over her shyness, or whatever it was that was eating on her, and she talked a blue streak.

"We lost the flour," she said. "But it's no use telling grandfather to get a mule that's not so wicked. I think he'd get rid of me before he'd get rid of the mule. He's a little tetched as you must have noticed by now. Sometimes he thinks that wicked mule is the same wicked mule he had fifty years ago. Claims it died and come back to earth and because it died once and came back it can't die again. He says he's going to do the same thing when he dies."

"They'll make an interesting pair," Lee said.

She gave him a stingy smile, like a miser

compelled to part with a nickel. "I guess you blame me for losing the flour. What I mean is, if you like pancakes now you can't have them. It follows that you can't have pancakes without flour."

Lee wondered if the entire Landry family might not be tetched, but if so, she wore it better than the old man. For one thing she was prettier.

"The hell with the flour," he said. "Only thing I wouldn't like as if he lost the coffee."

"The mule didn't lose the flour, I lost the flour. If I hadn't lost my hold it wouldn't have happened. You can't blame the mule. Grandpa wouldn't like you blamin' the mule. A mule is just a mule and can't help being what he is."

The storm hadn't broken yet and maybe it would pass over and break further to the west. But it was dark and cold and the wind had a real bite to it.

"He can't hear me," Lee said, "and neither can the mule." He liked mules because they were such brazen bastards. They were smarter than any horse that ever lived. Just the same, a conversation about mules had its limits. "Can we get off mules for a while?"

She was as bad-tempered as the mule. "We don't have to talk at all if that's what you want." Her face was flushed and it wasn't from the snap of the evening wind. "Would you like that? You won't talk, I won't talk. You can talk but I won't answer."

But a few minutes later she said, "Why does a man like you want to join the Jacks? If the law is after you, why don't you go to Canada or South America? Or Australia? Go to San Francisco and get on a ship."

"Using what for money?"

She had an answer for everything. "You could work as a sailor. Or you could go to the South Seas and become a slave trader. There is a great demand for slave labor in the plantations of the South Sea Islands. *The Century Encylopedia* says many men are in that business."

Lee said, "I don't know what I'm much in favor of slavery."

"Then what about diving for pearls? You wouldn't have to dive for them yourself. You hire the natives and they dive for them. They bring them up and give them to you. A handful of pearls or just one big pearl and your fortune is made. Exporting copra, dried coconut meat, is something else you could try."

"Wouldn't work," Lee said. "I got absolutely no head for business. I couldn't give away ten dollar bills on a street corner."

"You're just saying that so you won't have to try," Missy said, and he thought it was strange, or maybe not so strange, to be getting the same sort of bullshit from her that he used to get from Maggie. Women weren't too different after all.

"Right now I'm trying to keep from getting hung," he said, wondering where in hell they were going to make camp for the night.

Without being asked, the old man answered the question. He turned in his saddle and said, "We'll be there in a minute."

The minute stretched out to more than an hour, but the night camp was worth waiting for: a deep, sandy-floored ravine out of the wind, with plenty

107

of deadwood for the fire and a run of water not far away.

Missy got a fire going while Lee and the old man watered the animals and when they got back she was laying strips of thick sliced bacon in the skillet and had the coffee cooking. It was good not to have to bend against the mountain wind and to be warm, with food on the fire.

The old man ate in his blankets, as he usually did, and he did most of the talking, but now he was tired and just wanted to sleep. "Guess I'll saw some wood," he told them. "No need to stand any watches here, young fella, not yet anyhow. In a day or two we may have some nighttime visitors, but I'll know them they'll know me. That's the trick of it, to have a lot of people know you. Ever'body knows me. That was mighty respeckful of you, calling me *Mister* Landry. You're safe as houses long as you're with me. Otherwise . . ." .

Lee built up the fire while Missy scrubbed the dishes with a hot, wet rag covered with clean sand. Then he checked the animals, especially the rascally mule which was double-hobbled and tethered to a stout bush. Missy was already in her blankets, her slicker on top, when he got back. The old man lay on his back, snoring and grunting. Missy lay with her face in shadow and didn't answer when Lee said goodnight. He lay awake for a while listening to the crackle of the fire. It hadn't rained yet, but the sky was black with clouds.

He didn't know how long he'd slept when he felt her crawling in with him. Whatever time it was, it wasn't a time for talking. Talking, even a word,

108

might ruin it. Missy smelled of horses and wood-smoke and strong yellow soap. Her body stiffened when he kissed her, but when she knew he wasn't going to be rough with her, she kissed him back with a fierce longing that had finally broken loose and demanded satisfaction. They lay facing each other in the smoke-smelling, half-light of the fire. Her eyes were closed and she arched her back when he unbuttoned her Levis and pulled them down over her small, boyish backside. He slid his hand inside her drawers and took them off. His hand moved down to her bush and stayed there, stroking it, until a gentle pressure opened her legs. His fingers felt her wetness as they parted her love lips. One of her hands was around his neck, the other groping awkwardly until he took it and helped her to unbutton his pants, and when all the buttons were undone, his cock stood up like a rod. He lifted his backside and she pulled down his pants and under-pants, and moist with sweat, her hand closed over the head of his cock and played with it. Then her moist hand began to slide up and down his cock, making him shudder. It excited her as much as it excited him. So much love juice flowed from her that the inside of her thighs were wet and she sucked on his fingers when he put them in her mouth. She tasted her own wild longing and liked it and her legs opened wide as he positioned himself between them and her hand closed on his, guiding him into her, steadying his throbbing cock for the first thrust. He worked the head of his cock in slowly, wanting to be gentle, but she drove him in all the way with a sudden bumping motion that must have hurt her.

Her muscles contracted, gripping his cock and holding it deep inside her, and then finally she relaxed and he began a steady pumping. Her legs closed around his waist and his hands kneaded her ass and he sucked her breasts while her fingernails raked his back, and if his thrusting hurt her, it was pain she couldn't get enough of.

His swollen cock would have been too big for her if she hadn't been so wet. He knew she was close to coming when she took his face in her hands and raised it from her breasts. She looked at him in wonder, this stranger who was giving her such unbearable pleasure. Her eyes were wide and staring and frantic. Now his long fast thrusts were pushing her closer and closer to the edge, and in a moment she would be over it and falling, and then suddenly she came with a great, shuddering gasp, a convulsion that seemed to spread to her toes, and her heels drummed in the sand underneath the blankets and, still gasping, she began to relax . . .

A few moments later, still silent, she took her clothes and crawled into her blankets, and he smiled at the way she wriggled and pulled until she finally got them on and then turned on her side so he couldn't see her face.

Nothing much happened the next day, and even the mule behaved himself. Thunder rumbled and the peaks were lost in clouds. All they could do was bend their heads against the wind and keep going.

The next night they made camp in a cave the old man claimed was haunted by the ghost of a mountain man who had crawled in there with a broken back after a fall from a high place. Ghost or no ghost, the old man said, it was where they were going to spend the night because the long-threatening storm was likely to break before morning.

It was a long deep cave and a draft that went somewhere took away the smoke of their fire. "As good as a reg'lar house and you don't have to do no repirs," the old man said as if he had created it himself. "Wouldn't mind livin' here the year round. Make a few sticks of furniture and call it home sweet home. More than enough space for man and animal. No snakes up this high but even if there was a few snakes they don't hardly ever bite you when they used to havin' you around. Would have to fetch water from below though there's a nice drip of water when it rains, which is most of the time so close to the peaks . . ."

Missy hadn't been to Lee's blankets for two nights and had little to say when he spoke to her. He couldn't figure her and he didn't try. Now she was kneeling by the fire putting the evening meal together. The horses and the mule were in the back of the cave eating oats spilled into a natural trough in the smooth stone floor.

The old man insisted in talking about the ghost. As usual he ate in his blankets, old and dirty and garrulous. "This poor ghost I want to tell you about," he said to Lee. "Well sir, I was the one found him right after he died. Poor man had propped himself up by the mouth of the cave, right over there behind you, I guess in the hope that some fellow human would hear his howling and might come to help him. Such a howling he put up, must have been howling for days, Lord knows, maybe weeks. Sound come to me on the wind and so I figures it's only the wind squeezin' through a crack in the rocks. Then I decides that there is a real genu'ween ghost, a poor soul in torment up there. Curios'ty druv me to climb up here and take a look. Found him right there by the lip of the cave, nothin' left of him but a raggedly sack of bones. Starved to death, all the time howling for help, all the time thinkin' how he'd do himself to death and not havin' the means . . ."

Lee knew Missy must have heard this yarn at least fifty times, but now it seemed to bother her. It bothered her so much that she kicked over the coffee pot and then kicked it again.

The old man stopped talking and looked at her gape-mouthed. "What the hell did you do that for, you crazy girl? Been thinkin' on that coffee since it started to cook."

Missy kicked it again and it clanked against the rock wall. The horses whinnied, frightened by the racket. Missy yelled, "Why're you always jabbering about death and dying. Ain't you close enough to your own death to be afraid of it? You're not the last of the mountain men, you're the last of the undertakers!"

The old man winked at Lee. "Little girl, I ain't afraid of the hereafter. Ghosts don't bother me neither. Ghosts is just folks can't settle down on the other side. They're just restless and keep tryin' to come back. Some quit and make the best of it. The real restless kind keep at it till Judgment Day."

Missy had picked up the coffee pot and was examining it for holes. She had her temper under control, but she said, "Now we're going to hear all about Judgment Day."

The old man was having a good time, so good that he rolled in his blankets, making gobbling sounds. Finally he laughed himself out and sat up. Thunder rolled overhead and suddenly there was a salvo like an artillery barrage followed by a tremendous lightning flash.

"God's wrath loosed on the world," the old man shouted.

"Damn you, grandpa," Missy shouted back. "Damn you to everlasting hell!"

"I leave that to a higher judge not you, girl," the old man replied in the few moments of silence that followed the first tremendous report. He was about to say something else but the heavenly cannonade resumed.

Lee thought: He's a malicious old man, with his ghost stories and all the rest of it. He knows he is bothering Missy, yet he goes on with it.

Lee lay sprawled beside the fire with a cigar in his mouth. Taking no notice of the storm, the old man had gone to sleep. Missy was filling the coffee pot from a canteen. Home sweet home, Lee thought, but it was better than being out there in the storm. It was raining now and water ran down through the flue that carried off the smoke. A pool of water formed, but not close to the fire. Missy went on with her cooking and the instant the food was ready, the old man woke up.

The storm wore itself out after a couple of hours. The wind grew colder, the trail narrow and difficult, and there were long stretches where they had to dismount and lead the animals. They saw mule deer in small numbers and once a black bear showed itself before disappearing into a scatter of brush-choked rocks.

Lee spotted the first of the lookouts after they got across a whitewater creek swollen with storm water and melting snow from higher up. Even with fording ropes it took most of an hour before they got the animals to the other side. The lookout was high up at the top of a pile of great rocks, and though it wasn't raining and there was even some watery sun, he was covered by a tent-like oil-soaked cotton slicker of dark color that blended in with the gray rocks. Lee knew he wouldn't have seen him if he hadn't used binoculars that flashed in the weak afternoon sun. He knew, too, that the lookout was taking no trouble to evade detection.

They passed below him and the old man waved and got a wave in return. "That fella up there has a rifle with a telescope mounted on it," the old man told Lee. "And he's got one of them heliographs the army uses to flash messages from one point to another. Works in relays and works fast when there's sun. Not as fast as the telegraph line but fast enough. Was we a hostile force that managed to get this far, word would be flashing ahead of us by now. You got to give the Jacks credit for knowin' how to pertect themself."

Far ahead Lee saw what he expected to see: a vast expanse of badlands the area of which he could only guess at. It seemed to run clear to the base of one of the great peaks. Up here the eyes played tricks, but as near as he could figure it at least fifty miles of badlands had to be crossed, and that was the first really formidable obstacle any invading force would have to face. It had to be in there, in some twisted canyon, that the first war party of ranchers and farmers had met their end. It looked like a maze and was a maze of jagged stone. Up here there were no rivers that could be followed; plenty of water-courses, but no rivers. It could be treacherous even for men that knew it; for those that did not, it would be disaster.

They spent that night beside the ruin of a log and stone cabin some energetic trapper had built fifty years before. Or so the old man said.

"Fella that built it must've found damn little to trap by that time," the old man said. "The fur animals was goin' fast by the Forties. But he stayed anyhow and I guess he lived on what he could shoot. A mystery why he built it. Most trappers moved all the time, had to move as the fur animals moved, and I often think he was no kind of real trapper but some kind of a hermit with no interest in anything but bein' by his lonesome. One story is he went off to enlist in the Messican War, but I ask you how could he even know about the war, and if he did hear, how long can a war go on? I would say he just lived till he died and the animals carried off his bones."

That night after the old man had gone to sleep Missy was hacking at her hair with a steel comb. Lee watched her from the other side of the fire. Suddenly she said, "You'll be seeing the last of me in a few days. That ought to please you."

"Why should it?" Lee asked.

"Because I know the real reason you want to join the Jack Mormons. That's right. Deny it if you can."

"You haven't said what you think it is." If her hand even moved toward her gun he would kill her and kill the old man with the second shot. But all she did was keep hacking at her matted hair.

"You're just joining because of all those women they have. All this talk about having the law after you is horseshit. You're not running from a rope, you're running to all those asses and tits. God damn you to hell, I know what you're thinking of when you get a certain look in your eyes. You're wondering where am I going to start first? I know what you told Spargo, but you don't fool me. You can't convince me that you have to join the Jacks to escape the law. You're too smart not to be able to figure a way."

"Do tell." This was a new approach even for her, but it was better than what he had been afraid of a few minutes before. He didn't want to kill her unless he absolutely had to. He'd kill her if he had to, but he would do it with some regret. There had been good nights together and, besides, he liked her in spite of her craziness.

"You're not even a real outlaw," she said. For the moment she was cold and sarcastic and he knew that wouldn't last because she had a terrible temper. That was all right even if it meant dodging coffee pots or rocks or burning brands from the fire. All that he could handle. Just as long as she didn't reach for her gun.

"Don't you think I've seen enough outlaws and

116

law-dodgers to know a desperate man from a fake? You may have committed crimes, but that's not your reason for being here. Believe me, you won't get hung or shot, you'll fuck yourself to death. Like the drunkard who can't keep away from the bottle, you can't stay away from the crotch. You're nothing but a crotch fiend."

Lee didn't want to argue with her and he didn't want to get hit with the coffee pot. So he said, "I'm sorry you think that."

Her temper was rising. "Oh no you don't," she jeered. "You think you're God's gift to women. Get ready, ladies, here comes Ben Trask, the great lover from parts unknown. Spread them wide, ladies, so poor old Ben can creep into you and hide from the hangman. Shed a tear for him, ladies. If you don't like one story, he'll tell you another."

The old man made a choking sound, but she didn't even look at him.

"You sure have a mad on," Lee said.

She picked a shred of bark from the comb. "Why should I be mad? Why should I care about a crotch fiend? You don't have to listen if you don't want to?"

"What should I do?" Lee asked. "Take a stroll in the dark?"

"Yes, why don't you do that and why don't you stroll off the edge of a cliff." With a sudden angry gesture she shoved the comb into the top of her boot and jumped to her feet. Her eyes were fierce in the firelight. "You do as you please, crotch fiend. I'm going to sleep. Try anything dirty and I'll cut your balls off. You wouldn't be much good to the ladies without your balls.''

But for all that she came to him later. Much later, less than two hours before daybreak. She crawled in and shushed his mouth though he hadn't said anything and wasn't about to unless she spoke first. Crazy as a hoot owl, he decided. Crazy as a squirrel.

Her love-making was more like a catfight than anything else. Her nails drew blood and she slammed her crotch into his with the fury of a madwoman. It was all he could do to control her before he thrust and let go. What now? he wondered. What will she do next?

They lay together while the cold night wind whistled through the ruined cabin and a ground-nesting bird scratched nearby. The mule and the horses stirred, knowing that morning wasn't far off.

"You don't have to go in there," she whispered when he decided she wasn't going to say anything. "You'll be a prisoner and they'll never let you go. We can turn back now before it's too late. So far only one guard saw us, the one up in the rocks. We can go back and you can sneak up on him. He watches the trail coming from the west. He won't be expecting it. We'll go all the way back, get past Spargo and get away. You saw it's a good mile from the Springs to the break in the cliff. We don't have to go past the post to get away."

Lee said, "Spargo took all the money I had. We'd be leaving without a cent. You have money with you?"

"Then we'll kill Spargo and take his money. We'll kill him from ambush and kill Lem too. There's nobody else there. God damn you, don't you hear what I'm saying? Turn back or it'll be the finish of you." She took a deep breath. "It'll be the finish of me. Don't you see the sense of what I'm saying? Spargo doesn't trust banks and has his money cached in the supplies building. Gold and paper, thousands of dollars. Enough to get us anywhere we wanted to go. You can change your name and we can live for years on Spargo's money. There wouldn't be any need to rob or steal. You could start a business, make money, we could be rich. How would the law ever catch up with you? Ben Trask wouldn't exist. They'd stop looking for you. You're not that important. Will you say something for Christ's sake?"

"What do we do with your grandfather?"

"Tie him up, leave him food and water. He's a tough old man."

"How can he survive if he's tied? He'll die."

Lee could feel her anger. "Somebody will find him."

"We're way off the trail. The only travelers on it are the Jacks. He'll be buzzard bait long before they find him. A hell of a way to die."

She was silent for a good five minutes, but her anger and impatience was evident. She was out of control and knew it and didn't like it. She wanted what she wanted and here he was putting arguments in her way. She had given herself completely to a man and was furious that he didn't see things her way.

"Damn your arguments," she said. "We'll kill him in his sleep. He's old and crazy and better off dead. He can't last much longer. He nearly died last winter, so what's the difference? After he's dead we don't even have to think about him. We'll go back and deal with Spargo and go far away from Utah."

She's as murderous as Spargo, Lee thought, and as crazy as the old man. Years of loneliness and bottled-up feelings had driven her mad. No matter what she said or what she did, there would be no changing her.

"I won't do it," Lee said. "I won't murder an old man or stand by while it's done. There may come a time I wish I had, but not now. I won't do it. I'll forget we even talked about it. I wish you'd do the same."

"Son of a bitch! I won't forget it," she hissed at him. "What happened with us didn't mean a thing, did it? You just wanted to fuck me like you want to fuck every woman you can get your dirty hands on. You mealymouth bastard, I hope you get the pox from one of your women. It would serve you right."

Missy was sitting on a rock when the old man woke up and sleeved the sleep crust from his eyes. He was accustomed to waking up to hot coffee and a blazing fire. Now he blinked because there was neither.

"What's a-goin' on?" he complained. "Why ain't you fixed the fire?"

"You fix it," Missy yelled. "You and this gutless bastard can fix it. Fix your own fucking breakfast while you're at it."

Lee built up the fire and cooked breakfast and the old man, with no tact at all, allowed as how he was a hell of a better cook than his granddaughter. Missy refused to eat anything, or even to have a cup of coffee. Instead, she stuffed the pockets of her sheepskin with jerked meat that she chewed steadily throughout the day. The old man, with no idea of what was going on, continued to make up and to sing his two-line songs. Confidentially he told Lee that Missy was just in one of her moods. She had her moods, he said, but she always got over them. He knew that because he had been dealing with them for years.

"Wasn't right, her folks not coming back to look after her. Me and the wife done the best we could, specially the wife, but a young'un needs a mother's care."

They crossed sixty-five miles of badlands in three days, and Lee tried to forget about Missy as he tried to remember this turn or that back-track of this featureless wasteland. The old man went forward without hesitation, talking to himself, singing his songs. Lee couldn't write anything down, but he didn't know that it would have helped much. The great peak up ahead was the only landmark he recognized.

No matter how hard he tried to disregard Missy, she was always there, silent, and watchful and implacably hostile. There was one night when he thought he heard her coming close in the dark and whether to make love or to kill him he had no way of knowing. But it was just some small night creature moving stealthily.

They reached the Jack Mormon settlement on the afternoon of the third day.

SEVEN

It lay in a small valley south of the peak and far from being a jumble of log houses and shanties it had a planned, orderly look and the street was plank rather than mud and on the south slope of the mountain, shielded from the wind, there were cultivated fields with people working in them in the afternoon sun. East of the town, higher up, was an earthen dam that dammed a small lake. Below the dam were gold workings or workings of some other kind, and there were people here too, all visible from far away because the air was so clear and the sun didn't have the glare of the lowlands.

"There she is," the old man said as they rode in without challenge. He waved to a rifleman in a guard tower at the entrance to the village. In the Mormon fashion, an arched gate had been built at the entrance-way that led to the main street and it was surmounted by a great wooden eagle painted gold. The eagle's claws gripped the word

PALMYRA, which had been carved from wood and was painted gold like the rest of the gate.

"Ain't that somethin' now," the old man said. "They took the trouble to do all that work right here in the back of beyond."

Lee was leading the mule because Missy had refused to do any work for the last three days of the journey. She chewed the dried meat and drank water instead of coffee, saying nothing, and at night she took her blankets as far from them as she could. Lee didn't know how things were going to go with her, but he knew she could be a real danger to him. But what he could do about it he didn't know.

The old man said they would spend the night in Palmyra and start back for Eutaw Springs the next morning. That might take care of Missy, but Lee wasn't so sure. Back at Spargo's place she had seemed wild and dangerous and ill-tempered, but now there was something else that hadn't been there before. It was too bad about Missy, Lee thought, but he hadn't shaped her unhappy life and he couldn't be responsible for it. Odd thing was that he still liked her in spite of her craziness, her willingness to murder her own grandfather, the man who had done his best to care for her for all his own madness. But he had come too far to let her get in his way and he would do anything he had to to see that she didn't.

"That there's the meeting house they're building," the old man said, pointing to a half-finished stone and wood structure that stood on the lower slope of the mountain. It was bigger than anything in the settlement. "Only they call it a temple.

123

I'll tell you one thing, young fella, these people mean to stay. Well come on now, it's time for you to meet the head man if he has time to talk to you. He may or he may not, depends whether he's at his headquarters or out somewhere lookin' over the various properties.''

Lee looked to see what Missy was doing and saw that she had dismounted. The old man said nothing and it seemed that she had the run of the settlement, was under no kind of restraint. Lee wondered where she went, what she did in a place like this. The town itself had a curious stillness about it and there was none of the aimless bustle you generally found in a small place. In an ordinary village there would be the idlers, loungers, old people sitting on porches, or just gossiping. Nothing like that here; what there was, was a kind of blankness, a dull silence, though there were men in the streets and horses in a small corral beside a blacksmith shop down the street. Then he realized why Palmyra was different from other places he'd been. Everybody seemed to have some kind of purpose, a job he had set to do. He'd seen it before in the few religious communities he'd been in, and this wasn't something he liked or admired. Here in this strange settlement, founded on hate, it was something to be feared.

The building they were heading for was at the end of the main street, a two-storey log structure with another golden eagle on top. Nothing was as finished as it would have been in a regular settlement where all the right tools were available, but it was a fair copy. Once, in a tiny village in the wild country of northern Argentina, he had seen a building like this. The village was dominated by a bandit who called himself mayor and the building he ruled from was a kind of miniature palace made of dried mud-brick and painted with whitewash. It looked imposing until you got up close and then you saw the cracks in the walls, the balconies that weren't balconies, the doors that weren't doors. This building was a little like that; no matter how hard it had been worked on, it was still just a two-storey log house.

They got down and hitched the animals and went in. On the second floor a young man with greased hair sat at a desk in front of double doors with hammered-iron doorhandles. Once again Lee got the impression of rough copy. This Jack leader was doing his damnedest to give the impression of the real thing. It wasn't badly done, but the fact that he bothered to do it at all told you something about the man.

The man behind the desk wore a gray coat, a white shirt, a black tie. He was less than thirty but took himself seriously. "Wait," he said when the old man told him they wanted to talk to Bisiph Rankin.

"Bishop?" Lee said to the old man.

"That's what he calls himself," the old man said.

"Bishop Rankin will see you," the man said when he came out. He looked at Lee without interest and went back behind his desk. The affairs of state, Lee thought. He wondered if the man behind the desk carried a gun. He had the bright eyes of the religious fanatic. Lee wondered how many wives he had.

"Bishop" Rankin sat behind his desk, a squat, hammered-down man with wide shoulders and a great shock of red hair worn long and brushed back from a protruding forehead. He looked like a big man who had been shortened by about a foot. Behind him on the plank wall was a map of Utah; looming over the map was yet another golden eagle, its talons extended. There were two windows overlooking the street and a man standing at one of them turned when they came in. He was of medium height, ferret-faced, with quick, black eyes and had the look of a man always amused at something known only to himself. He wore a black sponge suit, a white shirt, a black bowtie with the ends folded under the shirt collar. He carried a .38 Officer's Model Colt in a black belt without cartridge loops.

"Hello, Bishop," the old man said when Rankin looked up. "Brought another man from the Springs. This is him. I'll leave you now."

The old man left and Lee waited to be questioned. Instead he got a short, fiery speech from the "bishop" who delivered it sitting down. The other man stayed by the window and watched.

"I am Joseph Smith Rankin," the bishop began. "I am the temporal and spiritual leader of this community. My word is law in all matters whether they be worldly or spiritual. Transgress against community law, which is my law, and you will be put to death. There is no other punishment here. We have no fines, no jail, no second chances. Break the law and you will be excuted. Do you accept that?"

'Yes sir," Lee answered.

"Not 'sir,' " the man by the window said. "It's 'bishop.' Say 'Bishop' or 'Bishop Rankin.' "

"What is your name?" Rankin asked Lee.

Lee told him Ben Trask. There were no other questions and Rankin, obviously a madman, explained why. The old Ben Trask no longer existed, his past life had been erased as if with a pencil eraser. It had been rubbed out, the crumbs or rubber dusted away, and now the page was clean and ready to be used again. It was what was written on it from now on that mattered. What was written from that point became indelible and could not be erased.

"Which means that you will be held accountable for your actions,." Rankin shouted, suddenly excited. "You have been wilful or you would not be here. You have broken the law and escaped punishment. Here there is no escape. It is possible to run but where can you run to? Back into the badlands? Farther into the mountains? However, if you obey orders absolutely there are many rewards: absolute protection from your enemies in the outside world since your enemies become our enemies. Money, the love of good women, good food, comfortable accomodations, freedom from such vices as alcohol and gambling."

Rankin paused. "We have established here a community based on the teachings of the Blessed Joseph Smith whose name I bear, the founder of the first and the only true Mormon church. In recent years his teachings have been disregarded, ignored and even mocked at. But now—*here*—there is a return to fundamental ways. We have returned to the teachings of the Book of Mormon, which is the rock the original church was built on and so it would have remained throughout the ages if traitors and apostates had not become greedy and disloyal. We

127

could have held this land"—here Rankin waved his arm—"all this land if certain leaders had been more resolute, if they had not become faint of heart in the face of adversity, if they had not been so eager to seek accomodation with our enemies in the outside world. We should have fought the Americans when they sought to subdue us, to force us to renounce the teachings of the prophet Joseph Smith. We should have fought and died by the thousands if necessary, and if we had, we would have prevailed because God was on our side if only our leaders had the courage to acknowledge it, and God is still on our side. I tell you he is on our side here as we attempt to reestablish the old faith and the old ways . . ."

Rankin stopped talking and poured a glass of water from an enamel jug on his desk. "We have declared war on the world," he continued, "and there is nothing the world can do to stop us. Here we are invulnerable. You have seen something of our community. It is called Palmyra after the birthplace of Joseph Smith, and it is just a beginning. What you have seen has been established within a year of its beginning. We are building an army of which you will be part. We have weapons and supplies and the gold and money we have taken from the outside world. We have gold here, our own gold. For years men have searched for gold in these mountains without finding more than modest amounts. Think of it: we chose this valley not with any thought of gold but because of its location, protected from the northern storms and winds by the great mountain, and yet here we found gold. You must take that as a sign as we have taken it as a sign that God is on our side and march with us into battle against our enemies . . ."

Another pause, another drink of water, and Rankin went on with: "When these new laws were passed against us by the Gentile courts, it was argued that we should retreat to the Mexican wilderness as many others have done in the past and where they remain to this day under the protection of President Diaz. But it came to me, as the Lord came to Joseph Smith in his humble home in Palmyra, that to skulk off to Mexico would be against the word of God, a slap in the face of God. No, I cried, let us remain in our native land but find a place where our enemies cannot find us, a place where all his might is of no avail. Well we have found it here. Like the Mormons of old we have journeyed off the maps. Even now we have been offered amnesty, through intermediaries, if we will lay down our arms. I say no. Let them send as many soldiers as they choose. We know these mountains and they do not. We will fight from behind every rock and tree. Their supply lines will be thin, their line of march extended, and always we will fall back if we have to, drawing them forward into the wilderness, beckoning them to their destruction . . ."

The man at the window said, "Excuse the interruption, Bishop, but you were to inspect the new gold workings this afternoon. They're ready to release water from the dam."

Rankin looked at his huge gold watch, which lay on the desk in front of him. "Captain Wingate will talk to you," he said to Lee, and went out. As soon as the door closed Wingate sat down in Rankin's chair.

"You can sit down too," he told Lee. "Get that chair over there."

Lee took one of the chairs that were placed along the wall and put it in front of the desk. Wingate gave him a sardonic smile that wasn't very different from his normal expression. "I used to be an infantry officer," he said. "That's all you have to know about me. Now you, what did you do to bring you here?"

"Killed two men while I was stealing horses in West Texas," Lee said. "One of them was the owner's son. The father had political connections and has been using them to try to find me. There was just no good place to hide."

He repeated the story as he had told it to Spargo. "That's what happened," he said when he finished.

Wingate lay back in the bishop's big chair. The high back had been carved by somebody who knew how to work well with wood. "Well it may be what happened and it may not," he said. "It doesn't matter a damn as long as we get some things straight. Rankin may be the leader of this outfit but I'm the man who runs it. Don't tell the bishop I said that because I'll call you a liar."

Lee nodded. "You're the boss," he said.

"The bishop has his ways," Wingate said, very sure of himself, very comfortable in the head man's chair. "My ways are to make money and see that the men that work under me don't make trouble for me or for themselves. Which comes to the same thing, naturally. Now a lot of them come in here because

Spargo really doesn't know what I want. He knows I don't want habitual drunkards or homicidal lunatics and he's been pretty good on that score. But as to sending me men with intelligence, ruthless but intelligent men, he hasn't measured up. Not that I'm blaming him: he doesn't have much to work with, and he doesn't have time, and he isn't so very intelligent himself. Cunning, certainly, intelligent no. You can talk if you like."

Lee said, "Are there as many rules as the bishop said."

"He likes to think so," Wingate answered. "But that's because he doesn't pay too much attention to detail. Oh he can surprise you from time to time, but most of the time he thinks of the glory to come. The bishop is more than a little cracked as all men of destiny are." Wingate smiled. "But he did start this settlement and the Jack Mormons will follow him anywhere. Therefore he holds the place together because the Mormons are the strongest element here. You'll be mistaken if you think otherwise. If he gave the order they would wipe us out."

"Us?"

"Men like you," Wingate said. "Outlaws, wanted men, non-Mormons. We could take them by surprise —maybe—but that isn't the idea. Some of them don't like us, which is understandable, but it hasn't been a problem except when some horse's ass does something to cause trouble. Only yesterday I had to hang a man who raped a Mormon's woman. Can you imagine that? The son of a bitch had three women of his own, all young and good-looking enough, and he had to go and unbutton his pants in the wrong

131

house."

"Was he drunk?" Lee asked.

"Of course he was drunk," Wingate said. "He brought it back from a raid and hid it. The hell with him! I was saying. I don't know what your plans are, but I don't intend to stay here until I grow a long white beard. But it suits me for the moment. The law is as much after me as it's after you, more so I would say, and having a certain amount of money isn't enough. I need time and a great deal of money. So you will help me and I will help you. Am I making sense?"

"A great deal of sense," Lee said. "You want men so loyal you'll want to throw money their way. Am I making sense? Do I call you 'Captain' or what?"

Wingate smiled. "I could do without the rank, but that's what they call me here. Rankin started it because I really was a captain, and everybody else picked it up. As to the question of money, yes I will want to throw money your way if you are loyal. The more loyalty, the more money. Naturally you will get your own share of what we take on the outside. Your share will be fairly small in the beginning, but I'll make up for that. Not all the money we steal finds its way into the community treasury. But don't try to cheat by yourself even if you get the chance. It's risky and I don't like it. Let me cheat for you. It's safer. I have been with Rankin almost from the beginning, so I'm trusted. If there's one thing I've learned from the politicians it's that every successful thief should earn a position of trust. You look as if you have an important question."

Lee nodded. "I do, Captain. Why are you telling me all this?"

"Simple. I need a second in command."

"What's wrong with the one you have?" Lee asked.

Wingate said, "I had to hang him yesterday. He was a good man before he fell in love." Wingate laughed bitterly, shaking his head in wonderment at the folly of mankind. "Can you believe such a thing? In a settlement teeming with women he had to go and fall in love with the wrong one. For God's sake, if he wanted a fourth or even a fifth wife he could have had her. If he didn't like the wives he had he could have changed them. But no, he wanted this woman. He absolutely had to have her and he did. He had her once. Any more questions?"

Lee said, "Don't you have other candidates for the job?"

Wingate said, "I did have until you walked in. You had a certain look about you and still do. I suppose I would have to call it confidence. You looked confident and intelligent. What you were doing stealing horses I can't imagine but"—again the sardonic smile—"we all do foolish things. I used to regret some of my foolish behavior, but it's too late for that. I don't know you and I'm sure I can trust you, but you will die screaming if you try to cross me. I mean that sincerely."

Wingate's voice was so quiet, his manner so mild, that Lee had no doubt that he meant every word he said exactly as he said it. He had no idea what Wingate had done to turn a career officer into a renegade boss of outlaws, but it must have been worse than any ordinary killing. He could not have explained why he knew that, but he knew he was right.

Wingate leaned forward in the big chair and his manner became confidential. "I intend to amass a great deal of money and to go far from the United States. What are your plans?"

"Much the same except that I might hire a smart lawyer and try to stay in the country."

"Then our goals are much the same," Wingate said. "The important thing is to be determined and steady in our efforts. Too many men come in here and become restless when they have as little as a thousand dollars. They come here because they are hunted and desperate and are glad to find a safe haven. But all too often it doesn't last, that awful feeling of being hunted, and some of them try to make a run for it while we are off on some raid. So far none of them has been successful. It would be bad for discipline if they were allowed to run off. Worse still, it would be bad for the military integrity of Palmyra."

"I won't try to run off, Captain. I know how well off I am just being here. What happens next? Do I have to be cleared for the job? Won't the bishop ask why this stranger?"

"He may or may not ask. If he does ask I'll explain my reason for choosing you. Don't let me down, Trask. It will be very bad for you if you do. I am sorry to make all these threats and I'm sure a time will come when we will laugh about them. Because of the poor fool I had to hang yesterday I

134

can't show you any special favoritism, but I will make it up to you. Like all new men you will be on probation for several weeks, but that won't last. Tonight you will have a cabin to yourself, but tomorrow you will have to bunk in with the other new men. Not a word to anyone about this discussion. Let me announce your new position as my second in command. While you are with the new men, gather all the information you can and report to me when I send for you. Any information you can pass along will only strengthen your own position."

"You suspect somebody, Captain?" What in hell was this Wingate up to? Lee wondered. Wingate had as much, or more, reason to suspect him as anybody else. But maybe that was it. Maybe this fucked up ex-officer was testing him as Spargo had tested him except that Wingate was better at it, and had more time. Wingate had said it himself: Spargo just didn't have the time.

"Let's just say that I'm careful," Wingate explained. "I want you to trust my judgment. Keep your ears and eyes open at all times. If you see or hear anything that doesn't seem right, make a mental note of it. Anything at all. Don't be embarrassed to bring it up. I'll decide if it's important. I think that covers everything."

"Captain, there are a few things you haven't explained. Can I just walk around while I'm on probation? Where do I eat?"

Wingate looked mildly surprised. "Sorry. You will have the freedom of the settlement. Why not? There's nothing to hide. Bunkhouse, call it what you like. The cabin you will stay in tonight is behind the blacksmith's. A bunk will be free in the barracks sometime tomorrow. One of the men on probation is to get his own cabin and his first wife. If you get hungry, go to the barracks and the cook will feed you. Good luck, Trask. You better find your cabin before it gets dark.''

It was far from dark, but Wingate held out his hand and Lee shook it. There was something strange going on, but he did as he was told and went out and down to the street. There was no sign of the old man, nor of Missy, and he wondered where they were. He was on his way to the blacksmith shop when a line of young women roped together crossed the street followed by a guard. This was no hard case guard, but a middle-aged Mormon with black clothes and a beard. The women wore shapeless dresses of some rough material and they were barefoot but didn't appear to have been beaten though the man behind them carried a short whip with a flat snake. The whip was intended to intimidate rather than to punish. The rope that linked the women together circled their waists and it wasn't pulled tight. The feet of the women were caked with dried mud and it looked like they had been working in the fields. Lee stood back to let them pass and some of them gave him defiant stares. He saw that Maggie was not among them.

"Back there," the blacksmith said in a surly voice when Lee asked him about the cabin. Obviously he was a Mormon who didn't like Gentiles even if they were, on the face of it, on the same side. Lee found the cabin and went in. There was a bed, a stove, a table and two chairs. Cut wood for the stove was stacked against the wall and there was a shelf with canned goods and a patent can-opener on it. Pots and pans and dishes were on another shelf. Everything was clean and neat and bare as a poorhouse chapel.

It wasn't cold yet so he didn't start the fire. He stretched out on the bed and thought about his situation. Wingate had tried to make their talk very man-to-man, but something was wrong there. It didn't make sense to offer the second in command job to a total stranger just in from the badlands. Just as it made no sense to have him bunk in here for one night and then join the new hard cases in the bunkhouse in the morning. He knew Wingate considered himself a very clever man, a man who knew how to play on the feelings and hopes of other men, but did he think everyone else was so dumb? Likely enough he did, and it was easy enough to understand that, given the brain power of most law-dodgers, who were generally a pretty lame-brained bunch. If they weren't so thick between the ears they wouldn't be law-dodgers in the first place and they wouldn't be found out in the second. There were some outlaws with brains, but for the most part they were small men with big ideas and no real idea of how to get out of the rut they were in. As Buckskin Frank used to say: "Most of them are two-bit gamblers trying to get into a high stakes game."

He got sick of lying on the bed and went down the street to see what the so-called barracks was like. The blacksmith, as surly as before, told him where he could find it. The blacksmith's log house was to one side of the smithy and four women, all in their

137

early twenties, looked out the door when he stopped to talk to the blacksmith. That man must be tired after a good night's rest, Lee thought, giving the women no more than a quick glance. But the smith didn't like even that much familiarity with his wives. He yelled at the women to close the door, then brought his hammer down on the bare anvil with a mighty clang.

Lee saw no one watching him, yet he had the feeling of being watched. It grew stronger as he walked down the street. After so many years in dangerous places he had learned to respect his feelings even when there was no hard evidence to back them up. But he didn't try to find out who the watcher was because it didn't make any difference. It could even be that all the Gentiles here were under observation all the time. Wingate didn't like the Mormons, but he probably trusted them more than his own men. A Mormon was just a Mormon, while a Gentile could be anybody. Spargo did his best to ferret out spies and government agents, but he couldn't see inside a man's head. Wingate took up where Spargo left off.

Every log house in Palmyra was on either side of the main street except for one house, bigger than the others, that faced down it. That would be Rankin's, the bloody bishop watching over his flock of vultures. Apparently Rankin had been some sort of church elder before he quit or was kicked out. It was sure to have been a little of both. Men like Rankin usually brought about their own downfall, and when it finally happened, they saw it as some sort of noble sacrifice on their part. In everyday life this wouldn't matter very much, but Rankin had gone on to find his own little murderous empire. He had gone on to wage war against the world that had no use for him and, Lee decided, for that he deserved to die.

Lee found the so-called barracks, a long log house with smoke coming from two stone chimneys. It was getting dark now and light showed from half a dozen unglazed windows. There was a corral without horses behind it. Steps went in from the side and when Lee went in men sitting at two long tables stopped talking and looked at him. Then the scattered talk continued, but it was listless and there was none of the rough humor of the ranch bunkhouse or the army messhall. These law-dodgers had bitten off more than they could chew and there wasn't a poker game or a friendly saloon in sight. Lee made a quick count and came up with fifteen men at two rough tables. There were no familiar faces anywhere. A cook, a law-dodger himself by the look of him, carried in a huge two-handled stewpot and set it down.

"Come and git it," he called out.

Lee got one of the tin bowls that had been set out and took his place in line. He wondered if the badmen who had been in prison felt as if they were back there. There was very little talking on the line. Two badmen got into a mouth fight about shoving, but it stopped when the cook banged his ladle on the rim of the stewpot and warned them to shut the hell up.

Lee took his bowl of stew back to the table and sat down. The man across the table had a livid scar from the corner of his right eye to the end of his chin. He dipped bread in the stew and ate it, making a lot of noise. Up and down the table there was some conversation. One man was telling another about all the money he made in shooting contests back in Tennessee.

"You couldn't shoot your mother," the other man growled.

"I just got in," Lee told the man with the scar who had been staring at him. "How long you been here?"

"That's my business," the man said. "Why don't you mind yours? Who are you, one of Wingate's spies?"

Lee ate his beef stew and it wasn't bad. At least there was plenty of it. Then he left and went back to the cabin. Once again he knew he was being followed. But he didn't look behind him because it didn't matter.

He felt his way to the hanging lantern and lit it. Then he took off his boots and stretched out on the bed. In a while he heard horses going down the street, their hooves hollow on the plank paving. Palmyra was a progressive little community, plank paving and all. He wondered what they did on Saturday night?

Hours passed and nothing happened. It was ten-fifty-five by his watch when he decided to take off his pants and get under the blankets. He was doing that when there was a soft knock, a single knock, and the woman with red hair came in.

EIGHT

There was something familiar about her, but he had no idea what it was. She didn't look like a field worker or any kind of worker and she carried a tray covered by a napkin and in the pocket of her unbuttoned sheepskin coat was a bottle of whiskey and when she moved glasses clinked in the other pocket. She bumped the door shut with her heel and smiled at him before she set the tray down on the table.

"I'll bet they forget to feed you, you poor man," she said. "There now"—uncovering the tray—"that should make you feel better. Steak and onions and mashed potatoes. It's not fancy but it's filling."

"I had a little stew at the barracks," Lee said. "But I'm still hungry. Thanks for thinking of me."

He didn't know who she was and he didn't ask. It had to be one of Wingate's tricks, but he wasn't going to play along with it by asking questions.

"It's the least I could do," she said. "Eat up now before it gets cold."

"Well you can't be hungry now," she said after Lee cleared his plate and put a woodie to a cigar. "My name is Clarissa. They tell me yours is Ben."

"That's right."

"You must be tired after the long journey from Eutaw Springs. Some day there will be a road from there to here."

This place was full of surprises. "You think so . . . Clarissa? It's going to take some fancy engineering before that happens. As well as other things."

"Oh you mean the legal situation. By the way, would you have a cigar for me?" Lee gave it to her and lit it for her and when she puffed on it it wasn't for show. "Thank you, Ben. Everything changes and there will come a time when we are recognized for what we are, the true and original Mormons. In time the federal government will be forced to recognize the validity of our claim."

Lee looked at her. What in hell was going on? "I'm afraid all this raiding and killing won't help. I've just come from Colorado and they're even talking about it down there."

"It will change," she said complacently, disregarding what he had said. "But I'm sure you don't want to talk Mormon politics. If you're tired I won't mind if you lie down on the bed. Why don't you do that? Don't be bashful. After all, Palmyra isn't just another village. Would you like a drink?"

"If I don't get shot for taking it," he said, and she laughed. It was a nice laugh, low and musical, and, he thought, completely insincere. He had pulled up his pants when she came in and now he lay down, leaving them unbuttoned. If she wanted to look at a

142

man with his pants half-off, then she was welcome to the sight. She herself was easy to look at, this red-headed Clarissa. Tall for a woman, she was good-looking in a confident, almost arrogant way, and her full red lips were set off by her bright red hair, which was made up into a bun that didn't look in the least prissy, and her body, clothed from neck to toe in shapeless gray cotton, was as sensual as if she had been wearing nothing at all.

She filled two small glasses and took them over to the bed. "Nobody gets shot for drinking whiskey, not even in Palmyra. It's discouraged but nobody gets shot for enjoying it, not even if you get drunk. I'm very proud to be a Mormon, but our laws aren't set in concrete. Drink up now and get into bed."

Lee drank up and got into bed after Clarissa pulled off his pants and undershorts and played with his cock. "One of the things I like most about being a Mormon woman," she told him, "is the freedom between men and women. You are not a Mormon so you probably have many wrong ideas about us."

"I don't know," Lee said. "We don't have many Mormons in my part of Colorado." He was enjoying the effect of the whiskey and the feel of her hand on his cock.

"At least the Mormons aren't puritans," she said. "Mormon men and women can't wait to go to bed at night. The outside world prefers to believe that Mormon women are slaves to their husbands' lust. But what about their own lust? Plural marriage was a heaven-sent institution, a system devised by the Almighty Himself to see that no woman spent a lonely life in unholy longing. There is no adultery among the Mormons who practice plural marriage, did you know that? Why should there be? If a man is not crazy he is happy with the wives he has if he comes to love yet another woman he doesn't sneak after her like a randy dog but takes her into his home as his wife, be she his third or fourth or fifth or sixth or sixteenth.''

Clarissa took off her clothes as she talked and there was no false modesty in the way she took off her bloomers and tossed them over the back of a chair. Lee's cock was already rod-stiff and throbbing with the urge to get inside her.

Before she got into bed with him, she refilled the glasses and handed one to him. "Here's to honesty between men and women," she said, and knocked back her whiskey.

They made love then and it was pure pleasure to fuck a woman big and strong enough to give as good as she got. There was no need to teach her anything; she knew all there was to know about making love and yet there was nothing mechanical or false about the way she responded to his powerful thrusting. Whatever it was that had brought her to his bed didn't matter any more, or at least it didn't matter for the moment.

She was quiet in her lovemaking. She expressed her deep-felt pleasure in the way she smiled at him and sometimes even laughed happily when he did something special or unusual to her or she to him. She found humor in lovemaking and there was no shame in the things she did to him with her hands or with her mouth and later after they came several times and got into new positions she continued to enjoy it as much as he did.

At last she lay back on the pillow, smiling at him. "You have exhausted me," she said. "I am happily exhausted. Are there many more like you in Colorado? If so, it must be a wonderful state."

"There's just me," Lee said, and grinned at her.

"You have made me so happy I don't know how to thank you," she said.

"You've thanked me ten times over. A hundred," Lee said.

She propped herself up on her elbow and looked at him. "Aren't you going to ask me who I am or the real reason I came here tonight?"

"Why don't you tell me?"

"I'm Clarissa Rankin and I came to warn you about Captain Wingate."

"Oh sure, the same red hair. I thought you looked familiar. If you came to warn me about Wingate, why didn't you?"

"By the time I got here I was no longer sure I should. I thought, how can I be sure he won't tell Wingate? Now I'm sure you won't. You won't, will you?"

"Not a chance," Lee said. He would tell Wingate as soon as he saw him. She might be Rankin's daughter, but he knew this was all Wingate's idea. She had to have a real hate for her father to throw in with a son of a bitch like Wingate.

"Warn me about what?" he asked.

"I believe he intends to kill my father and blame it on someone else. When I heard of the long talk he had with you this afternoon I realized it was going to be you."

"Why me? I saw a whole bunch of new men at the barracks."

"They're just stupid outlaws without an ounce of brains between them. The other Mormons here would never believe that any of them had the intelligence or was ambitious enough to kill my father."

"How do you know all this?"

"The man Wingate hanged yesterday told me his suspicions. The rape charge was just an excuse to kill him. But there was no rape. He came here a Gentile, but converted to our faith. He loved that woman, so why would he rape her? He could have added her to his wives. An exchange of wives is common among fundamentalist Mormons who believe in plural marriage."

Lee pretended to think. "But what can Wingate hope to gain?"

"Control of Palmyra."

"But how can he if he isn't a Mormon?"

"He is a Mormon," she said. "He had to convert or my father would never have trusted him. The other Mormons would never have accepted him. Don't you see, if he can get rid of my father and hang you for it, the way is clear to taking over Palmyra. None of the other Mormons is qualified to be leader. So it would have to be Wingate."

Lee did some more fake thinking. "Have you told your father?"

"Of course," she answered. "But he is afraid of Wingate and his Gentile gunmen. He hasn't told the Mormons because there would be so much bloodshed. You may think my father is a wicked man, but the villain here is Captain Wingate. It's Wingate who began the bloody raids, the burning and the killing. He is power mad and money mad. And lately he has turned my father to his way of thinking. Now that the world sees him as a bloody-handed renegade he thinks he has nothing to lose."

"Get me a drink, will you, please," Lee said. "My head is spinning with all this. This afternoon I didn't know a single soul in Palmyra. Then suddenly I'm in the middle of a plot to murder your father. God Almighty! I'm just a simple horse thief from Colorado. What do you want me to do?"

She came back to bed with two drinks. "Kill Wingate," she said, handing him the whiskey. "Kill him before he kills you. If you don't you will hang as surely as the sun will rise tomorrow."

Lee knocked back the whiskey. "Why can't you tell the Mormons and have them do it? There must be more Mormons than gunmen."

Clarissa Rankin downed her own drink. "There are but my father doesn't want an out-and-out fight between the Mormons and Wingate's men. It would tear Palmyra apart. What he wants to do is keep the gunmen under control and perhaps get rid of them altogether. Will you do it?"

"I'll think about it," Lee said. "You have to give me time to think. How can I kill Wingate without getting killed myself? If his gunmen are loyal they'll lynch anybody that tries to stop them."

Clarissa Rankin got out of bed and started to get dressed. "It's very late and I must get home before Wingate learns I'm here. Will you do it, Ben? You can do it by stealth so no one will ever know. Kill him quietly, a rope or a knife. Then take the body away at night and throw it into a crevasse. It will save your life and my father will be grateful. I'm sure he will give you Wingate's job."

"Let me think about how it can be done," Lee said.

"That's all I ask," she said, putting on her sheepskin coat. "I'll be back tomorrow night and you can tell me what you decide."

Lee made himself look worried. "Tomorrow night I'll be in the barracks. That's what Wingate said. What should I do?"

She said, "Wait for me to find you. Goodnight, Ben, and God bless you."

She opened the door and a gun spat yellow flame in the darkness. The bullet ripped through the door and buried itself in the wall. Before the shooter fired again Lee sprang from the bed and knocked her to one side. Then he slammed the door and dived after her. Now the gun fired fast, ripping the door with lead. Then—Sweet Jesus Christ—he heard Missy yelling out there in the dark:

"Ben Trask, you crotch-loving son of a bitch! Come out Ben Trask or send your whore out so I can kill her! Ben Trask, you bastard, can you hear me!"

It went on and on like that. She had fired six times and he knew she was reloading. Then the shooting began again and so did the yelling and cursing. The door sagged on its hinges and bullet-struck tin plates clattered to the floor. Lying beside Rankin's daughter he counted the shots as they came. The sixth shot struck the wall and he jumped to his feet and went crashing through the door. Just then a

148

revolver fired twice and Missy screamed and then Lee saw Wingate bending over her with a gun in hand. At the same time the old man came limping as fast as he could from the street. He had the old Henry in one hand and when he saw Missy's body sprawled in the light from the doorway he tried to raise the rifle. Wingate shot him twice and he was dead before he hit the ground.

Staring at Lee, Wingate took a handful of bullets from the pocket of his black coat and began to reload. "It looks as if she suddenly went mad," he said to Lee. His voice was quiet and unemotional. He might have been talking about a sick horse he had to destroy. "She was crazy and so was her grandfather, but I never thought I'd have to kill them. She was shouting your name?"

Lee looked at Missy's small body sprawled in death. "She was crazy to get some man," he said. "I just came along at the wrong time."

Wingate holstered his Officer's Model Colt and said, "I'll get some men to take away the bodies. Are you all right?"

"I'm all right," Lee said. "But wait a minute. I have to tell you something. Bishop Rankin's daughter came to see me tonight. She's still in the cabin and I know you sent her to test me. Come out . . . Clarissa."

She came out smiling and Wingate was smiling too. "You're a faithful lover, Ben, after all we've meant to each other. Better watch this man, Fletcher. He may prove too clever even for you."

Fletcher Wingate smiled at her and told her to go home before her father arrived. She said goodnight to both of them and left. By now Mormons, but no hard cases, were crowding around the bodies. Wingate explained what had happened and told them to take the bodies away.

Lee turned to go back into the cabin and Wingate followed him. Lee poured a drink and drank it. Wingate said, "Would you have told me if the crazy woman hadn't started shooting up the place?"

Lee nodded. "I would have told you even if her story had sounded more convincing. It wasn't a bad story, but it was too complicated. My guess is you gave her a straight enough story, but she kept adding to it as she went along."

Wingate smiled his sourly humorous smile. "Something like that, I guess. But you would have told me? I have to make sure."

"I would have told you no matter what she said. I couldn't take the chance and not tell you. I find the best way to work is to trust one man and keep on trusting him until he proves absolutely and beyond all doubt that he can't be trusted. If you keep jumping from one to the other you usually end up trusting nobody. Am I making sense?"

Wingate said, "You're making a lot of sense and if that crazy woman meant anything to you I'm sorry I had to kill her."

You came up behind her and could have knocked her cold, Lee thought. Instead you chose to shoot her twice in the back.

"She meant nothing to me," Lee said. "I guess you saved my life. I didn't have my gun."

He knew this wasn't true because if Missy wanted to kill him she would have killed him. She wouldn't have yelled and hollered and pegged bullets without taking aim. .

"I guess I did at that," Wingate said, getting up from the table. "About your gun, you'll get it back tomorrow. And forget about the barracks. You can keep this cabin until there's a better one available. You want a wife or have you had enough of women for a while?"

"I wouldn't mind a wife," Lee said. "Where do I find one?"

"We'll go and look at the women in the morning," Wingate said.

In the morning Wingate came to the door while Lee was opening some of the cans with the patent opener. "You want to go now or later, after you've eaten?"

"I can eat any time," Lee said.

"Then let's not keep the ladies waiting," Wingate said, and handed Lee his Colt. He checked the loads and holstered the Colt and it was good to feel its weight on his hip.

"I suppose you've been wondering where the men are," Wingate said as they walked up the street in the pale, early morning sun.

"Sort of. All I saw were the new men in the barracks. I have to say they're a sorry looking bunch."

"That's the truth. I lied to you about them. Most of them aren't going anywhere but away from here. They're unarmed so the Mormons don't see them as much of a threat. The men with guns I sent out of town to take more supplies to the caves and other strong points we may have to fall back to if the army ever gets ambitious. So far it hasn't but

151

political pressure may build to the point where it has to do something. It would be a costly campaign in men and money, but the commanding general northwest may be pressured into doing something."

Lee said, "I thought that decision would be up to Washington."

"You're right. But there is such a thing as initiative. General Strater doesn't have much of that. But if he's ever replaced we may be in for trouble. That's why we have fixed a line of withdrawal. Caves in the mountains east of here are stocked with ammunition, foodstuffs, winter clothing, weapons. That's where the men are, east of here. I didn't want them here for Baxter's execution. They might have run wild and tried to stop it. Or the Mormons might have run wild and attacked them. We have an uneasy situation here at the best of times. The rape and the subsequent execution could easily have caused an explosion. It's in my interest to see that such a thing doesn't happen."

"And the men in the barracks?"

"It wouldn't have mattered if the Mormons had vented their anger on them. In fact, it might have released some of the tension and ill will that's been building up. One thing is certain. The situation here can't last indefinitely. Either the army will move or there will be open conflict between our two groups."

"And I expected to find a nice safe hideout," Lee said.

Wingate found that funny. "You still may find it. I've been thinking that it might not be a bad idea to get rid of the Mormons altogether. If that sounds ruthless, it is. It's a difficult decision to make. This is an ideal place from which to raid, but the whole thing has become too political. As a rule the government shows little inclination to become involved in the suppression of outlaw gangs. Leave that to the states and territories, the men in Washington say. But this—what we have here—has become too political. I have tried to convince Bishop Rankin to stop issuing all these proclamations of his, but he refuses. So every time there is a raid these proclamations are left behind. Nailed to doors or trees, left with rocks to weight them against the wind."

Lee thought of the tree at Spade Bit and wondered if Wingate had been there.

"To be honest," Wingate continued, "I would prefer to turn this whole Jack Mormon business into highly organized banditry. Forget about plural marriage as a political cause and concentrate on taking all there is to be taken in the shortest possible time. They say the West is changing, and of course it is, but Palmyra is an almost perfect outlaw haven in a world that is increasingly being ringed by civilization. This is the kind of place outlaws dream about, so why shouldn't it be put to the greatest possible use?"

They were now close to the edge of town and Wingate said, "We'll get to where the unattached women are in a few moments. They are housed beyond the town limits, you might say. Our little settlement keeps growing. You see I take a certain pride in the place, having been here almost from the start. But hardly a day passes that I don't regret that somehow a potentially great idea is going to waste."

153

"You mean turning it into a completely outlaw town?"

"Exactly. All this talk about Mormon fundamentalism and the right of plural marriage is just claptrap. It's backward looking and the government won't hold still for it. But a wholly bandit community, now there's an idea that is ahead of its time. Of course, money is the key and why shouldn't we have all the money we need."

"But first you'd have to get rid of the Mormons," Lee said.

"It always comes back to that," Wingate said. "But it's an idea I can't let go of, or it can't let go of me. Utah is a sparsely populated territory, but it has great riches. Inevitably it will become a state, but even now gold is being taken from its hills, so much that the banks of several cities, large and small, are bulging with money. A bandit army, well disciplined and trained, with a secure base, could fan out across this territory taking what it wanted. Once again, it couldn't last forever but—ah—if it only lasted a year or two. Those of us who led it would become rich beyond imagining. You could hire your smart lawyer then, Trask. You could hire a whole battery of lawyers. Yes, yes, I know. But first we would have to get rid of our Jack Mormon friends."

Lee smiled. "Rankin's daughter said you were a Mormon."

Wingate laughed. "Yes, of course I am. And I would become a Muslim if it suited my purpose."

Wingate stopped talking and pointed to a long log house with barred windows and surrounded by a stockade. "That's where you will find your bride-to-be. It isn't as terrible as it looks and not all the women in there are prisoners. The women who resist discipline are prisoners and are held there and worked very hard until they see the error of their ways. The others are there simply because there are too many of them and we don't have anywhere else to house them. It's up to you which kind you want. I'll go in with you but I can't stay. I have to see the bishop about something he has in mind."

A Mormon guard let them into the stockade and they went into the main house which was divided into two sections. Wingate spoke to the young Mormon woman, not bad looking but hard-faced, who opened the door.

"Morning, Mrs. Smiler," Wingate said. "I want you to meet Ben Trask who is to be my second in command. He needs a wife. Show him the ladies and let him decide for himself. How have the difficult ladies been behaving themselves?"

"Not too bad, Captain," the woman answered. "They know better than to get too *difficult* with me."

Wingate smiled at Lee and went out. If Maggie isn't here then I'll have to look somewhere else, Lee thought. By now she could be the wife of a Mormon or a hard case. That would make it much more difficult.

The Mormon woman called Mrs. Smiler said the women were eating breakfast, but that didn't mean that he couldn't look them over. What kind of wife did he have in mind?"

"I don't know," Lee said. "I'll have to look before

155

I decide."

"That's what they're here for," Mrs. Smiler said. "Why don't you look at the sensible women first?' Was I a man looking for a wife, that's what I'd do."

She took Lee to the section where the "sensible" women sat at long tables eating breakfast. Most of the sensible women had a subdued look. A few of them ventured timid smiles when he came in accompanied by Mrs. Smiler. He wondered how many were captives, how many were here of their own free will. He looked them over, but didn't see Maggie.

"I'd like to look at the others," he told Mrs. Smiler, who pursed her thin lips in disapproval, but said nothing.

The door to the other section was bolted and Mrs. Smiler warned him that some of the women in there were pretty wild.

"They don't want a husband and a family," she said. "They don't know how lucky they are to have the chance. A lot of women never get it at all. Watch they don't throw something at you. I'll go first to quiet them down."

Lee went in when Mrs. Smiler called him. Not all the women there were openly hostile; some were just silent, lost in misery but determined to resist. Others, the ones Mrs. Smiler called wild, started calling him names as soon as he stepped inside the door. Nearly all the wild ones were farm women, by the sound of them.

The least offensive thing he was called was "dirty, stinking, shit-faced son of a bitch."

And then he saw Maggie at the same moment she looked up from her plate and saw him. Her face contorted and for an instant he thought she was going to cry out and give him away. If that happened there was no way it would escape Mrs. Smiler's attention because she was right beside him. But Maggie put her face in her hands and bent her head and she might have been praying or crying or both. There was no way to tell. He stood there until Maggie raised her head again and this time her face was calm and showed no emotion of any kind.

"I'll take that one," he told Mrs. Smiler. "That young lady over there. Do you know what her name is?"

"Maggie McIvors," the Mormon woman said.

The "wild" women howled when Maggie's name was called and the Mormon woman beckoned her to leave the table and come forward. They called her every dirty name they could think of and pelted her with biscuits. Mrs. Smiler yelled at them to be quiet, but that only made them worse.

"Take her out quick," Mrs. Smiler urged. "They'll tear the place to bits if you don't get her out fast. I hope you know what you're doing. My opinion is you'd have done a lot better on the other side. This one's been a troublemaker since the day they brought her to Palmyra."

"I'll take her anyway," Lee said, smiling at Maggie who did her best to smile back. "Is this all I have to do: just take her?"

Mrs. Smiler looked surprised. "What else would there be?" She pushed the bolt into place, muffling some of the noise inside. "What you do with her now is your business. Bishop Rankin will marry you if that's what you want. If you don't it makes no dif-

157

ference." Mrs. Smiler did her best to smile, but it wasn't easy for her. "Mrs. Trask, that's your name, isn't it? Will you do me a great favor?"

"What is it?" Lee asked. Maggie stood beside him in one of the shapeless Mormon dressed. She had no coat and she shivered in the morning chill.

"No matter what happens," Mrs. Smiler said, "don't bring her back here. If she doesn't suit you, trade her to some other man. Just don't bring her back here."

NINE

"Wingate led the raid against Spade Bit," Maggie said.

They were in Lee's cabin and he had a big fire going and he made her drink some of the whiskey Rankin's daughter had left. She wasn't used to liquor and it made her cough. But it also brought some color to her face.

"There were about twenty of them," she said, "and they came early in the morning, so they must have been riding all night. Wingate led them and he gave the order to kill old Mac and the others. They had taken them prisoner, so they didn't have to kill them. I was there when they killed them and burned the house. Then Wingate gave the order to shoot the horses and they did. I begged them to shoot me too, but Wingate just laughed and said I was cut out for better things. I think that man hates all women. On the way back here they raided another ranch north of the Bear Lake. They shot two women there because Wingate said they were too old."

"Drink the rest of the whiskey," Lee said. "Go ahead and cry if you feel like it. No, I guess you won't. You're different, Maggie. You hardly seem like the same woman."

Maggie swallowed the rest of the whiskey. "Everything changed when I saw them shooting the horses. Those beautiful horses! I shouldn't say this, but the killing of the horses affected me more than the killing of Old Mac and the others. Is that wrong, to feel like that?"

"No, it's not wrong," Lee said. "Things take us in different ways."

Maggie said, "I was so sad when they began to kill the horses. Then after it was over I wasn't sad any more. All I felt was anger. I would have killed Wingate without mercy if somebody had given me a gun. But they're all bad, all evil men. The Mormons are as bad as the outlaws. God, how I'd like to kill every one of them. They took turns raping me on the way here. One after the other, like animals. Worse than animals. By the time I got here I couldn't feel anything. But I knew they weren't going to break me. You have to believe they haven't broken my spirit."

"I know that," Lee said.

"It's very very bad here, Lee. A woman in our part of the stockade killed herself the other night. Cut her throat with a sharp piece of glass from a broken whiskey bottle. There was blood everywhere. They fed us like pigs because the Jack Mormons think women should be strong and heavy to bear children. Being fed like that is worse than being

160

starved. But you should have seen the women in my part of the stockade. They call them the wild ones or the difficult women. God bless them, they are wild and they are difficult. Most of them are from the farms. They would fight like men if they had the guns."

Lee had been thinking of Wingate. "What was that you said?"

"I said they'd fight like men if they had the guns. Some of them even talked about it. I'm glad to be with you, but I hated to leave them. That evil Mormon woman hates them and they hate her. I hate her so much I'd like to kill her with my bare hands. I don't care what you think. I'd like to tear her God damned Jack Mormon eyes out."

"Easy," Lee said. "I feel the same way about Wingate, but take it easy. We have to figure out how we're going to escape from here. The old man and the woman who brought me here are dead. Wingate killed them. But they knew the trail in and out of here and I don't. Just the same we've got to try."

"But what about the women in the stockade? You can't just leave them here. They'll have no chance."

Lee wondered if there was any way to settle her down. "I don't know if we can do anything about it. We'll be lucky if we can save ourselves."

Suddenly her anger boiled over. "The hell with saving myself. I don't want to save myself. Those poor women are my friends. They need to be helped. You can go if you like, but I'm going to stay. I didn't go through hell to run away from my friends."

Lee felt like a man swimming across an icy river

with an anvil on his back. He had come so far to bring this woman out and now she didn't want to go. It made him angry with the whole God damned world.

"What the hell can two people do? This may be the only chance we get. Wingate has sent his outlaws into the mountains to head off trouble with the Mormons. One of them raped a Mormon's woman and was hanged for it. But the Mormons are still ready to explode. So are Wingate's outlaws."

"I don't care about any of that," Maggie said angrily. "I want to talk about how we can save the women. I'm not just talking about the women in the stockade. I'm talking about all the women who are here against their will."

"Go ahead and talk."

"No, you talk. You know more about this sort of thing than I do. I'm asking you again. What can be used against these evil men?"

"Will you let me think a minute, for Christ's sake. There might be a chance of getting away if it came to open warfare between the Mormons and Wingate's outlaws. But I don't think that's going to happen, at least not in time to do us any good. You know where they keep the guns? Is there a place where they store weapons?"

"Yes, I do know," she said. "There are guns in that building Rankin uses as a town hall. The building where his office is. There are guns in a room on the ground floor."

"How do you know?"

"The women in the stockade talk about guns all the time. One of them was given to a Mormon who

162

didn't like her and put her back in the stockade as punishment. This man had charge of those guns. They must still be there."

"Did she say how many guns?"

"Damn it, Lee. She said a lot of guns. Guns and ammunition. There's a padlock on the door, but that can be broken, can't it?"

"The dam," Lee said suddenly. "God damn it, the God damned dam. Wait a minute, listen to me. They just finished building a dam east of town. It's high up, it dams a small lake, they built it to work the gold diggings. Must have something to do with pressure hoses. I don't know what it's for, but it's there. Did you ever hear any explosions? Dynamite? Explosions?"

She nodded. "There were some explosions when they brought me here, I heard them one afternoon and then they stopped."

"Good. They must have been blowing down rocks and dirt from the side of the mountain. It's no use asking you if that woman said anything about dynamite?"

"She just talked about guns, Lee."

"Doesn't matter. If you heard explosions, there must be dynamite. If we can get dynamite we can blow the dam and wash away the whole settlement. The dam is filled to capacity. I heard Wingate talking to Rankin about letting some of it loose. It must be capicity-full if they're letting it spill. If we can blow the dam this town will be hit by a wall of water. There won't be a thing left standing after it passes over. Christ! If we could only get at the guns and arm those farm women. I guess you know some of them will be killed if we do get the guns?"

"Of course I know it." Maggie was angry again. "Don't you think they know that and do you think they care? Like hell they care! The Jacks have been working them like dogs to break their spirit. But they haven't been able. Those women you saw me with this morning, they're out in the fields right now. They'll work there until the sun goes down. A Mormon with a whip and a gun stands over them. How do you think they feel? Do you think they're afraid to die?"

"Don't get mad at me," Lee said. "I'm beginning to think this can be done. But they have to be out of the stockade with guns in their hands before the dam blows. If not, they'll all die and we'll probably die with them."

Maggie took another drink of whiskey. "I don't give a damn. I don't care if I die as long as those bastards die with me."

"Don't be in such a hurry to die," Lee said. He wanted a drink himself, but didn't have it because he didn't want Wingate smelling it on his breath. When he looked across at Maggie he saw that she was falling asleep, worn out by the tension that had finally been released by whiskey. God damn it, she was all right. She was more than all right and she had proven him wrong. The iron he thought her character lacked had come to the forefront the minute she found herself in serious trouble. And that was where it counted most: when the chips were down.

He lifted her and carried her to the bed. She murmured something, but didn't wake up. He covered her with a blanket and sat down to think. Damn it, it could be done if all the parts came together at the same time and if they had the right amount of luck. You couldn't succeed at anything if luck wasn't with you. Being in the right didn't always bring luck, but he liked to think it did.

Someone would have to lead the women while he set the charges and buried Palmyra under a million tons of water. That meant Maggie unless there was some women in the stockade who could do it better. He didn't think there was.

They would have to be safe on the high ground when the wall of water hit. That meant the mountain slope where the fields were. But they couldn't be just on high ground, they had to be far up the slope, almost as far up as Rankin's God damned temple, when the dynamite-powered flood put an end to this evil place. He felt the old hot anger coming back as he thought of Wingate and Rankin and all they had done, all the human misery they had caused. He thought of decent ranchers and farmers he hadn't known and never would know because they were dead. He thought of the two women Wingate had murdered north of Bear Lake. Because they were too old, Wingate said.

He felt there would be no justice at all if Rankin and Wingate didn't die with the others. But he forced himself to be calm. He would do the best he could; he would kill them if he could. That was the idea: to kill as many of the bastards as possible. But he couldn't risk the lives of everyone just because he wanted to kill two men who deserved to die, if anyone deserved to die, and so he would give it up if

165

he had to. But if by some chance they happened to escape, well then he would have to catch up with them in some other place and at some other time. It was as simple as that.

He didn't know how much store he could put in his position as Wingate's second in command. Nothing was for sure. But right or wrong he would have to take it for granted that Wingate now trusted him and wanted him for the job. It could all be some elaborate lie, but he would have to assume that it was not. It was the only way he could put this plan into action.

First he would have to get into Rankin's town hall to see if the guns were there. Without the guns they didn't have much chance of pulling it off. The flood probably wouldn't kill every Mormon, every outlaw, and so there would be shooting. How much depended on how many men survived the flood. That some of the farm and ranch women could shoot he had no doubt, but how many could shoot well enough to go out against men? But they couldn't shoot at all if they didn't have guns. He would have to move fast because the Mormons, meaning the bishop, could remove the guns and ammunition at any time. With open warfare a very likely possibility Rankin might play it safe and move the weapons to a more secure place, where Wingate's men couldn't get their hands on them.

Breaking the women out of the stockade was another, different problem. According to Maggie the stockade was guarded day and night by a single guard whose position was just inside the gate. One man didn't mean much provided he could be killed silently. If he got off as much as a single shot the entire plan would be ruined. He knew he could trust Maggie to lead the women, but he didn't think she'd be able to kill a guard without making a sound. Well she might, of course, that is, if she got close enough and the guard was unsuspecting. That would free him for the work on the dam. He decided that it would be better all round if someone else killed the guard.

The dynamite presented the most difficult problem because he didn't know where it was, and there was even the possibility that all the dynamite had been used up during the blasting. No dynamite, no damn busting, no escape. Of course Maggie would insist that the women would fight anyway. Sure they would. They'd probably fight like tigers, but would it do any good, and the answer had to be that it would not. No matter how hard they fought, they would be beaten in the end.

Maggie woke up and asked what he was going.

"Planning the escape," he said, and he asked her if she thought she could kill the guard at the stockade. Then he explained how it had to be done, quickly and without noise. "I don't know if you'll have to kill that Jack Mormon woman. Is she armed?"

Maggie said, "She has a pistol, but she doesn't carry it into the dormitory. She's afraid somebody will take it away from her. Yes, I can kill the guard and I can kill her too. I want to kill her. It will be a pleasure to kill her."

"I told you to go easy," Lee warned her.

"I can't go easy, I don't want to go easy. What do you care how I am if I get the job done?"

"Suit yourself, Maggie. Just don't get everybody else killed. I think you have to be the one to lead the women back to the town hall to get the guns. Can you do it?"

She nodded. "I can do it."

"And later if there's fighting? What then? You've never fired a long gun in your life."

Maggie looked defiant. "Then I'll lead them with a pistol. I've seen you shoot a pistol at Spade Bit. I know how to load and fire. You point it and pull the trigger."

Lee grinned at her. "That's how you do it all right."

"What else do you want me to do?" Maggie was showing more fire than he'd ever thought possible. No matter what happened after this, she would be all right, a new woman, tough and brave and strong. The whiner and the house proud nag who wanted to be liked by "respectable" people was gone for good.

He told her about taking the women high up the mountain slope.

"You may have to fight your way up. They'll forget you're women when they see you have guns. The Mormons will show less mercy than the outlaws. The outlaws may or may not be in the settlement. Just don't expect any mercy from the Mormons. The sight of women with rifles will drive them wild. They're used to having women fetch and carry for them. That makes them think they have bigger balls than other men."

A few weeks before Maggie the prig would have objected to that kind of language. Now she just smiled.

"We'll shoot their big balls off if we get the chance."

"Move along the side of the mountain while the flood is boiling through. Head east and try to make the badlands before the flood ebbs. It's a small lake and the flood won't last all that long. I'll follow along as soon as I can. But make for the badlands. If you have to you can make some sort of stand there. Above all keep going, always heading east. Once we're in the badlands we'll all be equal. I don't know if I can find a way through any better than you can."

"Yes, but what if there is nothing to run from? If the flood destroys them, why should we lose ourselves in country where we may be lost for good?"

Lee smiled at her. "Then all you do is move east along the mountain and wait for me. Let the escape plan go for a while. There's something else I must ask you to do. You may find it harder than anything I've asked you so far."

She looked puzzled. "Such as?"

"I want you to be pleasant to Wingate when he calls. He'll be sure to come by to see what kind of wife I've picked. Can you do it? It's important to keep on his good side. The plan can't succeed unless I can move around freely. Maggie, do you hear what I'm saying?"

Instead of giving him an answer she stared into space. Her eyes narrowed and her face turned pale. She must be reliving the whole thing, he thought.

"Maggie, answer me. If you can't be pleasant to Wingate I'll try to head him off. I didn't mean you

169

have to kiss him and treat him like your dearest friend. Can you be civil? That's all I'm asking."

"All you're asking! I'm sorry, Lee. You're doing your best and I'm being dramatic." She sounded very tired. "Yes, yes, yes! The answer is yes, I can be civil to the dirty fucking cruel son of a bitch. I can be civil to him, but don't ask me to be more than that."

Lee said, "That'll do fine. He'd be suspicious if you were more than that. He may be suspicious anyway. Wingate is a suspicious man."

"If you can call him a man."

"Makes no difference what you call him. We need him for now. I know somebody was watching me the night the old man and his granddaughter were killed by Wingate. At the time I thought Wingate was behind it, but it could just as easily have been Rankin. He may be moving to protect himself. I have to find out who was following me or I won't be able to check on the guns."

Maggie was sitting by the fire with a blanket wrapped around her and he knew she was dreading the arrival of the man who was responsible for her degradation at the hands of the Spade Bit raiders. He had asked her to be "civil" to Wingate, but hadn't asked himself how he would take Wingate when he came to the door. He knew he could keep himself under control, but he would have to do much more than that. Since Wingate became his friend a sort of easy familiarity existed between them and the other man even made his little sour jokes about the Mormons and their ways, and that morning, walking to the stockade, he had done an impersonation of Rankin's speaking style that would have been funny under normal circumstances.

It was hard to think of Wingate as lonely, but he couldn't think of any other word to describe him. He seemed to have a need to talk not only about the situation in Palmyra but about himself, as if talking convinced him of his own importance, and when he talked of the huge amount of money he needed to leave the country, there was the feeling that he really didn't want to go because he would then be finally on his own, cut off from the past which he claimed was of no importance and yet seemed to haunt him.

Lee knew that Wingate's claim on his friendship might be genuine enough, yet it did not necessarily prevent Wingate from regarding him with deep suspicion. This wasn't all that hard to understand, but it could make it difficult to know when Wingate was just making a casual observation or when he was saying something with some deeper purpose behind it.

Maggie would have said that he was taking too much time trying to figure out Wingate's character when all that was needed was a bullet through his head, but he knew it was worth the effort because it was the only way he could even guess at how Wingate would behave in some future situation. So far he could only conclude that Wingate was a man who saw too many sides of the same question for his own good. The Mormons were a threat because their open defiance of the federal government would inevitably bring retribution and so the only logical thing was to destroy them, yet he always hesitated at taking that final step. Sending his force of outlaws to the mountains when he should by right have kept them in the settlement for his own protection and as proof of his power was another example of his reluctance to meet an important decision head-on, and while this kind of thinking might have been understandable in a civilian it was a puzzle when the man involved had been trained as an officer, someone accustomed to making decisions and then carrying them out . . .

Lee looked up and so did Maggie when there was the crunch of boots in gravel and a knock on the door. He nodded to her and she nodded back. She was ready to meet the man she hated more than any man in the world. Lee opened the door and Wingate stood there black-suited and sourly smiling and he said, "Well, let's have a look at the new wife, Trask. You can't have come back without picking one." He came in still smiling and when he saw Maggie his smile didn't change and didn't fade, and he said in a hearty voice that didn't suit him, "So this is the little woman."

Maggie stood up slowly and Lee said, "Maggie, this is Captain Wingate."

Maggie bent her head and Wingate said, "Please call me Fletcher. It's an unfortunate name but it belonged to my father and he decided to share some of his humiliation with me."

"I am pleased to meet you," Maggie said, and her lips were as drained of color as her face.

"The pleasure is mine," Wingate said, and Lee thought: God damn it, he doesn't even remember her or he's pretending he doesn't, but even as he looked at Wingate he knew he wasn't pretending. His smile was too casual to come from anything but indifference. He's playing the gentlemanly officer to the noncom's wife, Lee thought. He really doesn't remember her.

"I'm going to steal your husband for a while," Wingate told Maggie, still playing a part that didn't suit him. Maggie nodded stiffly and they went outside.

Lee got ready for questions about Maggie, but none came. "I just got word that the men are returning to Palmyra without orders," Wingate began.

"Maybe your information is wrong," Lee said, but Wingate cut him off with, "My information is not wrong. They are returning without orders and how soon they get here depends on how fast they travel. I'm assuming they'll get here some time tonight."

"You think they'll be trouble?"

"I don't know. It depends on how the Mormons see it. The men have had time to think about Baxter's execution. My information is they suspect me of selling them out to the Mormons. They don't realize I had to hang Baxter or the Mormon would have risen up and slaughtered them."

"What do you want to do, Captain?"

"Wait until they get here, they try to reason with them. That won't be easy, but I have to try. The worst news is they've been drinking. No, my information is not wrong. They've been drinking."

"Where would they get liquor in the mountains?"

Wingate gave Lee an impatient look. "It's not hard to make moonshine, raw alcohol. All you need

173

is copper tubing, some kind of mash, a fire. It can be made out of almost anything. You must know all that. They had plenty of time to make it between raids and now they're drinking it and threatening to kill all the Mormons. That may be just drunken talk or they may really intend to do it. The hell of it is they're our men and we'll have to back them if the Mormons start shooting at them. Some of the Mormons have wanted to get rid of us for a long time. They resent outsiders, any and all outsiders. There may be nothing for it but to seize Rankin and hold him as hostage. We'll seize their leader and seize their guns at the same time. Then we can bargain or try to. If that fails we'll hang onto Rankin and pull out of here."

"What guns are you talking about?" Lee asked, not liking the sound of this. "I would have thought each Mormon had his own weapons."

"Of course they do, but they also have a large reserve of rifles where Rankin has his office. You were there. That building. They're downstairs in a storeroom. Dozens of rifles, thousands of rounds of ammunition. The rifles are just sitting there. We have to get at them if a shooting war can't be avoided. The hell of it is they may grab it first. Damn that Baxter and his hot cock! He may have fucked us into a war."

It wasn't like Wingate to use obscenities and Lee could see how agitated he was. Seizing the guns would be an act of war that Wingate wanted to avoid.

"You know who the rabblerousers are?" Lee asked. "You know which of our men are trying to

174

force a fight with the Mormons? Every mob has its leaders?"

"Ferguson is," Wingate said. "He has his supporters, but he's been behind this all along. He's a thug and a bully and he was one of Baxter's closest friends. They belonged to the same gang in Montana. I should have done away with him when I had the chance, but he's loud and brash and well-liked by the other men. He's wild and dangerous but Baxter was able to keep him in line because they were friends. He's the one who's leading the men back here. I don't know how to stop him short of killing him. And if I do that the men will turn on me."

"I'll stop him," Lee said. "You won't have to kill him and you won't have to seize the guns unless you want to."

Wingate stared at Lee. "You don't even know Ferguson. How can you stop him? He's bigger and heavier, and stronger than you are. What do you think you're going to do, challenge him to a fist fight? He may not want to fight you with his fists or feet or anything else but a gun. He may just whip out a gun and kill you. Get into a fight with him and they may all pile on top of you. You're talking like a madman."

"I'll find a way to stop him," Lee repeated. "He can't be so much of a monster as you say he is."

Wingate was seething with impatience. "Talking to you is like talking to the wall. I'm telling you he'll kill you. Baxter told me Ferguson has killed and crippled men in saloon fights. Can you say the same? Of course you can't. The man is not civilized even by the standards of his kind."

"Let me try it," Lee urged. "Isn't it worth a try if it means buying us time? That's what you want, isn't it? You said yourself a shooting war with the Mormons can't be won. At least it can't be won the way things are now."

"No, it can't be won the way things are now. We'll wait until they get back and I'll try to reason with them. If that fails then you'll have your chance at Ferguson. Of course the Mormons may attack without warning and we'll be glad to have men like Ferguson on our side. You better lay low for now. That's what I'm going to do. You don't have to wonder what time the men will arrive. You'll hear them long before they get back."

Lee went back inside and repeated everything to Maggie, who looked alarmed when he told her he was going to take on Ferguson.

"He may kill you," she said. "Wingate must know what he's talking about. He knows this man and you don't. Don't do it, Lee. We'll find another way to escape."

"There is no other way," he said. "We need those guns, but if Wingate seizes them that's the end of it. Ferguson isn't John L. Sullivan, for Christ's sake. He's not the wild man of the woods. He's just a man."

"John L. Sullivan wouldn't try to bite off your nose," Maggie said. She didn't smile. "John L. Sullivan wouldn't try to break your spine. Give it up, Lee."

He didn't know where she got her information, but he knew she was right about Ferguson. Saloon brawlers used every dirty trick they could think of: teeth, boots, broken bottles, everything and anything. Biting off ears and noses were commonplace. Eye gouging was as common as drunken salesmen in day coaches. But if you expected all that, had seen it before, it came as no surprise.

"He may seize the guns no matter how your fight with Ferguson comes out," Maggie argued. "You may get killed or crippled for nothing. Then what will happen to me?"

He smiled at her. Women always said that when all else failed. "You'll be fine," he said. "You're one of the wild women from the stockade and nothing's ever going to get you down. You said that yourself, or have you forgotten so soon?"

"I have forgotten that you used to be pretty good in bed," she said. "Why don't we get under the blankets so I can make sure you haven't lost your touch?"

Later she said, "All right, you pass the test. However, there are other tests I would like to make . . ."

TEN

Lee was pulling on his boots when he heard them coming and they sounded like Texas cowboys at the end of trail, barreling into town with three months wages in their pockets. Their howling echoed up and down the valley, but there were no gunshots. At least they had enough sense not to push the Mormons too far.

"Be careful, Lee," Maggie called from the bed.

He put on his hat and went up the street to the log barracks where he knew Wingate would be waiting. Wingate was a vicious son of a bitch, but he wasn't a coward. He'd be there, ferret-eyed and sourly smiling.

"Let me talk first," Wingate said, stepping out of the shadows.

The street was deserted and there was a moon, but clouds threw shadows on the side of the mountains. Up above the great peak hung over everything. Mormons might be watching, but they didn't show

178

themselves. Lee eased the Bisley Colt in his oiled holster. As Wingate said, this thing might not be decided with fists.

The yelling came closer and soon they could see them coming in from the end of town, thirty-two likkered-up hard cases swaying in their saddles, drunk and angry and loaded for bear. Moonlight glinted on the liquor bottles in their hands and they traded obscenities. One man started to belt out a dirty song, but was shushed by the others. They had the solemnity of drunks, but these drunks were armed to the teeth. Lee and Wingate stepped into the street where they could be seen.

"That's Ferguson with the white Stetson," Wingate said before they got close enough to hear.

Lee saw a man about his own age, but wide and big and heavy. He was so big that he seemed to dwarf the big Morgan horse he was riding. Even on a horse and still at a distance he had the look of a man who kicks down doors and throws policemen through windows.

Ferguson was out in front and he saw Wingate and Lee before the others. He said something to the man closest to him and they all reined in. Lee and Wingate walked toward them.

"Well goodnight there, Captain," Ferguson called out in a low loud voice that didn't have much intelligence behind it. "Out for a stroll in the moonlight, are you, Captain? Who's your lady friend? Or should I say, Who's your gentleman friend? You do have gentleman friends, don't you, Captain? Anyhow, that's the rumor that's been going round. Nasty things, rumors, except with you they ain't exactly rumors, are they?"

So that was the trouble with Wingate, Lee thought. A few sneering words from a saloon brawler had explained everything.

"What are you doing back here, Ferguson?" Wingate said. "I told you to stay out there until I sent for you. You know what can happen here? They're ready to attack us, they want to attack us. Now take the men and go on back to the supply base. You have everything you need there. I see you have plenty of liquor. What's all this drinking about? I never knew you to be much of a drinking man."

Ferguson took a swig from the bottle in his hand. "Well you see, Captain, this is kind of a special occasion. Kind of an Irish wake so there has to be plenty of liquor. We're mourning the untimely death of our dear friend Tom Baxter. You heard of him, I'd say. You oughta heard of him. You hanged him, you man-loving son of a bitch."

The hardcases laughed and jeered, but Wingate stood his ground. He flipped his coat behind the butt of his Officer's Model Colt and his hand dropped to his side. "If you'd like to back up that kind of lying dirty talk with gunplay, here I stand. Come on Ferguson, make a try for your gun."

Ferguson just laughed and had another drink. "We all know how good with a gun you are, Captain, and you won't find me making the mistake of going up against you. That, sir, would be suicide. But that don't mean I'm the least bit afraid of you. You are ten times a better shot than I am and you can shoot me any old time you like only you'll be full of lead in three seconds. Isn't that right, boys?''

There was a chorus of approval and Ferguson said, "Captain, we're all through taking orders from you. As of this moment your little outlaw army is disbanded, meaning that you can go soak your head in a shit bucket. We're not going back to any God damned mountains and we're not going to check any God damned supplies. What we're going to do is stay right here in good old Palmyra and have ourselves a whale of a time. We're going to fuck all the ladies and kick the asses of all the men. And if they want to start shooting at us, well then, Captain sir, we're just going to have to shoot back. Tit for tat, like the girl said to the soldier. Now get out of our road, Captain sir, or we'll ride all over you."

Wingate turned to Lee. "Any time you like," he said.

Ferguson leaned his bulk forward and cupped a hand to an ear. "What was that you said to your gentleman friend, Captain sir? What's your name, Gentleman Friend? Are you of the same persuasion as Mr. Wingate?"

"Least all I don't fuck my mother like you, pig-face. That's right, you fuck your mother because your mother is a scabby whore that sucks cocks for a living. How'd you like them apples, pig-face."

Ferguson was so startled that he just looked down at him. This bear of a man was being grossly insulted by a man ten inches shorter and a hundred pounds lighter and he just stood there instead of running for the hills.

"What did you say?" Ferguson sounded so astonished that some of the hard cases chuckled. "Shut up!" he roared. "Everybody shut up. I see a cockroach standing in front of me asking to be stepped on."

"Try it, pig-face," Lee dared him. "Climb down and try it. I'm as good with a gun as the captain, but I'm not going to shoot you. Climb down, you tub of pig shit."

Ferguson was so heavy that it took him a while to dismount. Then he walked toward Lee, all three hundred pounds of him. "I'm going to tear your head off and cork your ass with it." He uttered other fanciful threats. "I'm going to tear your leg off and beat you over the head with it."

He was reaching for Lee when Lee drew the Bisley and cocked it right in Ferguson's face. The muzzle was only a few inches from his forehead, so he could see it. It was cocked and Lee's hand was steady. "All you have to do is grab it," Lee said. "It's cocked and this pistol has a hair trigger, but you might get lucky. Take a chance, pig-face. If you're fast enough you can grab my hand with both of yours and so stop the hammer from falling. I've seen that done, so I know it can be done. But speed is what counts. I'll give you thirty seconds to think about it."

There wasn't a sound as Lee held the pistol steady as a rock. Ferguson had been half-drunk, but he was sobering fast and though the night was cold beads of sweat ran down his booze-reddened face. One of the drunk hard cases called out, "We going to let this son of a bitch treat Fergy like that." Another man, less drunk, told him to shut up. Lee started talking again.

"What's the matter, pig-face, got no guts. You got a whole sackful of gripes but no real guts. Your pals want you to do something but you're letting them down. What's happening to Fergy the iron man? Why looka here, pig-face Ferguson done shit and pissed his pants. If you can get hold of my wrist you can snap the bones like twigs. But you got to take the chance, pig-face."

Ferguson's eyes rolled up to look at the barrel of the Bisley and his huge fists clenched and unclenched without doing anything. "Get a move on, Fergy," Lee said. "You get hold of me you can bend my spine till it snaps, you can toss me clear over the top of that mountain. All the things you were going to do to me, why ain't you doing them? I'm getting tired of this, Fergy. I'm going to pull the trigger in a minute. Goodbye, Fergy."

Lee pulled the trigger and the flat sound of the hammer fallling on an empty chamber echoed in the silent street. Ferguson didn't move and neither did Lee.

"Now the next one may or not be live," Lee said matter-of-factly, "but of course you have no way of knowing that. Now I got an offer I want to make to you. You want me to pull the trigger of do you want to strip off our clothes and do a dance buck nekkid. Don't see why you got to be shy about it seeing as how all your friends are here. I'll count to five and while I'm doing it you decide what it's going to be. One . . . two . . . three . . . four . . ."

"I'll dance," Ferguson said.

"Can't hear you," Lee told him. "Repeat after me and say it loud. I'm a big teddy bear and I want to dance for my liddle friends. Repeat after me and say it loud. I'm a big teddy bear and my iddle pecker swings when I dance. Repeat after me and say it loud. I'm a big teddy bear and sometimes I like to eat shit."

With one quick movement, Lee stepped back from Ferguson and ordered him to strip or get shot through the head. Lee taunted him with, "If you don't want to strip, why don't you tell your pals to open up on me. See, Fergy, you don't have the balls of a flea. Get off your clothes, Fergy, or do I start counting? One . . . two . . ." Ferguson began to take off his clothes. His large size pants dropped to the plank-paved street, revealing a very dirty pair of underdrawers. One item of clothes followed another until Ferguson stood naked in the middle of Palmyra's main street.

"Dance," Lee ordered. "Dance and sing, Fergy, your pals want some entertainment. Dance and sing. I'm a big teddy bear and I want to dance for my iddle friends." Ferguson began a slow shuffling dance. One or two men laughed, then the laughter spread through the gang of hard cases and there were whoops of approval or disapproval, and it was just as Lee had thought. Ferguson had enemies as well as friends.

Lee pointed the Colt at Ferguson's face and told him to dance out of town. "Just go as you are," he said. "Leave your clothes. I said leave them right there in the street. Don't come back, Fergy. If you come back I'll shoot you on sight."

184

Huge and naked, Ferguson stood there helplessly. "You can't do this. I'm cold. I can't go out there without my clothes. Some of you men help me."

"I'm going to kill you in ten seconds," Lee warned. "Now dance on out, Fergy. Dance and sing: 'I'm a big teddy bear and I want to dance for my friends.' Go on now, it's not so hard."

Lee waited until Ferguson disappeared into the darkness before he looked at the rest of them. He said, "You men go back to where you were and don't come back here till you're sent for. Do it now."

There was some hesitation but it disappeared as soon as he holstered his gun and turned his back to them. This was their chance to blow him to bits. But then he heard them turning their horses. Wingate was still there and he said, "You did it all right. Where did you ever learn a trick like that?"

"On the Mexican border. A local badman was terrorizing a small town and nobody was able to do anything about him. Then they hired a town tamer and instead of killing the bully he made him strip in the plaza right in the middle of the day. He probably found clothes somewhere, but he never came back. If Ferguson comes back I *will* kill him. What do you think, Captain?"

"It's over for now," Wingate said. "You've made yourself a lot of enemies tonight. But you know that."

"I know it and I don't care. It wouldn't have worked any other way. One shot and we'd be dead now. You want me for anything else?"

"Are you in such a hurry to go home?" Wingate asked.

"It's the time of night for it."

"They'll be thinking you're the one to obey," Wingate said.

"No, I don't want anybody to obey me. You're the captain as far as I'm concerned. Goodnight."

Lee walked away and Wingate called "Goodnight" after him. There wasn't a sound as he walked back to the cabin. He had carried off this bit of bravado, but he knew it had been a fluke. Ferguson had buckled but another badman with more pride might have defied him even with a cocked gun in his face. Ferguson had been a bully for so long that he hadn't ever really been tested. Being tested was what made a man tough.

"What happened?" Maggie said when he came in. "I kept waiting for the sounds of guns going off."

Lee told her what had happened and she turned pale. "And Wingate just stood there?" she said.

"That's what he did," Lee said. "The outlaws are gone, but they may not stay gone. It was the shock of what happened to Ferguson that made them leave town. Every man there was thinking, 'I don't want that to happen to me.' When I say thinking I don't mean really thinking. Men like that fear humiliation more than anything else. Sooner or later they'll know it couldn't have happened to them. They may decide to come back and kill me. Or when they get halfway sober they'll see the sense of not getting into a shooting match with the Mormons. You never can be sure what outlaws are going to do."

"So that's what Wingate is," Maggie said. "No wonder he hates women. I can feel it now, what's wrong with him. The trouble that brought him here must have had something to do with that."

"Probably. There must have been a killing or a number of killings. But I'm just guessing. Forget about what he did. We don't have much time. If I can find the dynamite we'll do it tomorrow night. If there is no dynamite we'll burn the town and try to use that as a cover. We'll have the Mormons after us, but if there's to be an escape it has to be as soon as possible. Tomorrow night may be too late, but I don't see how it can be done any sooner. I'm going out now to see if the guns are there."

"Wingate may be watching," Maggie said. "I know I said all those things, but I was talking about myself. I don't want you to get killed. What if Ferguson is waiting for you in the dark?"

Lee shrugged. He was tired of Wingate and the Mormons and Palmyra and everything. "If he comes back it will take him time to work up to it. You take my gun and watch yourself. If Ferguson comes in that door you shoot and keep on shooting. Aim at his chest. It's a big enough target. Just don't shoot me when I come back."

"How long will you be?"

"Not long," Lee answered. "It's just down the street. I just hope there isn't a guard. I'll have to think about what to do if there's a guard."

There were some Jack Mormon houses behind the houses that lined the main street. One good thing about Palmyra: it had no dogs. He moved quickly without making a sound. No lights showed anywhere. Moving and then stopping to listen, he got to the back of the town hall in a few minutes. The building stood squat and dark and ominous. He edged toward the door and found it padlocked.

He climbed to the second floor using notches in the logs as footholds. In place of glass the windows had hinged shutters that opened out. He tried two windows and found the shutters bolted from the inside. A third shutter was looser than the others and he used his knife to slide back the wooden bolt. He left the shutters open to give him light. He was in Rankin's office, with its big desk and carved chair. He went downstairs with a ring of keys he found in a desk drawer. The door to the gunroom was sure to be padlocked.

There were rooms on the ground floor, but the only one with a padlock on it was under the stairs. There were only three keys on the ring and the second one he tried opened the lock. He pulled the lock loose and went into darkness that smelled of gun oil. The room had no windows and he struck a sulphur match after he closed the door. There they were, the guns, all rifles, no handguns. They lay in factory cases. One case had the lid pried up and he picked up a rifle, a .44 caliber, the one with the long barrel. The rifle was new and had recently been cleaned. So had the others in the case. He put the rifle back.

Cases of ammunition stood against the wall. He had to light another match, taking care to put the charred stub of the other one in his pocket. And then, moving the light, he saw the case of dynamite. The case was open and some of the sticks had been removed. It was a hell of a place to store dynamite, but he saw that the sticks were new and not at all sweated. Stick dynamite wasn't like liquid nitro. It wasn't dangerous if you didn't expose it to too much heat or rough handling. They said it was possible to hit a stick of new dynamite with a hammer without causing an explosion. Lee had never tried that.

There were primers and fuses to go with the dynamite. He put four sticks and primers and a length of fuse in the pockets of his coat and looked around to see if he had left any signs of being there. There were none.

He put the padlock back in place but didn't lock it. It looked all right if you didn't look too close. Unless somebody checked it during the day it would be the way he left it when the women came for the guns.

He went back upstairs and put the keys back in Rankin's desk. Then he went out the window and used the knife point to bolt the window. Five minutes later he was back in the cabin after calling to Maggie before he opened the door. She was in a chair with the cocked pistol in her lap. He took the pistol and let down the hammer and holstered it. Her eyes grew wide when he showed her the dynamite.

"We're getting there," he said. "We'll go tonight. Are you sure you'll be able to go through with it? If you can't do it, say so now. It'll be too late after we get started. Answer me. Can you do it?"

"Yes, I can do it."

"It has to be a knife. This knife." He showed her the long-bladed skinning knife he always carried in his boot. "Take it, get used to the feel of it."

She took the knife and turned it in her hand. The lamplight was reflected in the blade. "I'll be all right," she said. "What time will it happen?"

189

"Late," he said. "After they've gone to bed. I'll give you my watch. Get the women out of the stockade and go along behind the houses on the main street. We'll walk around today and I'll show you where the town hall is. The front door will be padlocked and you'll have to tear it loose or break down the door. Those big farm women ought to know how to break down a door. But get it done because you have to be on the mountain when the dam goes up. The rifles are new Winchesters and are easy to load and shoot. Couldn't be easier."

Her eyes were bright. "We're finally going to get away from this horrible place."

"If all goes well," he said. "Here's how it will go, allowing for setbacks. Ten o'clock should be late enough. We'll leave here together. I'll head for the dam, you for the stockade. I'll give you a full hour and a half to break the women out, take the guns and start climbing the mountain. But make sure you have the rifles loaded before you start across the street. You'll be out in the open then and there's the chance you'll be spotted. If somebody challenges you don't try to do anything but kill him. Just open fire and keep shooting. You'll have all the ammunition you need, so just keep shooting. But get up on that mountain. That's the most important part of all. There will be nothing left of the town when the water hits."

"We'll be up on the mountain if we have to crawl there."

Lee smiled, feeling better now that he had the dynamite. "Run, don't crawl. Anyway, walk fast. Like I said, move along the slope and wait for me. If

I don't show up after the water goes down, head for the badlands."

Maggie stared at him. "Then we head west and keep heading west."

"It's the best you can do," Lee said. "If the flood destroys the Jacks we can come back and try to find what we can. It would be hell to start back without supplies. But that part has to come later. First we have to get out."

"Yes," Maggie agreed. "First we have to get out."

In the morning, they walked along the main street and he showed her where the town hall was. The doors were open, which probably meant that Rankin was in his office. Above the town the dam stood like some kind of fortification. On the way back they met Wingate heading for the town hall. "Morning," he said to Maggie, touching the brim of his hat.

"I'm going to talk to Rankin," he said. "It may still be possible to avoid trouble. I'll point out that the men have gone back to the mountains. That should convince the bishop that we have no intention of trying to seize power."

Lee thought it was strange to hear Wingate use such expressions as "seize power" when he was talking about a miserable little settlement populated by renegade Mormons and ragtag outlaws. "I hope you can convince him," Lee said, thinking of the dynamite he had hidden back at the cabin. He hated to let it out of his hands, but it was too bulky to carry around even in the big pockets of his coat.

They went back to the cabin and waited for night to come. Maggie said, "I keep thinking of all that's happened during the last few weeks. Less than that. It just seems like a long time. Remember how I used to talk about wanting to be invited to the houses of nice respectable ladies. We would have library parties and talk about the latest three-volume romances."

"I remember," Lee said, checking the primers. The door was closed and a chair back was wedged under the doorhandle. "Why not. Ladies are entitled to talk about books. But I know what you mean. Sometimes you were a pain in the ass."

She laughed. "I suppose I was. Thinking back on it I'm surprised you were able to put up with me. But I was good in bed, wasn't I?"

"The best," Lee said. "Why are you talking so much in the past tense? We'll go back to Spade Bit after this is over."

"We may," she said. "Or I may go somewhere else. I don't know that I wouldn't go back to being a pain in the ass."

The primers were all right and he put them away. "I don't think there's much chance of that. You've been through hell and it's changed you. For the better. People who change as much as you've changed hardly ever change back. Some of the old habits and ways come back, but that's only natural and doesn't matter a hell of a lot. Spade Bit is always there for you. It's your home."

"We'll see," Maggie said. "Whatever happens I know I'll be able to take care of myself. I couldn't before or I didn't try. I'll be all right."

They went back to talking about the escape because it was directly ahead and could not be avoided and so they had to talk about it. They both knew they might not live through it and these might be the last hours of their lives. Even now with death looking them in the face they knew they were an ill-matched couple and there was nothing they could do about it. But they had the escape in common and they had more than that. Looking at her he felt great affection and regard, and though these feelings were new, they were strong and would last.

"You are in charge and don't let anybody take away your authority once you get started," Lee told her. "I may not be with you when you start back west. Some woman may try to take away your authority because people are like that no matter what the situation is. There can be only one leader and that has to be you. Things will fall apart if you aren't strong."

"I'll be strong," Maggie said.

"Be strong tonight," Lee said. "After you leave the stockade don't let anybody go their own way. Some of those women are crazy and full of hate and may want to do wild things. Yes, I know I shouldn't talk like that about your wild women, but that's what they are: wild. Don't let them start burning the town or killing Mormons. They'll just get killed and you'll get killed and probably I'll get killed."

Maggie laughed in spite of the situation. "You certainly are cheerful, Mr. Morgan."

"You don't know what it's like when these things get started. There's a wildness, a madness that has a life of its own. Once the killing mood takes hold of people they don't know when to stop or even how to stop. Keep a tight rein on those women of yours."

"You make them sound as if they belong to me."

"Tonight they do and they may belong to you for a long time after tonight."

"What about Wingate?" Maggie said abruptly. "What if Wingate gets away?"

"What about it? I'll find him no matter how far he runs. Now that I know he was at Spade Bit it's a lot simpler for me. I had to know who was at Spade Bit and now I do. The other men who were there aren't so important. I can't spend my life hunting them down. Wingate will have to stand for all of them."

Maggie frowned. "I'm not like you, Lee. I can't look at things in long terms the way you do. I want justice now."

"You mean revenge," Lee said. "No real difference when you think about it. I'm not sure I want either. For me it's gone beyond that. I just want him dead or, to put it another way, no longer among the living. He shouldn't breathe the same air as other men. For me it's as simple as that. But you must put him out of your mind. There is no guarantee that we can kill him now. It's what you want and I want, but we can't dwell on it."

Maggie looked grim. "I dwell on it. I dwell on it all the time. I don't know that I'll be able to pick up the rest of my life knowing he's still alive."

"You'd better. Because I'm tellling you there may be no way to kill him. The flood may get him. Would that be enough for you? If he drowned in the flood. A lot of men are going to go under in that flood. Why should Wingate float to safety?"

Maggie said, "No, it wouldn't be enough, but it would do. It would have to do."

194

"Indian women were always worse than the men," Lee said. He smiled at his bloodthirsty woman from Massachusetts. "Forget about Wingate. Leave Wingate to me. You have to concentrate on leading your women to safety. Now there may not be enough rifles to arm all the women . . ."

ELEVEN

They waited into the evening and the sun went down and there were no sounds at all. Lee went outside and from the front of the cabin he could see the mountain and the great peak looming over it and when he went back inside Maggie had the knife in her hand and was looking at the blade.

"I'm getting used to it," she said.

He sat down and looked at his watch and it was nine-forty, so there were twenty minutes to go before they started out. He knew they could have started now, but he had said ten o'clock and they might as well stick it out. His horse was saddled and waiting outside behind the cabin. It didn't matter if Wingate came now and asked what the horse was doing there. Wingate could be killed and the body hidden.

Once again he checked the dynamite, the primers, the fuse. The fuse was already cut and everything was in place. He had cut long fuses, ten minutes fuses, that would give him time to head for the mountain where it sloped down to the dam at that point. It was too bad Wingate didn't come now so that business could be settled once and for all, and he wouldn't have to think about it any more. But Wingate didn't come and when he looked at his watch again it was five minutes to ten and he told Maggie it was time to go.

Outside, he eased the Colt in its holster and tucked his coat back behind the butt. With Maggie beside him, he led the stallion down to the street and they started toward the east end of town. He took care leading the horse, but even so its hooves made a clomping sound on the plank paving. No one was in the street and there were no sounds except those the horse made. He didn't see Wingate, but that didn't mean he wasn't there.

Facing the street, Rankin's house still showed lights and it looked like the bishop was up late. They reached the end of the street without being challenged and it was time to go their own ways. Off to one side the stockade was, a long, squat shape in the darkness. Maggie had the knife in the sleeve of her coat and she nodded when he asked her one last time if she was ready to do it.

"Go on," she said. "I'll be all right." She looked at the watch and it was ten minutes past ten. She hurried away from him and he mounted up and rode out in the direction of the dam. There was no planking here and the horse made little noise. Lee climbed down when he was a hundred yards from the dam because there wasn't time for scouting and coming in slow and careful. The dam bulked up big in the darkness and if there were guards they had themselves well hidden. But there were no guards because, there was really nothing to guard the dam against, and then he was right under the great thick wall of the dam. The wall went up from nearly seventy feet and he could hear the lake water lapping on the other side of it, at the top.

He placed the charges and waited, listening for sounds. There were none. He counted time in his head. He guessed half an hour had passed by the time he checked the charges again. He couldn't see the stockade from where he was, though it was less than a mile away. A low hill got in the way and cut off his view. But Maggie and the women had to be out of there by now, heading for the town hall and the guns.

He counted off more time and knew that most of an hour had passed. Fifteen minutes later, or what he took to be fifteen minutes later, he saw small dark figures on the side of the mountain. He took binoculars from his pocket and was able to see by moonlight. More and more figures went up the slope from the town. He waited while they climbed higher and higher and as he waited he kept counting. One last figure climbed the slope and after that no more came. That was all of them.

He had touched off the fuses when there was a wild howl from far out in the darkness. Then he heard the thunder of a lot of horses coming fast. Jesus Christ! Wingate's men were coming back except they weren't Wingate's men any longer. He looked at the fuses, all burning down fast. Out in the dark the howling grew louder and then they swept past in a black cluster of men and horses. They swept down into the town and guns started to go off. He didn't know if they were just loosing off bullets or were being fired at. It was too far to see. All to the good, he thought. They were all together now. All together in Palmyra.

He mounted up and headed for the mountains. The slope was steep where the dam was and he had to urge the stallion to make the climb. He was halfway up now, not yet safe from the flood when the dam blew, but he was getting there. From where he was now he had a good view of the town and it looked like the Mormons and the outlaws were finally at it. Guns blazed all along the main street and the hard cases might have been trapped. He couldn't see that far. The stallion was stumbling and kicking when the dam blew.

The four charges blew like small blasts of cannon-fire and the dammed-up lake literally fell forward. A great wall of water seventy feet high crashed forward and swept down as if a mountain had fallen. As he watched from high up, the town just disappeared. The enormous cliff of water didn't just flood the town, it swept it away like the hand of God. Then as the first great wave flattened out and passed over, the water covered the highest home and pushed it along in front of it. Lee started along the side of the mountain and then he was high up over the town. Except the town no longer existed. It was gone.

He rode along the mountain looking for the women, but they were well ahead of him. Now when he looked down the water was settling into a lake that would ebb and empty and dry-out as time passed. But for now it was a lake, flat and black in the moonlight. Nothing floated on it that he could see, but he was high up and the moon was down for the moment and there may have been bodies that he couldn't see. Well that part's over, he thought. He had come a long way to do this, and now it was done. The Jacks would raid no more.

He caught up with the women about a mile from what was left of the town. Lake Palmyra he thought of calling it. The women were strung out along the side of the mountain and up ahead he heard Maggie shouting for them to stay together. The women he caught up with carried Winchesters and they panicked when they turned and saw him and he had to do some shouting himself before they lowered the rifles. Maggie turned and walked back toward him and her eyes were alive with excitement. She carried a Winchester and she shook it at him like an Indian.

"We did it, Lee, we did it. We saw them fighting, heard them fighting down there and suddenly they were swept away. The water hit the town and it just disappeared. I feel as if we've won a great battle."

"Not yet we haven't," he said. "Tell the women to hold up. Now we have to go back and see what we can find in the temple."

Maggie talked to the women and came over to Lee. "They don't want to go back. They hate the place so much they don't want to go back."

"Tell them we're going the hell back. Ask them if they want to die of starvation in the badlands. That's what'll happen if they don't go back. We may have to go all the way west to the mountains to get supplies. Tell them to simmer down. You simmer down too."

They went back along the side of the mountain, the women fearful and reluctant. A climb up to the half-built temple turned up nothing. It stood there in cut-log grandeur, but it was empty. They were coming down the slope when he heard shouting down below and a tough looking farm women said to Maggie, "They've caught somebody."

Maggie went down ahead of Lee and then she called back. "They've captured Wingate. Do you hear what I'm saying? They caught the half-drowned son of a bitch."

Lee rode down and saw Wingate surrounded by women with rifles. He had pulled himself out of the water and had been caught doing it. Now he stood wet and shaking with cold and his beltgun was gone and so was his head. He didn't look like a leader of men. He didn't look like any kind. His already dull eyes dulled even more when he saw Lee.

Lee dismounted and walked to the man who had burned his ranch, slaughtered his horses, killed his friends. Lee had his gun drawn, but he put it away. The women cried out when they saw him holstering the Colt. The women crowded around again, clawing at Wingate, spitting in his face. His face was bloody with scratches and one ear dripped blood where it had been torn at the lobe.

"Kill me," he said to Lee. "Don't let them have me. Draw you gun and kill me . . . please."

"Not a chance," Lee said and turned away. A rock struck Wingate in the face and he dropped to his knees begging for mercy. Another rock struck him, and another, and another. Lee looked at Maggie and she had her face turned away.

"It's not so easy when you have to look at it," he said.

"The hell with you," Maggie said and stopped to pick up a rock. She threw it as hard as she could.

"Feel better now?" Lee said, but she didn't answer. Instead she went back to the women and stopped them from mutilating the body.

They waited on the side of the mountain until the sun came up. During the night it was cold, but nobody complained. The women, cold and hungry, had an air of satisfaction that Lee could understand, but didn't feel himself. Down below the floodwater was receding and what was left of the town came into sight. There wasn't much left, log stumps standing in the mud, a pile of rocks from a toppled chimney.

"We'll have to go west to the mountains," Lee said. "We'll be going the wrong way, but there's no help for it. When we get the supplies we'll have to come all the way back. That's the way wars are fought. This was a kind of war, I guess."

"But we won it," she said.

It took them three days to reach the caves where the emergency supplies were stored. The Mormons had put them there, thinking to use them in a retreat. There was food and winter clothing, weapons and other supplies. They stayed there for a day while the women rested and the supplies were laid out for the long journey west.

"We'll just go and keep going," Lee said. "An old man and a crazy woman brought me in here and now

I have to try to remember everything about that journey."

They started back early in the morning and at that hour the women looked tired. The war was over, with another, longer war dead ahead. "Keep them moving," Lee told Maggie. "They were fine during the escape, but now they feel let down and some of them will want to give up, but you can't let them because no one will come to help them and they'll just die."

They passed through Palmyra for the last time and Lee was glad to look back and see nothing. There were bodies in the mud and buzzards were busy. They started down into the badlands and two women died there before they finally found their way out of the rocky maze and were heading due west again. The supplies held out, but they made very bad time because the women were so tired. Another woman died, but she had been sick and would have died anyway. Then, because the pace was so slow, the supplies began to give out and everyone was put on short rations. There was a light snowfall and brought some hardship because they had no tents; there were places where firewood was scarce and that had to be rationed too.

It would all have been bearable if the women hadn't started bickering among themselves. Women who would have fought bravely against a common enemy now fought among themselves. Women who liked and admired Maggie at the start of the journey now resented her and some hated her. Lee, trapped in the middle of all those women, felt himself at a loss. He longed to be back at Spade Bit in the company of men: Sid Sefton and Bud and Charlie and Wes, listening to their bragging, their horse gossip, their dirty stories.

Maggie always came to him for support, but he didn't have much advise to give about women. "You're the boss," he would say. "You handle it." And she did handle it as best she could, but the role of the pioneer leader was new to her and as time went on she liked it less and less. One night, sitting by a meager fire, she said angrily, "Damn it, Lee, I'd rather be back in Massachusetts." Then she smiled and said, "See, I'm changing back to my old ways. Don't you hate me for it?"

"Just don't start hanging curtains on the mountain," he said, and they both laughed.

The supplies ran out and Lee shot a mule deer, but that didn't go far, and the meat was gone by the next day. Game was scarce in the mountains. It was there if you had time to look for it, but there wasn't time. It was late for snow, but that didn't mean it wouldn't snow. Lee remembered what Spargo said: "The weather doesn't run like a train schedule," and he was right: it snowed the next night and most of the next day and it was hard to start fires with damp wood, and there wasn't all that much wood to begin with.

"Maybe the would have been better off back in the stockade," Maggie said one night when she was feeling low. "There was plenty to eat and Mrs. Smiler didn't beat them if they behaved themselves. You said it would be hell, but I didn't listen to you."

"They're free," Lee said, "and those that make it back will be glad they're free. Some more are going

204

to die, but that can't be helped. If you can even get half of them back it will mean something. Only thing to do is keep going and hope we'll make it."

It snowed again and this time it didn't stop for two full days. It could be worse than that, Lee knew, and probably would be. Another woman died and they piled rocks around the body and left. No one had the strength to dig a grave for her even if there had been shovels.

Hunger and cold hammered at them as they bent their heads against the wind and kept going. Maggie seemed to be everywhere, helping women who had fallen and couldn't or wouldn't get back on their feet. Lee did what he could, but it wasn't much.

He figured they were about halfway back to Eutaw Springs. But it was still too far and he wondered if any of them would make it. They had camped in a brushy gully that provided some protection from the wind driven snow, but now it was morning again and the women were refusing to go on. They sat huddled in blankets with the snow on top of them, frozen and listless and despairing.

"It's no use," Maggie said. "They won't move. Do you think there's any chance of getting help?"

"Not a chance in the world," Lee said. "The closest place is Eutaw Springs and that's where Spargo is. Besides, I'd never get back in time. I'm going out now to see if I can shoot something. In the snow, there's not much chance. You want me to be honest. That's being honest."

He had gone several miles west of camp when he saw them coming from far off. It had stopped snowing, but there was fog and visibility was limited. They were at least half a mile away, a line of men coming down a long slope. Spaces out between them were pack mules and horses. They were all afoot because the slope was broken ground and the slope was steep. Infantry, he thought. A big party of infantry.

He rode out to meet them and they disarmed him before the officer in charge, a major, listened to his story. The major, a short, grizzled man in his forties, thought he was a renegade and wasn't inclined to believe him.

Lee was patient; he could see the major's point of view. "The women will tell you," Lee said, and they did. Only then, while the women were being fed, did the major open up.

"I'll have to continue on to the Jack settlement, but I'll send a detachment of men back with the women. You say it's gone, wiped out," the major said. "Sorry to hear that. I was hoping to engage the bastards."

"Yes, Major," Lee said, glad that he didn't have to fight anybody. "It's gone. For good."

The major, whose name was Catlen, said the Territorial Government had finally been forced to move against the Jacks. "We're militia," the major said. "But there will be regulars coming."

Lee didn't say they weren't needed because the major would not have liked it. He didn't say that the Territorial Government had sat on their fat political backsides for too God damned long.

"We arrested that man Spargo," the major went on. "He will be tried and hanged. We found graves, many graves. He is on his way to jail right now. I'm sorry to hear that an ex-officer was mixed up with this dirty business. You say his name was Fletcher Wingate. Never heard of him. But it could be an alias."

They had an infantry escort for the rest of the journey and when they finally reached Eutaw Springs the trading post had been boarded up and Spargo was gone. Lee thought of the men he had killed there, all the rootless outlaws who had died there. It was good to see the last of Eutaw.

After that the rest of the journey was easy. Lee and Maggie parted company with the women at the Logan Road and then went north to Idaho and Spade Bit. The men came running when they saw Lee and Maggie and Lee said, "Later, later" to all their questions.

There was a cabin, not fancy, but new. The horses were in corral, the ruins of the house had been cleared. A new house would go up there when he had the money. He would have to work hard now and make house-building money. It was good to stand and breathe the clear mountain air, to smell the pines and know that it was all over.

Maggie stayed for three weeks and then said goodbye and went away. She said she thought she would go back to Massachusetts, but she wasn't sure. Their lovemaking had been as good as ever, but he could see the old Maggie coming back. More and more of it returned with every day she stayed. They both knew it would soon be what it had been and that was no good. Everything worked fine for them as long as there was a common danger to be faced. But now the danger had passed and they found they had really nothing in common. It was a pity, Lee thought, but there it was: it couldn't be changed. Maggie felt it too, but she said it was all right. She was the same and yet she wasn't, if he knew what she meant.

Lee said he did.